SKIN | DEEP

MICHELLE HANSON

Cover Design Copyright © 2018 by Karri Klawiter
Book design and production by Art By Karri – www.artbykarri.com -
Editing by Teena Parker

Copyright © 2018 Michelle Hanson

All rights reserved.

Published by Fearopoly © 2018

Hanson, Michelle, 1979–

Skin | Deep / Michelle Hanson – 1st ed.

ISBN-13: 978 – 17216435703
ISBN-10: 17216435709

PROLOGUE

"HEY? YOU AWAKE?"

A single light bulb dangled perfectly still from a long cord in the center of the ceiling. It provided the only light in the desolate room. It was barely bright enough to reach the dark corner of the hotel-lobby-sized room I had been confined to, and I couldn't see the face that belonged to the timid, female voice coming from the opposite corner.

A blurry haze caked over my eyes as I tried to blink my vision back into focus. I could barely make out the contents of the room, as if I was looking through an out-of-focus lens. There was a damp chill in the air, and I was certain I was in a cellar.

"Hey," the voice whispered again.

Beads of sweat trickled down my face, mixed with tears that had already fallen. I slid my tongue over the thick film that had formed across my teeth and opened my mouth. A putrid stench of blood and mucus emitted past my lips. I gathered the sloshy blend of bodily fluids and spit it out. It pooled onto the cement ground beneath me, where I sat, shackled at the ankle. The cold cuff hung loosely around the ball of my joint. The thick, heavy chain coiled like a spring and stretched nearly ten feet. It connected to a large metal hook affixed to the blank cement wall I was propped against.

"You awake?" the voice repeated.

The rattle of the restraint echoed within the room as I dragged my leg closer to my chest. The long chain scraped against the cement ground as I brought my knee under my chin. I gripped the sturdy cuff and squeezed at the hinge. The dim light reflected off the metal cuff, sending streams of light rays against the wall. I placed my thumb over the keyhole and pressed down. The small groove imprinted in my thumb, and I ran my index finger over the impression.

It was a standard cuff, the kind my department used when transporting convicts. It wasn't easy to pick the lock, but it was certainly possible. All I needed was something to pry the lock with. A Bobby pin or a pair of tweezers. Anything flat and slender.

Instinctually, I reached for my gun—but it, along with the holster, was gone. My badge and cell phone were missing from my back pockets too.

I checked my pockets knowing it was pointless. If he took my badge and gun, then he took anything else I had on me. I slid my hand inside the breast pocket of my black blazer. Then in my pants pockets. I frisked myself in the hope that maybe there was something viable I could use. But nothing. I had nothing.

"Where—where am I?" I asked the voice.

My right cheekbone throbbed, and I placed my free hands against my face. I winced at my own touch. A welt, the size of a walnut, had formed on the right side of my face. With each shallow breath, strands of my dark brown hair flew around my face. It chaotically hung over my eyes and clung to the sweat that dripped from my pores.

"Did you see who took you?" she asked, slightly louder than a whisper.

"Who took me?" I repeated. How did I get here? I remember being in Mirror Woods, too anxious to call for backup. "I was in Mirror Woods," I said... my voice trailed off as the memory slowly came back.

After eleven months of piecing together clues, I finally had him. I'd wandered into the woods, knowing if I'd waited for backup, he would've gotten away.

I had stumbled into the woods with my gun drawn—ready to fire—and then it had gone dark, as if a hood or bag had been draped over my head. I'd spun around, blinded by the foreign fabric covering my face.

I remembered hearing a heavy crack just as I'd felt a blunt blow to my right cheek. It had felt as if a boulder struck against my face. A low hum had rung through the back of my head as I'd fallen to the ground.

Perilous to the darkened state, another blow landed hard into my rib cage. I'd gasped for air, the heavy fabric sealing my mouth from capturing air. And then everything had gone dark. Not as if someone had turned the lights out—but as if the light inside me had gone out.

And now I was here.

Adrenaline surged through my body, but I was too weak even to stand. I fought to keep my eyes open as my head bobbed up and down. *I can't fall asleep. I could have a concussion. I have to stay awake.*

"How long have I been out?"

"I don't know." The voice went low again. "An hour—a day—it all feels the same." She let out a low sigh. "It's *him*, isn't it?"

"Him?" I played dumb.

"The Faceless Killer," she answered. Hopelessness punctuated the end of her sentence. "It's him. I know it is."

The Faceless Killer had wreaked havoc on the citizens of West Joseph, Ohio, for almost a year now. It was the biggest case I had ever been assigned. With at least four homicides on his resume, he was notorious for his signature kill: Each of his victims—a female in her late twenties—had her face skinned off her skull.

The bodies were dumped somewhere in the thirty-three-hundred-acre state park known as Mirror Woods. Because we never had any faces to identify the bodies, it took weeks to put a name to the deceased, often having to use dental records if her fingerprints weren't already in the system.

I sucked in a shallow breath, and my chest ached as it expanded. It felt as if I had a thousand pins trapped in my lungs, and each breath sent them swirling like a tornado. They pierced my sides, trickles of blood filling my insides.

Panic coursed through my veins like a shot of espresso. If I didn't find a way out of here soon, I would end up like the others. I knew where I was, even if my denial didn't want to admit it. This reality was too monstrous to ignore.

"Who are you?" I asked. "How did you get here?"

"Rachel," she breathed out. "Rachel Sanzone."

"Rachel Sanzone," I repeated to myself. I didn't recognize her name from the long list of Missing Persons Reports I had read through this morning. "Is there anyone here with you?"

"No. Just me."

"How did you get here?"

"I was leaving work," she said. "I work at a movie theater as the closing manager. I was the last one to leave. I lock up. I'm the only one with a key...," she trailed off. "I got into my car and then I felt something wrap around my mouth. He was in my backseat." She started to cry. "I don't know how. My doors were locked. And then everything went black. I woke up here."

"How long have you been here?"

"I don't know," she snapped. "A day? A week? I've been fed three times since I've been down here. A salami sandwich each time. I'm a fucking vegetarian." She let out a loud cry. "What's your name?" she asked once she calmed down.

Before I could answer, a sharp squeak pierced through the room. I held my breath as a loud thud followed. Then another thud. Then another. Each thud became louder as the pace picked up.

Stairs. Whoever it was—he was coming downstairs. The pace of his steps matched the pulse of my heart as the beat rapidly increased. My lungs burned as they begged for oxygen. I took another shallow breath and quickly exhaled.

His shoes scraped against the soot-covered ground as he walked from the stairs to the center of the room. He stopped just at the edge of where the light succumbed to the dark. The only visible parts of him were the black tips of his boots. He paused for a moment, hidden in the shadows, then took another step, his torso and legs now highlighted by the light. He stood at least six feet tall with an athletic build. His navy blue coveralls were torn and covered with grease. He smelled of motor oil and gasoline, with a hint of stale cigarette smoke.

The West Joseph Police Department never did figure out what the Faceless Killer wanted with the faces of his victims. Some detectives hypothesized he wanted to keep them as trophies. I always feared he kept them for something more sinister.

The man in front of me took another step into light, making himself visible from head to toe. But it wasn't a man's face looking down at me.

My body involuntarily lunged forward as a string of bile rose from the pit of my stomach. It mixed with the blood that had coated the inside of my mouth, and I coughed out the foul mixture. It burned against my windpipe as another chunk spewed past my lips.

This man—this monster—was wearing the face of his first victim.

I recognized Angela Truman from the Missing Persons photos. Age twenty-seven. Disappeared in October of last year. Her body had been discovered in Mirror Woods Lake seven days after she had been reported missing by her boyfriend.

At first, West JPD thought the damage to her face had been caused by wildlife or fish feasting on her exposed skin, but further examination showed no other parts of her body had gnaw marks. And the slit around her neck had been too pristine for that skin to be missing by accident. The muscular tissue left on her face had eroded from being waterlogged for more than two days. In my ten years as a detective, it was the most horrific corpse I had ever seen.

That was until the other victims started popping up.

Angela Truman's skin now stretched taut across this man's face as he stood directly in front of me. Her blond hair, matted with blood and knots, recklessly dangled over his shoulders. Her thin lips cracked in the center, having been forced to fit over his large head. The bridge of her nose stretched over his, her nostrils slashed into tiny slits, barely wide enough for him to breathe through. His breath echoed inside his human mask as he inhaled and exhaled. It reverberated around the room, melting into my skin like acid rain on a statue.

A faint shimmer flickered across Angela's face, as if polyurethane had been smeared across her skin. Chunks of flesh were missing from the cheeks— undoubtedly his first attempt at skinning. Maybe a combination of nerves and lack of skill had caused the messy debacle of her features?

My lips irrepressibly contorted into disgust and sorrow. Was it his plan to wear my face? And Rachel Sanzone's too? Was her face to become part of his wardrobe?

And how long did we have? If he stuck to his original MO, in five days he would discreetly dispose of my faceless body in Mirror Woods. My coworkers would be forced to identify me by my fingerprints or dental records.

He took another step, this time to the right, and walked to the opposite side of the room. A burst of light popped on as he flicked a switch above a workbench, which was covered in engine parts and greasy tin cans. Above the work station, taped to the wall, were dozens of newspaper articles written about the Faceless Killer's victims.

MIRROR WOODS LAKE: HOME TO ANOTHER MURDER

I recognized the article about the second victim, Lisa Johnson. Age twenty-five. Grad student from Cleveland. Reported missing in January. The lake was too frozen for her body to be thrown in. She had been discovered fifty feet from a deserted hiking trail deep in the woods. Had she been placed there in the summer, she may never have been discovered due to overgrown weeds and shrubbery. The ground around her was too hard for a foot impression to be left behind.

THIRD BODY DISCOVERED IN MIRROR WOODS

Carmine Jenkins. Age twenty-eight. The oldest of the victims. Reported missing by her roommate in May and discovered on the gravel shore by the lake a few days later. She had been weighted down—rocks in the trash bag that served as her coffin. But he did a poor job sealing the bag. Instead of knotting the rope around the bag, he merely wrapped it around her ankles and abdomen. She, too, had been discovered without her face.

FACELESS KILLER STRIKES FOR FOURTH TIME

Sophia Good. Age twenty-seven. Reported missing by her husband almost a week after she disappeared. He said they were going through a messy divorce, and he thought she had skipped town because she could be "rather dramatic at times." When he checked the credit card statements and noticed no new transactions—along with no new outgoing calls or text messages on their phone bill—he called her mother to see if Sophia had contacted her family. When her mother said no, he reported her missing.

Her body had been discovered a few weeks ago, in late August, a few days before she had been reported missing. Classified as a Jane Doe, West JPD believed she had put up a fight, as she had several defensive wounds on her forearms. She also differed from the first victims in that she had been fully decapitated instead of just skinned. With no prints in the system, her husband had to come in to identify her body based solely on a tribal tattoo on her lower back.

With the exception of one, all of the other articles were follow-ups on each victim, with an emphasis on how frustrated the citizens of West Joseph had become with the police department for letting this psychopath run rampant. I couldn't really fault them for their frustrations. TV crime shows molded viewers into believing any homicide could be solved in two days. But killers rarely left behind the type of proof needed to catch them, and crime labs didn't have a turnaround time of thirty minutes after the evidence was collected.

The article that really stuck out from the rest was the one with my photograph in the center. Although I wasn't able to read the text from where I sat, I knew what it was about. I had that same article in the top drawer of my desk.

The reporter did an excellent job of letting the public know just who was responsible for this case, blaming everything on my "sloppy detective work." He gave a recap of all the victims, statements from their families, and a nice reminder that West JPD still hadn't named a suspect, let alone had anyone in custody.

If I was indeed in the Faceless Killer's trophy room, then who better to flaunt it to than the one person who was assigned to catch him.

On the workbench, mixed with the scattered pieces of car parts, I noticed my gun and badge. With his back to me, I could see his salt-and-pepper hair stuck to the back of his neck, below the three-inch gap that Angela Truman's scalp wasn't able to cover. He picked up my gun and slid the clip from the handle. He counted the bullets in the magazine and slid it into his back pocket. He placed my empty gun back onto the workbench and tapped the black leather case that held my detective's badge. He flipped open the leather case like a book and ran his fingertips over my ID. He caressed my photo for a few moments. Then, in a quick swoop, he picked up my badge and turned to face me.

One step.

Two steps.

Three steps.

He squatted in front of me. Angela Truman's face stared back at me as a subtle bump emerged from her cheekbones. Underneath her face, he was smiling at me—his teeth fully exposed between her lips.

"Detective Sergeant Lena Evans," he said, smirking under Angela's face. He held my badge at eye level as he examined my photo. From Angela's shallow eye sockets, his icy blue eyes shot back and forth from my photo to my face. "I like you better when you're all cleaned up," he said, a shallow tone of sympathy washing through his voice. He reached into the pocket of his coveralls and fished out a small bottle. The contents rattled inside. He gently shook it in front of my face and popped the lid open with his thumb. "It's just aspirin," he said. "It should help with the swelling and pain." His speech was articulate and distinct. The profiler assigned to the case had assessed the killer was likely educated, good with his hands, and a loner. So far the profiler was at least one for three.

"You know who I am," I dryly snapped. "So you know my entire department and SWAT will be looking for me."

"Oh, I'm counting on it." An ominous laugh grumbled from his throat. Dark shadows filled the gaps between his face and Angela's.

He clutched the bottle tight in his hand, the pills rattling once more, as he skimmed my swollen cheek with his fingertips. I jerked from his touch, my head hitting the back of the wall, and I kicked my leg out. The heel of my boot dug into his thigh, and he looked down at my foot, slowly shaking his head, as if debating whether to reprimand my feeble attempt at self-defense. He brought his cold stare back to my eyes. "Don't be stupid," he growled, caressing my jaw line and lightly brushing the tip of my nose with his index finger.

He held the pill bottle in front of me and waited as I held out my hand. He dumped three aspirin into my palm, the pills rolling around like dice on a Craps table, and he snapped the lid back onto the bottle. I studied the pills, as if somehow I could magically decipher if they were poisoned just by looking at them. Even if they were poisoned, that would be a better fate than what he had in store for me during the next five days.

With a sigh of disgust, as if he was offended that I didn't trust him, he took two aspirin from the bottle, lifted his mask at the chin, popped the pills into his mouth and dramatically swallowed. He exposed his whole mouth and opened it wide, sticking out his tongue to show me he had swallowed the pills.

If I was going to meet my demise at the hands of this maniac, it was going to be on my terms.

I slowly brought the pills to my mouth and let them fall past my lips. The bitter taste of chalk fizzed on my tongue, and I collected as much saliva as I could to dry-swallow the pills. A wave of coughing erupted from my chest. I leaned to the side, away from the monster in front of me, and tried to catch my breath.

He stood from his squat and walked toward the staircase where Rachel was.

Tears glazed over my eyes as I continued coughing, his actions only a blur. Within a few seconds, he had returned. He let a plastic water bottle fall from his grip then lightly kicked it in my direction. It was warmer than room temperature, but I was desperate for anything. The buildup of mucus and blood, now coated in chalky dust, had induced more bile to erupt from my stomach.

I reached behind me, searching for the bottle of water, and choked on my own spit. The thin plastic bottle crushed under my grasp as I brought it in front of me and twisted the cap. Water poured from the spout as I brought it to my mouth and began to drink. Between coughs, I swallowed the lukewarm liquid, letting it wash down my throat and slosh in my stomach. I swished another gulp, collecting the congealed bits of blood that had suctioned to my teeth, and spit it out.

I loosely held the half-empty bottle in my left hand as I got up on all fours and breathed in the damp air. I didn't care that my lungs felt as if they were going to split at the sides from a bruised rib. I needed oxygen. In two quick scrapes of his shoe, he kicked the bottle out of my hand, sending it—and all the water inside it—soaring across the room. Streams of water splashed against the concrete, and the bottle landed against the wall with a hollow thud.

My body collapsed at the deafening sound of defeat, and I wiped the tears from my eyes as I sat upright. He quickly turned away from me and walked toward the staircase. Angela's blond hair fluttered as he took each forceful step. He placed his hand on the wooden rail of the staircase and paused.

"Don't you two get any ideas," he said as he walked up the stairs, never acknowledging the state he was leaving me in. The door opened with the same high-pitched squeak and then slammed shut. A series of clicks rumbled down the staircase as he locked the door behind him.

With the room fully illuminated, I saw Rachel Sanzone cuffed at the wrist and ankles near the bottom of the staircase. Was that why I only had one cuff? Did he not have enough for two captives?

She sat on a tattered twin mattress, two rusty springs shooting through the fabric. Her cheeks were stained with mascara-colored tears. She bit down on her lip to keep it from quivering when we made eye contact. Her long, auburn hair slicked to the side of her head. It looked as if she hadn't showered in at least five days.

Five days, I thought. Was I to be her replacement?

With the light still on, I was able to see the room more clearly. The cinder-block walls reached from floor to ceiling. Not a single window in sight. The only escape was through the locked door at the top of the staircase.

I stood from the ground, using the wall to gain my balance before attempting to walk. This chain wasn't exactly quiet, and any scraping would be an invitation for him to come back downstairs. I picked up the chain to keep it from skidding across the ground as I took a step forward. The workbench was at least twenty feet away from me. The chain was ten feet, and I was five foot seven. Even if I lay down and stretched my arm as far as I could, I would be two to three feet short of being able to reach the workbench.

Even if I could reach it, what was on there that could be of use? He emptied my gun, and my cell phone was nowhere in sight. And I couldn't very well assemble an engine and drive myself out of here. Unless there was screwdriver or knife on the table, anything else was worthless.

"You're... you're a detective?" Rachel's voice shook.

She didn't have the hopeful tone I was expecting her to have. Instead, she sounded even more despondent—as if knowing her captor had also caught the person who was supposed to save her was the final nail in her coffin. In that one whimper of a question, she had come to terms with her demise.

"Yes." I answered.

"You'll have people looking for you," she said, hope slowly maturing in her voice. "They'll find you. They'll find us."

"Yeah," I lied.

Had I not been so eager to solve this case on my own—to show that condescending reporter and the rest of this town that I was good at my job—I would have waited for backup. I would have told Captain Fluellen what I had found.

I knew that skinning someone would require privacy and a lot of it. It had to be in a desolate area and probably one close to the dumping site. I highly doubted the killer would be daring enough to travel a far distance with a faceless corpse in his backseat. He may be psychotic, but he wasn't stupid.

After I had viewed dozens of satellite images of abandoned and foreclosed homes in the area, I found something: a ranch-style house nestled far away from the other homes in the neighborhood, with a backyard that led directly into Mirror Woods. It was just a spec on the screen from an aerial view, but when zoomed in, it had become the largest piece of the puzzle.

But if I was able to find this place—an abandoned house so rundown no one would think to look twice at it—then maybe another detective would be able to as well. Once they realized I was missing, they would search my desk and computer. It was only a matter of time before they figured out I had looked into this house.

How long it would take them to find me, though—and in what condition? Perhaps that's what the Faceless Killer meant when he said he was "counting on it." Would the officers see him—wearing my face—and initially think it was me?

Before I could swallow the thought, the bright overhead light suddenly shut off. It left a single bulb as the sole source of light. I picked up the chain as I eased back toward the wall and sank to the ground. He was toying with me. He had confined me to his workspace, and he left my empty gun on the table. He rationed water and light. He was trying to break me. It was worse than being a fish in barrel. At least the fish didn't know it was going to be shot.

I knew more than anyone what was in store for me. I had studied his victims. I could surmise the last moments of their lives with precise detail. I was the fortuneteller looking at my own demise as it played in the crystal ball.

"They'll come," Rachel said, as if singing herself a lullaby while being rocked to sleep. "They'll come."

Underneath the workbench, barely visible by the dull light, was a Styrofoam mannequin head. It's pale face— ghostlike and undefined— was covered in a rich red, resembling the color of blood.

Because that's exactly what it was.

My vision focused in and out as my eyes adjusted to this dimly lit tomb of a basement. I was sure that the mannequin's head had been purposely placed in my line of sight—as a daunting reminder that this was my fate.

And certainly Rachel's if I didn't act soon.

I brought my knees to my chest and lowered my head as I wrapped my arms around my legs. Thoughts of what this beast was going to do to Rachel—and eventually me—flooded my head like a dam that had been split in half. I caught myself rocking back and forth as the image of Angela Truman's face cut in between flashes of everything I was going to miss in life.

Family and friends, my girlfriend, the series finale of *The Simpsons*—I was going to miss all of it. Everything I had worked for—being an honest detective, saving for retirement. The hope of one day getting married. Mowing the yard—I hated yard work, but I was going to miss it. This creature was going to steal everything I had ever wanted away from me.

He had no right.

This was *my* life. Mine! What I had in life may not have amounted to much monetarily, but it was still worth fighting for. And that's exactly what I intended to do.

A sharp pain, like a dagger being twisted in my side, shot through my rib cage. I hugged myself tighter and hoped it would pass as the tips of my fingers skimmed the underwire of my bra, and I froze.

Something flat, I recalled. I needed something flat and slender.

I took in a deep breath and quickly took off my blazer. It fell to the ground as I reached behind my back and unfastened the two metal loops holding my bra together. Paste-like sweat glued the cups to my breasts, and a blast of cold air swept over my skin as I gathered the cloth in my hands.

I followed the underwire to the edge of the cup and worked the curved tip through the padded fabric. The thin wire gradually poked through the silky mesh, and I slid it the rest of the way out.

My bra fell to the ground as I measured the tip of the underwire against the lock. It was too wide. The underwire was too wide. With a shaky hand, I scraped the rounded tip against the cement wall. I sawed it back and forth until each side was a forty-five degree angle. The tip was now a sharp point that resembled a prison shank, and I pressed my index finger against it. It poked through the top layer of my skin, and I inserted the pointed edge into the lock.

"What are you doing?" Rachel asked from the dark corner.

"Quiet," I whispered. It was possible we were being listened to. Any inquisition from Rachel could send him barreling down the stairs.

I twisted and turned the makeshift key alongside the latch. The wire bent between my fingers as it fought against the lock. Suddenly a soft pop vibrated through the underwire, and the cuff loosened around my ankle. I wrapped my hands around the plates and slowly pulled them apart, a soft click-click-click resounded in the room as I separated the cuff's teeth from the latch. The hinge opened like a smile.

"Are you free?" Rachel asked, her voice echoed in the room.

"Shut up," I angrily whispered. The cuff lifelessly fell from my ankle.

I stood from the ground and tip-toed to the workbench where my gun and badge were. I picked up my gun, the cold metal absorbing into my skin, and I held it at my right side. Even without bullets, it was familiar, comforting, and better than nothing.

"What are you doing?" Rachel cried from her corner.

I placed my finger over my lips and mouthed *Sshhhh* to Rachel before making my way over her. The dim light barely led the way, and she was more shadow than person the closer I got to her. I squatted in front of her and cupped my hand behind her head, her greasy hair matted to her scalp.

"I'm going to come back for you," I said in a low voice. "I need you to stay here and keep quiet."

"No," she shook her head, her voice coated in tears. "He'll come down here."

"Stay quiet," I repeated. "I promise I will come back for you. I can't look after you and myself. You have to stay here," I pleaded.

She nodded as her breath became panicked puffs, and she trembled beneath me.

"Have you ever heard him talk to anyone?" I asked. "Does he have a partner?"

"No," she cried. "It's only been him."

Only him, I thought to myself. Good. I had a chance.

I stood from my position and lightly took three steps back. I felt around the workbench, looking for any type of weapon to give to Rachel in case I didn't come back. Not because I was going to abandon her but because I honestly didn't know if I would survive this.

I gripped my hand around the smooth, plastic handles of two flathead screwdrivers—too wide and thick to pry open her chains, but thin enough to stab him with. I placed one of the screwdrivers in my back pocket and handed the other to her.

"Just in case," I whispered as I squatted next to her again. "I'll be back. Stay here." I squeezed her hand as I stood once more and took in a deep breath.

I made one tiny footstep after the other until the tip of my shoe hit against the bottom step. A light pop echoed in the room, and I carefully stepped onto the bottom stair and lifted my body with ninja silence.

I pressed my back against the staircase railing and took one stair at a time. I froze in paralyzed fear each time a step would squeak. By the fifth step, I was able to see the gap between the floor and the bottom of the door. A half-inch of artificial light stretched in a horizontal line.

The light was too yellow for it to be sunlight. It had to be past sunset if he had a light on. It was early afternoon when I was abducted from Mirror Woods. I could have been down here for six hours or thirty-six hours.

I sat down on the third step from the top and peered through the gap. The light ricocheted off the linoleum floor that stretched at least ten feet until it reached a dirty baseboard. I held my breath as I scanned the length of the door. I looked for any movement or shadow that would indicate where he was.

Nothing.

I blinked twice. A surge of courage patiently waited behind my chest as I decided what to do next. Before I reached for the doorknob, a harsh shadow stepped in front of the door. Slowly, locks of blond, matted hair eased onto the floor, soon followed by the chunky, fleshy mask of Angela Truman's face.

His cold eyes stared at me through her empty eye sockets, and he rested his *and her* cheek on the ground as he peered into the gap under the door. I let out a shrill shriek just as he stood from the ground and unlocked the door. Before I could run down the stairs, he opened the door, reached inside, and grabbed the back of my head. He yanked me through the doorway, my hair pulling at the scalp, and he threw me into the wall.

My right shoulder landed against the wall, and I dropped my gun. It skidded across the floor as my back and head hit the wall. My breath shot from my mouth as my lungs hollowed. My vision went black then slowly came to a blur as I slid down the wall.

My head bobbed up and down as the room spun in slow motion. In the corner of my eye, I saw him charge at me. The grimy T-shirt under his coveralls fit tightly against his biceps.

He wrapped his right hand around my neck and lifted me from the ground, holding me high above his head, my back pressed against the wall. My legs kicked out as I gasped for air, his massive grip squeezing the air from my throat.

I slapped and clawed at his arm, but my meager attempts only made him squeeze harder. I kicked against the wall, trying desperately to break from his grasp. My lungs burned as they ached for oxygen, and my vision continued to blur as I struggled for air.

White noise coated the room. Slowly, my kicks came to a lingering halt, and my hands fell to my sides. My head lowered as I felt what little life I had left in me escape from my lips.

This was it. This was my end.

My body sank lower into his grasp. I locked eyes with him, my vision fogging over. His arctic blue eyes stared into mine, and Angela's face wrinkled at the cheeks as he smiled.

I can't, I thought to myself. *I can't let him win.*

A jolt of adrenaline coursed through my body and erupted from my hands. I reached behind my back and pulled the flathead screwdriver from my pocket. I swung my fist like a boxer delivering the final blow. The screwdriver stuck straight out from my fist, and I drove the long blade into his left ear. It crunched as it entered his ear canal, and I twisted the blade like a key starting a car engine.

He squealed out in pain, a scream so blood curdling it could've been heard from miles away, and he retracted the steel grip he had on me.

I fell to the ground and sucked in a tankful of air. I breathed out then took in another. The static slowly faded as my vision returned, and I looked around the room, my chest heaving as I continued to swallow air.

Lying on the ground next to me, with a six-inch screwdriver sticking out of his ear, was that vile and disgusting demon. His chest rose in uneven breaths as he coughed up a thick trail of blood. It slowly emerged from the thin lips of Angela's face.

His bleak eyes were barely visible as they rolled to the back of his head. With each cough, spurts of blood burst from his mouth, covering Angela Truman's chin and cheek. His shoulders and legs convulsed as he watched me slowly turn onto my stomach and army-crawl toward my gun, which was still on the floor.

He grabbed at my legs, his firm grip cutting off the circulation at my ankle, and he pulled me back to him. My gun was a little over an arm's reach away. I kicked out of his grip, my boot landing hard into his rib cage, and I continued to crawl on the floor, my stomach sliding on the dirty linoleum.

I picked up my gun, its cold barrel breathing life into my body. With my last bit of energy draining, I slammed the blunt end of the gun against the handle of the screwdriver. A piercing crunch exploded through the room as the entire blade drove deeper into his ear canal. The screwdriver pounded into the floor beneath him, and his skull caved at the temple.

His body shot upward as his head stayed nailed against the

ground. His backside landed with a thick thwack, a geyser of blood gushing from his mouth. I watched him take his final, labored breath as I stared into his cold, dead eyes.

CHAPTER | ONE

WITH A FEROCIOUS GASP, I shot up from the bed. The comforter rustled against the sheets as I sat paralyzed, my mouth agape, and I struggled to catch my breath. My chest was thick and heavy, like tar had been poured down my throat. Sweat trickled down my hairline and pooled in the pockets of my clavicle. My eyes shifted to the right and then to the left.

He was no longer next to me. I was alone.

I wasn't in Mirror Woods being terrorized by Lathan Collins, the man behind the mask and murders. I was home—in bed. The only light in the room was provided by the neon blue numbers on the alarm clock. 4:36 a.m.

A cascade of thunder rolled outside as raindrops bounced off my windowsill.

It was a dream.

I was awake.

It was a dream, and I was safe now. He couldn't hurt me.

I took a deep breath and let it out.

Water. I needed water.

I swallowed the desert heat that sizzled in the back of my throat and pushed the comforter off me. The down feathers stuffed between the two thin pieces of fabric crinkled as they bunched together. The flannel material of my pants caught between my thighs as I slid off the mattress, my bare feet hitting the cold wooden floor, and I walked into the bathroom connected to the upstairs bedroom.

I winced as I turned on the light. A burst of brightness reflected off the mirror, and I blinked away the sting as my eyes began to focus. Next to the chrome faucet handles of the porcelain sink was an empty glass and a prescription bottle. Both called to me.

I turned the handle marked "C" and put the glass under the spout. Air bubbles tumbled and rose as water filled the glass. I was too thirsty to wait. I took two gulps, the cold liquid gliding down my throat like an ice cube on scorching asphalt. I took another gulp—a chill traveled down my body as goose bumps collected on my skin.

I filled the glass again and took another gulp. Water gathered in the corners of my mouth and spilled down my face. I pulled the glass away and wiped the mess from my chin. I set the glass back onto the sink and picked up the pill bottle. Its contents rattled inside like checkers pieces in a cardboard box, and I pressed down on the cap with the palm of my hand. I twisted it open, a slight impression of the lid engraved itself into my hand, and I tilted the bottle to the side. One pill fell out.

My fingertips covered the instructions printed on the bottle. Although I had been off these pills since I went back to work six months ago, I could recite every word on the label—even the FDA's cautionary warning about accidental overdose.

PRAZOSIN 5mg: TAKE ONE PILL BY MOUTH TWICE DAILY

I popped the small pill into my mouth and pushed it to the back of my throat with my tongue. The capsule was hardly a mask for the chalky aftertaste from the powder inside. I turned the faucet back on and filled the glass a quarter full.

I had consciously made the decision to be off all meds before I returned to work. Did I really want to start taking these again? It was one dream. A fluke.

I leaned over, spit the pill out of my mouth, and poured the glass of water down the sink. The pill swirled around the drain before it disappeared.

I flipped the bathroom light off and let the lightening-stained sky guide the way back to the bed. I needed to go back to sleep, but the adrenaline coursing through my veins felt like tiny nitrogen-fueled racecars speeding up and down my arms and legs.

The mattress sank under my weight as I sat on the edge and stared at the clock. 4:44 a.m.

I could watch television, but what would be on at this hour? Infomercials about diet pills or home-shopping channels selling knock-off jewelry? I could watch a movie, but my brain was too fried. I didn't want to put in the effort of following a plot. I just needed noise. I needed something to fill the vacant maze inside my mind.

With Lathan Collins fresh in my thoughts, I knew I wouldn't be able to sleep. Every time I closed my eyes, I saw him. I *felt* him—as if he was lying next to me, cradling my backside, his breath hot on my neck as he smoothed my hair back; I lay there motionless and full of fear.

I reached for the slender remote control that sat atop the

nightstand and hit the "power" button. A jolt of laughter roared from the television, and I flipped through the channels. I stopped on Channel 10 to catch the tail end of the early-morning news.

What there was to report on before five in the morning was a mystery to me, one that was going to be solved rather quickly. As the anchors finished a segment on the best diners in West Joseph, I propped the pillows against the headboard and reached down to pull the blanket over me. I draped the feather comforter over my lap as I leaned against the pillows, my feet soaking up the heat trapped far beneath the covers.

"It's the one-year anniversary of the Lathan Collins murders, and someone wrote a book," the burly newscaster reported. His thick mustache hung over his upper lip as he peered into the camera, drawing the audience in with his charm. "Rachel Sanzone, the only victim to survive the Faceless Killer's terror, will be at Volume One Bookstore on Monday evening at six o'clock."

In the upper left-hand corner of the screen, the cover to Rachel's tell-all book, *The Face of a Killer*, appeared. A dark silhouette of a man's face wearing a tight black mask filled the entire cover. In white letters, just under the man's chin, was the title, followed by RACHEL SANZONE in all capital letters.

I let out a heavy sigh as I gritted my teeth.

"She will be answering questions and signing autographs for everyone who buys the book. Channel Ten will be there to cover the full story," the newscaster quickly added before the segment ended.

I muted the television as commercials filled the screen. The glow emitting from the screen lit the room, and memories of that night swarmed my mind like last-minute holiday shoppers down a toy aisle.

That night.

As Lathan Collins had been lying dead on the floor, I had gone into the basement to free Rachel Sanzone. She and I had run to the closest house on the street—a quarter of a mile away, the moon our only source of light. I had thought Rachel wasn't going to be able to make the walk. She had been so poorly malnourished, and her psyche had been too far gone to trust a midnight stroll through the woods.

But she made it. I didn't think she would—I honestly didn't think either of us would—but we did.

The neighbor, a kind and elderly man, had let me use his phone to call the police. We had waited in the elderly man's living room and used over-the-counter first aid ointment to mend our wounds before my department's Captain, Thomas Fluellen, and the rest of West JPD had arrived. Rachel had been sent immediately to the hospital. I had given

Fluellen the address to the house and then had been taken to the hospital by an ambulance shortly after.

"You're awake?" I heard Abi, my girlfriend of two years, say from the bedroom doorway. Her voice snapped me back to present time.

She rested her shoulder against the doorframe as she peered into the spare bedroom where I sat in bed. Her long, strawberry-blond hair fell to the middle of her back. The glow from the television bounced off the walls and highlighted her oval face. It sent a sparkle through her blue eyes. She gave a half-smile as she waited for my response.

"Did I wake you?" I asked.

She nodded. "I heard you go the bathroom. I wasn't going to come in, but then I heard the TV, so I wanted to check on you. When did you come in here?"

We hadn't slept in two separate bedrooms in more than six weeks. After the incident, it had become part of our routine for me to sleep in the spare bedroom. With all the tossing and turning from the nightmares, I didn't want to keep Abi awake.

"After you went to bed," I said. "I couldn't sleep, and I didn't want to keep you up."

"Did you have another dream?"

I nodded.

"About him?"

I looked to the floor and lowered my head. I didn't want to admit that I was having dreams of that night again. It was strongly encouraged by administration that I take a paid leave of absence for six months while I recovered. I went to therapy once a week, and when I was deemed well enough to go back to work, I did. In the five months since I'd been back at work, I had been nightmare free.

Until now.

"I'm sure it's because of the anniversary," Abi said as she walked further into the bedroom. She sat down next to me, the mattress sinking slightly, and I scooted over to give her room to join me.

But she didn't. She just sat there, her hand on top of mine, as she studied my face. As if looking deep into my eyes was going to give her the answers she needed to figure me out. "Why don't you take today and tomorrow off? Make it a five day weekend," she added.

"I can't." I immediately pushed the idea out of my head. "I know it's Labor Day, but I have to work this weekend," I said. "I'm sorry I woke you," I added and forced a smile.

"It's fine," she said as she scooted closer to me. I moved to the middle of the bed so that she had room to lie down. She lifted the covers and slid her feet toward the end of the bed, and she pressed her stomach against my back. The warmth of her body absorbed into my skin, and I nestled closer to her as I rested my head on the pillow. She draped the comforter over us, trapping the late-summer heat under the covers. It felt good to lie against her. I felt safe with her next to me, but something was missing.

Whether she knew it or not, I had slowly fallen out of love with her. And I didn't know why. Before that night with Lathan Collins, we were happy and in love. We were seemingly perfect. The connection between us ebbed and flowed, but it had never burned out. Somehow, we always found a way to reconnect. This time, however, I had strong doubts. The passion that had once ignited between us just couldn't catch fire, like sparking flint in an empty lighter.

It was as if someone had drilled a hole in my heart—and all the love I had for her was slowly leaking out. At first, I thought it was because of the trauma. I thought pushing her away was normal.

And maybe part of it was because of the trauma. For the past year, I had been holding onto the hope that something in me would change. That maybe the hole in my heart would heal and I could fall in love with her again. But nothing had changed. And I was beginning to think it never would.

Abi had simply faded into the background, like a piece of old furniture. If she was there, I didn't notice her. If she was gone, an unfamiliar emptiness lurked around me.

It's not that I didn't want her there—I just didn't know what to do when she was around. The monotony and tedious predictability of Monday morning through Sunday evening only amplified the fact that I wanted more than the comforts of consistency. I wanted mystery. I wanted to feel desire. I wanted to physically ache for someone. I wanted to feel in love again.

As unfair as it was to Abi, I forced myself to ignore those thoughts. I would be a fool to let her slip from my life, especially if my insanity was only temporary. I forced myself to go through the motions as if I was in love with her—because maybe, in time, I would be again.

That was my hope, anyway.

A part of me was convinced Abi felt the same but that she didn't leave because of guilt. How could she leave me after everything I went through? Or, if she wasn't staying out of guilt, I was sure pity played a part.

"Will you at least consider taking Friday off?" she urged.

Abi placed her head on the pillow and slipped her hand under my breast as she held me closer. I took a deep breath and closed my eyes. It was nice to be in her arms—but, again, it was a feeling as familiar as a well-worn sofa.

I was able to relax with her next to me. I knew she would never let any physical harm come to me. She treated me as if I was a wounded child, too fragile to face the terrors of the world, and I was okay with that. Aside from work, I didn't want to be a hero. I didn't want to put on a brave face. I wanted to hide from the world and everyone in it.

Abi gave me a way to do so.

"I'll see," I humored her, though I already knew taking a four-day weekend was out of the question.

Abi let out a soft sigh as she bowed her head against my neck. She lingered there for a few seconds then slowly sat up. She bent her legs at the knee and propped her arms on top of them, pulling the comforter with her.

I sat up from the pillow and moved to the bottom corner of the bed. I sat with my legs crossed and shoulders forward, the glow from the television highlighting the disquiet in her face.

Abi's smile slowly collapsed as she looked down at the bed and back at me. It was the look she gave whenever she was about to deliver bad news. She picked at her nails, a stalling tactic of hers that I recognized, and then tucked the loose strands of hair that had fallen in front of her eyes behind her ears.

"My brother invited us to his place this weekend." Abi continued to pick at her fingernails. "We could go there—make it a mini-vacation?"

Her brother lived in Pittsburgh and, although he was nice, he wasn't worth the three-hour drive. His house had three bedrooms, one for him and one for each of his two children. The basement had been converted to a guest area, but it was still a basement: damp and muggy, filled with insects I couldn't identify. It would hardly be a vacation.

"Is this why you want me to take today and tomorrow off?"

Abi nodded. "It's a nice drive," she said.

"Don't you have houses to show?" I hoped that maybe her busy work schedule would be a reason she couldn't go, and then I would be off the hook. Abi was a real estate agent—and a successful one too. It was the reason we met. She sold me this house and her heart within the same showing.

"I have an appointment later this morning, and then another one on Tuesday," she said. That was the nice thing about her career: She could take as much time off as she wanted. Not that she frequently did.

"Oh," I said. My plan had backfired. "I don't think I can take the time off." I scrambled for a reason. "I have a lot to do."

Since returning to work in April, I had immersed myself into each case I was assigned—staying late and going in early. I didn't care this much about my work life before Lathan Collins, but something had changed since that night. I wanted to catch the bad guys, sure, but it was the other officers' expectations of me being the constant hero that weighed me down. It was as if I was swimming in the ocean with a garbage bag wrapped around me. No matter how much I fought the currents, it was never going to be enough to stay afloat.

"I think it would be nice to get away for a few days, that's all." Abi shrugged as the inevitable defeat stiffened around her. The air conditioner kicked off and sounded like a tin can falling to the ground. Silence filled the room. Abi and I looked at each other, her lips drooping into a crooked frown, and I felt my face slump into an unsettling calm.

"If you really want to go, please don't let me stop you." I sat up from the bed. "Go without me. You should see your family." I crossed the room and headed toward the bathroom.

"They ask about you all the time," Abi said as she turned her body to face me. She sat on the edge of the bed, one leg dangling off the side as if she was prepared to bolt at any moment.

"It would be nice to see them. I just can't," I said firmly. I walked into the bathroom and flipped on the light. My eyes had already adjusted to the brightness from the television, so the sudden burst of fluorescent bulbs wasn't as jarring as I'd expected.

"Are you leaving?" Abi asked, more accusation than question.

"I'm already up." I shrugged. "I might as well go in early."

"Oh." Abi stood from bed and stared at me, disappointment staining her face. "If you change your mind, the invite's still there." She shook her head, as if she knew reminding me of the standing invitation was futile. She looked exhausted—not just from fatigue but from me as well. "I'm leaving tonight," she said as she left the room. "Have a good day at work."

Upsetting Abi wasn't how I wanted to start the day, but I knew I wasn't going to change my mind about the weekend. I had enough to worry about at work. I hoped Abi would understand— but if she didn't, then maybe we would reach our end sooner than I thought.

CHAPTER | TWO

THREE CEMENT WALLS COVERED in soot appeared on the large projection screen at the front of the room. Two archways on the back wall had been sealed off with maroon-colored bricks. A thin shadow cast along the top of the archway. Drops of water rhythmically splashed into a shallow puddle that could be heard off screen. Each drop echoed in the room, sending a chill up my spine. The hairs on the back of my neck rose as my shoulders quickly shuddered. Along the top of the back wall, between the two sealed archways, a burst of sunlight shot through a narrow glass-block window.

The rays of sun shone upon a petite female barely twenty-years-old. Her long blond hair was just as voluptuous as her breasts as it fell seductively over her shoulders. It sparkled each time she shifted in the aluminum chair that sat in the center of the dimly lit room. Behind the woman, camouflaged within the dull gray walls, a sharp hook hung loosely from a thick rope. It was barely noticeable at first but stuck out like pizza sauce on a white shirt once seen.

The young woman tentatively riffled through a small stack of papers she had rested on her lap. The pages crinkled around the edges, as if she had rolled and twisted them in her hands before taking a seat in front of the camera. She looked directly into the lens, her blue eyes filled with both uncertainty and ambition, then darted her eyes to the side.

"You may begin whenever you're ready," said an off-camera voice, deep and distorted, as if it had been electronically altered.

The young woman smiled, revealing her bold, white teeth, and looked down at the stack of papers on her lap. She cleared her throat and began.

"You said you would be home hours ago." Her voice shook as she read the script. "Where were you?" She scrunched her eyebrows together, shrugging off her nerves as the inflection in her voice changed from anxiety to anger.

"I had things to do," the deep off-camera voice replied.

"The kids ask about you all the time," she said as she raised the script from her lap and brought it to eye level, squinting.

"What do you tell them?" the distorted voice asked.

"Nothing. Because I know nothing...." Her eyes darted off camera as an eerie clash of clanking chains interrupted her audition. She smiled nervously and looked back at the script, the taunt of the rattling chains breaking her concentration only for a moment. "If you want a divorce, then just say it," she snipped. "Because I'm so tired of the lies."

From the left side of the screen, a long shadow stretched across the concrete floor, a silhouette of chains dangling at its side. The chains scraped along the floor as the dark shadow continued dragging them along. The young woman stopped reading as she slowly followed the shadowy figure with her eyes.

"Please continue," the voice said.

The young woman paused as she eyed the shadow, which was almost directly in front of her. She looked into the camera and shook her head. "I'm no longer interested in the part."

She abruptly rose from the aluminum chair. Its legs skidded against the cement as she stood, sending a chilling screech into the air. "What's he doing?" she asked as she took a step back. A large, black mass entered the shot.

This man, who could only be seen from the top of his shoulders down to his legs, appeared on screen. The young woman stiffened her posture as the man, dressed in all black, his beer belly spilling over the top of his black jeans, raised the chain in his right hand and swung it against the woman's face. It collided against her left cheek with a force so strong she instantly shrieked. The links wrapped around her neck like a noose, and the man gripped the chain tighter in his hand as he dragged her to the side of the room.

High-pitched cries filled the room as he wrapped the length of the chain around her neck and fastened a padlock through the last link. A loud click loomed in the air as it locked. The man, fully visible now, straightened the black mask over his face before lifting the young woman off the ground. He secured her onto the hook that hung from the center of the room. She twisted and squirmed as she grabbed at her neck, trying to pry the chain from around her throat.

She gasped for air as she choked on the restraint around her throat, her feet kicking in midair as she desperately searched for anything to stand on. Streaks of mascara trailed down her face as a barrage of tears poured from her eyes. She lifted her arms into the air and wrapped her hands around the thick rope. She tried to raise herself, a pointless effort to relieve the pressure off her windpipe. Her arms trembled as she lifted herself slightly.

The man stood less than a foot from her reach. She unsuccessfully kicked at him, her feet missing the target by mere inches. The mask clung to the man's nose with every breath he inhaled. He waited patiently for her to tire, standing there as if bored with her struggle.

As her kicks became less forceful, the man raised his left hand, and a long blade gleamed in the sunlight. He swiped the knife across the woman's wrists, and she let out a painful shrill as she released her grip from around the rope. Her body slumped closer to the ground as she dangled from the chain-link noose. Blood streamed down her hands, past her fingertips, and dripped onto the ground below. She brought her bloody hands up to her throat, gagging under the pressure of the chain, and clutched at her neck. Her fingers stiffened as if her hands and wrists had been paralyzed—likely due to severed tendons from the assailant's knife.

A loud cough released from her lips as her hands fell back to her sides and her head hung low. She slowly swayed back and forth, like a rag doll limply sagging from a rope, as the masked man raised his knife again and slashed it across her sternum. A flood of bodily fluids and organs spilled out of her. Her intestines plopped onto the floor and splashed upward with a sickening splatter. The camera picked up the sloshing sound, like water against a rowboat, as her entrails dangled from her midsection.

The masked man turned his head slowly toward the camera, the knife in his left hand dripping with blood, and he glared into the lens. His dark eyes stared blankly into the camera as if he tried to hypnotize the audience with his gaze. Then the video abruptly shut off.

My muscles tightened to keep the bile brewing in my stomach from rushing up my throat. The screen went black, and Captain Fluellen—"Flu" to his colleagues—cleared his throat.

"That's where the video ends," Flu said. The glow from the projector overhead highlighted the wrinkles around his eyes and the place where his bald spot met his receding hairline. He scrolled the cursor to the top right corner of the video program and clicked the red "X" with his mouse. He closed out of the program, and the randomly scattered icons on his desktop remained visible on the screen. "This is the second video we've received anonymously," Flu added someone turned the fluorescent lights back on.

"Does she have a name?" an officer asked from the third row of chairs.

"I'm sure she does. But we don't know it yet—mainly because we haven't found her," Flu said. "We scanned her image from the video, and we're running it through facial-recognition programs, but that takes times," he added. "We were, however, able to determine the name of the victim from the first video. Pamela Westlake, age thirty-three. Caucasian female, worked as a hair stylist part time. She lived in West Joseph her entire life. She was reported missing by her boyfriend in July." He paused. "We still haven't been able to find her body—so we aren't able to treat this as a homicide yet. As far as we know, this is some kid with a bucket of pig's blood playing a bad prank. But if the video is real—and I believe it is—it's safe to assume she's dead." Flu lowered his head and slowly shook it from side to side. "We received Pamela Westlake's video last week. Both videos were sent to the department's email address. Both were sent on consecutive Wednesday evenings between 9:00 p.m. and 11:00 p.m. Both were presumed auditions with the same nefarious outcomes."

"Can't we just look up the email address it was sent from?" the same officer asked.

"If it were that simple, we wouldn't have received a second video, now would we?" Flu snapped. "Perhaps I'm not the best person to explain this…." Flu motioned toward the back of the room.

Abram Myers, West Joseph Police Department's most recent Information Technology hire, had been with the department since February. My first interaction with him was the second day I came back to work. He gave me a department-issued laptop so that I could work from home if I wanted. I took the laptop without protest, knowing this job didn't have banker's hours. He looked me up and down and politely complimented my investigative skills. He didn't specify which investigation, but I knew he meant the Lathan Collins case.

Abram sauntered up the aisle as he made his way to the podium at the front of the room. He barely made eye contact with anyone as he strolled past each officer. His curly, auburn hair neatly skimmed the collar of his checkered shirt. When he approached the podium, he scratched his right cheek, his nails scraping along the scars embedded in his skin from what must have been years of bad acne.

"To answer your question, yes. We can look up the email address it was sent from. And we tried. But the service provider has up to ninety days to respond to our subpoena requesting more information about the user's account." Abram paused, then continued more confidently. "What we do know is that the first video was sent from a laptop that used a coffee shop or a fast food restaurant's Wi-Fi. I'm sure you all know what Wi-Fi is?" He paused again, as if he was teaching a class. "It allows for users to connect to the internet wirelessly. In every email header, there's a detailed log of the network path between the sender and the receiver. We usually see 'To,' 'From,' 'Date,' and 'Subject.' But beyond that, there's more information, like the IP address."

A wave of contrasting reactions washed over the room. The younger officers, who knew the internet well, crossed and uncrossed their legs as they listened to Abram explain something as everyday to them as brushing their teeth. The older officers, the ones who could barely turn on a computer, let out sighs of confusion as Abram continued his lecture.

"The Internet Protocol, or IP, address is a numerical code that resembles longitude and latitude on a map. The numbers are something like, one-four-two dot eight-two dot one-nine-two dot two. Unfortunately," he said, "the IP address isn't as precise as longitude and latitude is. It can only pinpoint a user within a five-mile radius. But I was able to narrow it down by the city block, and it's somewhere in the West Joseph Shopping Plaza," Abram said in a boastful tone. "There are a few fast food and coffee shops there that provide free Wi-Fi to customers. And any one of those could have been where the video was sent from."

"Can't we just ask the coffee shops for their IP addresses?" one of the elderly officers asked.

"We did," Flu interjected, "and none of the businesses are willing to give up that information without a warrant. It's *likely* the Wi-Fi being used is in the West Joseph Plaza, but we don't know for sure. And we don't have the manpower to go knocking on every door within a five-mile radius."

"Even with each business's actual IP address," Abram said, taking back the proverbial microphone from Flu, "it would be easier to find a needle in a haystack than to track down whoever might've used their Wi-Fi. A coffee shop has over two thousand sales a month. We know the date and time the email was sent, but the coffee shop doesn't keep track of who uses their Wi-Fi. We could subpoena their sales receipts for that date, around the time the email was sent, but there's a possibility the sender didn't buy anything or could have paid cash. And not every shop has a camera. Whoever's sending these videos could be anyone tech-savvy enough to connect to Wi-Fi—so, basically, anyone."

"There is some silver lining, though," Flu said, walking back to the front of the room where Abram stood. "The sender sent each of the two videos on the exact same day, one week apart. It's too early to say this is a pattern, but it's not too early to dismiss it as a coincidence."

"Is there an established motive?" I asked from the back of the room. A domino effect of heads turned to look at me.

"Each video we received was some type of audition gone wrong," Flu said. "We'll have an agent from the Bureau of Criminal Investigations here in a few days to assist. Until then, everyone keep your eyes peeled—especially around the West Joseph Shopping Plaza. We don't have it in the budget to add extra patrol, but if you're acquainted with the shop owners, see if you can get a little more information out of them about their customers. Ask if they remember anyone using their Wi-Fi who may have sat in a secluded area. Abram says that video file of this size would take around twenty minutes to upload, especially on a shared network, and whoever sent it would want their privacy," Flu said and then dismissed the second-shift officers.

A cacophony of chairs skidding along the linoleum pierced my ears as the officers made their way out of the briefing room. It was early afternoon, and the first-shift officers were headed back into the station. They had received the same briefing prior to their shift this morning, along with Flu's instruction to patrol the Shopping Plaza carefully. It was my hope that they didn't return empty handed.

I waited for the officers to leave before I maneuvered my way to the front of the room. Abram was still there. "Any calls?" I asked Flu.

"One, but not about the video," Flu said. "We're needed in Mirror Woods. They found a body in the lake—the dive team is already there."

"Mirror Woods," Abram said. "You do your best work there." He patted my shoulder. I looked at Flu as I tried my best to ignore Abram's compliment.

The Lathan Collins case had been closed for nearly a year, but it seemed like I was the only person in West Joseph willing to move on. I felt as if I was the star quarterback who threw the winning touchdown in the championship game. Back in high school. Two decades ago. More than a few restaurants in town refused to charge me for my food, and star-struck residents offered to buy me a drink. I was a local celebrity, but I didn't want to be.

"Let me know the moment you ID the woman in the second video," Flu said to Abram. He turned to me. "Evans, let's go."

I sat in the passenger seat as Flu drove us to Mirror Woods. After the horrific murders that happened here last year, the West Joseph Planning Committee entertained the thought of changing the name of Mirror Woods to something less haunting. But City Council quickly dismissed the idea. Instead, they had an enormous slab of marble, engraved with the victims' names, placed by the entrance of the park. On the anniversary of each victim's death, friends and family would place bouquet of flowers, stuffed animals and other tokens of remembrance along the stone.

In the past year, West Joseph had slowly grown in popularity—mostly among individuals who are intrigued by serial killers. The increase in local tourism meant more business for the city: hotels, restaurants, even a Lathan Collins Bus Tour that went through Mirror Woods.

Soulless residents who lived near Mirror Woods profited the most from the tour. They would tell tourists tall tales of what it was like to live by Mirror Woods during the murders—some even went so far as to say they saw Lathan Collins lurking nearby after victims were found. The tourists would shell out dollar after dollar, sliding the cash into the residents' hands like a vending machine that spat out gumballs. And the tourists sucked down every last bit of the residents' fables.

The winding road that led through the thick forest of Mirror Woods twisted like a serpent's spine as Flu and I made our way toward the lake. I stared out the window, the trees blurring as we whizzed by, and I felt my chest start to close in. A sudden surge coursed through my body as the back of my throat tightened. I shut my eyes and counted backward from ten.

Ten, I thought to myself. My hands and legs started to tingle into a familiar numbness.

Nine... eight. I took in a deep breath and held it in hopes that would control my shallow breathing.

Seven. I opened my eyes—the trees still a blur and I blinked back the tears that formed in my eyes.

Six... five. I exhaled, my heart slowly retuning toward a normal beat.

Four... three. I dragged my palms against my pant legs and wiped the sweat from my fingertips. I clenched my hands into a tight fist, my knuckles turning white from the strain.

Two. I swallowed hard, and the pressure in my chest eased.

One. I took another deep breath and let it out slowly. My heartbeat eased to a natural rhythm, and I felt calm again.

Flu parked the car, and I stared out the window. A blanket of water and spectators stretched before me. My head throbbed as my vision returned to normal.

"You all right, Evans?" Flu asked as he opened the driver's side door.

"Yeah," I said, my throat dry and itchy.

A light breeze blew through the late August air. An orchestra of birds chirped as I opened the passenger door. I followed Flu down the dirt path toward the lake. Grapefruit-sized stones lined the way leading to the man-made beach. The "beach" was mostly loose gravel, and the deepest part of the "lake" reached a maximum of ten feet. Locals used to argue whether to call the lake a "pond" instead, but most everyone referred to it as "Mirror Woods Lake," so the name stuck.

"Captain," the responding officer said to Flu as we approached the shore.

"This is Sergeant Evans," Flu said, officially introducing me to the officer. Beads of sweat formed along the officer's hairline. "What do you know?" Flu asked him.

"We believe it was an accidental drowning," he said, his overgrown buzz cut revealing the dark bristles of hair sticking out from his head. "The dive team found algae wrapped around the woman's ankle. Her arms were outstretched, so she must have run out of oxygen as she fought her way to the top."

"Her name?" Flu sighed.

"We believe her name is Wilma Reynolds," the officer said.

"You believe?"

"Yeah," the officer replied. "The ranger said he remembered seeing the same blue Corolla parked in the lot for a few weeks now. We ran the plates and came up with Wilma Reynolds."

"Why didn't he report it weeks ago?" I chimed in.

"I don't know." The officer shrugged. "He doesn't sound very good at his job," he added.

"Has the family made a positive ID?" Flu asked.

"Not yet. She's still in the water. We checked Missing Persons for her name, and she was reported missing by her husband on July eleventh," the officer informed us.

"That's over a month ago," Fluellen pointed out, clearly flabbergasted.

"Yep," the officer concurred.

"Is that her family?" I gestured to a small huddle of people standing on the dock on the other side of the lake.

"Could be?" The officer shrugged again. The ranger wasn't the only person here who wasn't very good at his job. "We told them to meet us at the station, but somehow they showed up here."

The family—presumably Wilma's mother, husband, and daughter—watched the dive team's boat bob up and down in the middle of the lake, which stretched over an acre wide. The crystal blue gleam of the water's surface rippled as the breeze blew a steady wind across the lake. One of the dive team members, dressed in a red windbreaker, sat along the edge of the boat as he peered into the water. He held a thick, white rope that hung off the side of the boat and into the water.

Next to the family stood a local reporter. The slender brown-haired woman was dressed in a gray pantsuit and held a wireless microphone as she smoothed back her shoulder-length hair. The lone camera operator, a chubby man with a backwards cap, had his camera hoisted onto his shoulder as he fiddled with the buttons on the side. Their white news van was parked in the grass along the white picket fence that separated the parking lot from the dock entrance. Next to it, looking like its twin, was the coroner's van.

The coroner leaned against his van as he took a long drag off his cigarette. A thin trail of smoke lingered above the red bud as he sucked on the end of the filter. Large bags had formed under his eyes, and his poorly combed-over gray strands of hair wisped in the wind. He sighed heavily as he took one last puff on his cigarette and threw it on the ground. He lifted his foot, stomped on the butt with his black shoes, and ground it into the pavement before walking toward the dock.

A series of large bubbles broke through the water near the shore as the second member of the dive team surfaced. His scuba tank glimmered in the sun as he swam toward the boat. Alongside him, tucked under his arm, was the victim. Her matted brown hair stuck to her bloated pale-blue face, which had chunks of skin missing from her cheekbones. Large welts ranging from dark red to light pink popped around her eyes, which had turned yellow from the submersion. The victim's arms were locked upright due to rigor mortis, and as the member of the dive team swam toward the boat, her arms swayed from side to side, as if she was waving.

"Look, Dad!" the little girl called out. She couldn't have been more than five or six years old, and her blond hair had been pulled into a high ponytail that curled at the end. "It's Mom! She's waving to us." She threw her hands in the air and waved them above her head. "Hi, Mom!" she shouted.

"Oh, thank God. It's her," the dad said and clutched his heart. His wavy black hair fell slightly past his shoulders, making his round face stand out. "Wilma!" He waved his arms. His cheeks stiffened into a tight grin.

"No...." Flu's eyes bulged as he watched the family cheer for the dive team. "No."

Flu ran along the perimeter of the lake, cutting through the crowd of spectators, as he tried to shield the family from the sloppy search-and-recover mission. Even though Wilma Reynolds had been submerged for almost two months, her family must've been in such denial of her passing that they thought it was plausible she could still be alive.

"Get them out of here!" Flu flailed his arms in the air as he ran along the bank. Deep imprints of his shoes sank into the loose gravel as he continued to yell. "You have to bag her first," he muttered.

The news reporter snapped her fingers several times at the camera operator and spoke into the microphone as soon as the camera was on her. The cameraman stood close in front of her and panned the camera across the lake, recording the cheering family who waited to embrace their loved one.

I gave the responding officer one last look and jogged around the lake, following Flu's prints in the gravel. The diver had reached the boat, and he passed Wilma Reynolds' body to his partner in the red windbreaker. He wrapped his hands around Wilma's arms and lifted her into the boat before helping the diver out of the water.

White streaks of water rose across the lake's surface as the boat's motor kicked on and the boat made its way to the dock where the family, news crew and two officers stood. The officers gently pushed the family back from the dock once they saw the body hadn't been bagged. Flu pushed his way through the officers and the news crew as he ran down the dock toward the boat.

"Get them out of here!" he barked at the officers.

The responding officer and I were close behind Flu as the three of us ran down the short dock. The officer assisted his partners in keeping the family and news crew from seeing the decomposed body.

"Sir," the officer said. "You and your family need to step back. Let the officers do their job."

Flu stood at the edge of the dock, the soles of his shoes covered in soot and pebbles, and he glared at the diver, who was taking off his flippers. The boat continued to bob in the water as the dive team bagged the rotting corpse of Wilma Reynolds. The moldy smell of decayed, water-logged flesh burned in the back of my throat and made my eyes water. A faint taste of raw sardines soaked in oil crept over my taste buds as I took in quick breaths, trying to shield my nose from the stench.

"What were you thinking?" Flu hollered at the diver. "You are to bag them underwater. Never break the surface with an exposed victim."

"I'm sorry, Captain. He's new," the man in the red windbreaker said sheepishly.

"I can't believe this." Flu sighed as he threw his hands down to his sides. "If the family sues us, it's coming out of your pay," he snapped, then walked up the dock toward the now grieving family.

The rubber soles of my shoes squeaked on the dock as I followed Flu. He pushed past the cameraman as the reporter shoved the microphone in Flu's face and asked him a series of ill-mannered questions. He ignored her and continued walking.

"Sergeant Evans," she said as I walked past her. "What's it like to be back in Mirror Woods with *another* dead body?" She stood in front of me with the microphone a fraction of an inch away from my mouth. The cameraman stood alongside her and pointed the camera at my face.

"Have a little respect for the deceased," I said as I grabbed the lens and twisted it in my hands. The camera shifted from the man's grasp and fell to the ground with a loud cracking sound.

That's going to cost me, I thought to myself as I followed Flu to the coroner's van.

CHAPTER | THREE

"CAPTAIN," ABRAM SAID AS he walked into Flu's office. "We got a name for the second victim." He slapped a rolled piece of paper against the door, interrupting my conversation with Flu. A sudden *pop* echoed through Flu's office as the paper-smacking sound ricocheted against the metal doorframe.

Flu pushed his chair away from his mahogany desk, a cluttered mess of case files, legal pads, and crumpled napkins from several days' worth of lunches. The wheels of his office chair skidded along the tile floor as he stood up and took the paper from Abram's hand. It crinkled as Flu unrolled and smoothed out the sheet of paper. He looked over it several times and nodded, then handed the sheet to me.

It featured a woman's picture in a square box—along with her name, address, and date of birth. Her long blond hair wildly framed her face, and her sparkling blue eyes reflected the flash from the camera. Her age, height, and weight were also listed.

"Fionna Michaels," Abram said. "Reported missing in late July by her boyfriend. She's local. Her boyfriend's number is on the report if you need to talk to him."

"Thank you. Good work," Flu said. "Send this to me in an email."

"I already did, sir—I printed this off for your convenience." Abram said, much too pleased with himself.

"Evans, I'm putting you on lead. Abram, send this information to Evans," Flu said as he sat back down in his chair.

"Certainly." Abram nodded and left the room.

"Go home, Evans," Flu said. "I'll finish up the Reynolds case."

I waited until I was sure Abram was nowhere within earshot before I turned to Flu. "I was thinking about the videos...." I said. That was the truth, but it wasn't the whole truth. Really, I just didn't want to go home. Not yet, anyway.

We had returned from Mirror Woods less than an hour ago, and I wasn't ready to call it a day. After the mishap with the dive team—and then bagging the evidence, which concluded the death was an accidental drowning—I was too wired to go home.

"What about them?" Flu asked.

"Something seems… off. Why would someone send us the videos but not the identities of the people in them?"

"Pride," Flu simply stated. "Whoever this is wants to create a cat-and-mouse game. He's proud of what he's doing, and he wants to flaunt it in our faces." Flu paused before he motioned for me to close his door. I leaned back, pressed the tips of my fingers against the edge of the door, and pushed it closed.

"Since you're here," he said, "there's something you need to know. I haven't made this public, and no one aside from Abram knows." Flu paused again, as if searching for the right words to reveal his big secret. "The videos are being addressed to you."

"Me? Why me?"

"Aside from the obvious reason?" Flu answered.

After the Lathan Collins' case, I had become the most well-known detective in the city. If Flu was right about pride being the sender's motivation, then addressing the videos to me added a bit more flavor to the meal.

"Why haven't you told the rest of the department?" I asked.

"I don't want anyone to get carried away. We have some of the best officers around, but even the best can be tempted by the media. We can't let these videos get out to the public."

"I understand," I said. I completely agreed with Flu. The less attention I received, the better. "Is that all?"

"Yeah," Flu nodded, curiosity suddenly striking his face. "How are things at home?" he asked with a shift in the tone of his voice.

"Fine," I quickly said.

"Uh-huh," he said, as if he was humoring me. Flu knew me well enough to know when I wasn't being completely honest with him. "I noticed your panic attack in the car today, when we were headed into Mirror Woods. If things aren't so good at home with Abi, that could be the reason—"

"Things are fine," I snapped.

"After everything that happened, it's a lot for one person to go through. Are you still seeing that psychologist?"

"I don't have time to see one now," I cut in. "I went through the mandatory sessions and was given the all clear."

"Find the time," Flu said, "before the time finds you." He paused before locking eyes with me. "How many divorces have you seen in all your years as a cop? Too many, I'm sure. And it's all for the same reason. This job can cost you everything—but only if you let it."

I nodded. Flu was right—I just didn't want him to be. In the twenty years I'd been in law enforcement, almost all the divorces within the department were due to the officer putting the job first. But that was part of the job; it had to come first.

"We're fine," I said, shrugging off the thought. "Somehow it'll work itself out. I have too much going on at work."

"Don't use your job as an excuse to let the people you care about slip away."

I let my eyes drift toward the floor. So much had changed in the course of a year. Sometimes I wondered if I made the smart choice coming back to work. Maybe Abi and I should have moved to Pittsburgh when her family suggested it. We could live in her brother's basement—insects and all.

"How could a town this small change so much in a year?" I asked. It was mostly rhetorical. But for some reason, I wanted to hear Flu's answer.

"Maybe it isn't the town that changed," he said.

I should have known better than to seek understanding from Flu. Although I knew his intentions were good, I didn't want a boss-turned-friend lecture from him. "I should get home," I said and stood from the chair.

"Think about what I said," Flu said, making no attempt to back off. He was on a mission, and he was going to make sure I heard him loud and clear.

"Yes, Captain," I mustered as I walked out of his office.

As I drove home, a fluorescent mauve hue coated the cloudless sky as the sun sank past the horizon. From the busy intersection that raced with cars traveling in all directions, I turned onto my street that had all the quiet and calmness of an abandoned church. The streetlights hovered over the beat-up brick road, and an elderly woman walked down the sidewalk. She clutched her purse that was tucked under her arm as she shielded it from potential would-be thieves.

I pulled into the driveway and sat in my black Jetta as it ran idle. With the car's air conditioning still running, I was able to tolerate the stifling humidity that lingered just outside the door.

My modest two-story Victorian-style home sat in the middle of the yard, and it looked rather welcoming as I gazed out the window. The paved walkway that led to the front door was a shade darker than the light-gray siding, and the burgundy shutters coordinated well with the weather-beaten brick chimney. Along the front of the house, a small flowerbed contained purple sage blossoms and black-eyed susans swaying blissfully in the shallow breeze.

I shut off the engine and opened the door. The sweet scent of freshly mowed grass filled my nose, and a thin layer of sweat instantly formed under my arms as the scorching heat beat down on my face. I took a deep breath and walked along the path leading toward the front door. My body immediately cooled as I reached the shaded section of the front porch, and I quickly opened the door.

Sheer white curtains draped along the large window in the living room. The thin slats of the wood floor stretched vertically through the living room and led toward the back of the house, which is where the kitchen and home office were. Under the window, crushed potpourri sat in a glass jar atop a long and narrow console table. An oversized white doily dangled off the sides of the table. Just in front of the table was a tan suede couch with dark red pillows. The large flat-screen television on the opposite wall stood on top of a small entertainment center with a DVD player and cable box resting on the shelves below.

"You're home?" I said, shocked to see Abi on the sofa.

Abi sat with her feet curled under her legs and her hair wrapped in a tight braid that fell over her left shoulder. "Yeah, I got home about an hour ago," she said.

"Oh," I nodded. "That's right. You met co-workers for dinner," I reminded myself. She had told me of her plans several days ago, but it had slipped my mind until now.

"Just one co-worker," Abi said. "How was your day?" she asked as I closed the front door behind me. A coy smile slipped from her lips.

"You saw?"

"It'll be on the eleven o'clock news too." Abi held in a laugh. "My favorite part was Flu," she added. There was no doubt that she knew about the mishap with the dive team this afternoon.

I didn't have to guess how comical Flu looked as he flailed his arms in the air and frantically hollered at the dive team. I had hoped the news crew would show some mercy and not air that part. Apparently, after my clash with the cameraman, mercy was not their style.

"Am I in it?" I winced. I already knew the answer, but confirmation was the salted dagger I was missing in my side. Abi's lips contorted into more of an apologetic smile as she slowly nodded. It wasn't just because of the media attention I had received from the Lathan Collins' case that I didn't want to appear on the news. It was also because having footage of law enforcement destroying private property, such as a news camera, didn't sit well with the administration or with the public.

"You looked really good," Abi said. That was one of the great things about Abi. Deep down, I knew she was mad at me—maybe even more than mad—but she wasn't going to kick me when I was down. No matter how tempted she was.

"Thanks," I said as I walked into the kitchen.

Light-colored wood cabinets with glass doors formed an "L" shape that hung above the gray-speckled countertop. The black gas stove and matching microwave reflected the sun that peeked through the window on the opposite wall. White subway tiles covered the wall space between the cabinets and the countertop. I walked toward the refrigerator and grabbed a beer from the full six-pack on the bottom shelf. I held one by the neck and lifted it from the pack. The sharp sting from the cool bottle nipped at the palm of my hand.

I reached into the drawer adjacent to the dishwasher and picked up the bottle opener. The metal clacked against the glass as I snapped off the cap. A refreshing *tsst* sound escaped from the bottle, and an almost translucent layer of smoke fogged around the bottle. I clenched the cap and bottle opener in my hand and placed them on the granite countertop as Abi walked into the kitchen.

I took a sip from the bottle. The foam bubbled in my mouth as the cold liquid washed over my tongue and down my throat. The back of my head tightened slightly as I took another gulp, the suds building in my stomach. I twirled the bottle between my fingers as drops of condensation pooled around the base, and I looked at Abi.

"I thought you were going to Pittsburgh" I said.

"I'm leaving tomorrow morning."

I picked up my beer, which was still more than three-quarters full, and I walked past Abi as she stood in front of the stove. Walking past her was the only way out of the kitchen, and I knew if we stayed in the same room much longer, it would turn into a passive-aggressive argument. My shoulder grazed hers as I walked toward the office.

With the sun setting and the curtains drawn, the lamp cast its light over the wood floors as dark shadows hid in the corners. My department-issued laptop sat in the middle of the oak desk, which took up the entire right corner of the room. The modem and router, tucked under the desk, cast a soft green glow. I pulled back the chair, and its wheels rolled smoothly along the plastic floor protector.

I sat down and opened the laptop. I thought tonight would be as good a time as any to start researching the videos.

If only it was that easy.

Although access to my work was less than a foot in front of my face, it was the furthest thing from my mind. I wasn't able to concentrate—not with the thought of Abi being mad at me. I was surprised she hadn't called me out on my behavior. She usually did by now, but maybe she was tired of being the one to make the first move.

Abi walked into the office. "Hey."

"Hey." I matched her tone, but I didn't look at her.

"I don't want to leave for Pittsburgh with you mad at me," she said

"I'm not mad at you." I turned toward her. Abi leaned against the doorway and crossed her arms. Her lips dropped into a subtle frown as she looked at me, her blue eyes full of worry.

It was impossible to feel nothing when I looked at her. She was beautiful—no amount of trauma was going to change that fact. But the emotions were missing. My arms ached to hold her, but my heart fell hard into my stomach, like a bowling ball dropped off a cliff. Whatever wall I had built around my heart couldn't crumble with just one look from her.

"I'm sorry," I said and lowered my head. "I want you to go see your family. I know how much they mean to you."

Abi walked farther into the office, her pant legs rustling together. "Everything okay at work?"

"Yeah." I hesitated. "I was assigned to a new case."

"Is that what's getting to you?"

"Partly," I said. She was right. There was something getting to me—eating at me—but I didn't know what it was. It was as if there was something living inside me, like a carnivorous parasite and I was its host. But instead of devouring me in one gulp, it took one morsel at a time, digesting me at its leisure before taking the next bite. "It's this case, it's work, it's the entire town of West Joseph," I said.

"I thought you liked it here?"

"I did." I shrugged. "I do."

"Maybe you just need time to adjust?"

"It's been a year," I said as I leaned back in the chair.

"Have you thought about talking to someone?"

"I did."

"Maybe you should go back," Abi suggested.

"You sound like Flu." I rolled my eyes.

"Maybe he's right," Abi said sternly. "He knows the stress of your job more than anyone."

41

"I know." I sighed. "I'll look into it."

But I already had.

Dr. Rosenthal and I had been meeting monthly since the incident with Lathan Collins.

The initial six sessions did nothing to help my emotional detachment from everyone—and Abi was receiving the worst of it. I was constantly agitated. I barely slept; when I did, my dreams were so violent and vivid that the strength it took to survive them made it feel as if I hadn't slept at all.

And I hadn't told Abi—or anyone else—that I was still seeing Dr. Rosenthal. I needed this to be something that was just mine. I didn't want their opinions or their encouragement for better mental health. I had fallen into a pit of mistrust, especially with those closest to me. And no matter how hard I tried to climb out, my hands were too weak to grab hold. I felt smothered and coddled by Abi, and my only defense was to push her away—not because I didn't want her to love me, but because I didn't want to be *here*. With her, or with anyone.

CHAPTER | FOUR

DR. MARLENE ROSENTHAL PUSHED her thinning gray hair behind her ears as I sat across from her. Neatly framed psychology degrees hung on the ivory-colored wall behind her desk. Pamphlets detailing various mental-health disorders were sprawled on the end table adjacent to the oak double doors. Dr. Rosenthal crossed her legs at the knee, her plaid skirt draped loosely around her thigh, as she twirled a pen in her hands.

She brought a certain sense of comfort whenever I talked to her. It was more than her psychobabble that made me feel at ease—I actually trusted her. Maybe that was because our relationship didn't go any further than these four walls. Only her pen and pad knew what was in my head. She was my personal diary in a way, a shoebox filled with memories that only opened when I wanted it to.

The oversized chair creaked as I sank into the cushion. A soft scent of sage permeated her office as I waited for our session to begin. The heat from the sun through her large office window soaked into my skin. It convinced my muscles to relax. Throughout the day, I'm stiff and on guard, like an attack dog waiting for the command to strike. The pressure on my chest and shoulders feels insurmountable, as if I'm going to crumble at any moment.

"How are you?" Dr. Rosenthal asked.

"It's Friday," I said with a shrug.

"How have you been since the last time we spoke?" She stopped twirling the pen as she sat quietly in her chair.

"The same."

"No changes at all?"

I shook my head and bit down on my lower lip as I gazed out the window. The cloudless blue sky created a brilliant backdrop for the adjacent two-story buildings that stood across from Dr. Rosenthal's office window. A small silhouette of an airplane soared above, its stream of white smoke trailing across the sky.

I envied the passengers in a way, the way I envied birds or any

43

other being that could take flight. Whether the passengers were coming or going, they weren't here in this town. At this moment, and for as long as the flight stayed suspended in air, they were free.

I knew that if I really wanted to leave, I could. Abi never said it, but I knew she would leave in a heartbeat—if I made the suggestion first. There was something holding me back, though. I was somehow anchored to this town. I had never been one to run from my demons, but this time I wanted to.

I hoped Dr. Rosenthal would be able to help me figure out why.

"How are you sleeping?" Dr. Rosenthal asked, which brought me back to the conversation.

"A little better." I sighed. "I'm able to sleep for about five hours a night... sometimes for two hours straight."

"And your dreams?"

"Normal," I said. "Until last night, I'd been dreaming about fire a lot. Either I'm trapped by it, or people are trapped in a building with fire all around it. And I can't get past it to save them."

"Why do you want to save them?"

"Because that's what I do," I said. "It's my job to save people."

"Fire has several meanings," Dr. Rosenthal said. "Depending on the context of the dream, fire can mean destruction, passion, anger, desire. What does it feel like to you?"

"Hot," I mocked—which was met with a disapproved look from Dr. Rosenthal. "The fire is chasing me," I conceded. "Not like it has legs or anything... but like my footprints are soaked in gasoline, and it follows me. It's destroying where I've been. I'm in a building, just trying to get away, turning corner after corner... and then I run into a dead end. The fire is still there, racing toward me. But before I'm engulfed in its flames, I wake up."

"You said 'until last night.'" Dr. Rosenthal paused. "Did you dream of something different last night?"

"Him," I answered. "I dreamt about that night again."

"It's approaching the one-year anniversary," Dr. Rosenthal said as she wrote in her notepad. "What happened in the dream?"

"It was a replay of everything that happened. I could hear him. I could smell him. I could *feel* him."

Dr. Rosenthal continued to write in her notepad. "How's your mood in general?" she asked. "The last time we spoke, you said you felt a lot of pressure—and were easily angered."

"The same. But I'm not angry, I'm... irritable."

Dr. Rosenthal raised one eyebrow as she looked at me, giving her

44

pen a break from feverishly writing. "Are you downplaying your emotions?"

"Maybe?" I smirked. "Okay, I'm angry." Anger had become an intuitive reaction to anything I couldn't control. Whether it was at work or at home, if the situation wouldn't allow me to control it, my body tensed, and a surge of rage coursed through my veins. I knew how to control my anger—usually by leaving the situation. But sometimes it stuck with me, like a leech sucking the blood from my skin.

"Your relationship? How's that going?"

"Oh," I said and sighed louder than intended. "She's going to visit her brother this weekend."

"Are you going with her?"

"No." I shook my head.

"What do you think of this time spent apart?"

"It's for the best." I shrugged. "Maybe I'm holding onto something that no longer fits."

"How so?"

"I don't know." I sighed again. "I… we…." My voice shook. A bout of nerves quivered in my chest and flowed through my fingers as my hands clenched into fists. A shallow pool of tears welled behind my eyes as my throat tightened and an army of chills ran up my spine. I lowered my head. "It's like, I'm surrounded by a sea of familiar faces, but I have no idea who they are or who I am." I took a deep breath and held it in. My lungs burned under the pressure as I kept myself from crying. I counted to five—something Dr. Rosenthal had suggested to do when I found myself in an uncomfortable situation—and then I slowly breathed out.

"I could recommend someone for couple's therapy," she offered.

I shook my head almost immediately. "No more therapists. I don't even know if we can be fixed."

"Couple's therapy isn't always about fixing. Sometimes it's to help break a relationship into as many little pieces as possible," Dr. Rosenthal explained. "What seems to be the main problem between you two?"

"I'm pushing her away, and I don't know why."

"Just her?"

"No." I shook my head. "Everyone. I don't trust anyone."

"Why not?"

"I don't know," I said, laughing through the tears that yearned to fall, and then I glanced out the window again. The plane, and its trail of smoke, had vanished. "I can't be who this town wants me to be."

"Who do they want you to be?"

45

"The hero," I answered. "The way the other officers look at me, and the way I'm treated, like I'm royalty or something. Like, I have all the answers and could walk on water if I wanted to." I sighed. "I'm not walking… I'm drowning."

"From?"

"Their expectations," I snapped. "You said I had posttraumatic stress disorder… from what happened that night with Lathan." A rotten taste, like spoiled meat, filled my mouth whenever I said his name. "I don't understand how I could have PTSD when I beat him? I won."

"It's the events that are traumatic, not the outcome. Although, taking a life doesn't sit well with most people either."

She had a point. Lathan Collins deserved to be dead, but that didn't bring comfort when I remembered I was the one who did it. "I've been doing the breathing exercises you suggested, and they're working," I informed her. "I was called to Mirror Woods yesterday. I hadn't been there since that night." I swallowed back the bile produced by thinking of that night. "And I could feel myself getting worked up. I was anxious and felt crushed, like I was having a panic attack. So I counted backwards from ten. And it worked. I was fine."

"I'm glad it worked," she said. "Have you given any more thought to In Vivo Exposure?"

"I'm ready to try. If you think it will work."

"I do," Dr. Rosenthal said. "In Vivo Exposure isn't as easy as counting to ten." She locked eyes with me. "In Vivo is a form of cognitive behavior therapy, and it's the most effective treatment for PTSD, along with medication."

"I don't want to be on meds," I said firmly. "Not with my job."

"In Vivo is used to reduce the fear and triggers associated with the traumatic event," she explained. "In your case, you have a series of traumatic events with a climactic end. There are two types of exposure therapy: 'flooding' and 'prolonged exposure.' Flooding involves flooding the mind with triggering memories, and prolonged exposure gradually introduces triggering memories coupled with relaxation exercises when the anxiety becomes too intense."

"So, diving-in versus an-inch-at-a-time?"

"Yes," Dr. Rosenthal laughed.

"Are you going to hypnotize me?"

"No, nothing like that." She smiled. "We'll come up with a scale from one to one hundred that measures your distress. Zero is relaxed… no distressing emotions. One hundred is the most distressed… you see red and are more upset than you've even been. Fifty is the halfway point, halfway between relaxed and distressed… manageable, but you still know the distress is there."

"Is fifty the goal?"

"Fifty or less is considered successful, yes." Dr. Rosenthal paused to write in her notepad. "If this is something you want to try, I would recommend coming in once a week instead of once of a month. We've spent a lot of time processing your trauma in order for you to understand your negative thoughts and feelings. The next step is to break the negative thoughts—by identifying them as they happen and then changing them to be less distressing."

I felt guilty enough withholding a monthly appointment with Dr. Rosenthal from Abi, let alone having to withhold weekly visits. Abi never pried, so I knew I could easily cover my appointment by saying I had to work late. But the omission was the lie—and I wasn't a liar. I knew what it felt like to be the fool in a relationship, and I didn't want to do that to Abi.

But I also didn't want to continue feeling this way.

"What would we do for prolonged exposure?" I asked.

"Talk about the trauma."

"We do that now."

"Repeatedly talk about the trauma," Dr. Rosenthal elaborated. "We would start each session talking it out, piece by piece, until the memories were no longer upsetting."

The nightmares, irritability, and loneliness were enough to warrant a change. I wanted more than a change, though. I wanted to feel like myself. I wanted my life back. I was tired of being so withdrawn from the people I cared about.

"If this doesn't work?" I asked.

"There are other treatments. But, for now, let's see how you do with prolonged exposure," she said. "We can start next week," she added.

"Okay," I finally agreed. "Once a week," I mumbled as I massaged my temple with my fingertips.

"In the meantime, think about what you want from your relationship with Abi," she said, "and whether you can be honest with her about your feelings. A relationship isn't going to work if both people aren't working toward the same goal."

Before I left, I made another appointment with Dr. Rosenthal for next week. I knew I would eventually tell Abi, but I wasn't ready. She would have questions that I didn't have the answers to yet. I needed to see how the exposure treatment went. Then I would tell her.

As I drove home, I couldn't help but project my problems onto passersby. A muscular man wearing jogging pants and a tank top waited at the corner for the light to change. Did he have a recent traumatic experience? Is that why he was out running? Two women walked close to one another as they traveled down the opposite sidewalk. What devastating life event had they gone through? Did they see a psychologist once a week?

Dr. Rosenthal's words about Abi were something I needed to hear. Stringing her along was crueler than ending the relationship. Maybe Abi was waiting for the right time to break up with me?

I pulled into the driveway and walked up the short walkway to the front door. The hard metal key pushed into the grooves of my thumb as I turned the lock. The tumbler clicked as the dead bolt slid back into the door, and I turned the handle, the brass knob cool to the touch from soaking in the shade. The waning sunlight seeped into the living room, and my shadow stretched across the floor like a trail of black tar. I plopped my house keys and 9mm onto the table underneath the front window.

My shadow vanished as I shut the door. The drapes had been closed all day, which made the house stuffy with stale air. I pulled the curtains back and opened the window. The screen was splotched with dust that had collected between the tiny squares. Fresh air trickled into the house, and a gust of cool wind rolled in through the open window. I locked the front door. A soft neon glow from the setting sun now filled the lifeless room.

Abi left a small note taped to the inside part of the front door. The ink faded as she neared the end of the sentence. *I'll call you tonight.* Abi was old fashioned in the sense that she preferred handwritten notes over text messages. I pulled the note off the door and crumpled it in my hand before stuffing it into my pocket. I preferred text messages.

Without Abi, the quiet inside the house was almost haunting. It lingered from room to room and amplified the somber sounds of a settling house. The living room seemed to expand, creating an abandoned abyss, like a lonely ghost lurking in the open air. It was invisible to the naked eye, but dark and sinister to the mind.

I walked the six feet from the front door to the couch and fell face-forward onto the cushions. A loud *puff* of exasperation escaped my lips, and I swept my hands under the throw pillow. The soft fabric felt silky against my cheek as I rolled over and stretched my legs down the couch. Before I could fall into a daydream—or a day terror as they usually were—a mechanical melody chirped from my front pocket. I would have let the call go to voicemail if I didn't recognize the tune assigned to Abi.

"Hello?" I answered.

"Hi," Abi greeted. "Were you sleeping?"

"No." I sat up straight on the couch. "I just got home. How was your drive?"

"Good," she said.

Normally, Abi was rather talkative and would go into great detail about her day. But I could tell there was something holding her back. It was more than the quick answer followed by dead silence on the other end. This conversation felt different. Before, even with Abi being hundreds of miles away, I still felt close to her. This time, she felt farther away than Pittsburgh. She might as well have been on the moon.

A soft hum of dead air swept through the phone. There was so much we needed to say to each other, but I couldn't find the words to tell her how I was feeling. The once-comfortable silences between us had turned into an agonizing lack of conversation. It felt like the end of us. I didn't want it to be, but there was no other reason for the wall of despondency that had been built between us.

"My brother says hello," she said after a few moments of silence. "And the kids. Everyone says hello. They miss you."

"Tell them I said hello too."

I remained tight-lipped, mostly because I didn't want to talk about my day. I could tell her about the new case. But without being able to go into detail, there wasn't much to talk about. I would be forced to tell her about my sessions with Dr. Rosenthal, and I wasn't ready yet. I needed more time to wrap my head around it.

"I'll let you go," Abi said. "You sound tired."

"I am. Tell the kids…." My voice trailed off. I wasn't tired enough to end the conversation, but what was the point? If I couldn't honestly tell Abi that I missed her and that I loved her, what was the point? Our relationship had been reduced to using familial bystanders as a way to convey our feelings.

A thin coat of tears rose from the brim of my eyes, and I held my breath. I couldn't let myself cry. If I did, I didn't know when I would stop.

"We aren't good, are we?" Abi quietly asked.

"No," I said as tears rose in my throat. "We aren't."

"I thought this was going to be temporary." Her voice cracked.

"So did I."

"But it isn't, is it?" Abi cleared her throat. I could only assume she must've had a long chat with her brother when she got to his house. He was the kind of guy who always advised ripping off the Band-Aid. Given Abi's burst of bravery to say the thing I couldn't, I didn't know whether to smack him or thank him.

I wanted to tell her that I didn't know if this was temporary. But the truth was, I did know. We weren't good. This wasn't temporary.

"I don't think it is," I finally answered. With that sudden confirmation, I had ripped the bandage off myself—and slapped her in the face with it. "I'm sorry, Abi. I don't know what else to say."

"That's the problem, Lena." She paused and sniffled softly. "You can say anything you want to me. But you choose not to." With that last sentence, her voice filled with anger. Not that I blamed her. She was right.

Abi was right, and Fluellen was right. Everyone was right but me.

"I want to. I just can't," I said. I heard a low, distant sigh from Abi—as if she had brought the phone away from her mouth, possibly debating whether to hang up on me.

"We'll sort this out when I get back," she quickly said.

"When will that be?"

"I don't know," she said, the sound of tears glazing her voice. "I have to figure a few things out. I'll let you know when I decide to come back."

"I don't know what you want me to do."

Was I supposed to give her space? Did she want me to check in with her every day? She was part of my daily routine. I didn't know how to get through the day without her being a part of it.

"I need some time, Lena."

Before I could respond, her end of the line went dead. I sighed as the phone slipped from my hand and fell onto the couch.

My face burned under the ache of my eyes as they filled with tears. The sleek outline of the phone soon blurred as I continued to stare at it. A trail of tears fell down each cheek. They dripped over my cheekbones, down my face, and slid along the curves of my neck. It wasn't just because of the silence in the room that I was able to hear my heart break. It was also because the crack was so brutally deafening that it echoed through my chest and rang in my ears like a shotgun. It was all I could feel. My body numbed as the sting in my heart twisted and turned like a vine of thorns wrapped around a brittle trellis.

I clenched my fists together as I brought my knees to my chin. I slowly rocked back and forth as tears poured from my eyes. Raking my hands through my hair, my body trembled, and my mouth filled with thick saliva. My nose began to clog, and I took a deep breath. I felt more than heartbreak over our inevitable break-up.

I felt relief.

I no longer had to play this charade. I no longer had to act as if I was happy and in love. She tried so hard to give me what I needed—what I wanted. But it wasn't enough. I stayed with her because I was too much of a coward to face her. I could face a goddamn sociopath, but I couldn't break someone's heart, even if it was the kindest thing I could do.

I was sure a part of her was relieved too. She no longer had to put me first. She was free of me and my fragility. I was no longer a cement block she had to carry as she swam to shore.

I couldn't let myself fall apart. Abi had been my protection plan for so long that I had lost my own sense of security. Whether I was with her or not, I was going to be okay. I had to be.

A sharp pounding hammered through my head, and I dragged my hands and fingers across each cheek to wipe away the tears. I took another breath, my sinuses clearer, and I smoothed back my hair. Even if my world had crumbled beneath my feet, I had to be strong enough to stand.

I picked up the remote control and turned on the television. An hour or so of mindless entertainment would help to clear my head.

The flat, dry aftertaste from my tears saturated my mouth and fizzed on my tongue. I walked over to the living room window and pushed it closed. The musty, stale stench no longer lingered inside the living room, and the evening air had a sharp chill to it. I picked up my gun and walked into the bathroom.

My gun had become a part of me as of late. I didn't trust being alone in a room without it. Even if it was just a quick visit to the bathroom, my gun was in my hand. The hard metal clanked against the porcelain sink as I set it down. I stood in front of the medicine cabinet, and an unfamiliar woman stared back at me. She was tired and pale, with dark circles under her eyes. Defined lines were permanently etched in her forehead.

When did forty land on my face?

I opened the medicine cabinet and pulled out my toothbrush and toothpaste. The faucet erupted with water as I drowned the bristles. I smeared a thin glob of paste across the brush and started scrubbing. A blast of cool mint gel foamed over my teeth and tongue, and I spit the excess into the sink. I let the foam and running water swirl down the drain before I turned off the faucet.

I placed the toothbrush back inside the medicine cabinet and picked up my gun. The faint sound of sitcom banter grew louder as I entered the living room. Before I could sit back onto the couch, a newsbreak interrupted the show. A sudden strike of cymbals clashed as the local reporter spoke.

"A breaking story you won't want to miss," the newscaster said. She was dressed in a navy blue blazer and a white blouse with a ruffled collar. Her short, brown hair curled at the ends. "Local police officers have received several videos depicting horrific homicides," she said as they cut to Pamela Westlake's audition tape. It was the same video we had received.

"No," I mumbled aloud. *How did they get this footage?* "No...." I stood there, frozen, staring at the screen.

"The videos are too graphic to be shown on television," the newscaster said as the camera panned out to show another reporter beside her.

Her co-anchor sat upright, his gray suit jacket bunched around his arms. He adjusted his navy blue tie and charmingly looked into the camera. "It sounds like we have another Faceless Killer on our hands," he said.

"Tune in tonight at eleven o'clock," the female reporter continued, "for more information on the Casting Call Killer targeting West Joseph residents."

"No...." I slowly shook my head.

My gun hung loosely in my hand as it dangled at my side. My heart shot into my throat as a loud ring blasted from my phone. My eyes slowly unlocked from the television as I walked back to the couch and picked up the phone. I didn't need to look at the Caller ID to know who was calling. The roar from my phone wasn't a mere coincidence.

"Evans," I said into the phone.

"What the Christ is going on?" Flu screamed.

"I take it you saw the news?"

"Now is not the time for jokes," he hollered. "My office—first thing Monday morning!"

"Monday is Labor Day," I reminded him. I was supposed to have the day off.

"Murder doesn't take a holiday, and neither do you," he said before the line went dead.

CHAPTER | FIVE

"EVANS," I SAID WHEN I answered my desk phone.

"My office," Flu said and hung up. He wasn't in his office when I had first arrived this morning. Murder may not take a holiday, but apparently it was allowed to sleep in.

His office was fifteen feet from mine, but that didn't deter him from using email or the phone to summon me.

I had spent the rest of the weekend barricaded in my house. The local news crew had anxiously tapped at my door to get my thoughts and comments on the person they had dubbed "The Casting Call Killer." I had been able to avoid their attempts, but I'd had a close call this morning walking into the station. I had a feeling my luck would wear out, though—and sooner more so than later, they would eventually find me.

It had been four days since we'd received the second video, and I had just opened the case file for the victim, Fionna Michaels. I pushed the chair back from my desk and sighed. Flu liked to start his Mondays with a bang, and I had no doubt something big was going on—especially after a phone-call summons like the one I'd just received.

Vertical blinds covered the large picture window in my office. It allowed small slivers of sunlight to slip through the gaps. The sun peeked through, trying to warm my iced coffee. A ring of condensation soaked into my desk calendar. Among the miscellaneous pens and wadded pieces of paper filled with scribbles and reminders, my computer monitor rested neatly in the center of my desk. The Official Seal of West Joseph, Ohio, served as the desktop's wallpaper.

Three black filing cabinets, each standing five feet tall, rested against the wall to the left of my desk. On top of the filing cabinets stood stacks of new binders and manila folders waiting to be used. There was nothing personal in my office, aside from a coffee spill that stained the beige carpet tiles. A soft hum buzzed from the fluorescent light just outside my office door. The sound followed me the fifteen feet to Flu's office, and I politely knocked on the closed door.

"Yes," Flu said. I turned the handle and walked inside. His layout was similar to mine, with the addition of a wilted plant on the vent under the window. And his furniture was much nicer than mine. In front of Flu's desk sat two chairs clothed in maroon leather with brass nail heads along their perimeters. I was surprised to see that someone was sitting in the chair closest to the door.

"Agent Porter, this is Sergeant Evans. Evans, this is Special Agent Caitlyn Porter with the Bureau of Criminal Investigations in Lyons, Ohio. She's going to assist us with the video case," Flu said. Lyons is an hour west of here, and Flu was notorious for mixing things up, especially partners, to keep perspectives fresh. But he'd never involved BCI before.

"Special Agent Porter?" I said as I looked at Flu and then to the person sitting across from him. If it was who I thought it was, we didn't need a formal introduction. Our paths had crossed many years before. "Cait," I confirmed when I saw her, my lips slowly parted in disbelief.

Her green eyes, thinly outlined in black liner, slowly looked me up and down as a smile stretched from her full lips, revealing a beautiful set of perfectly aligned white teeth. Her meticulously plucked brows matched her dark hair, which flowed flawlessly around her heart-shaped face and down to the middle of her shoulder blades.

"Cait Porter," she said, extending her slender, olive-skinned hand—and ignoring the fact that she knew me just as well as I knew her. We briefly locked eyes, and I debated whether to play along with her charade. But I had to. I couldn't make a scene in front of Flu.

I slipped my hand into hers, and the warmth of her fingers absorbed into my skin. She was dressed in a black suit with a BCI pin fasted to the collar of her white blouse. Next to the pin, a visitors' badge adorned the lapel of her tailored blazer, which fit snugly around her flat stomach and formed neatly against her small breasts. Her pant legs brushed together as she uncrossed her legs and stood from the chair. We were nearly eye-level, each of us five-foot-seven, and we locked eyes again.

A sudden burst of skipped heartbeats fluttered from my chest as she squeezed my hand in hers. I was already warm from the sun soaking into my back via Flu's large window, but a surge of unceasing warmth rushed from my head down to my toes. I lightly bit down on my lower lip, a smile broke through, and I let go of her hand. Cait clasped her hands together and took her seat. I bowed my head and slipped past her to the vacant chair. For a few seconds, I had forgotten Flu was even in the room.

"Agent Porter specializes in cybercrimes," Flu said as he passed

Cait a two-inch thick manila file folder. I had the exact file already sitting on my desk, so I didn't need to ask what was inside. Information on the first and second victims, along with screenshots of their audition videos, filled each page. "We don't have much on the case and could really use someone with your expertise," Flu said, appealing to her ego.

"Thank you," Cait said and graciously smiled. "Perhaps Sergeant Evans and I can go elsewhere to get started?"

"Certainly, certainly," Flu said. "Evans, go over the files and videos with Agent Porter," he ordered as he looked at Cait. "We'll get you a temporary badge so you have more access to the building," Flu said and gestured to her visitors' pass. She nodded and stood from the chair.

A light breeze flew through my hair as I quickly led "Agent Porter" the short distance between Flu's office and mine. She nonchalantly walked into my office, and I closed the door behind her. She had always been better at keeping her cool than I was.

"It's been a long time, Lena," Cait said as she leaned her backside against the front of my desk.

"A *very* long time," I confirmed as I tried to mask how completely dumbfounded I was to see her. "Almost twenty years."

Cait and I met in the police academy. We'd been paired up during self-defense training. We flipped and rolled one another so far down the mat it was no surprise we ended up in bed together. She was the first woman I had ever been with. In my heart, at least at the time, I had wanted her to be my last.

Back then, when I was with Cait, every part of my body ached for her. It was my first introduction to lust, and I craved her as much as any addict craved their drug. Simply watching her walk into a room was enough to make me buckle at the knees. Whenever I stood next to her, my heartbeat pulsed between my legs, and I instantly shuddered whenever her skin grazed against mine. Kissing her became a compulsion, and one that I welcomed. I wanted to be saturated in her— consumed by her. If I could have devoured her whole every time I tasted her, I would have. That's how much I'd wanted her.

After the academy, Cait and I were assigned to different departments, but our relationship stayed the same. For six months, we feasted off the hunger of being in love, but it wasn't enough to satisfy her appetite. Cait quickly bored of the lesser criminals in West Joseph, and she transferred to the BCI. She didn't tell me she was leaving. One day, she was just gone. And all that remained of her in West Joseph was a broken heart trapped inside my chest.

"You look good." She smiled. "West Joseph is treating you well. And 'Sergeant,' that's impressive."

"Not as impressive as 'Special Agent.'" I stared at her, and an uncontrollable twitch curled my lips into a smile. "Cybercrimes... that's fitting for you."

She confidently nodded.

"I'm sorry about what happened," she said and lowered her head. She could have been referring to her moving to Lyons without telling me all those years ago, but something in my gut knew better than to believe she would actually apologize for such a thing. "Last year... with your case?"

Apparently she knew about Lathan Collins.

"I should have called," she said.

"I stopped expecting a call from you twenty years ago," I said, letting my resentment accidentally come out. I sighed as I composed myself. "We hadn't seen each other in a long time. You didn't need to."

"But I wanted to," she said. "I didn't know if you'd want to hear from me... or if you'd even remember me."

"I'll always remember you," I said. And that was true. I could never forget my first love.

She bowed her head as an apologetic smile spread across her lips. "I don't want our history to cause a problem," she replied.

"It won't. We've both moved on," I declared. "Have a seat, Agent Porter." I gestured toward the chair behind my desk. Cait sat behind my desk and set the case file Flu had given her to her next to my laptop. I stood behind her and leaned over her shoulder. The warm fragrance of her perfume nipped at my nose as I opened the folder on my computer that contained the two audition videos. "This is the first video we received, two weeks ago," I said.

I had recently watched the video of the second victim, Fionna Michaels, in the briefing room with Flu and the rest of the department. But it had been a few weeks since I'd watched Pamela Westlake's video.

I stood next to Cait with my arms crossed over my chest as the file began to play. Pamela sat alone in front of the camera as she reviewed a few sheets of paper she held in her hands. Her dark brown hair fell softly around her oval-shaped face, and she nervously pushed loose strands behind her shoulder as she continued to read quietly to herself. Her glasses reflected the glaring lights shining on her from behind the camera. She was in the same room that Fionna Michaels would later be filmed in.

The narrow glass-block window, located on the far wall where one of the two archways was sealed off, was completely dark. This video must have been shot at night. Pamela adjusted her glasses, the glare from the lights followed in her lenses, and she set the papers on her lap. She peered into the camera, and she smoothed her hair around her face, massaging her scalp to add more volume at the roots. Her lips were heavily coated in a dark shade of peach, and the bright lights behind the camera highlighted her flawless tan skin.

"You may begin," the same distorted voice said. Pamela shifted her eyes to the left and smiled at the man off camera. She looked down at the papers on her lap and closed her eyes as she quietly mouthed a few words to herself.

"Okay, I'm ready," she said. "I won't be home until late tonight. I have to study," she said without looking at the script.

"You're always studying. I never get to see you," the distorted voice answered.

"I have one semester left, and then I'll be finished with grad school. I'll see you tonight." She paused as she adjusted in her seat. A dark figure, who wore a black mask over his face that looked more like a pillow case with eye holes cut out, stood next to Pamela. She looked him up and down, and although there was tinge of fright locked in her eyes, she remained seated.

She jumped slightly when the dark figure put his left hand on her left shoulder. She looked into the camera and then off to the side where the distorted voice was and nervously smiled. The right side of her lips curled upward and her eyes darted from the lens to the man next to the camera.

"In the next scene, you're walking alone on campus. It's dark out," the distorted voice said.

"Is this when he grabs me?" Pamela broke from character and gestured to the man standing behind her.

"Yes," the distorted voice quickly answered. "The scene ends with your throat being slit. Can we play that out, please?"

"Okay." Pamela sighed. A rustle could be heard off camera as Pamela nodded and stiffened her posture. She brought her chin upright, exposing her long, defenseless neck, and she closed her eyes as the masked man gripped his left hand around her chin and quickly slashed her throat with the knife in his right hand.

Pamela sputtered and coughed as blood poured from her neck. It spewed from her mouth like oil erupting from a well. The slash mark looked like a gruesome grin, and the masked man let go of Pamela's head. She clutched at her neck as blood seeped through the cracks between her fingers. It gushed over her hands and down her arms as she gasped for air, and tears trickled down her cheeks. Her pale blue shirt soaked up the blood like a lobster bib absorbing butter. The ends of her hair, now saturated in blood, created a sharp ombre effect. Blood pooled on the sheets of white paper on her lap. She sank back and slid off the chair, and her knees cracked as she landed hard on the ground. She swayed back and forth, the once rich color in her face faded into a pale white, and she slumped forward. Spurts of blood splashed around her and landed on the lens before the video cut off.

Cait set her elbows on the desk, her hands clasped above her chin, as she rested her thumb nails along her bottom lip. She stared at the screen, her teeth clenched so tightly that her heartbeat pulsed in her temple, and she reached for a pen and notepad that was next to my desk phone. She clicked the pen, the ball point shot out of the tip, and she started to write. The blue ink scrolled quickly over the pad and I leaned forward to read the words.

> *script*
> *altered voice*
> *warehouse*
> *at least two*
> *female victim*
> *caucasian*
> *actress*
> *suffer*

She wrote on individual lines of the notepad. "There's another video?" she asked as she looked at me over her shoulder.

I nodded. "It's in the same folder."

Cait scrolled the cursor to the folder that contained the videos and clicked on the second one. A large box filled the monitor as the video played. She made checkmarks next to the words "warehouse" and "female victim" when Fionna Michaels appeared on the screen. Fionna sat in the same cement room as Pamela Westlake. Cait watched the second video with the same horror and compassion for the second victim as she did the first, and she placed checkmarks next to every word and phrase on her notepad.

"When did you receive these?" she asked when the second video ended.

"The first one was on August twenty-fifth at seven in the evening. The second was September first at nine o'clock," I answered. "Each video was sent from a different email account. We subpoenaed the host site, but they—"

"Have up to ninety days to respond," Cait interrupted. "And they take their sweet time too." She wrote the date and time of each video next to their associated words. "When did you put in the request?"

"As soon as we received the first video," I replied.

"Flu said the IP came from a local shopping center?"

"We believe so, yes."

"And the victimology reports are…," she trailed off as she reached for the manila file next to the computer. "Here," she said as she opened the file.

Cait leafed through the pages, licking her fingers after every fifth page as she separated the victims into individual piles. She tapped the tip of her index finger on the date of each woman's Missing Persons Report, and she stared at the information as if she was calculating the significance in the dates. She crossed and uncrossed her legs as she swiveled lightly back and forth in my chair. She ran her finger down the information listed on each Missing Persons Report. She looked over her shoulder again and shook her head when she saw me.

"You probably want your desk back," she said more to herself as she stood from the desk. She collected the two piles she had made, walked around to the other side of the desk, and sat in the empty chair across from me.

"Agent Porter, you're welcome to sit wherever you'd like," I said, emphasizing just how professional I could be when it came to working with her again.

"Cait," she corrected me. We locked eyes again. A smirk danced in the corner of her mouth as she shook her head.

"Cait."

I sat on the edge of the warm seat cushion as it sank under my weight, and I leaned forward to open the original case file that sat on my desk. I pulled out the Missing Persons Reports for both victims.

"I'm on the Pamela Westlake file," Cait said as she waited for me to get situated. I picked up a pen to write down the pertinent information as Cait read aloud. "Reported missing on July eighteenth," she continued. "Local West Joseph resident. Age thirty-three. Hair stylist. Living with her boyfriend, who reported her missing. Mother and father both alive. No living will, assets worth less than ten thousand dollars."

"She had been missing for over a month by the time we got the video," I said.

"That's a long time to hold someone hostage," Cait said. "It's possible… but why go to the trouble?" she mumbled to herself. "Fionna

Michaels," Cait continued. "Age twenty-seven. From Akron, Ohio. Recent college graduate, BFA. Reported missing July twenty-fourth by her mother. Father lives in Wyoming. No living will, life insurance, or estate." Cait sighed. "It's safe to assume ransom wasn't the motive. Neither of these women had anything of real value."

"Just their lives," I muttered. "BFA? Bachelors of Fine Arts—that's acting, right?"

"Anything creative," Cait answered. "Writing, drawing, design, acting."

"Is there anything in Pamela Westlake's file regarding drama or acting?" I asked. "They were both very comfortable in front of the camera. They were both in some kind of an audition—whether the audition was real or not."

Cait thumbed through her Pamela Westlake pile, and the papers rustled together as she scanned each page for anything that would indicate an interest in theater or film. The light above my desk reflected in the highlights in her dark auburn hair. Her eyes darted from one side to the other as she continued to read. Her lips parted as she breathed in and looked up at me.

"Here," she said. "In the statement from her boyfriend. He said she auditioned for local plays but had never been offered a role."

"We have her computer too." I said. "Our tech guys have it. We can run a search on her hard drive to see if she responded to an ad or emailed anyone regarding an audition."

"It's textbook Mardi Gras," Cait said.

"Mardi Gras?" I asked.

"Mardi Gras Effect," she said. "When the assailant uses the internet to mask his or her true intentions. Like, in a chat room or an ad. The anonymity of hiding behind a screen, a mask, allows the offender to be whoever he or she needs to be in order to carry out the mission." Cait clasped her hands together and set them atop the case file. "The Craigslist Killer here in Ohio," she said. "He placed job ads on Craigslist in order to lure victims to his house."

"I remember," I said. "One of the victims got away. Who knows how many more victims there would have been if he hadn't."

"Pedophiles, rapists— they all fall under Mardi Gras. I have yet to come across a pedophile who goes into a chat room and announces his full intentions to underage victims," Cait said. "Prostitution is another one—she, or he, will use code terms that aren't as easily identifiable by those not active in that world. Terms like 'escort,' are too familiar, so they'll use internet slang and rose symbols to announce their presence."

"Rose symbols?" My interest piqued.

"It's a way to publicize pricing," she answered. "A rose, or the 'at' symbol." She drew a lower case A with a circle around it, followed by two dashes, a less-than sign, and three more dashes. "It's used to show pricing," she said. "Each 'at' symbol is how many hundreds of dollars the night will cost. So three 'at' symbols is equal to three hundred dollars." She then wrote an example headline: LET'S CHAT @@@-->---

"Is this what you specialize in? With the BCI?" I asked.

"I deal with anything cyber-related," she said. "Hacking, identity theft, solicitation, stalking. This is just information I've picked up along the way. How soon can you get the victims' computers from your tech guy?"

I locked eyes with Cait as I picked up the phone and dialed Abram's extension. She looked down at the desk, the soft glow from the sunlight that snuck through the blinds struck shadows across her face as she read over her notes from the videos. I wedged the phone between my ear and shoulder as it rang. It hummed in my ear until Abram picked up on the third ring.

"Myers," he said.

"It's Evans. I need Pamela Westlake's computer. Do you still have it?"

"I'm walking it back down to Evidence after my lunch," Abram said. "I can send you what I pulled from it." He struck a series of keys on his keyboard. "You should have it in your email now," he said.

"I need the laptop too."

"Just give me a few minutes to finish my lunch," he said.

"Thank you," I said before I hung up. "We'll have it soon," I told Cait. "I'll send a request to Evidence for Fionna Michaels' computer too," I said as I dragged the keyboard in front of me.

The printer made a loud grinding noise as if it were digesting the paper as it printed the form. The paper flipped and flopped as it traveled through the large machine, ink swiped across the paper as it scrolled across it line by line, and fell onto the loading tray. I reached across the gap between my desk and the printer and grabbed the request form off the tray. I placed it on my desk as I read over it. I signed my name at the bottom of the sheet and placed the form into the "OUT" bin that sat on my desk.

"Here you go," Abram said as he walked into my office without knocking. He set a silver and black laptop onto my desk. The computer had been sealed in a clear plastic bag with red lines across it. On the top red line, written in black marker, was Pamela Westlake's name, along with the date of admittance and her case number. Abram loosely held a clipboard in his left hand as he backed away from my desk. "Hello," Abram said as he turned to Cait when he realized I wasn't alone in the room.

"Abram, this is Special Agent Porter. She's with BCI," I said. "Agent Porter, this is Abram Myers. He's a tech analyst."

"Agent Porter," Abram said. The way he said her name made it sound like it was synonymous with beautiful. "It's lovely to meet you." He offered his hand to Cait. He cocked a smile as he looked her up and down, as if he was trying to dazzle her with his charm.

"It's nice to meet you," she politely said and shook his hand—although I had a feeling she was less than impressed with his cocky demeanor.

Abram lingered next to Cait, a goofy smile stretched across his face as he looked at her. As I set my pen down, a soft thud broke the silence in the room and snapped Abram out of his trance. "Oh," he said as he shook his head. "Sign this," he passed me the clipboard.

Pamela Westlake's case number was written in black ink along the top of the sign-out sheet that was attached to the clipboard. I signed my name, along with the date and time, under Abram's name before handing him back the clipboard.

"I'll walk this down to Evidence," he said with a nod. "It was nice to meet you, Agent Porter."

"You too." Cait smiled.

Abram let the clipboard hang from his hand as he excused himself and left my office. I lifted the seal across the plastic bag that was wrapped around the laptop. A high-pitched rip filled the room, and I pulled the laptop from the bag. A white index card, taped to the lid of the laptop, had Pamela's password written on it. I opened the lid to her laptop, typed in the password from the index card, and a series of icons appeared on the screen.

A black and white photo of Pamela Westlake and, presumably, her boyfriend filled the screen behind the program icons. They sat on cement porch steps, Pamela on the third step, nestled between her boyfriend's knees, as her boyfriend hugged her from behind. His backward baseball cap fit snug around his head. Wavy strands of brown hair fell around his face. Pamela rested her head against his chest as they both looked into the camera and smiled, her boyfriend's goatee jagged down into a point. Pamela's hair was just above her shoulders, much shorter than it was in the video. Dry leaves scattered around the cement steps, and a pot of decayed flowers sat along the brick doorframe of the front porch.

I clicked on a series of folders until I reached her internet history and opened each webpage.

"Do you want to look at this?" I motioned for Cait to stand next to me. She stood from her chair and walked around my desk. She blocked the sun's reflection off the laptop's monitor. She set her arm across the back of my chair and leaned forward as I opened each webpage from the week of her disappearance.

"She looked at a series of online ads searching for an actress," I said as I scrolled through the first page. *"Indie Director and production crew looking for actress, age eighteen to thirty, to play lead role in upcoming horror film. Must be able to scream, work nights, and not afraid of gore,"* I read aloud.

"That sounds like the video," Cait added as she leaned in closer to the screen. Her left breast lightly skimmed against my shoulder. "What about the next one?" she nodded.

"Film maker seeking actress for adult film. Please respond with stats," I said.

"Did she respond?"

"No. The link to respond isn't in her history. But she did respond to the horror movie," I said as I turned in my chair and opened the email Abram sent me. "Abram sent me copies of her emails," I told Cait as I opened each document attached to the messages. "Here," I said. "She responded to the horror ad on July twelfth and received a response from the director the next day with his phone number."

"Is that a local number?" Cait asked.

"Yeah, the area code is West Joseph...." I trailed off as I searched the phone number in our system. "It's assigned to a pre-paid phone."

"Practically untraceable, especially if he paid cash for it," Cait added. "Is that it? Just his phone number? No address or name?"

"It doesn't look like it," I said. It was smart—any verbal communication between him and Pamela would be untraceable. Cell phone companies didn't keep transcripts of conversations or text messages. If the director verbally told her where to meet him, there would be no way for us to know. Unless....

I moved through each webpage from the week of her disappearance as I looked for a mapping site. If the director had given her a place she wasn't familiar with, she would have searched for directions.

"Nothing," I muttered.

"Do you have her cell phone? Or her car?" Cait asked.

"No to both. But she hasn't made any incoming or outgoing calls since the day she was reported missing."

"Any abandoned warehouses in the area?" Cait asked. "It's a needle in a haystack at this point, but it's a start at least."

"There are a few," I said. "Who knows if this warehouse is even in West Joseph," I added. "I'll have Abram create a list of vacant warehouses. We can go tomorrow." I had to assume—since the videos were being sent to West JPD and the two victims were from West Joseph—that the murders were also taking place in West Joseph.

"Evans," Flu said as he sharply knocked on the door before he walked into my office. He nodded toward Cait and smiled. "Agent Porter, do you mind if I speak to Sergeant Evans?" Flu's potbelly spilled over the waistline of his black trousers as he eyed Cait.

"Of course." Cait stood from the chair and walked out of my office.

"We need to discuss the media," Flu said as he closed the door. "How did the video leak?"

"Are you asking me, or accusing me?" My defense clamped around me like a suit of armor.

"Asking, Evans. What's gotten into you?" Flu invited himself to take a seat across from me. He set his left ankle across his right knee and folded his hands over his belly while he waited for my answer.

He might have been asking, but his tone, at least how I took it, sounded more like an accusation. As if I was the one who could've leaked the video to the media. Of all people, Flu should know how much I despise reporters. They meddle and interfere with our investigations. They harass victims and their families solely for an increase in ratings. They strip away the victim's dignity just to get what they want. In my eyes, they were just as bad as the perpetrator.

"I don't know," I answered. "Has anyone called them? Maybe the station will reveal its source." It was a shot in the dark, but maybe one person working there had an ounce of decency.

"Abram did," Flu nodded. "They told him it had been sent anonymously via email."

"Do you believe them?"

"I have to," Flu said. "It's the same way we received it."

He had a point. Had we not received the video in the same fashion, I would have argued the news station was lying to protect its source. But in this case, they may be telling the truth.

Flu lowered his voice: "I don't have to tell you how important it is that we get to the bottom of these videos."

"I think you just did," I pointed out. For some reason, I had an impulsive and uncontrollable urge to challenge Flu's authority. There had been a chip on my shoulder since the Collins' case, but maybe that chip had grown into a boulder.

"You're a good detective, Evans. But watch yourself." Flu stood from the chair. "Don't think I haven't noticed the attitude you've been handing out these past six months. At first it was tolerable, but now you're really testing your boundaries. I'm not the only one who's noticed either." He turned the doorknob and opened the door slightly. The roar of office conversations trickled into the room. "I know you went through something terrible. But I'm not the one who hurt you. This department isn't the one who hurt you. Just remember that. We're a team—nothing gets solved if we turn on one another." Flu pulled the door open and stepped into the hallway. "I'll tell Agent Porter she can come back," he added before leaving.

Within a few seconds, Cait returned. She looked over her shoulder toward Flu's office and watched him walk away. "Everything okay?" she asked as she came back in to my office.

"Yes," I said. The reprimand from Flu was absolutely none of her business. "I'll request that list of warehouses from Abram," I added as I sent Abram an email with the request. "He should have it for us by tomorrow morning."

I picked up my phone and looked at the screen. It was a quarter after one. Not a word from Abi. No text, no call, nothing.

I hadn't heard from her since Friday evening. The last thing she'd said to me was that she needed time. I thought I would've heard from her over the weekend. But here it was, Monday afternoon, and nothing. This was the longest we had ever fought for—although this was more than a fight. This was a break-up. The feeling of permanency had finally sunk in.

From the corner of my eye, I noticed Cait watching me. "Are you hungry?" I asked. "We could grab something to eat." Normally I didn't eat lunch this early.

"I could go for something light," Cait said.

"There's a great bistro by the bookstore. I think you'd like it."

"Lead the way," Cait said as she stood from the chair.

How many times had I gone to lunch with a co-worker? Too many to remember. So why was my heart suddenly in my stomach? Why was there sweat forming between my fingers? I certainly didn't have romantic feelings for Cait. It would be impossible for all those feelings from twenty years ago to come racing back.

I grabbed my car keys off the desk and led her to the elevator. She followed closely behind, as if we were a packaged deal. Maybe as colleagues, we were. I tried not to think too much about her or why she was walking so close. It felt good to have her near me—like we were those same rookie recruits again, ready to save the world.

I pressed the "down" arrow for the elevator, and we waited in silence for the door to open. The commotion from the department's chatter would have drowned out any conversation between us. I kept my eyes to the ground and watched her through my peripheral. She had the same cool demander she'd always had. She stood with purpose, as if being in her presence was more than a compliment—it was a privilege to be standing next to her. I didn't detect a single insecurity in her demeanor, and I found myself feeling somewhat envious.

Where was that elevator? I pressed the illuminated "down" arrow again and nervously smiled at Cait. She didn't seem to notice or mind that the elevator was taking forever. Maybe she didn't feel awkward standing next to me. I assumed she saw me more as a temporary co-worker than an ex-lover at this point. That's the way I saw her. So why was I behaving like a schoolgirl with a crush?

The elevator doors finally opened, and I quickly stepped inside. Cait took two steps in then turned so her back was facing me. My eyes slowly scanned her backside, not just to marvel at her athletic physique but also at her. She had accomplished a lot since I'd last saw her. I was proud of her—I was proud of myself too. We both had accomplished a lot in the past twenty years. If we had stayed together, who knows if we would be where we are in our careers now.

The doors slowly closed, sealing us into a private room of sorts. There's something incredibly sexy about being in an elevator with someone you might be attracted to. It replicates the same type of closeness and proximity as sharing a bed. It's hot and stuffy, even with cool air blowing around us. It was a lot like being tangled beneath the sheets with someone. The warmth of her body, the chill in the air....

I shook the thought from my head and pressed the button to the garage. As nice as it was to be that rookie recruit head-over-heels in love with Cait, that time in my life had passed. And I knew without a doubt there was no sense in being that naïve girl again.

CHAPTER | SIX

"WOULD YOU LIKE TO sit outside?" Cait asked.

"Sure."

After ordering and purchasing our meals, Cait and I walked through the bistro to the small outdoor patio encased by a low wrought-iron fence. We each carried our red trays, with paninis and soft drinks, and sat at the only vacant table outside. The square, four-person table had recently been wiped down. Streaks of cleaning spray slowly vanished into the marble tabletop as the sun soaked up the solution.

The bistro was busy feeding hungry Labor Day shoppers. I was surprised the plaza was this busy. Shoppers gathered in groups and maneuvered around one another like passengers just let off a plane.

A cool breeze carried birds' chirps and mild conversations through the air. As the sun bore down on us, I realized why this table had been vacant: absolutely no shade. Cait sat in the seat next to me, as opposed to across from me, and I assumed it was because she didn't want to stare into the sun while she ate her lunch.

"Sergeant Evans?" A round gentleman in his late twenties approached me. He was carrying a backpack slung over his right shoulder. He looked down at me with a goofy grin across his face.

"Yes?" I said with curiosity—although I knew what he wanted.

"I can't believe it's you!" He continued to grin. "You're a hero," he excitedly exclaimed. "I have every article written about you. You caught Lathan Collins." His breath quickened with each word he spoke.

"Thank you." I humbly nodded. Aside from the hero part, he was simply stating facts. Flattering facts, but facts nonetheless.

"If anyone can catch the Casting Call Killer, it's you," he said. "Are you close to catching him?" His wide-eyed grin grew two sizes bigger. News of the newest murders had traveled quickly, but I wasn't surprised. With actual video footage to accompany the story, I was amazed there wasn't someone selling bootleg copies of the videos outside every grocery store. They could set up a stand right next to the Girl Scouts and their cookies.

"I really can't comment," I said, which was true. Even if I did have any information, I couldn't relay that to... "What's your name?" I asked.

"Jimmy Coffer," he beamed. His cheeks turned bright red, though I couldn't tell if that was from blushing or from the sun beating down on us. "I have to get going," he said and looked to his right. Three hundred feet from us was the Volume One Bookstore. I assumed he was here to get a copy of Rachel Sanzone's book, given that his interest in me stemmed from Lathan Collins. "It was nice to meet you," he said. "Wow. You're just...." He paused as he looked me up and down. "My friend and I talk about you all the time."

"Thank you," I repeated.

"Wow. Lena Evans," he mumbled to himself as he walked toward Volume One. By the time he turned around, I had already forgotten his name.

I watched him walk toward the bookstore to stand at the end of a line at least thirty people deep. Had I not known better, I would have assumed a new tablet or smartphone was being released today.

But I knew exactly what that line was for.

The poster-sized cover art of Rachel Sanzone's book left no room for confusion. I remembered hearing on the news that she would be at the bookstore to sign autographs starting at six o'clock. It was hard to believe her book was in such demand that fans were willing to wait in line for more than four hours.

The line was roped off and being managed by a scrawny teenage boy with a clipboard. His khaki pants fit loosely around his hips, and his belt was more of a fashion statement than an actual way to keep his pants up. His white button-down shirt was tucked in his pants, and he paced back and forth as he greeted the customers patiently waiting in line.

A large van was parked on the sidewalk in front of Volume One. Written across the side of the van was WEST JOSEPH TOURS. I knew that van only gave one type of tour: driving past the homes of Lathan Collins' victims, then bringing tourists to Mirror Woods for a walking tour of the "dump sites."

From a marketing point of view, it made perfect sense to advertise in front of the bookstore. After all, that's where Lathan's biggest fans would be. But from humanity's point of view, their business model was repulsive.

"Does that happen often?" Cait asked, her mouth still ajar. I could almost see the bruise forming along her jawline from when it hit the table in disbelief. The shock of my stardom stained Cait's face as she waited for my answer.

"Not as much as it used to." I shrugged. "They stopped asking for photos, so that's an improvement."

"What's going on over there?" Cait gestured over my shoulder with a nod, and her normal demeanor resumed.

"It looks like a book signing," I casually answered, avoiding the fact that I knew exactly what was going on.

"A book signing?" Cait paused. "Here?" she asked, ending her sentence with a high-pitched question mark. She tilted her head so that she could see the line behind me more clearly. I followed her eyes as she scanned the excited patrons. Her brows gathered as if she was trying to decipher what famous author would come to West Joseph to sign books.

Her eyes suddenly stopped, and she slowly nodded. She must have seen the poster of the book cover. *"The Face of a Killer,"* she said quietly, more to herself than to me. I swallowed back a wave of jitters so filling that I no longer wanted my sandwich. She sat back in her chair then looked at me, her stare stricken with worry. "Do you want to leave?"

"I'm fine," I said as I picked up my sandwich. Losing my appetite was irrelevant. I wasn't going to let on how uncomfortable I felt.

"Do you want to talk about it?" Cait asked.

"No." I cleared my throat.

Cait nodded and began to pick at her sandwich. She watched me take a bite, my teeth sinking into the toasted ciabatta. I bit off a chunk of roasted tomatoes with pesto and melted mozzarella, and I slowly chewed. Nothing was going to make this sandwich taste good, but I swallowed it back as if it was the best sandwich I'd ever eaten.

"You know I'm going to make you talk about it." Cait bit into her sandwich and confidently ogled me. She made chewing look so easy. We locked eyes as my heart hammered away at her determined stare.

"I know," I said as I set down my sandwich. I wasn't going to bother to protest. It was typical Cait. If she wanted something, she rarely took no for an answer. It was annoying and endearing at the same time.

She wanted to talk about that line behind me. She wanted to talk about that book—and what had happened that night. She wanted to get to know me again. But the only way to do that was to relive what I had gone through the past year.

"How'd he do it?" Cait asked. "Get to all those women?" she clarified, followed by another bite of her sandwich.

"He was a mechanic. Owned his own shop. Collins Auto

Garage," I said. "He made a copy of his victims' car keys and just waited. Sometimes a few weeks, sometimes a few months. He just waited to make his move."

"Any history of violence?" she asked, taking bites of her sandwich between each question.

"Sure," I said. "He was bullied in middle school and high school. And he was expelled for eventually attacking the kids who made fun of him. No arrest record once he turned eighteen, so his prints were never in the system." I clasped my hands together as I waited for the interview to continue. Part of me expected to see Channel 10's newscaster come out of the bushes with a microphone.

"Why did he do it?" Cait lowered her voice.

"Skin their faces?" I asked.

"Yeah...."

"The removal or covering of eyes, even in post mortem, means the perpetrator is ashamed of his actions. He doesn't want the victim to see him, or his actions."

"But he *removed* their faces," Cait said, disgust dusting her voice. "Why?"

"Vanity?" I shrugged. "His victims were attractive—not gorgeous, but attractive in that girl-next-door way. Their faces were never found, so we don't know what he did with them after removal." I knew firsthand what he did with one of the faces, but it didn't seem like appropriate lunch conversation to bring it up. "We searched his property. His auto shop, his house. Even the abandoned home in Mirror Woods—"

"Where he held you?" Cait interrupted.

"Yes," I quickly answered. "We found nothing."

I knew why she was curious. It's natural for anyone, especially law enforcement, to want a motive for such a violent act. But I didn't have the answers she was looking for.

"To answer your question as to *why*," I said, "I don't know. I don't think anyone knows." I paused. "We had a profiler working on the case. He said Lathan would be intelligent and good with his hands. As a mechanic, I assume both are true. The profiler also said Lathan would be a loner. So far, we haven't discovered anything to indicate he had a partner."

My knowledge of Lathan Collins, post death, was vastly limited. I didn't want to know anything more about him than I already did. I was curious to know the reasons behind his killings too. But when it came to knowing him as a real person—his hobbies or favorite restaurants—I preferred to be in the dark. To see him as a human being, instead of the monster he was, made coping with his actions even more difficult.

Cait chewed on the end of her straw as if she couldn't wait to hear the climatic ending. She looked at me, her face coated with a mix of empathy and sweat. "What was it like?" she asked. "Being that close—"

"To death?" I cut her off. I had been asked that question so many times by interested townspeople who lacked tact and manners. As if they felt I owed them an entertaining story. Talking to me was better than reading a tabloid. I was the real deal. I lived it. I breathed it. I *was* it.

"Yeah," Cait said sympathetically, as if the need to fulfill her curiosity was greater than her guilt for asking.

It was a loaded question. Whose death did she mean? Killing Lathan? Or the fact that Lathan himself was death incarnate; he created death. Rachel Sanzone's death was close too. None of Lathan's previous victims had made it past day five, and I didn't get the impression Rachel was special. So had I not been there—had I not gotten free and killed Lathan—Rachel wouldn't be here right now.

I wouldn't be here right now. And that was the other death: my own.

"If I could answer that question, I'd have my own book out right now." I smirked.

Cait laughed. "Why don't you? It would be a guaranteed bestseller," she said, referencing the line behind me. In the five minutes we'd been sitting here talking, at least a dozen more people had lined up.

"I don't want the attention," I answered honestly. "The people in this town…." I paused. "People want to buy a book about a hero, not a bitch."

"A bitch?" Cait cocked her head. "Who thinks you're a bitch? Fluellen had nothing but praise when he told me about you. So did the other detectives in your department."

Cait mentioning the department and our assignment sparked a question I was bound to stir over late at night.

"Did you know it was me?" I asked. "When you were given this assignment… did you know it would be with me?"

"I had a pretty good idea. There aren't many 'Lena Evans' in West Joseph." Cait smirked as she sucked on the end of her straw.

"So why'd you take it?"

"And miss the chance to work with *the* Lena Evans?" Cait joked as she set her drink down. "Everyone said I would be lucky to be working under you." She raised an eyebrow with a grin. "I couldn't pass that up."

I stifled a laugh. A large cloud floated past the sun and cast a dark shadow over the table. "I'm not who this town thinks I am," I said, returning to the initial conversation.

"You're a hero to a lot of people. Why shy away from that?"

"Because." I paused. Did I really want to get into this with Cait? She was eager to hear my story—not because she wanted to be entertained, but because she genuinely cared. "Heroes don't fail. I feel like a part of me did."

"How so?" Cait leaned forward.

"I don't know." I shrugged. "What I did—killing Lathan to get away? It robbed the victims' families of the answers they needed. The answers they deserved. I took that away from them. We'll never know why Lathan did what he did, or where the victims' remains are. I failed them."

"You *saved* them," Cait said. "How many more victims would there have been if you didn't stop him?"

Deep down, I knew Cait was right. But that didn't matter. The families deserved closure. They deserved answers. And I took that away from them. "It was sloppy work on my part," I said.

"No one expects you to be perfect," she said. "Your department looks up to you. The victims' families are grateful for what you did, I'm sure. Take pride in that. Not just anyone would have been so self-sacrificing. Even with a badge."

"I appreciate what you're trying to say. But I'm just not who this town wants me to be," I reiterated.

"Would you take a bullet for a stranger?" Cait asked. She sat up straight, as if prepared for a long interrogation.

"I would like to think so."

"When your entire life is at stake? Everything you ever wanted to do. Giving it all up for a stranger?" Cait added as if she was trying to persuade me to say no.

"It's my job to take the bullet," I said.

A smile stretched across Cait's face. "That's why you'll always come out the hero."

"Any further questions, Agent? Or am I free to go?" I grinned.

"Just one," she chuckled and then dropped into a serious tone. "Why did you go alone?"

As I stalled to answer the question, sunlight peeked past the edge of the cloud that floated by. The rays bounced off the table and soaked into my skin as beads of sweat gathered along the bridge of my nose.

"You'll have to buy the book to find out."

Cait laughed as I stood from the table. My hands had become sticky from the sandwich, and running cold water across my face was worth the pinball journey through the crowded restaurant to the restroom.

"I'll be back," I said. "Do you need to use the restroom?"

"I'm good," she said. "I'll wait here."

A blast of cool air hit me as I opened the back door to the bistro. Large windows made up the majority of the walls. Customers sat at every table, their sandwich wrappers and drink cups waiting to be thrown away.

I walked through the maze of patrons as I made my way toward the back of the restaurant where the restrooms were. The smell of cleaning solution burned the back of my throat as I inhaled. I turned to the right and walked down the small, desolate hallway. The cinder block walls were painted dark red on the bottom and white on the top. A plastic rectangular sign fixed to the wall had "men" with an arrow pointing to the left and "women" with an arrow pointing to the right.

I pushed down the metal handle of the door, and it opened with ease. A soft squeak hummed from the hinges as it opened wide and revealed a small room the size of a studio apartment. A soft ambient light hovered over me, like a lonely streetlight brightening a dark alley. The rubber soles of my shoes squeaked against the white tile floor as I walked toward one of the two vacant hand-washing stations.

I turned the knobs for both hot and cold, and a mixed rush of water flowed from the faucet. I stood in front of the sink, where a large rectangular mirror hovered over the dual vanity, and I watched myself as I pushed the lever on the soap dispenser. The syrupy gel gathered in my right palm, and I clasped my hands together as I placed them under the running water. Suds emerged from the pocket in between my palms and spilled over my knuckles as I lathered my hands.

In one of two stalls behind me reflected in the mirror, I noticed a shadow under the door. The sound of a sandal scraped against the tile floor and echoed in the small bathroom. I watched two feet, complete with manicured toes, turn toward the back of the stall as flushing water roared.

The stall door unlocked, and I brought my eyes back down to my hands and turned the hot water off. Cold water pooled in my palms, and I swiped my wet hand over the bridge of my nose, wiping the sweat from my face. The humid air quickly evaporated the drops of water on my face.

A woman stepped out of the stall. She kept her head down, the soft light too dim to show her face. She had a small frame, and she gave off the impression that she was easily intimidated. An overwhelming feeling of familiarity swept over me.

"Rachel?" I muttered when she lifted her head, and the dim light revealed exactly who she was. I looked over my shoulder to make sure the mirror wasn't playing tricks on me. But there she was—standing right there. This was the first time I had seen Rachel Sanzone since that night.

My vision began to blur as the room wavered in slow motion. I could no longer feel my heart beat, as if my heart had disconnected from every vein that held it in place. It fell from my chest and drifted deep into the contents of my rib cage. My eyes widened as I took in the image of the woman standing next to me. A thin film of surrealism glossed over her eyes, and she robotically took several steps forward. We stared at one another's reflections in the mirror, wide-eyed and pale. Rachel gripped the counter to support her weight, her eyes still locked on me.

"Sergeant Evans," she gasped.

In one motion, too quick for any radar gun to capture, a coat of armor wrapped around my body and prepared for a battle I didn't know I was going to face. I knew being in West Joseph brought the inevitability of seeing Rachel. I just wasn't prepared to see her right here, at this very moment.

As the earth moved in slow motion, my chest caved in. I just stared at her. She looked exactly the same, although her beauty was mercilessly hidden behind her disheveled appearance. Her long auburn hair had been thrown back into a loose braid, and tendrils of split ends poked out the bottom. She was without makeup, her complexion pale, as if she had purposefully avoided the sun during the past twelve months. Her lips had grown into an almost permanent frown.

I turned off the cold water and walked to the left side of the sink where the paper towels were. The towel immediately absorbed the layer of water on my hands as I tugged on it. It ripped from the roll, and I rubbed the dry part over my hands. I knew I should say something to her, but I didn't know what. What could I possibly say to her that wouldn't dredge up memories of that night? There wasn't anything I could say.

"Your book signing," I finally said. "It doesn't start for another four hours." I didn't understand why she was here.

"I just got here… I need to eat before hair and makeup arrive," she said.

More silence fell over us. It was strange to look at her, as if I was staring at a figment of my imagination. A part of me urged my subconscious to wake up. Was this a dream? If it was, then seeing Rachel meant I would soon see him. Was he hiding in the other stall, waiting to make his move?

"I hope it goes well." I forced a smile. Maybe if I left the restroom before Lathan could make his appearance, this delirium would remain a dream instead of an aspiring nightmare. "It was nice to see you, Rachel." I turned toward the doorway.

"I never told you thank you," Rachel blurted as my fingers tightened around the doorknob. I was almost out of here. Just ignore her and keep going.

"I got your letter," I said against my better judgment.

"Yes, but I never did say, 'thank you,' in person." Rachel's voice shook.

"You don't have to." Why couldn't I open the door and end this conversation? Why did I have to put myself through this? Was it to give her closure? She was the only one of Lathan's victims I could give it to.

"I need to," Rachel said. "I want to." She swallowed hard as I imagined her coming up with the words she needed to say to me. She could write an entire novel about her experience, but she couldn't come up with one damn sentence to thank me? "Do you have nightmares?" she asked. Her voice was weak and barely louder than a whisper. "I do," she confided.

I froze in place with my back still turned to her. I couldn't answer her question. Doing so would only confirm I was just as much his last victim as she was. And I couldn't be his victim. I wouldn't let him have that over me.

The back of my throat tightened, and I squeezed my eyes closed in a quick attempt to keep the tears from pouring down my face. The weight of her honesty crumbled the armor I had placed around me. I took a deep breath and let it out slowly as my eyes began to dry. I couldn't do this—not here, and not in front of her. I held my breath in an effort to keep my emotions intact, and I turned my head over my left shoulder.

"Congratulations on the book," I said coldly. I gripped my hand around the metal knob and opened the door. I lowered my head and stepped into the barren hallway. The steel door closed behind me with a thunderous crunch and created a barricade between Rachel and me.

I walked past blurry images of people sitting at their tables. I felt like a drunken fool leaving a bar. If only I was drunk, maybe that would make this feeling more bearable. I didn't understand where this anxiety was coming from. My hands and legs tingled as my body fought to stay in control of my thoughts. Images of Lathan wearing Angela Truman's face—mixed with images of Rachel shackled in the basement—erratically played in my mind, like a child playing with the television's remote control. Each image flashed too quickly to actually know what was going on, but I could feel it. The images were so engrained in my brain that I could paint a picture based purely off memories.

I opened the patio door and saw Cait. She had gathered both our trays and placed the crumpled food wrappers on the top. She was walking toward the trash bin.

"Are you ready?" she asked. She was calm and completely at peace with her surroundings. She wasn't trying to hide from her past. I envied the way she could just *be* in the world. Completely at ease, as if tranquility was in her blood.

"Yes." I forced another smile.

Cait led the way from the patio to the car. I hadn't realized how close we were to the bookstore until I noticed the line now wrapped around the building. Out of curiosity, I glimpsed at the people standing in line. I couldn't help but wonder why they were so fascinated with a killer. What was it about Rachel's story that intrigued them so? Was it the fact that good conquered evil?

That was my hope, anyway.

"There she is," I heard a voice say.

"Sergeant Evans!" a woman shouted.

I looked more closely at the people in line. I couldn't quite determine who had called my name, but I gave a general wave in that direction. As I unlocked the driver's side door, I looked at Cait. Her eyes darted from me to the crowd, then back to me again, as a stunned smile crossed her face.

I pressed the automatic unlock button, so that Cait could open her door, and we both got into the car at the same time. The heat trapped inside the car clung to us like plastic wrap, and I quickly started the car to turn on the air conditioner.

"I had no idea it was like this for you," she said as I navigated out of the parking lot, purposefully avoiding eye contact with anyone in line.

"It's a lot better than it used to be," I replied. "It's also the anniversary of his death. I'm sure that has a lot to do with it."

"I wanted to ask you about that," Cait said. "Do you think it's more than a coincidence that the videos are being sent at the same time as the anniversary? Could they have anything to do with one another?"

"These murders are just as violent as Lathan Collins' were," I said.

"But the nature of the crimes, the location, the MO—that's all different."

"Why do you think the videos are being addressed to you?" Cait asked.

"Flu told you about that, huh?" I had hoped that piece of information would stay between he and I.

"Yeah," she said. "I think there's a reason why they are. I just don't know what it is."

"Me neither," I admitted. I knew she was right. It was no coincidence these videos were being sent to me on the anniversary of Lathan Collins' death. Unless another video arrived, I didn't know if I would ever figure out why.

But another video would mean another murder.

CHAPTER | SEVEN

THE NEXT MORNING, THREE reporters huddled by their respective vans as I drove my car in front of the police station. One newscaster held a black umbrella over her honey-blond hair as the cameraman next to her was showered in raindrops. I recognized the reporter from the news channel that broke the story about the Casting Call Killer last Friday night. She was also one of the reporters who had lurked outside my house over the weekend.

The cameraman had his hair slicked back into a low ponytail, although that might have been from the rain. He wore a plastic poncho over his jean shorts and yellow short-sleeved shirt, which fit cozily around his pudgy waist. The camera that rested on top of his right shoulder was also covered in plastic. He and the reporter stood close to their van, with CHANNEL 10 NEWS written in tall bold letters. The reporter had her face pointed toward the ground when I pulled onto the street. But with some sort of sixth sense, her head quickly snapped up when my car approached the entrance to the parking garage.

It was my strict personal policy not to speak to the media. No matter what I said, they would twist my words into a misleading segment to boost their ratings.

"She's here," the reporter said to the cameraman. That alerted the other two television crews to my presence. Channel 6 and Channel 4 also had reporters and camera operators positioned in front of the station. They, too, wore the same plastic ponchos to shield their clothes and cameras from the light rainfall. It was Channel 10, however, that had relentlessly clung to my front yard over the weekend as they'd tried desperately to get an interview from me.

"Sergeant Evans," Channel 10 said as she ran to the front of my car. She stood in the street, a few feet in front of the car, and blocked my entry into the parking garage.

The cameraman stood close by her. He closed his left eye as he looked into the viewfinder and pointed the camera at me inside my car.

The reporter walked to the driver's side door, her heels scraping against the asphalt, and knocked on my window. "Sergeant Evans," she repeated, the microphone gripped tightly in her hands. "What are your thoughts on the Casting Call Killer?"

The cameraman moved to the side, unintentionally granting me access to the parking garage. It was the first clear shot I had to get away from them. The other news crews waited alongside the sidewalk, where they were permitted to be. Channel 10, however, were the rule breakers—and ruthless at it too.

I stepped on the gas pedal, and my car lunged forward. The honey-blond reporter *tsk*ed her teeth at the cameraman for moving out of my way. She followed closely behind my car as I entered the garage. I parked three rows over from the metal door that led into the station, and I shut off the engine. I was at least a hundred feet away from the door.

My knuckles turned white as I gripped the steering wheel. I took three short breaths and breathed out slowly. A knot grew inside my stomach and traveled up my esophagus before it loosened. It broke into long tentacles that fastened along my throat and locked themselves around my vocal cords. I sucked in a deep breath, my vision clouded with dark specs, and I squeezed my eyes shut.

Ten... nine, I counted to myself. My arms began to shake as my fingers stiffened. A layer of sweat built up between my hands and the leather steering wheel.

Eight... seven... six. I breathed out and then in again. I forced my eyes open and peered into the rearview mirror. The black specs faded from my vision, and I focused on the reporter, who stood behind my car. The cameraman stood next to her.

Five... four. The sea urchin unraveled its tentacles from my throat, and the strain behind my vocal cords eased.

Three... two. I breathed out and glared at the reporter through the rearview mirror. I clenched my teeth, and my jaw pulsed with fury.

One.

With a body still full of rage, I opened the door and lunged out of the car. The door slam echoed through the garage, and I steadfastly walked toward the reporter, who was now moving toward the entrance of the station. She smoothed her hair back as she switched the microphone from her left hand to her right. She motioned for the cameraman to stand next to her, and they blocked the path from my car to the station's door.

"Sergeant Evans, can you tell us more about the Casting Call Killer? Is it just a coincidence these murders are surfacing on the anniversary of Lathan Collins?" Four silhouettes emerged from the entrance of the parking garage. Channel 6 and Channel 4 must've decided to press their luck alongside Channel 10. "Sergeant Evans, do you have a potential suspect?"

I ignored her questions as I walked past the cameraman. I was less than seventy feet from the station's door. Once I was there, I would be safe. I only had to make it seventy more feet. One foot in front of the other—keep my head down, keep walking.

Sixty more feet.

From the corner of my eye, I noticed a silver Lexus pull into the garage. The dark, tinted windows hid the driver as the car turned down the center aisle to park in a vacant spot.

"Sergeant Evans, Channel Six news—should the citizens of West Joseph be worried?" asked a reporter with long red hair before she shoved a microphone in front of my face. The cameraman for Channel 6 stood directly in front of me; the light on top of his camera shone in my eyes, making it impossible to see the door.

I looked at the ground. Six pairs of feet huddled around me. I looked up. Bright lights from the three cameras blinded my sight. I clenched my hands into fists, and I continued to move forward. I could make it fifty feet with my eyes closed if I had to. My neck stiffened, and the knot in my throat returned as I took another step. My foot collided with the cameraman in front of me. He wasn't going to move. The news crews tightened their huddle around me, and my lungs collapsed inside my chest.

I took a deep breath, but there was nothing to breath. There was no oxygen around me. I was in a vacuum, surrounded by these vultures. I couldn't breathe. I opened my mouth to tell them to go away, but nothing came out. My throat tensed as I choked on the barbed wire slicing into it.

"Sergeant Evans," Channel 10's voice echoed in my head. The bright light turned my vision from white to black, and then to red. "Can we expect a more thorough investigation than the Lathan Collins case?"

The entire world stopped. The six people around me slowed to a dead halt as that question haunted my mind. The woman's voice dropped to a low pitch, each word coming out slower than the last.

I swallowed the barbed knot stuck in my throat and cocked my head in the direction of that vile excuse for a human being. I stared into the light that shone in my face. I didn't need to see her to know where my fist was going to land. My fingernails dug into my palms as I tightened my hand and brought it back before I shot it forward with all my might.

A sudden force closed in around my shoulder and bicep, blocking the punch before it could land on that beast's face. "Lena, don't..." I heard someone whisper into my right ear. I tried to break from the grasp around my arm. Heavy pressure seized my shoulder as my arm was brought down my side. "You're harassing an officer," the voice said as I was pushed forward.

I clenched my body. My abs burned as I tried to break from the person's grasp. The camera lights that were once in my face had been turned off, and the news crews backed away as I was pushed through their suffocating huddle.

Forty feet.

Now thirty feet.

The door was just thirty feet away.

"It's me, Lena. They're going. They're gone." I recognized the voice now.

"Cait," I whispered.

"Keep walking," she said.

My muscles relaxed as the strain through my body eased. I took a deep breath. I could breathe again. The oxygen had returned.

Twenty feet.

I looked back and saw the news crews being escorted from the garage by a uniformed officer. They were so willing to cooperate with the officer's request. Where was their compliance when I was alone?

Cait loosened her gripped around my arm once we reached the metal door that led into the station. I fished for my badge inside the front pocket of my black trench coat and swiped it over the key pass. A low beep chirped and the metal door unlocked. Cait pushed the door open with her free hand, and I walked into the stairwell with her close behind me.

The door closed quietly behind us, and I stood in the center of the stairwell as I peered up the staircase. The floodlights reflected off the metal handrails that hugged the cement walls. My head ached as I tried to blink away the assault from the camera lights. White spots clouded my vision as I concentrated on the stairs. The fragmented spots slowly blurred together, allowing the sharp lines of each step to come into focus.

"Are you okay?" Cait asked as I stood in place. I tightened my body again to keep the uncontrollable shake from taking over.

I slowly nodded and kept my eyes locked on the stairs. A harrowing memory suddenly burst in front of me. "Did I... did I punch a reporter?"

"Almost," Cait said as she took a step forward. She placed her hands gently around my arms. I instinctively jerked back, but she tightened her grip and held me in place. This was the first time I had looked at her since she rescued me from the reporters. She smiled softly.

Dark shadows from the poorly lit stairwell cast over her face as we looked at one another. The brim of my eyes swelled with tears. They lingered on the edge and pooled around the ridge before they slowly drained behind my eyes where they belonged. Cait took another step, closing in the arm's length of space between us, and I lowered my head against her neck. She wrapped her arms around me as I leaned against her. I kept my arms at my sides.

Had Cait not been there—had she not intervened—there's no telling what would have happened. I almost assaulted a reporter. I was on the verge of blacking out. I had no control over my actions. But I was safe now. I was with Cait, under her protection. The warmth of her body seeped into mine, and I listened to her heartbeat. It thumped in my ear as my boiling blood cooled. I took another deep breath. Cait lightly squeezed her arms around me before letting go.

"C'mon," she said. "It's over."

I stood up straight before taking the four flights of stairs. I needed to walk off the anger and frustration bottled inside me. I couldn't go into the office with fists full of fury. If my face looked as red as it felt, I needed some time to cool down.

Each step echoed in the stairwell. By the time we reached the fourth floor, the rage that raced through my veins had subsided. Whenever my mind wandered to the reporter asking her degrading question about Lathan, my muscles tensed and my breaths tightened in my chest.

"I'll meet you in your office in a few minutes," Cait said once we stepped onto the fourth floor from the stairwell. She slipped past me and walked toward the elevator.

Every eye in the office bored into me as I walked into my office. Had they witnessed the entire scene on television already? Is that how the uniformed officer knew to escort the reporters from the garage?

I set my badge on my desk and placed my coat across the back of the chair. Abram must have been in my office prior to my arrival. A two-page list of vacant warehouses and an access badge for Cait sat on top of the piles of miscellaneous paperwork sprawled across my desk.

Ten minutes had gone by before Cait walked into my office with two cups of coffee in her hand. She placed a paper cup with its plastic lid on my desk. "I just got you black. I couldn't remember how you like it." She smiled. Her entire demeanor had returned to normal, as if the incident in the parking garage never happened.

"Black, with two sugars. Or a caramel latte with an extra shot." I appreciated her attempt at normalcy. I picked up the coffee cup from the edge of the desk, its warmth saturating my cold fingers. Drops of rain cried from the sky and landed against the office window behind me. They slid downward in a zigzag pattern. Heavy, gray clouds rolled in front of the sun and blocked its rays. "Thank you," I said. Her simple gesture had somehow made the morning more tolerable. I opened the top desk drawer and pulled out two sugar packets before I lifted the plastic lid.

A thin trail of steam rose from the cup, and I breathed in the warm aroma. I gripped the sugar packets together at the edges and shook, sending the grains to the bottom. I ripped them both open in one motion and tapped the contents into the cup, a small sugar island building in the center before quickly submerging into the steaming liquid.

"This is for you." I handed her the cream-colored badge. "You can access this floor from the parking garage, or any other floor in the building."

"Thank you," she said. She took the badge from my hand and clipped it to her lapel. In black, bold letters TEMPORARY ACCESS was printed under her name, along with her grainy black-and-white photo. "Is this the list?" Cait asked as she stood next to the vacant chair across from mine. She placed her cup of coffee on the desk and picked up the list. She counted the locations as she read over the addresses on each page. "Eleven." She frowned.

"We can head out now if you're ready," I said. It wasn't ideal weather for scouting warehouses, but it was better to get started now. In the off chance that the videos were actually filmed in West Joseph, perhaps a rainy day would discourage the video maker from moving to a new location— if he hadn't already.

"I'm ready," Cait said and took a sip of her coffee.

I picked up my black trench coat from the back of the chair and slipped my arms through the sleeves. I wrestled with the collar before it straightened out, and my hair fell against my back. I picked up my coffee and opened my top drawer again. The keys to my favorite city vehicle were toward the back of the drawer, and I reached my hand inside to fish them out. Cait held the list in one hand and her coffee in the other. She followed me out of my office, down the hallway, and back to the stairwell we had just come from.

"What's the first address?" I asked Cait once we were in the garage. Thankfully, there were absolutely no signs of the reporters.

Rows of cars sparkled under the fluorescent lights mounted to the cement ceiling. Trails of rain-soaked tire marks pooled on the ground toward the entrance of the garage, and a gray haze lurked at the opening.

"There are a few listed on Woodward Avenue," Cait said as she passed me the list.

"We'll start there," I said and paused as I looked over the two pages of paper.

Cait walked to the passenger's side of the black Impala and waited for me to unlock the doors before she got in. The leather seats were cool from the damp air, and I slid into the driver's seat before I started the car. Cait reached behind her and pulled the seatbelt over her chest and lap. She smoothed her hair as she nestled into the seat. It was strange having her sit passenger-side in a car with me again. Almost twenty years had passed since the last time we drove around the city together. But in one quick click of her seatbelt, I was transformed into a smitten twenty-year-old again.

After the academy, Cait and I had spent the majority of our time together at my apartment, which had been cheaply stocked with hand-me-down furniture. Although Cait had aged since the last time I saw her, I couldn't help but see the same twenty-three-year-old that I had been so mesmerized by. She was my first of everything when it came to women. I trusted her enough to actually be myself around her—to let down my guard and explore my sexuality without restraint or shame. I had allowed myself to be fully exposed when I was with her. And, until now, I had forgotten what it was like to have the entire world in front of me. I had forgotten there was a time in my life when a missed opportunity didn't exist—because, at that time, at that age, every road we traveled had a fork in it.

Over the past year, I had wished for my life to go back to normal—back to before the Faceless Killer murders. But maybe I had subconsciously wished for my life to truly go back to normal—long before the stress of my career had sunken its claws into me. Maybe Cait was who I needed to feel normal again. While I felt zero romantic feelings for her, there was a huge part of me that couldn't deny how easy it was to be around her.

The monotonous click of the turn signal ticked like a time bomb before I turned left onto Woodward Avenue. I dodged numerous potholes that lay like traps in the broken asphalt. The road stretched one-mile long, and abandoned warehouses towered on each side. Gray clouds loomed over the rooftops and outlined the chipped and decayed buildings as rain splashed over the gutters that were full of nature's debris. This area had been deserted for five years, and each warehouse was a victim of gang graffiti and damaged construction.

Something felt off about this area. Why would anyone voluntarily come here? Especially a young woman who was alone? If I had been invited to audition somewhere around here, I would have turned around and gone home by now. But I wasn't desperate for stardom.

I turned into the parking lot to the first warehouse on the left. The car bounced in and out of potholes disguised as puddles. The wheel jerked from my grasp, and the car bobbed up and down as the front and rear driver's side tires rolled over a massive pothole. A wave of rainwater splashed alongside the car. Cait clutched the handle above her head and held on until I put the car into park.

The engine ran idle as we peered out the windshield; the wiper blades cleared the window with each swipe. A monstrous warehouse hovered over us like a haunted house on Halloween night. Spackle covered the chipped and peeling paint that covered the exterior of the building. The four corners of the square building met sharply together, with random rows of shattered and cracked windows that looked like a corroded checkerboard. Thin plywood covered three or four of the broken windows, and exposed iron rods pierced out of the wall like rusted jail bars.

Something was definitely off about this place and this entire street. The type of warehouse we were looking for couldn't be here.

"Something feels off," I said aloud. "It doesn't feel right."

"You feel it too?" Cait asked. She leaned forward in her seat, the seatbelt stretching from its base, and she eyed the building as if she was trying to memorize its every detail. "We should look anyway." She unbuckled her seat belt and opened the passenger door. Thick raindrops fell onto her shoulders and dripped down her jacket. Her water-soaked hair stuck to the sides of her face as she motioned for me to follow her.

I braced myself for the rain as I turned off the car and opened the driver's side door. The rain landed hard against my face, like sharp pellets of ice, and I jumped over large puddles in the parking lot to catch up with Cait. She stood by the only door located in the front of the building. The gray metal door had rusted at the hinges, and it screeched a high-pitch squeal when Cait turned the handle and pulled.

Support beams covered in chipped red paint lined up uniformly down the center of the open room. The checkerboard windows randomly covered by plywood on the outside were coated in soot and cobwebs on the inside. Rusted hanging lights dangled from the ceiling, like a rotted noose. Along the large brick walls, which were once evenly painted white, tattered and torn mattresses laid on the floor, with blankets and garbage bags carelessly strewn about. On the floor, ripped paper, fallen paint peels, and an array of junkyard electronics piled around each mattress.

"It doesn't look like anyone's here now," Cait said. "Anyone in their right mind would have turned around if they saw this place."

"Expert fallacy," I agreed. "The killer is coming across as a director—someone professional. That's how he gains the victims' trust. He uses all the lingo of a movie maker in his ad. He's trustworthy," I added. "This place wouldn't make me trust him."

"He would lose the victim's trust if he had her come here. A director, even for an amateur film, wouldn't use a condemned building, or any place like this, to hold auditions. I don't feel safe here, and neither would the victim," Cait agreed.

That was why something felt off when we pulled up. Pamela Westlake and Fionna Michaels were both too comfortable in their audition videos. They truly believed the killer was a director. If he had convincing camera equipment, the location would have to be convincing too. It would have to be in a safe area.

"Out of the eleven warehouses on the list, only two are in reputable neighborhoods," I said. "The list isn't exhaustive, so it still could be a needle in a haystack."

Cait walked to the right corner and squatted next to the mattress. "We should call Narcotics, have them look this place over. The smell of urine and bile alone is evidence that only junkies live here."

"Some of these junkies are good people," I snapped. "They need help… not judgment."

"I didn't mean anything by it," Cait said. "What's with you?"

"Nothing." I shrugged off her question. I had one moment of weakness with her this morning, and now she acted as if she was my shrink. I already had one therapist—I didn't need another. Maybe the twenty-year-old me didn't defend "junkies" or their poor hygiene, but the forty-year-old me certainly did.

"Those reporters. They really got to you, didn't they?" Cait asked.

"I don't want to talk about this." I took a step back from her.

"You don't want to talk about this? Or, you don't want to talk about this with me?" Cait insisted.

"Does it matter?" I snapped.

The soles of my shoes crunched on top of the paint peels and debris that was scattered across the cement floor. Both Cait and I agreed there was no cause for suspicion here—at least not in regard to the Casting Call Killer. My eyes immediately rolled to the back of my head. The catchy name the media conjured up to boost ratings had stuck so well that even I referred to him by it.

I made my way to the metal door, turned the slender handle, and pushed it forward.

Nothing.

The handle turned all the way down, but the door didn't budge. I shook the handle and pushed again. The door was stuck.

"Let me," Cait said. She walked over and moved me to the side. She pushed down on the handle and leaned forward as if she expected the minimal effort she put into it would actually open the door. It didn't budge for her either.

I cleared my throat in a petulant attempt to declare my victory. Cait whipped her head back at me and glared before she turned her attention back to the door. She placed her left hand against the door and pushed down on the handle again before she slammed her right shoulder and hip against it.

She bounced off the door. A dull thud echoed throughout the titanic tomb we were trapped in. I took a deep breath and held it; laughter tickled the back of my throat.

"Don't laugh," she snapped. "The door is stuck." She motioned for me to stand by her as she gripped a firmer hold on the handle. "One, two, three," she counted. On three, she pushed down the handle and we both slammed our bodies into the door in the hope that our combined weight would be enough to separate the warped trim from the door. "This doesn't make sense," Cait said.

She slid her 9mm from her holster and walked to the opposite side of the warehouse. I took my gun out of its holster and held it loosely at my side as I followed her to the back corner that led to another part of the warehouse.

The rain had finally stopped, and the sun had peeked far enough past the gray clouds that it lit the warehouse through the broken windows. Cait turned the handle of an identical door at the back of the building, and it screeched open with ease. We looked out the door that faced the back parking lot. Gravel mixed with broken glass created a stone beach that stretched twenty feet before landing against a set of train tracks.

Cait walked outside, sharp beams of sunlight hitting against her as she moved. I walked alongside her as we made two left turns toward the front of the building where I had parked. My shoes scraped along the gravel and left uneven footprints behind us. A gentle breeze picked up and created ripples in the puddles in the parking lot.

My lips parted as my jaw fell open. The driver's side back window to the car had been shattered. Broken glass dangled around the frame of the window, like dead leaves on a tree. Cait pointed her gun at the car as she slowly walked closer to it. With my gun drawn, I searched the area and looked for any sign that someone might be close by.

Across the street was another vacant warehouse. Overgrown weeds stood three feet tall in the cracks of the sidewalk. The only car in sight was mine. There was no sign of who could have done this. We would have heard another car pull up, and no one had followed us into the warehouse—at least not that I noticed.

"Cait," I said and gestured to the warehouse door we couldn't open earlier.

Underneath the door handle was a small shovel, not more than four feet tall. It was wedged between the ground and door handle. That would explain why we couldn't get the door open.

"There's a note," Cait said as she stood next to the car. She put her gun back in its holster and reached through the broken window.

"Be careful," I warned. My gun was still drawn as I continued to scan the horizon.

Cait stood from the car, a white note folded into fours gripped in her hand. She unfolded the paper carefully and smoothed out the crease in the center. "It's a picture," she said as she held it out.

I placed my gun back in its holster and took the paper from her. It was a pixelated screen capture. A young woman was in the same warehouse from the previous videos—but this wasn't Pamela Westlake or Fionna Michaels. This woman had bright green eyes and dark brown hair. She looked away from the camera as a nervous smile crawled out from her thin lips, and she wore a form fitting T-shirt that accentuated her large breasts.

"Do you recognize her?" Cait asked.

"No," I shook my head slowly. "We haven't received this video yet."

CHAPTER | EIGHT

"BEFORE WE BEGIN, I want to create your Distress Scale," Dr. Rosenthal said. The curtains, which were usually open to allow the bright sun to step into her office, had been drawn closed. Instead, thin fragments of light outlined the sides of the heavy curtains. Small dust particles, illuminated by the slivers of sunbeams, danced in the air as the strips of sun reflected off the beige carpet.

Dr. Rosenthal sat in the chair across from me, her legs crossed as she balanced her notepad on her knee, and she began to write. "Zero is the most comfortable you've ever been," she said, "and one hundred is seeing red—you're in extreme emotional distress," she clarified. "How do you feel right now?"

"About twenty," I said.

Inside Dr. Rosenthal's office was the only place I felt relaxed. Once I was past her office doors and in the real world, my Distress Scale—as she referred to it—was at forty or higher. No matter where I was or who I was with, I was constantly on edge, as if I was waiting for a bomb attached to my chest to go off. My muscles were constantly tense, and my arms dragged at my sides as if I was carrying fifty-pound dumbbells.

"During the session, I'm going to ask how you're feeling... that's when you can give me a number—twenty, thirty, fifty, and so on," Dr. Rosenthal said as I placed my hands on my lap and took a deep breath.

Dr. Rosenthal stood from her chair and walked to the corner of the room. Her heels scraped against the carpet as she made her way to the doors and dimmed the lights, making the space feel more like a massage room than a psychologist's office.

"I want you to lie back and close your eyes," Dr. Rosenthal said as she returned to her chair, "and tell me what happened that night. I want you to speak in first person, present time. Describe the situation in detail, as if it is happening to you right now."

"Okay," I nodded and took another deep breath. I closed my eyes as a silent tug of cynicism lurked in the back of my mind. It rose from my head and hovered behind me as it looked down at us with a crooked smile. It silently taunted me, like a playground bully who mocked the attempts I made to get past him.

"Where are you?" Dr. Rosenthal's asked.

I squeezed my eyes shut harder and concentrated on the black abyss in front of me. A thin white light formed, and it stretched across the center of my vision. It slowly grew wider, as if I was subconsciously walking toward it.

Gradually, sharp lines in the shapes of dry leaves appeared before me. They dangled off the decaying tree branches, which looked like malevolent arms trying to grab me. I envisioned myself pushing past the branches, twigs snapping beneath my feet with each step. The edges of the leaves scraped along my face and pulled at the loose strands of my hair.

"I'm in Mirror Woods," I said.

As if I was actually there, I saw myself maneuver through the dense cluster of trees and bushes that served as a barrier between the road and Lathan Collins' lair.

"Good," Dr. Rosenthal replied. "What are you doing there?"

I envisioned the same dusk sky from that night. It rolled over in dark shades of red, creating a threatening filter. My heart pounded inside my chest like a hammer against a cement wall, and my lungs tightened with each whack. The menacing sky hovered over the backyard of the abandoned home, which looked like a lonely rowboat stranded in the middle of the ocean, waiting to be rescued.

That's where I was headed.

"I'm looking for the house," I answered, my eyes still closed.

"Describe the area."

"It's warm. The sun is coming through the trees. Every step I take, I can hear the leaves crunch beneath my feet. I see it."

"See what?"

"The house. It's hidden behind the trees, but I can see it," I said. "It's farther away than I thought it would be. I'm walking toward the backdoor. The screen door is broken at the bottom. The wood trim is decayed. No one has lived here for a long time." I paused. "I'm looking around—making sure not to even blink. I hear him."

"Who do you hear?"

"Him!" I repeated. A snap of a twig from behind me echoed in my head, and then it went dark. My vision had been taken from me again. I couldn't see him. I couldn't hear him. I could only feel him.

90

The cold, muggy floor of that basement. My ankle, shackled to the wall. Rachel's voice, pleading for help. All I could do was sit there.

I sat there, frozen with fear, as I waited for Lathan to come down those stairs. I sat there as I waited to see Angela Truman's face stretched over Lathan's head, her skin full of silent screams from the strain.

Behind my closed eyes, a wall of tears formed. It sealed my eyelids further shut, like a coat of glue had been smeared across my lashes. The pressure in my jawline grew to a throbbing ache as I clenched my teeth tighter. The room had become more suffocating than a sauna.

It was as if a heavy boulder had rolled onto my chest, and I took a deep breath to try to get it off me. My chest rose as my lungs tightened, and a sharp pain pierced my rib cage. My lungs—they couldn't expand. They couldn't lift my chest high enough to move the boulder.

A soft pop escaped from my mouth as my lips parted and allowed more air to fill me. It still wasn't enough. This weight was crushing me.

"How are you feeling?" Dr. Rosenthal calmly asked. How could she be so calm when I was trapped under this thing? "What number are you?" Her voice became more concerned.

"I don't know," I gasped. "Seventy?" I tried to take a deep breath. The boulder had sunk so far into my chest that it was now resting on my spine.

"Where are you?" she asked again.

"I'm there. I'm with Rachel. I'm with *him*." The ghastly echo of Lathan's footsteps coming down the stairs seized my mind.

"I want you to remain still, with your eyes closed. And I want you to walk out of the house, Lena. Leave Rachel there. Leave Lathan there. He can't hurt you. You're in my office, and you're safe." I heard Dr. Rosenthal adjust in her chair, as if she was now sitting on the edge of the cushion, ready to lift this boulder off my chest at any moment.

Sweat dripped from my palms. But knowing I was outside the abandoned house, away from Lathan, made the boulder crushing through my chest slowly shrink to the size of a cinderblock. I envisioned myself walking away from the house, through the dense woods and toward my car.

The cinderblock was only a pebble now.

I saw my car parked on the side of the road. Waves of sunlight reflected off the hood. I opened the door and sat in the driver's seat. I took a deep breath. My lungs filled with air, and my chest stretched out until I couldn't fill it any more.

The pebble was gone.

My eyelids, which had been suction-cupped together at the base, slowly opened. My vision blurred as I focused on Dr. Rosenthal. I was no longer in Mirror Woods. I wasn't even in my car. I was with Dr. Rosenthal. I was in her office. I was safe.

"That's enough for today," she said from the edge of her cushion, just as I had imagined. Her eyes fixed on me as her lips pouted into a concerned frown. She held the notepad and pen loosely in her hands, as if she was ready to drop them on the floor in case she had to call for medical assistance.

I sat up from my reclined position in the chair, and my head throbbed as if it had been filled with wet cement. Dr. Rosenthal stood from her chair and walked toward the corner of her office. A burst of brightness shone down on us as she flipped the light switch, and I blinked back the blinding glare. The thin beams of sunlight around the edges of the curtains drowned in the artificial light that now filled the office.

"How are you feeling?" Dr. Rosenthal asked after she sat back down.

"Um...." I tried to clear my dry throat. A thin coat of film covered my tongue as I gauged a number. "Thirty? Thirty-Five."

"Is that normal for you?"

"No." I shook my head—and immediately regretted my honesty.

"What is?"

I didn't want to tell her. I was certain that, if I did, she would send me to the psych ward with a complementary straightjacket. But to hell with it. If that's where I needed to be, then so be it. I wasn't going to put myself through another exposure session. No way—not happening.

"Forty... on a good day," I answered.

"What's a bad day?"

"You just saw it."

Dr. Rosenthal leaned back in her chair. As she crossed her legs, she brought her two index fingers together in a point, and slowly nodded.

Here it was. She was going to send me packing.

"You said you're at a thirty now... thirty-five. Why is that?"

"Because I'm with you," I confided.

"That's quite common," she said. A rush of assuredness washed over me. "I don't pose a threat. The real world is stressful."

I nodded. I was finally talking to someone who understood.

"When you feel yourself getting worked up, there are home remedies that can help alleviate some of that stress. Going outside, leaving the situation that's causing your stress, sound therapy—"

"Sound therapy?"

"Tranquil music. Or noises, like ocean waves or—"

"What?" I snapped. I couldn't believe the audacity of her suggestion. Was I, a sergeant with the West Joseph Police Department, supposed to leave the middle of a crime scene in order to listen to a whispering waterfall?

Is this what my life had become? Harmonious plucks of guitar strings and soothing sounds of nature? If this was all I had to look forward to—envisioning myself chasing puppies along a creek through a field of wheat—then why fight it? Bring on the straightjacket and tiny paper cup of valium. I would rather be out of my mind and emotionally numb than listen to some gurgling-water soundtrack that would inevitably make me wet the bed.

"Sound therapy is just one of many options," Dr. Rosenthal calmly replied.

I shook my head as I glanced toward the window. The damn curtains were still closed. How was I supposed to find peace and relaxation if I couldn't even look out the window? My chest became tight again, and I held my breath to control my breathing.

My thirty-five was at a forty. Now fifty. Maybe Dr. Rosenthal had sounds of a babbling brook I could listen to.

"It's common among those who suffer from PTSD to avoid situations that remind them of the event. In your case, that's Mirror Woods."

"Sometimes I don't have a choice," I retorted. "If I'm called, I have to go."

"Yes, I understand," she said with a slight adjustment in her tone. "Is it possible that when you're called to Mirror Woods, you could listen to something that will help keep you calm?"

"I guess." I shrugged. She wasn't letting this sound-therapy thing go. "What else do people with PTSD do? You said it was common to avoid situations—what else?"

"You might try avoiding people who trigger memories of the event," she said.

"It was just me there," I reminded her. "And Rachel Sanzone."

"It isn't just the people who were physically there. People who were pertinent in your life at the time may also cause triggers," she added.

The only pertinent person in my life at the time was Abi. Until five days ago, she still was. "I live with Abi," I said. "I have to look her every day." Abi and I had yet to discuss what our living arrangements would be once she got back from Pittsburgh. I would be content with her living in the house until she found a place of her own. Just because we broke up didn't mean I wanted her gone.

I had a clear opportunity to tell Dr. Rosenthal about my pending break up with Abi, but I didn't. Telling Dr. Rosenthal would have made it too real. And I wasn't ready to admit I may soon be on my own.

The harsh truth of my newfound autonomy was that I forgot how to be independent.

I remembered Dr. Rosenthal telling me that co-dependency was a symptom of PTSD. Had co-dependency cost me my independence? I needed Abi to make decisions and guide me through life. She was my shelter. She was my sanity.

But I couldn't tell Dr. Rosenthal any of this. Not yet, anyway. Besides, Abi and I were technically still together. We had been through too much together to break up over the phone. This was something that deserved to be done face-to-face.

"But do you *see* her?" Dr. Rosenthal asked.

I braced myself for the windows to shatter as the office began to cave in. The weight of Dr. Rosenthal's question was almost as heavy as that boulder. Do I see Abi? I may look at her every day, but do I really *see* her?

"No," I finally said. "I avoid her. I barricade myself in the office while she's in the living room. She goes to bed without me because she's tired of waiting."

"How does that make you feel?"

"Relieved, in a way. Resentful in another."

"How so?"

"Relieved that I don't have to face her or talk about it. Resentful because she doesn't go the extra mile to figure me out." But it was more than just an extra mile she'd have to go. She could travel around the world and still wouldn't get anywhere with me.

"Is that fair to her?"

"No," I quickly answered. It wasn't fair. Not to her, not to me—not to anyone. But it was how I felt. She was the one person I could take everything out on, and I knew she would still be there to sweep up the broken pieces of our relationship.

"What do you want to say to her?" Dr. Rosenthal began to write in her notepad again. The room quieted as I thought about my answer. The only sound was the scribble of a pen across paper.

What did I want to say to Abi? *I'm sorry* was definitely a start. I had apologized to her—but not for everything I should have. "I want to say,

'You have every right to leave,'" I said. "And that just because I've given up on us doesn't mean I want *you* to.'"

"Have you really given up on your relationship?" Dr. Rosenthal continued to write.

"More yes than no. I just can't fight anymore. I need her to do all the work."

"Who's to blame for what happened with Lathan?" Dr. Rosenthal put down her pen and focused her eyes on me. I was unprepared for her shift in questions.

"Ultimately Lathan is to blame. He's the one who chose his actions…." I trailed off.

"But…."

"But I blame Abi too. I blame her because I wanted to make her proud of me." Tears began to form. "Deep down, I wanted to catch him. I wanted to catch the bad guy all by myself." I swallowed back the tears and forced a smile. "I wanted to make her proud to be with me."

"Did you want to make anyone else proud?"

"I wanted to make everyone proud. My boss, my co-workers, the entire town. Everyone." I slumped back in the chair.

"Do you place blame on your boss, your co-workers, or the town?" Dr. Rosenthal asked.

"No." I paused. "Only Abi," I sullenly admitted.

"Why?"

"I don't know." A tear fell. "I know it's not fair to her."

"Let's go back to my original question: What do you see when you look at her?"

I paused as I thought more about her question. "I see someone who pities me," I said. Dr. Rosenthal became a blur as my eyes filled with tears. "I *feel* her pity." I took a deep breath and held it in as I tried to get my fifty back down to a thirty—or at least forty. I would settle for forty.

"How has your anger toward her been? Any physical symptoms?"

"Like, have I hit her? Absolutely not." I exhaled, completely appalled at the suggestion.

"What about your tone? Your words? When those who suffer from PTSD get worked up, they become jittery. They're often on edge, as if they're anticipating a dangerous situation to occur. This can cause a person to become angry or irritable. It's called hyper-arousal."

"I'm easily irritated," I nodded. "Abi walks on eggshells around me. I can hear it in her tone."

"During your next session, we'll discuss your attitude and

perception of Abi. Until then, I would like for you to start seeing things from her perspective. You don't have to keep a journal per se, but make a few mental notes on how Abi may be interpreting your actions."

"Okay," I said. I was so physically and emotionally exhausted that I would have agreed to anything Dr. Rosenthal said. I felt as if I had completed a triathlon in less than an hour. My eyes burned as I fought to keep them open. I was completely drained, as if someone had knocked the wind out of me. But at least this would buy me some time before I had to confess to Dr. Rosenthal that Abi and I had broken up. "Thank you," I said as I stood from the chair.

"I'll see you next week," she said, politely reminding me of our now-weekly appointments.

I checked the clock on Dr. Rosenthal's wall as I exited her office doors. The thin minute hand moved past the number twelve, and the hour hand pointed directly at the number five. Cait and I had plans to stake out the West Joseph Shopping Plaza in the hope that we could find the person who'd sent the emails. I was supposed to meet her at the police station at 5:15. And if I didn't hurry, I was going to be late.

***

"Any luck with the photo?" I asked Abram when I walked into my office.

He was sitting behind my desk, and the glow of the amber sun coming from the back window highlighted his gelled hairline. A high-pitched squeak pulsed from underneath the seat as he rocked back and forth, as if this was his office and *I* was the intruder.

Cait sat across from him, on the visitors' side of the desk—where anyone other than me should be. I took a deep breath, half-expecting to smell urine from where Abram had marked his territory. But I decided to let it go. I glanced at Cait, and she gave me a simple nod. She was too engrossed in the file in front of her to notice that Abram had made no attempt to give up the seat behind my desk.

"Yes," he answered. "Her name is Kristen Valeri."

He handed me back the photo that had been left on my car at the warehouse, along with a Missing Persons Report on Kristen Valeri. I held the photo in my left hand and the Missing Persons Report in my right, comparing the two images. Shallow dimples dented her cheeks in both photos. The Missing Persons Report must have featured her driver's license picture; the plain, soft blue background made her dark hair and bright green eyes stand out.

96

The two photos were clearly of the same person.

"I'm reading over the Missing Persons Report now," Cait chimed in, though she never looked up from the file.

"My chair?" I said to Abram as I placed the photo and report on the desk. His eyes widened, as if he had just now realized I was the rightful owner.

"Oh, yes. Of course." He sat forward in the chair as he adjusted his tie and stood up. He took a step to the side. I scooted my chair back and sat down, the cushion warm and sweaty, and I looked at the sheet of paper in the center of my desk. I didn't recognize it from the victims' case files.

"What's this?" I asked Abram as I picked up the piece of paper.

"I made a list of each restaurant and coffee shop at West Joseph Plaza that offers Wi-Fi, along with their hours of operation," he said. "And it's Wednesday. So if the sender follows suit, he or she will be sending another video tonight."

"He'll be sending us Kristen Valeri's video," Cait added. She closed the file and placed it on her lap. "I think we should have a few undercover officers sitting in the coffee shop or the restaurants. Maybe someone will see something."

"That is a great idea," Abram said and smiled at Cait. "I'll run it by Flu."

I glanced up and gave him a puzzled look. Organizing a stakeout was definitely above his pay grade. Although Abram may have meant well, everything about him irritated me today. He was like a best friend's kid brother: a constant annoyance.

"I'm authorizing the stakeout," I said and turned my attention back to the sheet.

"Of course, Sergeant," Abram said. "I'm on my way to Flu's office now. I can let him know your plan if you'd like?"

"No need," I said. "Thanks for the list." I forced a smile, hoping he would notice the fact that his presence was no longer needed.

"Certainly," Abram nodded. He strolled past my desk and brushed against Cait's leg as he walked out the door.

"It's six o'clock," Cait said. "We should get there soon. If the videos are being sent between nine and eleven—"

"We'll need to set up early, I know," I cut her off. I was mentally exhausted and emotionally drained from my session with Dr. Rosenthal, and I didn't need Cait and Abram both telling me how to do my job.

"Don't let him get under your skin," Cait said. "For as annoying as he is, he's also a big help." She gestured to the list of restaurants in my hand.

"You're right," I sighed. I picked up the handset and began to dial Flu's extension. The cold plastic cupped my ear, and the captain answered on the second ring.

"Evans," he said without a greeting. "Abram said you're running a stakeout tonight. Excellent idea."

I took the phone from my ear, squeezing the handle with both hands as I envisioned myself choking Abram. I gritted my teeth together and brought the phone back to my ear. "I'll need four undercovers," I said.

"Sure thing," Flu sad. "I'll make the calls and have them meet you in the conference room in about—" he paused, and I imagined him looking at his watch as he estimated the time. "—thirty minutes."

"All right. Thanks." I hung up the phone and looked at Cait. "Thirty minutes in the conference room. We'll be at the plaza no later than seven."

"Will that be enough time to set up?"

"It has to be." I knew as well as she did that we were against a ticking clock. Maybe I should have scheduled the undercovers sooner, but there was nothing we could do about it now. "Is that Kristen Valeri's file?" I gestured to the manila folder in Cait's lap, though I knew full well it was.

"It is." Cait handed it to me.

"What do we know?" I opened the folder and read the first page.

"Kristen Valeri, age twenty-eight. Originally from Dayton, Ohio, but moved here five years ago," Cait said, reciting the details of Kristen's life as I turned each page. "She's a full-time nanny during the week."

"When was she reported missing?" I flipped through the pages until I reached her Missing Persons Report.

"July eleventh of this year."

"July?" I asked. "The other two victims were reported missing in July as well."

"Their videos weren't sent until late August," Cait added.

I opened the bottom right-hand drawer of my desk and pulled out the files for Pamela Westlake and Fionna Michaels. Their Missing Persons Reports were the front page of each file. "Pamela Westlake," I said. "Reported missing July eighteenth. We received her video August twenty-fifth." I opened Fionna Michaels' report. "Fionna Michaels, reported missing July twenty-fourth. We received her video September first."

"Kristen Valeri," Cait chimed in. "Reported missing July eleventh, and we'll probably receive her video tonight—September eighth."

"All abducted in July," I mumbled as I stared at the files in front of me.

"Why abduct someone and wait to kill them a month later?"

"I don't think he did wait," I answered. "Those girls are clean in the videos. Makeup is fresh, hair is perfect. Not a spec of dirt on their clothes. He isn't waiting to kill them. He's waiting to send the videos."

"If Pamela Westlake replied to an ad for an audition, I think it's also probable the other two victims responded to the same ad or a similar one," Cait said. I could hear her wheels as they turned. "Do we have Fionna Michaels' computer?"

"We do. I.T. is running a scan on it. We'll be able to look at it tomorrow," I said.

Cait nodded. "How many people respond to an ad? A dozen or so, depending on what it is? How many of those actually follow through... maybe half?" She was more or less just talking to herself at this point.

"He's killing multiple women with one ad." I pieced her thoughts together. "But how many women responded to his ad? If he's already killed them all and is just waiting to send the videos, there's no telling what his body count is up to."

"No bodies have been found. So that begs the question—where are they?"

"I don't know," I said. "If he dug graves somewhere, who knows when we'll find them?" It seemed no matter how many questions we were able to answer, it wasn't going to be enough to have a solid lead. We were at the mercy of the Casting Call Killer making a mistake or being sloppy if we had any chance of catching him.

I looked at the clock above Cait's head. "The undercovers will be here in ten minutes," I said. "We should head to the conference room." I stood from the desk and led the way down the hall. As we walked, I thought about the killer's motive for sending the videos.

If he hadn't sent the videos to West JPD, we would be completely clueless as to what had happened to these women. They would just be one of the thousands of people reported missing each year. That thought alone was enough to make me feel completely defeated. Unless the killer threw in the towel, we were going to lose the fight before it had even begun.

CHAPTER | NINE

CAIT AND I SAT in a city-owned blue sedan in the front parking lot of the West Joseph Shopping Plaza. She was in the driver's seat, and I sat in the passenger seat with the three case files on my lap. It was late enough in the evening that we didn't need to have the air conditioner on in order to survive a few hours in a vehicle. With all four windows halfway down, a gentle breeze blew into the car and provided us with enough fresh air that it was hard to remember we were there for work purposes and not a date.

The shopping plaza was the length of two football fields, configured into an "L" shape. Each store alternated between light stone and dark brick exteriors. Storefront windows neatly displayed the current week's sale items, and customers walked back and forth from their cars to the store like ants marching toward a melted popsicle.

It was completely impossible to have a visual on all four locations that offered Wi-Fi to its customers. Three quick-service restaurants and one coffee shop each had one undercover officer posing as a customer. The undercovers were instructed to choose a seat that overlooked as much of the restaurant as possible. If they saw someone with a laptop, they were to keep their eye on him or her—and, when the moment was right, walk past that person to see what was on the computer monitor. If something was suspicious about their behavior, they were to radio me and Cait, and we would intervene.

It sounded like a good plan, in theory. In practice, the odds were against us. We didn't have the manpower for such an intricate stakeout over this large of an area. We had to make the best of what we had and hope that luck was on our side.

I looked at Cait, who had both hands on the steering wheel, her right thumb tapping intermittently against the wheel. She looked out the front windshield as she stared toward the naïve patrons walking by.

"Is it bad that I hope the video we receive *is* of Kristen Valeri?" Cait dropped her hands from the steering wheel and looked at me. "If it's her, then maybe she's the last of them. Maybe there aren't more women to be found." Cait shook her head. "If we receive a video of someone other than Kristen Valeri...."

"We're going to catch him," I assured her, although I didn't necessarily believe it myself. It was how I felt during the Lathan Collins murders. To the public, and to my department, I acted as if I was one step ahead of Lathan. But the truth was: I never was. And now, here I was, a year later, and it was as if I was chasing Lathan Collins all over again.

But the Casting Call Killer was smarter and more cunning than Lathan. He took more pride in his work than Lathan ever did. And that scared me. I had a feeling this killer considered himself to be a god. He wanted to be worshipped, either by his victims or by the public—maybe both.

It was 8:37 p.m., and the dusk sky, with its beautiful purple and orange hues, had faded to dark blue at the horizon. Soon it would be pitch black. I had intended on reading the case files while we waited for information from the undercovers, but with the darkened sky approaching, reading was impossible. We would no longer blend in with the crowd if we sat in the car with the dome light on.

Neatly trimmed hedges outlined the parking lot and created a barrier from the busy street that led into the plaza. Newly developed condos and hotels broke the clean skyline, and I noticed the name of the hotel where Cait said she was staying. The "Westerly Inn" sign proudly shone in bright white letters over the parking lot where we had parked. It was eight stories high, with ten tinted windows across each floor.

"Is that where you're staying?" I gestured toward the hotel.

"Yeah," Cait answered. She rested her elbow on the driver's side door and propped her head against her fist. She kept her eyes on the plaza, as if she could zero in on the suspect just by what he was wearing. "I've counted seven people with laptops so far."

I sank into the seat and looked out the side window. The stores closed at nine o'clock, but the coffee shop and restaurants stayed open until eleven. We were camouflaged by the dozens of cars parked around us. But once the stores closed, most of the cars would be gone, and we would be among a handful of patrons still parked in the lot. Hiding in plain sight wouldn't be as easy.

"Can we see the plaza from your room?" I asked.

"Hm...." Cait broke from her trance. "Yeah, I think so."

"When the stores close, we'll need to be somewhere less obvious. Whoever's sending the videos is careful enough to mask his identity. I'm sure he's smart enough to check his physical surroundings too."

"You're right." Cait picked up the black two-way radio that sat in the cup holder between our seats and pressed the button with her thumb. A low beep chirped from the speaker, and she brought the radio close to her mouth. "This is Agent Porter to all units. Changing location to Westerly Inn. Proceed as normal. Over." She slid her thumb off the button.

A few moments of silence resonated before "Copy" emitted from the radio four times.

Cait set the radio back into the cup holder and started the car. The air conditioning roared from the vents, and I quickly turned down the controls. Cait put the car into drive and flipped on the headlights before she pulled from the isolated parking spot and maneuvered through the lot toward the hotel.

The narrow driveway into the hotel blossomed into a full-sized parking lot. Bushes and floral landscape outlined the fifty-plus available spaces. Cait pulled into spot in the side lot and turned off the ignition. She opened her door without saying a word, and I followed her toward the front of the hotel.

The glass double doors automatically separated as we approached the hotel's vestibule. The cream-colored marble tiles reflected the light from a large chandelier, which cast a soft yellow glow over the lobby. Maroon club chairs surrounded three sides of a large coffee table on the right side of the lobby. The front desk was off to the left. The clerk wore a stark white button-up and a kelly green vest. He nodded at us as we walked by, and I followed Cait to a pair of gold-colored elevator doors, which were adjacent to a hallway with a sign that pointed guests toward the fitness and pool areas.

A deep scent of chlorine and cleaning solution permeated my nostrils. Cait pressed the "up" button and tapped her foot as we waited for the doors to open. I held the case files in my hand, seeing this as a good opportunity to inconspicuously read over them. The elevator on the right opened first, and I stepped inside after Cait. She pressed the button for the sixth floor, and the doors quickly closed.

Dark wood paneling covered the three walls of the elevator. Each had advertisements for nearby entertainment as well as the hotel restaurant's breakfast and dinner menus. Cait and I were alone, which was good. The elevator was the size of a golf cart, and as soon as the doors closed, I felt myself gravitate toward Cait. I firmly planted myself in the corner farthest away from her, and I gripped the side railings on the wall. I remembered feeling this aroused by her the last time we were in an elevator together. Maybe it was the thought of being in such a confined space, behind closed doors, with her. I hadn't felt an urge to be with her when we were alone in the car together—or any other time we were alone together. It was just inside elevators when my mind wandered.

The doors opened as soon we reached the sixth floor, and I bolted like a dog from his crate first thing in the morning. I stopped once I reached a fork in the hallway and turned around. I didn't know her room number.

Cait walked effortlessly past me, and I followed her down the narrow hallway, odd-numbered rooms on the right, even-numbered rooms on the left. Cait stopped in front of room six twenty-eight. She reached into her back pocket and pulled out a key card.

She slid the white plastic into the slot, and a low grinding noise grumbled from the door. She pressed down on the brass handle and pushed the door open with ease. The handle collided against the inner wall of the dark narrow entryway. She reached her hand inside to flip on the switch, and a burst of fluorescent light reflected off the mirrored closet doors. She stepped inside the entryway, and I waited until she was a few feet in front of me before I followed her.

I peeked inside the bathroom to the right. Her toothbrush and toothpaste were next to the chrome sink. Tiny bottles of shampoo, soap, and lotion neatly lined the counter. Disheveled hand towels clumped together under the sink next to the plastic trashcan. The off-white tiles stopped at the edge of the door, where they met light brown carpet with black paisley-esque swirls. The carpet stretched from the narrow entryway into the rest of the room.

The door closed behind me, and an abrupt click echoed through the tiny room as the latch locked into place. The room was smaller than I expected it to be. Part of me imagined she would have stayed in a luxurious suite; the logical part of me, who knew the state wouldn't pay for such extravagances, wasn't surprised by the small double bed and basic complimentary toiletries.

Coconut white curtains covered the large window on the opposite side of the room from the front door. The bed had been neatly made, probably from an early-morning housekeeping visit. The bottom corners of the comforter had been tightly tucked underneath the mattress, as if a military sergeant had supervised the staff. Six white pillows were stacked in rows of two against the oversized micro-suede headboard. A large three-foot-by-two-foot horizontal painting hung above the bed. The canvas portrayed a log cabin surrounded by a blossoming forest. The deep blue sky was cloudless, and the sun was left out of the painting—as if the artist didn't see the need to include it.

On either side of the bed was a nightstand with a lamp atop each. The one between the window and the bed had an alarm clock and a telephone on it. I assumed that was Cait's side of the bed—the remote control was also on that nightstand. Across from the foot of the bed was a large dresser with a flat-screen television on top of it. To the left of the dresser was a small table with a coffee pot and four Styrofoam cups wrapped in plastic. Between the window and the dresser was a desk and an office chair. On the desk was another lamp and a leather-bound book, presumably containing information on local attractions and restaurants. And I knew if I opened the nightstand drawer, a crisp, clean bible would be resting inside.

The room was complete—except I couldn't help but notice something was missing.

Whatever feeling of lust I had for Cait inside the elevator was no longer with me. Here we were, inside a space whose sole purpose was for sleeping—or for sleeping with someone—yet I felt nothing. No ache to kiss her. No yearn to touch her. I was completely void of all sexual desire to be with her.

That scared me more than my momentary urge inside the elevator. Maybe it wasn't just Abi whom I no longer wanted to be with. Maybe I no longer wanted to be with anyone. Had I become so emotionally detached from romance that I no longer felt anything when I was with a beautiful woman? Even someone whom I was once in love with? Even a grieving widow still aches for her spouse. How dead inside was I?

As I looked at the bed next to us, wanting so badly to want Cait, I couldn't picture myself with her, or with Abi, or with anyone. My heart was so dry that it had become ashes at the bottom of a fire pit.

As I forced myself to try to remember what it was like to feel something for someone, all I could do was remember my session with Dr. Rosenthal from earlier this afternoon. Reliving the moments, the moments of stupidity that allowed Lathan Collins to catch me, had finally caught up to me. I thought the stress and fear that I felt in her office this afternoon would stay there, in her office, but I was wrong. They had wrapped themselves so tightly around my body that it felt like a coating of liquid latex. I couldn't breathe—I couldn't move. The only signs of life I had were the tears that had formed behind my eyes.

A throbbing ache hammered at the back of my head. I could leave, but what excuse could I give? I was working. This was my job. If I didn't want another person to go through what I did, to feel what I was feeling now, I had to stay and catch the son of a bitch responsible for those videos.

The dull *woosh* from the curtains drawn apart broke the trance I had cast over the bed. Cait stood in front of the large window. The curtains no longer covered the city view, and she rolled the office chair in front of the glass. She sat down and peered out the window.

"You can see everything from here," she said. "Come look."

My feet felt glued to the ground as I slowly took a step toward her. I watched my reflection in the window as I approached Cait from behind. The fluorescent light cast a dark shadow over the right side of my face, as if I was wearing a mask. I leaned over Cait, and she pointed out the window.

I looked at the alarm clock. 9:09 p.m.

All the stores were closed now, except the restaurants and coffee shop. The parking lot was practically bare. It was good that we had moved locations. Less than a dozen cars were scattered in a parking lot that could easily hold two hundred. We definitely would have stuck out to anyone looking over his shoulder.

The coffee shop was closest to the hotel. Green umbrellas covered the patio tables along the outside corner of the shop. A soft, amber light glowed from inside the building, and its wall-length windows made it easy to peer inside. Patrons sat at tables as they drank coffee and snacked on scones. One man, with a white baseball cap, hid in the front corner of the shop with his laptop on the table. He leaned his whole body into the corner as he furiously typed on his keyboard. We were too far away to see what was on the screen. Whatever it was, the man wanted his privacy.

I reached my hand over Cait's shoulder and down into her lap where the radio was and brought it close to my mouth.

"Unit Three, this is Twenty," I said. "Over."

"Go for Three, over." White noise filled the background.

"In the front corner, the man in a white hat. Do you see him? Over."

"I do. Over"

"Can you see what's on his screen? Over."

Within a few seconds, Unit Three, dressed in dark jeans and a black windbreaker, walked past the man in the white baseball cap. Unit Three dropped his wallet on the ground when he was behind the man and bent down to pick it up. As Unit Three pretended to put the wallet's spilled contents back together, he eyed the man's monitor. The man turned around and looked at Unit Three and quickly closed his laptop. I couldn't see the man's face, but I assumed the look he gave was not a friendly one. Unit Three quickly put his wallet in his back pocket and walked toward the back of the coffee shop, completely out of sight.

"This is Three," he said through the radio. "He's looking at photos from what appears to be a camping trip. Over."

My head instinctually leaned forward as I let out a sigh of defeat. I knew it wasn't going to be that simple to catch the person who sent the videos, but that didn't mean I was looking forward to a night of wasted time. "Thanks. Over," I said into the radio and tossed it onto the bed.

"The night's still early," Cait said with a tone of disappointment in her voice that mirrored my own.

"Two hours to go," I said. "Two hours filled with potential suspects that will turn into a letdown."

"You knew this was a shot in the dark. Why are you getting your hopes up?"

"I'm just tired." Even if this was a shot in the dark, as she put it, that didn't mean it wasn't worth a try.

"Tired of what?" Cait swiveled her chair to face me on the bed. We were very much sitting the same way as Dr. Rosenthal and I were this afternoon. All Cait was missing was a notepad—and the necessary degrees to be a psychologist.

"Just tired," I said. "I'm tired of feeling like we're one step behind. Maybe we're ten steps behind," I muttered. "I'm tired of the bad guy winning."

"He isn't winning."

"Well, we certainly aren't. So who is?" I snapped.

Cait turned back around and continued to look out the window. "He only wins if we let him," she said quietly.

I lay back on the bed, and my head sank into the middle of the mattress. The springs creaked under my weight. I didn't want to reach for a pillow. If I did, I would fall asleep.

Instead, I stared at the popcorn ceiling. The stippled points of paint hung like stalactites in a cave. It was the same type of ceiling I had in my bedroom as a teenager. I would lay awake at night and stare at the ceiling design, hypnotized by the thought that if there was an earthquake, the bits might fall off and stab me in the eye. It was an irrational fear, but one that had seemed so possible at the time.

"Keep an eye on the cars," I said. "It's possible whoever's sending the videos is doing it from their car."

"I am," Cait said with her eyes on the parking lot below. "So far, nothing."

I continued to stare upward. My thoughts drifted from the popcorn ceiling to the possibility that we were playing right into a trap.

The Casting Call Killer, for lack of a better name, was smart. He had to know that we could pinpoint his IP address—and that, when we did, we would wait for him. Why would he come back to the same location if he knew we would figure it out?

He wouldn't. He wouldn't be here at all. A cat can't catch a mouse if there are no mice in the house. So why did I expect to catch a killer when there was no killer here to be caught? Deep in my gut, I knew tonight was a futile effort. He wasn't here. We were a week too late.

"Talk to me," I said. The silence in the room filled my head.

"About what?" Cait didn't take her eyes off the parking lot.

"About anything." I needed to hear something else other than the voice in my own head.

"Anything?" Cait repeated. I looked at her reflection in the window. Her lips turned into a half-frown, half pucker as she raised one eyebrow. "Are you a fan of horror movies?"

"No," I scoffed. "I mean, maybe during Halloween. Why?"

"I'm just trying to come up with a rational reason why someone would send those videos to your attention."

"Because they think I like horror movies?" The thought was absurd. "It's obvious why they're being sent to me."

"What if the obvious is what's causing the confusion?" Cait said. "What if he wants you to think it's because of Lathan Collins—but, really, it's for a different reason?"

"Like what?"

Cait shrugged. "I don't know. Maybe they want your fame."

I laughed aloud. "*My* fame?" I continued to laugh.

"Don't laugh. I'm serious."

"The fame I have in this town amounts to nothing. I have no pull within my job. Hell, I wasn't even awarded Employee of the Month after catching Lathan," I said, stomping all over her idea. "If it's my fame they're after, then not only are they crazy, but they're also delusional."

"Okay, it was just a thought." A wounded Cait went back to her surveillance.

"I'm sorry," I said. "I shouldn't have been so—"

"Mean?" she cut me off.

"Dismissive," I corrected her as I lifted my head from the bed and sat on the edge of the mattress. I was less than three feet from the window that overlooked the plaza's parking lot. Streetlights lit the busy street beyond the parking lot. The cars that coasted by blurred as they traveled down the road. "Where do you think he lives?"

"Who?" Cait kept her back to me and her eyes on the parking lot.

"Who do you think? The Casting Call Killer."

"He's local."

"Why do you think that?" I asked.

"I don't know. I get the feeling he likes this area. Something is either keeping him here, or he's just drawn to it."

"Maybe both. The videos take place in a warehouse."

"So?" Cait said. "Does that make you think he's *not* local?"

"No, no." I shook my head. "I mean, he needs privacy for what he's doing. If he had a house, then he would have the type of privacy he needed. But he's using a warehouse."

"Go on," Cait said.

"So, if he's local, like you said, he probably doesn't have a house. He has an apartment."

"Or maybe he lives with his parents?" Cait looked over her shoulder at me and smirked.

"Maybe?" But that didn't feel right. "The women he's targeting are all local," I added. "They're in their late twenties and early thirties. He isn't afraid of mature women. So that makes me think he's older too. At least in his late twenties."

"Why do you think that?" Cait asked and turned her chair to face me.

"Let's say you're an eighteen-year-old aspiring serial killer. Who would you target?"

"I don't know. Little kids and animals, probably."

"Why?"

"Because they're weak. And I don't have the confidence to go after someone older... someone stronger."

"Exactly." I sat up.

Cait shifted her eyes to the floor as if she had to process her thoughts. "Okay, detective," she laughed. "He's in his late twenties."

"Sergeant," I playfully corrected her.

Cait grinned. "Okay. But if he's older, like you say, he likely would have a house rather than an apartment."

"Not necessarily. If he's a recent transplant, he wouldn't buy a house right off the bat."

"You think he has an apartment," she said, "and I think he has a house." Cait whipped the chair around to look out the window.

Typical Cait. Even if she had nothing concrete to support her argument, it would take mountains of contradicting evidence to change her mind.

As I watched Cait look across the parking lot, a sudden calmness came over me. Talking about the case helped. Most of the lingering stress from my session with Dr. Rosenthal had eased to a manageable level. My headache and the irrationality that flowed through my veins were gone.

"I'm going to read over the case files," I said. "Let me know if you see anything?"

"Of course."

I picked up Kristen Valeri's case file. Even with a more relaxed mind, I knew I wasn't actually going to read it. I had read over the same ten pages so many times that the letters and words had become nothing more than black smudges on the pages. They no longer made sense whenever I looked at them.

After an hour of silence and pretending to read, Unit Three came across the radio. I looked at the clock. 10:58 p.m.

"Unit Three, heading out. Over."

"Unit One. The night manager is leaving soon. I'm heading out too. Over."

"Unit Two. All clear here. Sorry, Sergeant. Over."

"Unit Four calling in. All clear here too. Over."

I picked up the radio and held in front of my mouth as the insurmountable feeling of defeat hovered over me. "Unit Twenty. Copy. Thank you. Have a good night. Over." I tossed the radio onto the bed and looked at Cait.

"Just because we didn't see anything doesn't mean he wasn't here. You instructed Dispatch to call Fluellen if they receive a video. It's just a matter of time," Cait said.

"Time we don't have."

"Time is *all* we have," she retorted. Regarding an investigation, she was right. Sooner or later, the perpetrator always messes up. Ninety percent of cases are solved because the perpetrator gets sloppy or brags to the wrong person. It was only a matter of time before this one got sloppy too.

But the longer we waited, the higher the victim count would be. And that didn't sit well with me. We couldn't wait for him to solve the case for us. We needed to act, and we needed to act now.

"Maybe that's how you do it at BCI, but that's not how we do it here," I challenged.

"Why do you keep snapping at me?"

"What are you talking about?"

"Just now, and earlier with the horror movies. Yesterday at the warehouse too." She paused. "You were never like this."

"I was never like this? We haven't talked in twenty years. How do you know what I'm like?"

"Because I know you, Lena. I've always known you. A hundred years could go by without us talking, and I would still know you."

My jaw locked as I glared at her. Who was she to say she knows me? I barely knew myself anymore—how could *she* know me?

As I stared at her, my teeth ached from the tension of my clench. I couldn't help but see the Cait I had always known. We met when we were just starting to find ourselves—we were young and impressionable. We were soft molds in need of sculpture. We found ourselves, together. She knew me during a time when I was lost. I was lost when I was twenty, and I was lost now.

"I'm sorry," I said softly. "You always did know when to call me out." I chuckled and then paused. "I should go." I stood from the bed.

"You don't have to go." She gestured for me to sit back down. "You may be on to something with that apartment theory of yours," she said.

I knew the game she was playing. It was a favorite of hers.

"I know what you're doing," I said as I reluctantly sat back on the bed.

"And what's that?" She tried to hide her smile.

"Telling me what I want to hear so you'll be back on my good side." I laughed. "You don't believe my apartment theory any more than I believe your house theory."

"You're right." She leaned into the chair and held up her hands in surrender. "Did you find anything else in the file?"

I shook my head. "Can't we just be regular people tonight? No Sergeant Evans. No Agent Porter. Can we just be *us*?" I slid the case files to the center of the bed. I feared my judgment was clouded from the letdown of this evening, and I didn't want to force a profile detail just to feel better about the case.

"Special," Cait said as she let her hands drop to her lap. "*Special* Agent Porter." She smirked and kicked off her shoes. "We can be whoever you want to be tonight, as long as it includes food. I'm starving."

"I'm hungry too. Where are we going to get food this late?"

"I don't know." She turned the chair so it was facing the desk. "Too bad we didn't think of this an hour ago when the restaurants were still open. We could have gotten coffee too," she said, playfully joking about our unsuccessful stakeout. "There's always room service?" She flipped open the leather-bound book and turned through the pages until she reached the menu. "Chicken tenders are only fifteen dollars." She laughed.

"Do they come with fries?"

"Yes."

"I'll have that." It was my favorite comfort food. Some people couldn't resist brownies—I couldn't resist breaded chicken and a side of fries.

"See. I know you." She cocked a smile as she walked to the phone on the nightstand. She dialed the number to room service and twirled the cord in her fingers as she placed our order.

There was a welcomed calm whenever I was around Cait. The more I thought about it, the more I remembered always feeling safe around her. It wasn't the type of safe I felt with Abi though. Abi was someone I could hide behind. Cait was the shield I needed to slay my own dragons.

In the thirty minutes it took for room service to deliver the food, Cait and I carefully walked down memory lane together. It wasn't a leisurely stroll. It was more like the kind of pace a soldier takes when walking through a minefield. I was cautious not to ask if she was seeing anyone, and she didn't ask me if I was seeing anyone either. I assumed she didn't want to know. Sometimes knowing an ex has moved on, regardless of the amount of time that's passed, can put a real damper on an otherwise enjoyable evening.

"Do you remember my brother?" Cait asked as she ate the last bite of her turkey sandwich. She and I both sat on the bed. She was toward the bottom, sitting on the edge with her left leg dangled off the side and I was propped against the headboard.

"I do. I met him just once—at your mom's funeral," I confirmed. Her mom had passed away when we had first started dating. At the time, I wasn't sure if I should go to the wake, considering I had never met her family before then. But there had been a sorrow in Cait's eyes that told me she couldn't have survived the day on her own. "He went into the army, right?"

"Right," she said.

"How is he?"

"He's good. He has kids now."

"Aunt Cait?" I mocked. "I can't see you as an aunt."

"That's a popular opinion." She laughed.

"With whom?"

"My dad. My brother. Everyone I've ever dated."

"Are you dating anyone now?" She left the door wide open for that question. Or maybe I saw it as opportunity that had to be taken.

"What do you think?"

I studied her face as I thought about the answer. "No," I said. I tried to make my guess sound like a verified fact. "You wouldn't have taken such a long assignment if you were."

"Why do you say that?"

"Wouldn't you miss her?"

"It's not like I wouldn't eventually see her again." She smirked.

A scoff escaped my lips as I shook my head. There was the Cait I knew, the one who was incapable of showing romantic emotion. Not because she didn't know how to feel it, but because she didn't know how to own it. To let the person she cared about most know just how much she cared for them in return was a weakness in her eyes. She was like this back when we had been together, and I would be lying if I said I didn't find some pleasure in knowing she hadn't changed. It wasn't just me she refused to show emotion for. It was everyone.

"Here," she said. "I have photos of my nieces." Cait picked up her phone from the bed. The comforter rustled underneath her as she scooted herself closer to where I sat.

She leaned her shoulder against the pillows underneath me. Her head was level with my bicep as she stretched her legs down the length of the bed. She was close—physically closer than we'd been in twenty years. Her head was just below my nose, and I took a deep breath. Her coconut- and raspberry-scented shampoo filled my lungs.

"Photos?" I asked as Cait held her phone above my lap. She tilted her phone so I could see the image on the screen. She swiped through a series of miscellaneous photos, mostly pictures of buildings and landscapes, until she reached a photo of two young girls. The youngest, no more than four, wore a pink shirt and cut-off denim shorts. She held two dandelions in her hand, her golden hair wrapped in a side ponytail, and she grinned as she looked into the camera. The oldest, another blond-haired girl around ten, stood next to her sister, and she beamed the same smile. "They're adorable," I said.

"There's more." She scrolled through her photos and landed on another picture of the girls, this time at the beach. Cait was also in the photo. She sat behind a shabby sandcastle. As cute as the girls were, it was hard to ignore Cait in the background. Her olive skin complimented her black bikini as she held a red plastic shovel in her hand. The soft outline of her abs was covered in grains of sand. And her hair, wet from the ocean, was pulled into a low ponytail. She wasn't as thin as I had remembered her being, though that was a given. Twenty years and being middle-aged doesn't always allow for a perfect beach body. But what Cait had hidden under her white button-up and black blazer was just as arousing and gorgeous as the body she had when we were in our twenties.

"How old are they?" I placed my hand under her phone.

"Ten and five," Cait said. I meant to take the phone from her hand, but she kept hold of it. My fingers now rested on top of hers. Her skin was warm and smooth, and she placed her fingers between mine as we both held her phone. The photos had become just an excuse for us to stay in this position, but neither of us moved. After several seconds of unwavering silence, Cait finally spoke. "I'm not seeing anyone," she said as she looked up at me.

She pulled the phone from my hand and sat upright. Her mouth was less than a foot from mine as I sat paralyzed. Not from fear of the possibility of kissing her, but from anger at the possibility that she was about to ruin a perfectly innocent evening. We were just old friends catching up. There was no pressure to be more than that—at least not until now.

"Cait…."

"Do you remember the first time we kissed?" she casually asked. She kept her distance as she opened her body more toward me.

"No," I answered honestly.

"It was the last day of self-defense training. I remember because you gave me a nice-sized bruise on my hip."

"It's not my fault you didn't know how to land," I cautiously teased.

A singe of heat picked up behind my neck and traveled down my spine as I watched Cait smile. She was incredibly beautiful. And this would have been the perfect moment for her to kiss me.

Except it wasn't.

As much as I wanted to feel her body against mine—as much as I wanted to feel normal and allow myself to get close to her—I just couldn't. It was as if that part of me, the part that knew how to connect to another human, had been ripped from my chest and set on fire.

"We were alone, in the elevator," she continued. "I had wanted to kiss you all during class. Each time you slammed me into the ground or put me in a restraint." She paused and her cheeks turned a pale pink. "All I could think was, 'three more hours,' 'two more hours.' I was petrified to make the first move. I didn't know how you felt about me—

"

"Wasn't it obvious?" I interrupted. It was baffling to me that she didn't know how infatuated I was with her from the first moment I saw her. It was a different time back then, so it came naturally to hide those kinds of feelings until utmost certainty the feelings were mutual. But I thought it was blatantly obvious how ridiculously and brutally attracted I was to her.

Cait shook her head. "As soon as we were alone, I counted to three, closed my eyes, and hoped for the best."

"That's when you kissed me," I confirmed. I remembered not knowing what was going on until I felt her hand cup the back of my head. I didn't know a kiss could be so passionate. Maybe that's why I felt the way I did whenever we were alone in an elevator. Somewhere deep in my subconscious, I remembered that kiss. And maybe, somewhere deep inside of me, I wanted that kiss to happen again.

"Are you seeing anyone?" Cait asked as she scooted closer to me, her knee brushing against my outer thigh. She leaned forward, her mouth less than five inches from mine.

"Cait…." I stood from the bed as I rejected her advances. She stood from the bed too and studied my face as I stared at her. My heart dropped into my stomach, and I could taste her breath against me.

"You *are* seeing someone." She eyed me up and down. Leave it to Cait to think that the only reason I wouldn't want to be with her was because I was with someone else. As if the thought of someone not being into her wasn't even a possibility.

She stared at me, and I could feel her trying to figure me out, like one of those magic-eye posters. I sensed a hint of jealousy sweeping through her. And I found myself enjoying it.

"It's not that," I said. I stopped short before a smirk of victory spilled from my lips. "It's just that your jealousy tastes better than you ever did."

With her mouth agape, she slowly sat back down on the bed, as if her ego had been so severely bruised she needed somewhere soft to land. She looked at me, completely speechless and humiliated. I turned away from her and headed toward the door.

The springs in the door handle popped as I pushed it down, and a low rustle came from the bed.

I turned around to look at her one last time. She stood at the brink of the entryway, her eyes locked on me. Her stare lacked the intimidation I expected. Instead, she looked at me as if I had unexpectedly served her divorce papers.

"I'll take a cab back to the station," I said. I didn't want to be near her. I would have rather walked a hundred miles back to the station than be in the same car with her.

Before she could respond, I stepped into the hallway. The dry scent of cheap laundry detergent permeated my nose as the door latched behind me. The grumble of the deadbolt echoed down the hallway, and I walked toward the elevators.

The farther I walked away from Cait, the more I started to regret my rebuff. It's not that I wanted this to turn into a romantic evening, but my cruel reaction would certainly have an impact on our working relationship.

But that was something to worry about tomorrow.

CHAPTER | TEN

THE LIGHT FROM THE floor lamp shone through the large panes of glass and illuminated the window of Cait's hotel room. I sat in my car with the windows rolled down and stared into the thin air. It was the type of evening perfect for sitting outside, sipping lemonade, and listening to what nature had to offer. But I was too consumed by grief to feel the joys of the outdoors.

Cait wasn't expecting me, and I hadn't planned on staying here. The low tick of the idling engine filled my head as I zoned out. Daydreams were the only defense I had against the day. My heart had been shattered before. But it had always healed itself, like hearts are supposed to do. Not this time.

My heart was permanently broken.

The pastel glow of the twilight sky swept over the Westerly Inn as I looked toward the lobby. As if she knew I was here, Cait walked through the automatic sliding doors and stood in the vestibule. Her hair laid flat against her back, with loose strands that curled past her shoulders. She tilted her head in curiosity as she looked at me.

Her lips fell into a frown as she glided through the second set of doors and walked toward my car. She wore her academy shirt from our training days—a gray polo with the West Joseph seal embroidered on the right breast pocket. Her jeans were tight around her legs, and her black shoes vanished in the dark driveway. The last time I saw her in that shirt was twenty years ago.

Heavy clouds formed above us and coated the night sky. The passenger door to my car quietly opened, and Cait sat in the seat—uninvited, but still welcome. The door closed with a quick click, and I rolled up the windows. I wasn't able to look at her. I couldn't. It took all my strength just to hold my head up.

"You changed out of your dress," Cait said. I looked down at my clothes and noticed I was also wearing my academy shirt from twenty years ago.

I nodded. "I threw it away." My voice choked as I held back tears. "I don't ever want to see a black dress again, let alone wear one."

"It was a beautiful service."

The horizon that blanketed us seemed only vaguely familiar. But I had been here before. I had heard these words before. This was the conversation I'd had with Cait after her mother's funeral.

I nodded again. The tears, once trapped behind my eyes, were now free. They slid past my cheekbones, down my face, along the curves of my chin and to my neck. Cait adjusted in her seat to face me, and I continued to look out the front windshield in a hypnotic stare.

"I'm sorry about the victims, Lena." Cait reached over the console and held my hand. Our fingers intertwined, and she hugged my hand with both of hers.

"I failed them," I muttered. My shattered heart fought to beat.

"No, you didn't." Cait squeezed my hand. "How are the families?"

I shook my head. "Not good."

"Where is he?" Cait looked out the window and scanned the parking lot.

"Gone," I replied. She didn't have to say his name. I knew who she was referring to. "I don't want him to see me like this."

Thick raindrops plopped against the roof of the car, covering the windshield in a layer of tears. I could relate to how hard the clouds were crying.

"How do people do it?" I asked. "How do they get past what's holding them back?"

"You have to get past yourself," Cait answered. She placed her hand on my cheek and swept her thumb under my eye as she caught my tears. "Why did you come here?"

What did she mean? Didn't she know that I needed her? Not the "her" she is now, but the "her" she was then. Before Lathan. Before my heart forgot how to love. I needed her to wake the part of me that had been knocked unconscious. I needed her to help me feel again.

"I need you to tell me I'm not always going to feel like this," I said. "I need to know there will eventually be an end. Because this is unbearable." My voice echoed behind my sinuses. I winced as my stomach tied itself into a knot, and my lungs ached under the pressure of holding everything in.

"It will stop," Cait said with a half-smile. "But only if you let it."

My elbows rested on the hard console between us, and I buried my face in my hands. Cait placed her hands around my jaw line and lifted my head. My vision blurred behind the layers of tears stuck to my eyelids. Cait locked eyes with me. I wrapped my hands around her wrists and looked down as raindrops pelted the car and thunder echoed across the sky.

Was I allowing myself feel? I had smacked away every helping hand that came my way. It was no wonder I felt as if I had to fight this battle alone.

I lifted my head and looked at Cait. My eyes fixated on her mouth, and I leaned in to kiss her. I needed to feel something—anything—besides the numbness in my heart. Long ago, Cait had brought emotions out of me I never knew I could feel, and I needed to feel those now. I didn't want to feel dead inside.

Her lips softly pressed against mine. I took a deep breath and kissed her harder. Something inside me slowly started to wake. It rose from its slumber as it stretched its cramped limbs. My lips smacked against Cait's.

After a year of starvation, she presented me with a grand feast. I grabbed at the food in front of me and shoveled it into my mouth. With each handful, the serving dish somehow refilled itself. I was dining from an endless banquet of desire, and Cait invited me to get my fill.

Warm teardrops fell onto my cheeks. I pulled back from Cait and looked at her. She was crying too. We stared at one another, our lips and eyes mere inches apart, and I eagerly resumed our kiss.

I let everything I felt—all the ache, all the hurt, all the emptiness—flow through my body and out of my mouth. Cait had become a blank canvas and I the artist. My kisses had become the paint, and I covered my beautiful canvas with tears of lust, love, and sorrow.

Cait broke from the kiss, and I hung my head low. Her lips skimmed my forehead, and I felt my temperature rise. The passenger door opened, and I looked up at her. She stepped out of the car and opened the back door. My hand instinctively pulled on my door handle, and I followed her into the backseat of my car.

I sat in the middle, and she straddled herself across my lap. She leaned in and kissed me as I smoothed back the wet strands of her hair that stuck to her face. A thin film of fog covered the windows as Cait slid from my lap and leaned against the door. She stretched her arms out and invited me to lie with her. A few cries escaped my mouth as I leaned against her for support.

She raked her fingernails along my scalp as I unabashedly cried into her chest. I sobbed into her cradling embrace as she combed her fingers through my hair, and I fell apart in her arms.

"You'll get through this," she finally said. "There's no magic cure. You just... get through it."

I squeezed my eyes shut. If I had any tears left to cry, they would have fallen. But my eyes felt like sandpaper when I blinked. I lay against Cait, with my head pounding and my neck sticky from the stale air. Her soft bosom slowly went stiff, as if I was cradled by a cement floor instead of a person, and her embrace wrapped tighter around me—tighter and tighter, as if she was trying to squeeze the life out of me.

I lifted my head in protest, and my muscles tensed when I opened my eyes.

I was no longer lying with Cait.

Angela Truman's matted blond hair flowed over Lathan's shoulders. Her decaying, oatmeal-gray face masked his. I tried to scream, but no sound carried from my mouth. I gasped for air and swallowed gulps of oxygen, but my lungs refused to expand.

I scrambled back and broke from his embrace. My eyes locked on Lathan as he continued to lean against the car door. I fumbled with the handle and pounded on the back window with my fists as the door remained locked. I was trapped.

I continued to bang on the window as I silently shouted for help. But no one could hear me—no one was coming. I looked at Cait's hotel. It was gone. Instead, in its place, I saw Cait's old home in West Joseph, where she'd lived when we were in the academy together. It was less than twenty yards away. If I could break the car window, I could run to her house. I would be safe.

The back windshield absorbed the force of my blows, and I jerked back when fiery flames sprouted from the ground. Fire circled the car and created a blistering barricade. The car shrieked as the flames engulfed its metal frame.

There was no way to escape. At least not alive. If I stayed in the car, Lathan would surely finish me off. If I left the car, I would burn within seconds.

The fire rose over the car. Its scorching heat filled the space between me and safety. I yanked on the door handle. The scorched metal sizzled in my hand, and the door opened. As I prepared to jump from the vehicle, Lathan lunged on top of me, his breath hot against my ear.

As I fought to break free, I saw Cait standing on her front porch, wide-eyed and calling for me to get out of the car. I took a deep breath. Smoke and ash filled my lungs as I slipped from Lathan's grip and fell to the burning ground.

I pushed myself up. My eyelids broke from their crusted seal as my hands sank into the malleable surface of the mattress. My stomach lay in a pool of sweat that had formed between my chest and the bed. Daylight slipped past the thin opening of the closed curtains. It struck my face and blinded my eyes. I shot up from the bed.

With uneven breaths, I looked around the bedroom. I was alone. My heartbeat pounded through the room. I reached for my cell phone on the nightstand and looked at the time. Across the screen were several notifications of text messages from Flu. He had even called twice.

What time was it?

I cleared out the notifications so that I could see the time on the screen. 9:13 a.m.

I'd overslept by two hours. Why hadn't my alarm gone off?

Because I hadn't set my alarm.

With all the mixed emotions of being around Cait last night, along with the disappointment of the stakeout, I had been too focused on sleep to worry about waking up.

I sat on the edge of the bed and called Fluellen's office. He answered on the second ring. The taste of my metallic breath lingered in my mouth as I spoke.

"It's Evans. I overslept. I'll be there in half an hour," I quickly said. I knew an apology would mean nothing right now.

"See that you are," Flu snapped and hung up.

I paused as I sat on the bed. The cool air absorbed into my skin and evaporated the sweat that had trickled down my neck. I felt as if I had just run a marathon. The thick pounding of my heartbeat rose to the back of my head. As desperately as I wanted to lie back down, I couldn't. I had to start the day.

The cold hardwood floors soaked into my bare feet as I walked out of the bedroom and into the bathroom. Of all the days to sleep in, it had to be this one. Cait was surely already at the office. Flu didn't mention whether he had received a video this morning, so maybe it wasn't a big deal that I was late.

The sun shone through the bathroom and bounced off the white tiles, lighting the room with little effort. I drew back the shower curtain. The plastic hooks clanked together as they slid across the metal bar, and I turned the faucet handle. A gush of water poured from the showerhead and landed on the base of the tub. It sent an echo through the room, like marbles falling onto the floor. As the water hit the tub, I opened the medicine cabinet and reached inside for the toothpaste and my toothbrush. I scrubbed at the morning residue that had coated my teeth and tongue, then slipped out of my tank top and baggy sweatpants and into the shower.

As I let the lukewarm water run down my face, thoughts of last night flashed through my mind. Aside from the stakeout being a waste, I had rather enjoyed the time spent with Cait. Not just on a professional level but also talking to her. It wasn't only talking about the case that had kept me there so late; it was also being around her. Finally, a human being who didn't look at me as if I was damaged and in need of being rescued.

The more I thought about the evening with Cait, the more I couldn't help but forgive her for the attempted kiss. Looking at her, having her skin against mine, it felt like old times. I was a cadet with a crush again—I still had my entire career in front of me, and I could make it whatever I wanted. There was no Abi. No Fluellen. Certainly no Lathan Collins. It was just Cait and I. We were optimistic and safe, like we had always been.

Maybe that's what the dream was trying to tell me.

In the dream, I had specifically sought Cait for comfort. I didn't have a sex dream about her—I had a therapy dream about her. Cait could have rescued me from the car, but she didn't. She stood on the porch and encouraged me to fight back. It was as if I had to prove to her, and everyone else, that I actually wanted to live. That I actually wanted a normal life.

When she and I were in the car, she consoled me in ways I needed to be consoled. She was the bandage my wounded heart needed. It wasn't about the sexual release—although that part was nice. It was that I felt desired and human again. I was no longer a frigid and hollow shell. The lust and want I felt for Cait had sparked a fire inside me. And it felt good. It was so good that I began to crave that feeling for her while awake.

I wasn't ready to be with her last night, but that didn't mean I wouldn't be ready down the road. Would she wait that long? Would it be fair to ask? After we solved this case, she would go back to Lyons, and I would go back to being a part of her past—and she a part of mine.

After I rinsed out the shampoo and conditioner, I let the water run down me. Once I turned off the water, I wouldn't have an excuse to stand here. And I wasn't ready to start the day. I wanted to stay inside the shower, shielded by the curtain. I wanted to stay here, accompanied by just my thoughts. Although I was naked and rather vulnerable, the narrow tomb created by the shower walls had become my sanctuary. As soon as I slid the curtain open, I would be defenseless against the world.

The steam from the shower began to evaporate, and the cold air from the air conditioner filled the room. I could either be defenseless and warm or shielded and freezing. I turned off the faucet, squeezed the excess water from my hair, and opened the shower curtain. I reached for the towel that hung on the wall and wrapped it around my bare body.

Before I could think about another evening with Cait, I had to get through the day. In record time, I finished getting ready for work. As I grabbed my car keys, I received a text from Abi.

I'll be home tonight. We can talk then.

Even if I didn't know her as well as I did, I would know that she was definitely still mad. I thought about what to respond with. A simple "OK" felt dismissive. I was already late for work, so I couldn't respond with anything that might lead to an ongoing conversation. I slipped the phone into my back pocket as I opened the front door and braced myself for the heat wave that would soon crash against me.

I quickly got into my car. The leather seats felt like oven mitts that had just taken a pie out of the oven. I turned on the air conditioning before I pulled out of the driveway. As I drove down the highway, I realized the pro to being really late for work was no traffic. But as I drove into the parking garage, I realized the con was having nowhere to park. All the spots closest to the building entrance were occupied. I drove through the entire parking garage and made a series of left-hand turns until I finally found a spot, on the third floor. That would add another five minutes to my tardiness.

When I reached my department, I walked into my office. I half-expected to see Cait waiting for me, but she wasn't there. And if she wasn't in my office, there was only one other place she could be.

"Evans, have a seat," Flu said when I walked into his office. Cait sat in one of the two empty chairs across from him. She barely made eye contact with me. It was as if we were forced to sit in study hall together after a break-up. I had severely bruised her ego—maybe even cracked it a little. She would be professional for the sake of the investigation, but when it came down to being friends or evenly friendly toward me, that was out of the question. The days of her bringing me coffee were probably over too.

"What's going on?" I asked after I closed the door and sat in the empty chair next to Cait.

Flu looked at the monitor on his desk, then to Cait, then to me. He had the same dread in his eyes that a parent has when telling the kids the family dog had been hit by a car. Cait crossed her legs at the knee and turned in her chair so that her body was closed off to me. How long had she been in Flu's office? Did she tell him what had happened last night? It would be pretty stupid on her part if she did. She was the one who'd tried to initiate a kiss—not me. So why did I get the feeling Flu was about to lecture *me*?

"We got Kristen Valeri's video last night," Flu said with a sigh.

"When?" I asked. "We were at the plaza until it closed last night." I trusted the undercover officers. If there had been even a hint of suspicious behavior, they would have radioed us.

"Around ten o'clock," Flu answered. "It's a different IP address than the others. Abram is trying to pinpoint the location now. Whoever sent this didn't do it from the plaza."

"Last night was a waste then," I said.

"According to the investigation? No. According to taxpayers? Yes," Flu answered. "If I thought it was going to be a waste of time, I wouldn't have authorized the stakeout. It's part of the investigation process, and it needed to be crossed off the list. We used the information we were given, and we tried to use it to our advantage. That's not a waste."

"Do you have the video?" I asked.

"I do. It's here." Flu turned the monitor on his desk so that I could see it. Cait uncrossed her legs and leaned forward. She still made no acknowledgement that I was in the room, let alone sitting next to her. "Agent Porter hasn't seen it yet, but I have." Flu cleared his throat as he hesitated to play the video. "I should warn you both." He paused again. "It's… it's as horrific as the others." He took a deep breath and exhaled as he pressed play. He sat in his chair, facing the back of the monitor, so that it was impossible for him to watch the video with us.

The grainy resolution filled the monitor as Kristen Valeri sat upright in a metal chair in the center of a warehouse. She wore an identical outfit as the one she was wearing in the printout that had been left in the backseat of my car. Her coal-black hair laid flat over her shoulders. She held a script in her hands as she read over it. Then she closed her eyes and silently mouthed a few sentences to herself.

A bright light shot over her, casting a dark shadow inside two hollow archways that led into small nooks no bigger than jail cells. I assumed the nooks were used for storage, but they were too dark to see if anything was inside. I hadn't noticed the two nooks in the videos before, but I was certain this was the same warehouse where Pamela Westlake and Fionna Michaels had been. And I knew Kristen was going to meet the same fate as Pamela and Fionna too.

My eyes locked on the screen, and my stomach churned. It was like watching the nature channel: The viewer can see the coyote hiding in the forest, ready to strike, as the naïve deer drinks from the brook. No matter how much the viewer wants to warn the deer of the danger lurking behind it, it's useless. Just like the deer, Kristen Valeri couldn't hear me. Her death was inevitable. Everyone knew it except her.

"You may begin when you're ready," the familiar distorted voice spoke off-camera.

Kristen nodded and took a deep breath. She exhaled slowly. She looked as if she was trying to shake out all her nerves—and to silence the voice inside her head telling her to run.

"I'll be home late," Kristen said as she looked up from the script in her hand. "The car is acting up again. Alternator, I think."

"Why don't you just get a new car? That lemon is going to send you to the poor house," the voice said.

"Because that lemon is all I can afford." Kristen smirked. "Are *you* going to buy me a new car?"

"I would if I could, babe. You know that."

"I know—that's not how I meant it." Kristen looked back down at the script. She mumbled a few words to herself before she looked at the person off-camera. "I'm leaving work early to drop it off at the mechanic, and then I'll be home."

Kristen sat still in her chair, as if she was waiting for the next line to be delivered, when a sudden skip in the video showed Kristen standing in the middle of the room. The chair was no longer there. The jump must have been caused by the person operating the camera. He must have hit "stop" and then resumed recording once Kristen had taken her place for a new scene.

Kristen paced the empty room. She acted scared. But I didn't know if that was part of the character or her actual state of mind. Either way, "scared" would only be temporary. Within a few moments, she would feel real terror.

"Feel free to adlib the dialogue," the distorted voice said.

Kristen nodded as she continued to pace. An echo of chains skidding against the cement whistled from the recording as an expression of pure horror spread across Kristen's face. She walked backward as the hooded man came into frame. He dragged the chains that I was most certain had also been used in Fionna Michaels' video.

"Please," Kristen begged. "Don't." She looked toward the off-camera man as a look of uncertainty replaced the terror on her face.

"Good, keep going," the distorted voice said.

"I won't call the police. Just let me go," Kristen pleaded as the masked man stood less than ten feet in front of her. He looked down at her and gripped the chain in his right hand. "Please," she cried. "Let me go!"

There was another sudden jump in the video, as if the recording had been stopped and restarted again. Kristen was kneeling in an execution pose. Both her arms were outstretched, crucifix-style, the chains were now wrapped around her wrists and anchored to a wall off-camera. Kristen faced the lens, and the masked man stood behind her.

She was crying—and they weren't fake tears. Her voice trembled. Between sobs, she pleaded for them to stop. "I no longer want the part," she cried. "Please, let me go."

That poor, foolish woman. Somewhere, buried far beneath her fear and terror, was hope that maybe this wasn't real. That maybe the two men who held her captive had just taken the audition too far. She was the fish at the end of the hook, beseechingly looking at the fisherman to throw her back into the lake.

Kristen lowered her head in tear-soaked defeat as she squeezed her eyes closed. The masked man reached behind his back and pulled out what looked like a wire cheese slicer. The wire was thin, like piano string, and had a wooden handle on each end. He brought the wire underneath Kristen's chin. His arms crossed over one another, and he tightened the wire around her neck. She kept her head down, her arms outstretched, drool dripping from her mouth as she began to beg.

"Please," she sobbed. "Don't...."

In the seconds that felt like an eternity, Cait and I both leaned forward, as if the video had a magnetic pull to it. My voice caught in my throat as I debated whether to demand that Fluellen turn it off. I didn't want to see this. I couldn't watch this woman suffer through her death.

But I had to.

The masked man took a deep breath, his beer belly hanging over the waistline of his black pants. He squeezed the wooden handles and slowly uncrossed his arms. The wire cut into Kristen's neck. Blood began to trickle toward her collarbone as the wire embedded itself into her skin. She tried to scream, but only a muffled gurgle choked from her throat as blood pooled in her mouth and seeped down her chin. As the man pulled tighter and tighter, Kristen's body began to shake. She was no longer able to plead for her life. As her body violently shook, her face turned red and then a pale shade of blue. Her meadow-green eyes bulged from their sockets, and her eyeballs erupted into bloodshot vessels.

I briefly turned my head away in an attempt to force down the vomit that had shot up from my stomach. I just needed a moment to regroup. I had to watch this. Not just for credibility as an officer, but because I needed the image of Kristen gasping for her last breath to fuel the fire of this investigation. I needed to have her tear-stained face engrained in my vision. If I ever felt like giving up or wanting to wait until tomorrow to follow up on a clue, I needed her death to remind me who I was fighting for.

I slowly brought my eyes back to the monitor, and the beat of my heart echoed inside my chest. I watched the masked man dig his knee into Kristen Valeri's back. Her chest shot forward as the wire sliced deeper. Blood spurted from the gash around her neck. The masked man let out of a deep sigh as he let go of the handles. Kristen's body slumped forward, and her hair matted to her neck like a bandage.

The man took a step away from her and turned to his left as he walked off-camera. My eyes filled with tears as I stared at the cold, somber image on the screen. I wanted to jump into the video and carry Kristen out of there. She didn't deserve to be left alone in that room, discarded and forgotten, like a carcass on a butcher's table. I wanted to jump into the video so that I could strangle the men who did this to her.

As rage and sorrow coursed through my veins, the monitor went black. Flu leaned forward in his chair.

"I know this was upsetting to watch," he said quietly as he focused his attention on me. I understood why he chose not to watch the video a second time. Once was enough. I blinked back the tears in my eyes and sat back in my chair. Cait remained forward. "Once Abram has a location for the new IP address, I'll let you know." Flu turned his monitor back toward him.

"Has this been sent to the media?" Cait finally said, her voice caked in empathy.

"Not that I'm aware of," Flu said. He adjusted his monitor and clasped his hands on top of his desk as he spoke to us. "This guy wants attention. More attention than what we're giving him." He knew as well as I did that sending the video to the media would ensure a great deal of attention. "I can't put a gag order on every news station in the state, so we'll just have to hope this case doesn't get as big as…." Flu paused and his eyes slowly drifted upon me. "Well, you know…." He trailed off, as if he didn't want to say Lathan Collins' name in front of me. "Let's just figure this out so that we can put a stop to it," he said.

Cait finally looked at me, her eyes glossed in tears. "Should we go to your office?" she asked.

I stood from the chair and led the way down the hall to my office. Cait's footsteps clunked closely behind me. As much as I wanted to address what had happened last night, I couldn't get the images of Kristen Valeri out of my mind. The video was a shock, even to a seasoned officer, and I was no exception.

I walked into my office and stood behind my desk. I looked at my phone to see if I had any missed calls. Cait walked in seconds after me.

The door clicked closed as Cait stood opposite of me, her head down as if she was trying to remember the words of a well-rehearsed speech.

"I'm sorry," she said and paused to look at me. "About last night." She wasn't the type of person who often apologized. If it was a formality, she could do it. If the apology was to a victim of a crime, for instance, the words "I'm sorry" rolled off her tongue like a soccer ball down a steep hill. But when it came to actually admitting she was wrong—that happened as often as civilians actually getting out of speeding tickets. "It won't happen again." She forced a half-smile.

Did she really mean that? I had finally warmed up to the idea of getting close to someone. "It's fine," I said, trying to save face.

"No, it isn't." She sighed. "I just... got caught up in the moment. We were talking and getting along, and a part of me felt like I was twenty-three again. It was nice."

"It was."

"Still—that's no excuse."

"Really, it's fine," I said. "It was very much needed. I haven't felt wanted for a long time." That was true. Abi had tried her hardest to keep us close during the months I had taken off work, but I just didn't feel it. So it was nice to feel wanted by someone—and by someone I wanted in return.

"I find that hard to believe." Cait smiled. "So, we're good? Back to being partners?"

"Back to being partners."

"Good," she said as she sat in the chair across from my desk. "This case needs our full attention."

It was impossible to disagree with her. Part of me wanted to focus on the possibility of us being together, but the more I thought about it, the more I realized Cait was right. We had both been caught up in the magic of reminiscing. She didn't want me; she wanted to be twenty-three again. And I didn't want her; I just wanted to be normal again. We could provide that for one another.

"That video... it got me thinking," Cait said.

"About what?"

"How much do you know about the Internet?" she asked. Her

mouth parted at the lips like she was deep in thought.

"I know enough to get by. Why?"

"Just thinking, that's all...."

"Do you have a theory?" I recognized her behavior. She stopped her speech, as if there was something more she wanted to say.

"More like a hypothesis." She licked her lips and zoned out, as if she debated on whether to tell me. "Do you know what the Deep Web is?"

"The part of the Internet where pedophiles and drug dealers rub elbows?" I shrugged. I didn't need to know much about the World Wide Web to know that the Deep Web was an all-inclusive resort for career criminals.

"More or less," Cait laughed. "There are two parts of the Internet: the Surface Web and the Deep Web."

"Okay...." She had started to lose me. I knew enough about the Internet to utilize it for my job. But once the fancy lingo came into play, I was out.

"It's usually described like this," she said. "An iceberg has two parts. The tip, above the water. And the bottom, which is underwater. The tip of the iceberg is the Surface Web. The bottom of the iceberg— the part that's underwater—is the Deep Web."

"Where's the Deep Web?"

"Um, it's kind of like the bottom of the ocean."

"So the Surface Web is all the good parts of the Internet, and the Deep Web is all the bad parts of the Internet?"

"Not necessarily, no." Cait shook her head. "The Surface Web is anything that can be found through a search engine, like Google. Recipes, obituaries, movie show times, stuff like that. The Deep Web is for anything that the search engines can't find. It can be something as innocent as a status update on a private profile. Or court records."

"That's why I can't find police records on a person unless I go to the court's website?"

"Yes. Those records are part of the Deep Web."

"Okay, I think I've got it."

"Good, because we're going deeper."

"To the Deeper Web?"

Cait smiled. "The Deep Web is for sites that are purposely hidden. It isn't just for drug dealers and sex offenders. Some of what's on the Deep Web is less harmful. Sometimes it isn't harmful at all."

"So why have it?"

"Anonymity," Cait confidently answered. "Some countries are

more restrictive with what their governments allow people to do online. Some people may want to complain about their leaders, but doing so on the Surface Web would get them executed. So they go to the Deep Web, to organize protests and the like."

"I'm sure that's few and far between," I scoffed.

"In America, it is," she said. "But that doesn't mean U.S. citizens use the Deep Web solely to plot terrorist attacks or sell babies. Some people use it to download music and books. Other people, like your typical conspiracy theorists, use it because they think the NSA is spying on them and they want their privacy."

"Privacy for what?"

"Anything. Even to send family members pictures of their vacation. They want to communicate privately without the fear of the government hacking their email."

"That's ridiculous."

"To you, maybe. But not to them. Anonymity is vital."

"But if they believe the government can hack into their email, then why don't they believe the government can hack into the Deep Web?"

"If you had your own website, so that anyone could get ahold of you, what would you call it?"

"I don't know. Lena-Evans-dot-com?"

"Exactly! But what would you call it if you *didn't* want people to find it?"

"Why would I have a website if I didn't want people to find it?"

"Okay…." Cait paused with a chuckle. "What would you call it if you only wanted *certain* people to find it?"

"I don't know. I'm-*Not*-Lena-Evans-dot-com?"

Cait laughed. "Close." Her laughter continued. "You might call it a series of letters and numbers. Jargon, basically. H-four-nine-sixteen-A-seven-dot-com, for example."

"Wouldn't the government be able to find that?"

"Eventually. But it's a very small needle in a very large haystack. We don't even have the manpower to do a proper stakeout, let alone dozens of people to randomly type in letters and numbers, hoping to stumble upon a website."

"Maybe not, but I think it would be beneficial. Those sites are just sitting ducks."

"Drug dealers' houses are sitting ducks too, but we don't go knocking on every door in the country just to find them," Cait countered.

"Good point." I chuckled. "What does all this have to do with the Casting Call Killer?" I loathed using the media's attention-grabbing title, but that was still the only identifier we had for him.

"I think that's where he's getting his attention," Cait said.

"How so?"

"Flu said he wants attention, right? And we aren't giving it to him. But the Deep Web has areas specifically for this kind of stuff, where viewers see it as entertainment. Like snuff films." She paused. "But I don't know if *he's* the one sending us the videos. Maybe it isn't him—maybe it's a viewer who all of a sudden grew a conscience."

"So you think someone is sending us the videos so that we can put a stop to it? But why send us just one at a time? Why not send all of them?"

"Maybe the killer only posts them once a week," Cait offered.

"Let's say you're right. Why didn't he just send us a link to the website where they're being posted?"

"You need a special web browser," Cait answered. "Internet Explorer or Safari won't work."

"Why not?"

"Do you speak German?"

"No."

"So if I gave you a book written in German, would you be able to read it?"

"No," I sighed. My patience had become unbearably thin. She was getting into the type of computer talk beyond my comprehension.

"Neither can your web browser," Cait said. "Deep Web sites are written in German, metaphorically speaking, and your browser only speaks English. But if you install a web browser that understands German…"

"Then I'll be able to go to the Deep Web."

"Yes."

"So your hypothesis is that the killer recorded his victims, put the videos online for people to watch, and one of the viewers is sending us the videos?"

"Basically, yes."

"So why not just tell us the killer's name and location?" I asked. It all seemed more complicated than it needed to be.

"Because he may not know it," Cait answered.

"Okay, but that doesn't explain why he's killing them."

"I know." Cait sighed. "It's the 'why' that's the most difficult to solve," she muttered.

"Can we go on this Deep Web of yours and find the answers?" I was ready to throw in the towel—not permanently, but definitely for the day.

Then I remembered Kristen Valeri's face. The horror in her eyes as she realized her life was coming to an end. It's the reason I forced myself to watch the video. I had to keep going—for her sake, and for the sake of the other victims.

"Not from this computer," Cait replied. "We would have to get admin's approval to download the program. And they'd probably say no. The program isn't a toy."

"Can the program be downloaded on my laptop at home?"

"It can be," Cait said. "But you'll still need admin's permission. And I don't think you realize how serious this can get." Her tone shifted. "There are very smart and very dangerous people on the Deep Web. And they don't like newcomers. Promise me you won't get on there without me."

I wanted to laugh at her sudden shift in concern, but the worry in her face made me believe she was actually quite serious. "Okay, I promise," I said. "But let's just download the program onto my laptop. We don't have time to waste on admin's red tape, so I'd rather ask for forgiveness than permission."

"Okay." She let out a sigh. "When do you want to do this?"

"Well…." I paused as I thought about what the day had in store for us. "I want to cross a few more warehouses off the list. How about after that? Do you have plans tonight?"

"No," Cait shook her head. "I'm all yours."

131

CHAPTER | ELEVEN

CAIT AND I SPENT the entire afternoon and early evening checking out vacant warehouses on the list Abram had given us. We batted oh-for-eleven at the eleven warehouses. Some of them were impossible to get into because the door hinges were so rusted. The ones we were able to get into didn't match the warehouse from the video, or the inside was so dilapidated that it was clear no one had been there for years.

As the day progressed, I couldn't help but feel that our canvassing was a waste of time. But, as Flu had pointed out, it was all part of the investigation process. Leaving no stone unturned meant coming up empty-handed nine times out of ten.

Feeling defeated and a little car sick, I drove us to my house. It was a little past eight o'clock, and I wasn't particularly looking forward to a night of Deep Web research. But if it led to even one answer, then maybe this entire day wouldn't feel like such a failure.

Cait and I sat in my home office, both exhausted from the day. "Who," "what," "when," "where," "why," and "how"—or the 5W-H—was written on the white board affixed to the bare wall. That wall, and this entire room, was one of the features that sold me on the house. Most people are interested in a large backyard or a spacious living room for entertaining. I, however, wanted a wall big enough to hold a white board that I could use to map out my investigations.

Cait sat at the desk and began to download the program we needed to search the Deep Web. I sat across from her in the oversized chair and rhythmically brushed the micro suede fabric with my fingertips. It was soothing, like drawing lines in the sand. We both faced the white board, and I stared at the sheer lack of information we had. Every time we got one step closer to solving a piece of the puzzle, another mile grew between us and the final answer.

We barely had a grasp of the "when" and the "where." The "who" was still a mystery, and the "why" was taunting us like a class clown during recess. The videos—or the "what" in this investigation—were the only concrete facts we had. And although we might be on our way to discovering the killer's "how" via the Deep Web, we were still just as clueless now as we were the day we received the first video.

"Are you ready?" Cait said as she turned her chair to face the monitor on the desk. I stood up and walked behind her chair, and I stared at the laptop's monitor. The screen displayed a plain white website with a simple search bar in the center. "Do you have any masking tape or duct tape?" she asked. "Anything that isn't clear?" She scanned the top of my desk as she fumbled through the bin that housed paper clips and rubber bands.

"Side drawer," I said. Cait opened the top left drawer and pulled out the roll of masking tape. She tore off a piece about an inch long and placed it along the top of the monitor's frame. "What did you do that for?" I asked.

"Webcams are easily hacked. You don't want anyone looking in, especially without your knowledge." Her deadpan tone was alive with earnest.

"I thought I was anonymous?"

"You are. But there's no such thing as complete anonymity," Cait said. "This site has a proxy server that reroutes your IP address to over a dozen places. When we start our search, you'll notice how slow each page is to load."

"What do you mean 'a dozen places'?"

"The Surface Web is like following someone who's driving a straight line from Point A to Point B. But an anonymous site, like this one here, is more like following someone from Point A to Point Z."

"Okay…."

"Here, watch. If we search for social security numbers," Cait said as she typed "SSN" onto the screen, "the search starts at *your* IP address, Point A. Then it goes to points B through Y—an IP address in Rome, then Spain, then Africa, then back Rome, then to a dozen other IP addresses before it finally lands on the search result. Point Z."

As she explained, her search for social security numbers slowly loaded onto the screen. The speed was worse than the days of dial-up. Line by unbearably sluggish line appeared on the page, with more than fifty links to Deep Web pages on how to purchase fake identities.

"It's just like buying flowers online," I muttered. "You just type in 'flowers,' and a hundred florists come up."

Cait nodded as she typed "drugs" into the search bar. At a snail's pace, the results loaded onto the screen. Hundreds of links came up, describing various types of illegal drugs—along with prices, how soon they could be delivered, and customer reviews.

"Sellers receive feedback from their customers?" I asked aloud. It looked like any online marketplace—complete with red, green, or yellow stars next to the sellers' accounts.

"Mm hmm," Cait confirmed. "Red stars are new sellers, green stars are VIP sellers, and yellow stars are confirmed VIP sellers—they're the most expensive but the most trusted by buyers," she explained as she continued to scroll through the page.

"They sell everything," I said, letting my astonishment ooze. "Oxy, heroin, cocaine…," I rattled off as Cait continued to scroll. "Marijuana, Vicodin…."

"Crystal, Molly… they have it all," Cait said once she reached the end of the page.

"How do people pay for this?"

Cait chuckled to herself. "It's called cryptocurrency. It's a digital payment system that can be transferred into real money. It's like…." She paused. "Pac-Man eats pellets. Those pellets are worth points."

"Okay…."

"That part really isn't important. It would take all night for me to explain the payments." Cait laughed. "We shouldn't snoop on here for too much longer. Like I said, the people who monitor these sites don't like newcomers—or voyeurs."

"I can see why." I took a few steps around the desk and returned to my chair.

We had been working on this case nonstop since ten o'clock this morning, and we had little to show for it. The warehouses were a bust, and this dip into the Deep Web was a frightening and potentially pointless journey. Frustration flowed through my body like water from a ruptured pipe. Images of Kristen Valeri's murder flashed in my mind like clips from a horror film. But I had to keep climbing this hill. For her. I was exhausted, though, and my brain was on the verge of shutting down. I needed to walk away from the case and regroup—even if it was just for an hour.

"I know it seems like a long shot," Cait said, "but I *know* this is where the answers are. I can't explain it. It's just a feeling I have."

"I know that feeling," I assured her. It was stronger than a woman's intuition. It's the proverbial sixth sense, which some investigators are just born with. For whatever reason, when we blindly walk down the right path, a feeling deep within the gut awakens. It screams "warm," warmer," "hot!" whenever we come close to the answer. "But I need to walk away from this, just to clear my mind for a bit."

"That's fine," Cait said. "I have a little fuel left. Do you mind if I stay here to work?"

What did she mean by "stay here"? And how long did she want to stay? It was close to ten o'clock. And if Cait worked much longer, it would just make sense for her to sleep here. She could sleep in the spare room. I had an extra toothbrush she could use in the morning.

"That's fine. Do you want to stay the night?" My voice went up an octave. "That way you can work as late as you want."

Cait paused as if she seriously considered the offer. "A hotel bed or a bed here, it doesn't matter to me." She graciously smiled. "As long as it isn't an inconvenience."

"Not at all."

"Okay," she said. "In that case, a glass of wine might help with the search." She smiled again.

"Is red okay?"

"That's fine." Cait nodded and typed on the keyboard.

"I have a few extra pairs of pajama pants." I gestured to the closet next to the whiteboard. "You're welcome to whatever you want."

I walked down the short hallway that led past my bedroom and through the living room to the kitchen. I grabbed two wine glasses from the cupboard above the sink and a bottle of cabernet from the pantry. I returned to the office with two full glasses and found Cait scrolling through a site that I could only imagine was filled with perverse and illegal requests. I set the glass next to her and took a seat in the oversized chair.

The way she sat in the chair, leaned forward, her legs crossed at the knee, she was completely absorbed by the work in front of her. The ends of her hair fell tamely against her back, and her fingers punched each letter on the keyboard with rapid precision.

From time to time, she would pause and take a sip from her glass. I was afraid to ask questions for fear that I might break her concentration. It was fascinating to watch how engrossed she was. I envied her in a way. She was able to take her hobby and turn it into a career. When we first met, the Internet craze had just begun. She quickly took an interest and worked her way from novice to expert in just a few months.

When Cait had finished her glass of wine, she stopped typing and looked at me. "I have an idea," she said. Hesitation tainted her voice. "Do you trust me?"

"That depends on what with," I said and drank the last bit of wine from my glass. Her sudden allusiveness had piqued my curiosity. Trust her with what? My life? I didn't need any time at all to come up with the answer. I did trust her with my life. She was my partner. It was a given that I did. But did I trust her with my heart? Maybe I should answer that when I hadn't just downed a glass of wine on an empty stomach.

"It involves your name." Cait locked eyes with me. Her tone was sympathetic but stern.

"Okay…," I reluctantly said.

"I want to search your name."

"Why?" I asked. "What's that going to do?"

"The videos are being addressed to you. Somehow the sender knows you… he trusts you, maybe."

"I'm still not following."

"I've been searching for snuff ads," she said. "Nothing has come up. But I haven't tried the forums." She began typing again.

"Forums? Like, chat rooms?" I sat upright in the chair.

"Yes," Cait answered. After several keystrokes, she forcefully struck the "enter" key with her pinky and waited for the results to load. Minutes of my life ticked away as I waited for the forum page to load. The screen scrambled as the results appeared, and flashes of black and green lines filled the monitor. Cait pressed the "escape" key then hit a series of keys before shaking the mouse, as if that would somehow bring the screen back to normal. "I lost the connection," Cait said when the screen went completely black.

"Why did it go out?"

"Your processor couldn't handle the data, I assume. If your computer isn't built for this type of activity, it's common for it to lose connection." She sounded like a college professor. "I can reboot and try again?" she offered.

"If you're up for it," I said. "Would you like a refill?" I stood from the chair, my empty wine glass in hand.

"Yeah." She nodded. "Thank you. I'll get changed while the computer starts back up."

There was an abrupt chill throughout the house as I made my way to the kitchen. If this Deep Web Deep Throat knows me, it's because he or she knows about my involvement with the Lathan Collins case. That could be either good or bad. Usually thoughts of Lathan resulted in an instant queasiness followed by a distinctly bad mood. I still had that lightheaded feeling from the first glass of wine, so maybe that's why I was more relaxed than usual while thoughts of Lathan lurked in my mind. Hopefully, with a second glass, I would be able to maintain a tranquil demeanor when it came to talking about him.

I set the glasses on the granite counter and pulled the cork from the wine bottle. It opened with a soft *pop*, and I filled each glass halfway. As it poured from the bottle, the rich fermented scent lingered around my nose.

I picked up the two glasses and walked from the kitchen into the living room. As I passed the front door, a sudden *ping* came from the doorknob, as if someone was trying to pick the lock. My gun was in the office with Cait. Unless I was going to offer the intruder a glass of wine, I was rather defenseless.

"Cait?" I called, unsure if I was loud enough for her to hear me. Before I could call for her to bring my gun, the front door slowly opened.

From the porch light, a thin shadow stretched onto the living room floor as the door opened wider. I stiffened my posture and waited to see the intruder's face before kicking the door against him. Or I could temporarily blind him if I threw wine in his eyes. Just as I was about to throw my body against the door, I recognized the figure walking in.

"Abi?" I stood in the living room. I clutched the wine glasses in my hands as I stared at her in disbelief. "You're home?"

"Yeah," she quickly confirmed. "I texted you this morning." Between oversleeping this morning and getting a crash course in the Deep Web, I had completely forgotten to answer her text. "I see why you didn't have time to reply." Her tone turned cold as she stared past me.

I didn't have to turn around to know who she was looking at. Cait must have heard my call for her and walked into the room before I had a chance to tell Abi that someone was here. Abi had never been the jealous type, so I didn't understand why she would have a problem with my co-worker being here—until I remembered I was holding two wine glasses.

I looked back at Cait as Abi continued to stare her down. Cait wasn't wearing a black blazer, black slacks, and white button-up shirt. Instead, Cait looked rather comfortable in a pair of my gray sweatpants and a white tank top. To anyone other than me, it looked as if Cait was my date for the evening, not my colleague.

"Is everything okay?" Cait asked at a cautionary speed. Abi's death stare was alive with fury.

"It's fine," I said. "Abi, this is Cait, my partner on that case I told you about," I casually reminded her. But I could have said Cait was my cousin, and it still wouldn't have mattered. Abi's eyes narrowed, as if she'd caught us in bed together. Her chest rose with each breath. Even if Abi did believe Cait was my co-worker, it was obvious by her glare that she had a feeling something else was going on between us. I had never invited a case partner to the house, and definitely not one who traipsed around the living room in my clothes at ten o'clock at night. "Cait, this is Abi...." I paused, the wine glasses clattering together as my hands subtly trembled. I didn't want to give Abi a formal title—because, until now, Cait had no idea Abi existed.

"Her girlfriend." Abi stamped the title on her forehead.

"Girlfriend?" Cait questioned as she turned her gaze to me.

Every moment Cait and I had spent together was an opportunity for me to tell her about Abi. I didn't have to go into specifics, but why didn't I ever mention that I did, in fact, have a girlfriend? Maybe I didn't think they would ever meet. Maybe I didn't want Cait to know that I was with someone—although the term "with" wasn't exactly accurate, either.

Cait and I had walked straight into the office when we got to the house. Any and all photos of Abi and I were on the refrigerator or in the bedroom. Cait hadn't walked into either of those rooms. The only way Cait would have known about Abi is if I'd told her. And I had accidentally on purpose kept that piece of information to myself.

"Do you mind giving us a minute?" I asked Cait as I set the wine glasses on the entertainment center behind me.

"Sure," she said with temporary complacency in her tone. She looked at Abi and back to me. There was no doubt Cait, too, was interested in an explanation.

"Don't bother," Abi said. "I'm leaving."

Before I could object, Abi tightened her grip around her car keys and walked out the front door. My legs had somehow turned into cement blocks, and I was too paralyzed to go after her. I turned to Cait, a plea in my eyes for her to stop this. Couldn't she use her two working legs to go after Abi?

"You have a girlfriend?" Cait asked accusingly once Abi was outside. "Nice, Lena. Thanks for telling me."

"It's not that simple," I tried to defend, though I knew it pointless. Cait had the right to know I was seeing someone. Whether anything was going to happen with her or not, Abi was a huge part of my life. And Cait was becoming a daily occurrence. The two were bound to collide. I was leading a double life, and keeping that part of my life from Cait was an insult to the trust we needed in order to work together. "Wait here," I said. "I have to talk to her." My legs unlocked from their hardened position.

"She's already gone," Cait said. "Let her go."

It was a suggestion that I very much expected Cait to say. She was notorious for letting people go. She let me go; she let every girlfriend after me go. She had let go of so many people in her life that there was no one left for her to hold onto. As much as I envied Cait's autonomy, I didn't want that to be me. I wanted Abi to know I still cared about her.

"I'm not like you," I snapped. "I can't just walk away from people I care about."

The front door let out a high-pitched squeak as I pulled it open. Abi was already at her car in the driveway by the time I stepped off the porch. Gray clouds formed around the edges of the moon, which dangled in the sky like a coin in a slot machine. Its glow lit the front yard as I jogged to catch up with Abi before she could make her escape.

"There's nothing going on with Cait," I said as I tried to catch her attention. "She's my partner. That's it."

"Why should I believe you?" Abi whipped around, her jaw tight as she glared at me.

"It's the truth." I stopped walking. At least ten feet was between us.

"What do you know about truth, Lena?" Abi shot back.

I didn't know what she was referring to. I had never lied to her about anything. "What truth haven't I told you?"

"I know you're seeing a psychologist." She delivered that fatal blow, and my heart went as still as the earth felt. All this time I thought I'd covered my tracks in an attempt to convince myself that my omission wasn't a full-blown lie. All this time, she must've known where I was going and who I was seeing, but still she didn't say a word. A sudden shift in betrayal switched between us, and I understood why she questioned my honesty. But she had lied to me just as much as I had lied to her. "You can talk to a stranger, but you can't talk to *me*?" she asked.

"It's not the same." I searched for the words to answer her question. A thick coat of tears grew in the back of my throat. It traveled up my sinuses and landed against the back of my eyes, like a dam trapping a flood of water. I swallowed the tears and looked at the ground. I broke from the staring contest with Abi. As much as I wanted to tell her why I kept my appointments a secret, I just couldn't. Each time I took a breath to try to explain my actions, the words caught in my mouth like hair in a thorn bush. "I can't do this right now," I sighed.

"When can you?" she shouted. This was the first time I had ever heard her raise her voice—at least to me. "It's always on *your* time, isn't it?" She brought her tone down as if she knew she needed to compose herself as to not alarm the neighbors.

Why didn't she understand that I couldn't do this? Not now, not here. My body trembled as I held my breath, a last-ditch effort to hold everything bottled inside me. All the pressure inside my body was coming to a boiling point. I wanted to scream and shout, kick and curse. I wanted to run away from her—and this conversation. I just needed her to shut up and let me walk away before I burst.

"Why do you keep pushing me away?" she pleaded.

"Because!" The emotional volcano trapped inside me finally erupted. "Because you're a reminder of what my life could have been—should have been."

If it wasn't for Lathan and the twisted torment I went through to beat him, I would still be normal; *we* would still be normal. I would be able to sleep through the night. I would feel safe and secure. I would be happy. But all of that was gone. Simplicity had turned into complication with a single punch from Lathan Collins' fist.

"We can still have that." Her plea sung through the growing space between us.

"No, we can't." I lowered my head as the truth carved its way out of me. "I'm broken."

"*We*, Lena. We're broken—because *you* destroyed us. With your bare hands, you destroyed everything by doing nothing." She paused, as if she was waiting for me to defend my actions, but I couldn't. She was right. Lathan may be dead, but the monster inside him was still alive, destroying my life and everyone who got close to me. "We could have left West Joseph, but you chose to stay. *You* did this. You broke us." Abi took a step back and ran her fingers through her hair. She stared at her car as tears flooded from her eyes. I knew she wanted to leave, but her vision was too blurry. She sniffed back the tears that hadn't yet fallen as she gradually composed herself. "I almost wish there was something going on between you two." She gestured toward the house where Cait was still inside. Abi's cold stare pierced my eyes. "It would give me a solid reason to hate you."

"I don't want you to hate me," I said as I kept my distance. I wanted to hug her and tell her how sorry I was for everything. But I knew she wouldn't believe me.

"Then why does it feel like you do?" She wiped the tears from her eyes. "I love you, Lena. I really do."

"I know."

"But I'm tired." She sighed. "I'm just so tired of feeling like I'm never going to be enough. Maybe the truth is I never will be."

"Abi, don't. That's not true. It's not about being enough."

"Yes! It is. I'm not enough for you… and you're not enough for me either. I'm tired of loving this relationship for the both of us," she said, then paused as she regained her composure. I more than knew the words that were coming next. I could feel them being imprinted onto my heart, the way initials are carved into a tree trunk with a pocket knife. "I can't do this anymore."

And there it was. She had finally reached her breaking point. She had endured as much of my neglect as she possibly could.

"Abi…."

"I assume you're going to work tomorrow?" she asked as she looked down at the car keys in her hand.

"Yes."

"I'll get my stuff then."

She walked to the driver's side of her car and opened the door.

"You don't have to leave. Where will you go?" I took a few steps toward her car. Abi looked up from the ground, and her eyes locked onto me as if she was in attack mode.

"Bye, Lena." She sat in the driver's seat and slammed the door behind her. She started the car, and the engine roared like a lion defending its young. She peeled out of the driveway, loose gravel spitting from under the tires.

As she drove down the street, I stood in the front yard and watched her leave until the car's taillights were no bigger than the stars above me.

Abi was gone.

For months, I had felt this coming. At times, I had even wished for it. Not because I didn't want her in my life, but because I didn't want to be in *her* life. She deserved better than I could ever give her.

My heart slumped to the bottom of my chest as I stood in the front yard. I looked into the night sky and blinked back the tears as I tried to make sense of what I was feeling.

My heart was caught in a vicious game of tug of war. "Who I am" was the home team, and "who I'm supposed to be" was the visiting team. No matter who won, the result would be the same: somewhere, lying torn and beaten inside my chest, would be my heart, useless to anyone—including myself.

CHAPTER | TWELVE

"I WAS SURPRISED TO see you were gone when I woke up this morning," I said when I saw Cait in the parking garage.

We hadn't said anything to each other last night after Abi had left. Cait had already made her way to my home office by the time I'd walked inside, so I'd grabbed what was left of the wine and brought it to my bedroom. I hadn't been in a position to drive Cait back to her hotel. So hiding in my bedroom, wine my only companion, had seemed like the most practical solution at the time. My throbbing headache this morning told a different story.

"It didn't feel right to stay. I took a cab back to my hotel last night," she said as we walked toward the station together.

"You could have said something." The fact that we were in the parking garage didn't deter me from leaving my sunglasses on. I needed as much shield from Cait's disappointed glare as I could get.

"I sent a text message when I left. I didn't think you wanted to be bothered."

"I didn't. But still." I gave up trying to receive an apology. I knew she would never give one. "You sent that text at one o'clock in the morning. Is that when you left?"

"Yes."

"Were you in the forums all that time?"

"Yes," she said and then paused. "We'll talk about it upstairs—in your office."

Cait held the stairwell door open as I walked through it. It was the same stairwell where I'd sought refuge when the news crew bombarded me. Cait was the one who'd led me to safety that day. If she hadn't have intervened, I would have undoubtedly been charged with assault. Even if that reporter would've deserved it.

Since that day, all news crews had been banned from coming onto the station's property without prior approval. Once I was a hundred feet from the station's front door, however, I was fair game.

142

I stepped inside the stairwell with Cait close behind me. Once the door closed and we were shielded from potential eavesdroppers, Cait placed her hand around my elbow and gently pulled me back.

"We need to talk about last night," she said when I turned to look at her. She let her hand fall from my arm.

"I know." I sighed. It was a conversation I'd hoped she would forget about. "I should have told you about Abi. I'm sorry."

"Why didn't you? I thought we trusted each other," she said, referring to the type of unconditional trust partners are supposed to have with one another. In order for her to trust me with her life, she had to believe I had her best intentions in mind. I had to be open and honest with everything in my life—there are no secrets between partners. Once secrets come into play, trust starts to fade. And only doubt can fill that void.

"We do—*I* do," I stammered. "Everything… is just really… complicated."

"Why are you so closed off to me?" she asked, a subtle plea glistening in her eyes.

"It's not *just* you," I defended. "It's everyone." I knew she had taken it as an insult, even though I hadn't meant it that way.

Cait took my unintentional right hook with grace. She lowered her head in a defensive nod and then locked eyes with me. "What happened to you, Lena? You were never like this." Cait knew what had happened with Lathan Collins, but she didn't know exactly what I went through. She didn't know about the nightmares or the panic attacks. She didn't know there was a constant well of tears behind my eyes so tall it hurt to blink.

As I debated how to express to Cait why I had changed, the door behind us opened. Two uniformed officers stepped inside and walked up the stairs. Cait followed the officer's pace with her eyes and then turned back to me. "Maybe another time," she said. She despondently smiled and walked up the stairs.

She was five steps ahead of me the entire way to my department's floor. When we reached the door, she held it open, silence staining her lips. I walked past her and took a deep breath before I walked through the door. It was as if I was a performer, taking that last breath of confidence before running onto the stage. Unbeknownst to my co-workers, they had become the audience for whom I was performing. It was easy to fool them into believing I was the same person I'd always been. Cait, however, was different. The more time we spent together, the harder it was to maintain the act—and she'd caught on to my façade.

143

Once inside my office, I let out a low sigh. My office had become backstage, past the curtain, and out of the audience's sight. I was able to regroup here, to relax and regain my strength for the next performance. Cait closed the door and sat in the chair opposite of the desk. I took that as my cue to take a seat.

"Your name," Cait said, "is in the forums." She sounded as if she'd just told me my phone number had been scribbled on a bathroom stall.

"What does that mean?" I asked.

"Before we get to that, there's more." Her tone sang of bad news. "I found an entire forum dedicated to Lathan Collins." She paused, and I took a deep breath and held it. I wasn't sure where she was going with this, but I knew it wasn't going to be good. If forums really are like chat rooms, then that meant people were chatting about Lathan Collins.

"What about?" I asked. Normally, I wouldn't be alarmed. Good people talked about Lathan Collins all the time. It was one thing to research him and his murders for a college essay, but I had my doubts whether anyone in those forums was there for scholastic conversation. This was talk on the Deep Web. What could people possibly be saying about Lathan Collins that they wanted to remain anonymous?

"Singing his praises," Cait said. "He doesn't have a cult following," she added, "so that's reassuring. But he does have a fan club." She paused as if she was waiting for me to ask another question. "There are several conversation topics. One is about his childhood, a few are dedicated to each victim… and there's one about you."

"Me?" The entire thought was ridiculous. "Is that where you found my name?" That would make more sense than finding my name associated with these new murders.

"Yes," Cait nodded.

"What do people say?"

"Some feel that you murdered a legend. That you stole the one person they had to look up to," Cait said slowly, as if she feared repeating their words would somehow mean that she shared their delusion. "No one has threatened revenge, per se," she quickly added, "so I don't think you're in any real physical harm. Most of the conversations are at least six months old—some more than nine months."

"Are they local?" I asked.

Cait shrugged. "There's no way for me to know."

"Anonymous," I mumbled to myself. That was the whole point of the Deep Web. "What about the victims?" I asked. "What does his fan club have to say about them?"

"They say the victims should be honored that they died at the hands of a true artist." Cait closed her eyes, as if she was trying to recite the text from memory. "They go into detail about the ways the victims were murdered. They even go so far as to critique the killings, like they're at an art gallery or something." She shook the thought from her head after opening her eyes. "I saved what I could from the forums, mostly screen captures of the conversations. I was going to give the flash drive to Fluell—"

"No," I quickly said. "Please, don't tell him. Not yet. He'll overreact and put me in witness protection or something." It was extreme but something I could imagine Flu doing. "I'll be taken off this case," I added.

"Lena…."

"You said yourself that you didn't think I was in any real harm." I used her words against her. "Let's just ride it out." I paused as I thought about the last time I intentionally didn't bring something to Flu's attention. I had thought I could take on Lathan Collins by myself, but all that got me was a bump on the head and a lifetime worth of PTSD. "If something happens, then we can tell him," I said.

"Like what?" Cait asked, as if she wasn't convinced she shouldn't pull the trigger.

"Anything," I quickly said. "The first sign that someone is after me, we'll go straight to Flu."

"There *is* a first sign," Cait said sternly. "The most recent post. It was written in April, I think. Someone with the username 'Alfa Mike,' with an F," she added. "He wrote 'In honor of Lathan's one year, there will be a big surprise coming.' But I don't know what the 'one year' signifies… Lathan's death, or when Lathan started killing." She shrugged. "There's no telling what these people see as an anniversary worth celebrating."

"Okay, then, the second sign." I tried to joke, but the harsh look across Cait's face told me she wasn't in a mood to laugh. "Please, Cait," I begged. "I can't be taken off this case. Not yet. Not without warrant."

This case was the only thing worthwhile in my life. It gave me purpose. I could use what I went through as the driving force to help the Casting Call Killer's victims. No one in the department had the same dedication and drive I did. I was the best person for this case, and I didn't want the victims to suffer any more than they already had. The victims didn't deserve to be dumped on the caseload of another detective who didn't care about them as much as I did.

Cait clenched her jaw and looked out the window, her knee bouncing in unison with the ticking clock above her. "Okay," she finally conceded. "But I mean it." She slightly raised her voice. "The next indication that you are in any harm...." Her voice trailed off, but her eyes stayed locked on mine.

"I promise," I agreed. "You can go to Fluellen."

A momentary silence broke through the room as Cait continued her deadlock on me, her posture stiff and full of dominance. She shook her head, as if she couldn't believe she'd actually agreed to stay quiet for now, and she let her body sink into the chair.

With the threat of Lathan Collins behind us, I shifted my thoughts to the Casting Call Killer. There was something bothering me about Kristen Valeri's video—aside from her brutal murder, that is.

"Do you remember the video from yesterday?" I asked Cait.

She perked up in her seat. "Who could forget?"

"Remember the jumps in the tape? Like the recording had been stopped and started again?"

"Yes. What about it?"

"I don't know...." I paused. "That was the first video that had a jump in the middle. Almost as if they purposely had to stop the recording."

"Maybe they did. Kristen was in a completely different position after the jumps."

"You're right," I said. "Maybe she put up a fight? And the person behind the camera had to intervene?"

"But why wouldn't they leave that in?"

"Because he doesn't want to be seen," I said. "If he isn't wearing a mask..."

"...then we'll see his face," Cait nodded along.

"I was planning on re-watching the videos today. You're welcome to join me if you're up for it."

"I am." Cait looked at the clock above her. "Can I get coffee first?"

"Sure. I'll meet you in the conference room." My office was too small and my desk was too cluttered to have two people hovered over it all day. Cait and I stood at the same time, and I followed behind her as we walked out of my office.

Once I stepped foot into the hallway, I kept my distance from Cait as she made her way toward the elevator. As I walked down the hallway, I saw Flu standing outside his office.

"Evans." He motioned for me to come over. I turned to the left and walked the twenty feet between Flu and I. Cait was alone in front of the elevator. "I'm glad I caught you before I left," he said. It was unusual for Flu to leave the station early, even if it was a Friday.

We stood just outside his office door next to the bulletin board reserved for department announcements. Headshots of all the new hires from the past year were evenly spaced apart along the board. Along with Abram's headshot from his February hire date, the newest detective was also on the board. He and I had never been assigned a case together, but from what Flu told me, the detective was extremely knowledgeable—except when it came to proofreading his own reports.

"You're leaving early?" I asked.

"Yeah," he admitted. "I'll be back early Sunday afternoon—I'm going to my daughter's house for the weekend," he added. "Anyway, I talked to Abram about the new IP address from the most recent video."

"Did he find a location?" I asked.

"Yes… and no." Flu shrugged. "He narrowed it down to somewhere near Mirror Woods. There's another plaza there, so the person who sent the video probably used a restaurant's Wi-Fi," Flu explained. "Same MO, just a different location."

"Should I organize another stakeout for Wednesday?"

"Hold off for now, but I wouldn't rule it out." He scratched his head as he looked over my shoulder. I turned to see what had caught his attention. Cait was waiting by the elevators, in route to her morning coffee. "How are things going between you two?" he asked.

"Fine…." I scrunched my eyebrows together. "Why do you ask?" He had never asked me about a case partner before.

"Just curious," he said. "She must have really wanted to work with you." A low chuckle came from his mouth.

"Why do you say that?"

"She asked to come here," Flu answered. "Another Agent had initially volunteered to come, but she pulled rank to get the assignment."

"I wonder why?" I played dumb.

"So do I." Flu fell silent as we watched Cait get into the elevator. "I don't want to keep you. I just wanted you to know what Abram found," he said once the elevator doors closed. "Oh, Abram also said to tell you that he checked Fionna Michaels' computer. She answered a series of ads looking for an actress. No one answered her inquiries, though. If you have any questions, Abram said he'll be at his desk all day."

"Thanks," I sighed. "Have a nice weekend."

"You too, Evans," Flu said and went back to his office.

My shoes clicked against the tile floor as I walked into the conference room. It was surprising to learn that Cait had "pulled rank," as Flu described it, to work on this case with me. She did say she was aware that I was the detective assigned to the case—did she really want to see me that badly? After all the time and distance between us, why would she care to go to such an extreme measure to work with me? If she wanted to see me, why didn't she just call?

In the twenty years that had passed, I had only thought of her a couple of times. I'd wondered how she was and had hoped she was happy, but my curiosity was never strong enough to actually look her up. I'd assumed it was the same for her. Apparently I was wrong.

As I waited for Cait to return to the conference room with her coffee, I decided I wasn't going to mention that I knew she pulled strings to come here. It was best for us to concentrate on the case. But the more time I spent with Cait, the harder it was becoming to see her as just a case partner. The feelings I had for her, no matter how dust-covered they were, had started to resurface. New life had been breathed into them, and I had to keep myself from wondering if we were meant to find each other again. We had both matured since we were in our early twenties. Maybe our time was now.

The laptop in the conference room was already on, and I logged into the shared server. I navigated through folders until I found where the video files had been stored. As I clicked on Pamela Westlake's video, Cait walked into the room, a cup of coffee in each hand. She closed the door with the heel of her foot and walked to the center of the room. She set one cup on the table and slid it in my direction before she took a seat across from me.

"Black, two sugars, right?" She scooted her chair closer to the table.

"Right." I smiled as I reached for the cup. "I pulled up Pamela Westlake's video," I said as Cait made herself comfortable. The laptop was attached to a projector that would play the video on the large dry-erase board on the wall in front of us. My intent was to watch every single video until I could make sense of the "why."

"I'm ready whenever you are," I said.

Cait looked around the room. She stopped when she noticed the stack of notepads on the corner table. She stood from the table and walked to the corner of the room and picked up two of the notepads and two pens. She came back to the table, notepads and pens in hand, and slid one of each to me, like a bartender slinging beers to the patrons at the end of the bar. "I'm ready," she said.

As the video played, I paid close attention to the dialogue and background. The scene that Pamela read revealed that the character she played was a grad student. The warehouse was bare; only the chair she sat in filled the room. Behind her were two small storage areas. One had been sealed off with bricks, and the other was wide open.

The next video was Fionna Michaels'. From what I could tell from the script, her character was a neglected wife on the verge of divorce. The warehouse was bare, except for the chair she sat in and the hook that dangled from the ceiling. The hook was incredibly noticeable now that I knew its purpose. The cement walls were covered in soot, and the storage areas were both sealed off with bricks.

I scrolled the cursor over Kristen Valeri's video, and I prepared to watch one of the most brutal murders I had ever worked on. Kristen sat in the same warehouse as Pamela and Fionna; the two archways above the storage rooms lurked in the background like ghostly black eyes. They were completely vacant as Kristen read the role of a woman on her way to the mechanic.

After Kristen Valeri let out her last breath, I stopped the video and turned off the projector. I stood from the chair, and nausea curdled in my stomach, I walked to the dry-erase board. The felt-tip marker squeaked as I wrote "Pamela Westlake," "Fionna Michaels," and "Kristen Valeri" on the board. Next to each name, I drew a hyphen and wrote my corresponding notes.

"Pamela Westlake," I said aloud. "Grad student." I jotted it down and turned to Cait. "Anything else about her video or her character?"

"Her character is killed on campus," Cait added.

I nodded as I wrote down the information. "Did you notice the wall behind her? One of the storage areas was sealed—the other wasn't."

"I didn't notice that in her video, but I did notice it in Kristen Valeri's," Cait said as she flipped through her notepad.

"Fionna Michaels," I wrote as I spoke. "Arguing with her husband. And both storage areas were sealed."

"Strangled and then gutted," Cait added and shook her head as if she sympathized for the victim. "Potential divorce."

"Kristen Valeri, on her way to the mechanic—neither storage area is sealed."

"That's when I noticed the difference in the wall behind her," Cait said. "Strangled with a wire. And there are the jumps in her video," she added.

I finished writing the additional information and took a few steps away from the board. I read the notes silently to myself, over and over, until the words sounded like a séance in my mind.

"What if...?" I mumbled as I stared at the number of vacant storage areas in the videos. "Pamela had one area sealed. Fionna had two. Kristen had none." I continued to stare at the board. "But how can that be? Did he knock the bricks down to open the areas?"

"That wouldn't make sense," Cait added. "It's easier to lay brick than it is to knock it down."

My eyes widened as Cait's words sank in. "Kristen was reported missing July eleventh," I recalled from memory. "Pamela, July eighteenth. And Fionna, July twenty-fourth." I grabbed the dry-erase marker from the tray and wrote the number "1" next to Kristen's name, the number "2" next to Pamela's name, and the number "3" next to Fionna's name. "We didn't get the videos in the order they were made," I exclaimed.

What had seemed like a minor detail at the time might have become a major turning point in the case. Noticing the differences in the warehouse walls may have also solved an important unanswered question.

When we received the first video, some officers thought it was a joke. Who would send us a video of their own crime? And where was the body? No body, no crime. But the videos may have held the answer to where the bodies were buried—we just didn't know we were looking at them.

"The bodies," I said. "They're in the walls. Behind those bricks." I looked at Cait, a horrific epiphany in my stare. "That's why we can't find them. They haven't been dumped anywhere. They're still at the original crime scene."

"So once we find the original crime scene, we'll find the bodies," Cait reiterated. "So that still leaves the question—where's the crime scene?"

Her question was like a pin to my overinflated balloon. Our small victory had just been popped. We may have known where the bodies were, but we didn't know how to get there. I was holding a map with a giant "X" on it, but none of the roads had names. "You really know how to knock someone off their horse, don't you?" I walked back to the chair and plopped down, my victory deflating as quickly as it had filled.

"I'm sorry." Cait refrained from ending her apology with a laugh. She knew what it felt like to take one step forward only to be pushed two steps back.

I sat in the chair and broke up the information next to each victim as I concentrated on the characters they'd played. This time, however, I read through the information in the order of their disappearances—not in the order we'd received their videos.

"In need of a mechanic," I muttered. "Grad student. Divorcee." I repeated the words over and over in my head. "Mechanic. Student. Divorcee." I read them so fast, I wanted to add *oh my!* at the end.

Cait and I sat in silence as we both stared at the board. *Mechanic.* The more I said the roles, the more familiar each seemed. The last time the word "mechanic" was associated with a case, it was Lathan Collins. He was a mechanic.

As thoughts of Lathan lurked in my brain, a tight pressure rolled through my body, like a can of pop shaken by a hyperactive seven-year-old. But it wasn't carbonation that bubbled and fizzed through my body. Disquiet coursed through my veins, ready to explode.

I moved on to the next word, to try to rid my thoughts of Lathan. *Grad student.* Pamela Westlake played a grad student. That, too, seemed eerily familiar, as if I had read those words a hundred times before. I let the words sink into my memory, hoping something would surface. The last time I'd dealt with a grad student was… Lathan Collins.

The memory of Lathan's second victim, Lisa Johnson, came flooding into my mind. She was a grad student from Cleveland. Her body had been found on the hiking trails in Mirror Woods. I didn't need her case file in front of me. I remembered everything about her—and the other victims too.

Was Lathan's association with "mechanic" and "grad student" just a coincidence? I moved on to the last word. *Divorcee.* Lathan wasn't divorced. As far as West JPD knew, he was a friendless hermit who liked to repair cars—and skin his victims.

Although Lathan wasn't going through a divorce, Sophia Good was. Lathan's fourth victim. She had been reported missing by her soon-to-be ex-husband. Was it also a coincidence that Fionna Michaels' character was going through a divorce too?

I went through the similarities again. Kristen Valeri was going to the mechanic in her "audition"; Lathan Collins was a mechanic. Pamela Westlake played a grad student; Lisa Johnson was a grad student. Fionna Michaels played a potential divorcee; Sophia Good was getting a divorce.

"We need to re-watch these again." I quickly turned to the laptop and brought up Kristen Valeri's video. "But we need to watch them in the order they were reported missing," I added.

"What's going on?" Cait said, as if my sudden excitement to watch the videos was cause for alarm.

"I don't know," I lied. "Maybe nothing." I stalled as Kristen's video loaded. I took a deep breath and let it out as I came to the conclusion that I should tell about Cait my suspicions. Even if I was wrong, she needed to know where I was going with this. "Lathan Collins' second victim was a grad student from Cleveland," I said. "Pamela Westlake plays a grad student. His fourth victim was going through a divorce—"

"—and Fionna Michaels plays a woman headed for divorce." Cait nodded but didn't seem completely sold on the notion. "What about Kristen Valeri?"

"She's going to the mechanic," I said, "and Lathan *was* a mechanic. It's how he found his victims."

"Okay." She paused. "I see the correlation, but you said his second and fourth victims—what about his first and third?" Doubt washed over her face. "We only have three victims, and only two of them have any similarities to Lathan's four."

"I know." More air escaped my balloon. I understood Cait's doubts, but there was something deep in my gut telling me there was more to explore here. "You know how you're absolutely positive the Deep Web is involved?" I reminded her.

"Yes."

"I can't explain it, but I'm just as sure about the victims being connected to Lathan."

Cait nodded as if she knew not to argue with intuition. She perked in her seat as her eyebrows rose. "Alfa Mike," she said clearly. "From the forums."

"What about him?"

"He said there was a big surprise to come." Cait paused. "A big surprise for the one-year anniversary."

"Okay…?"

"The one-year anniversary of Lathan's death is now, right?"

"Yes."

"What do you remember about Lathan's first and third victims?"

"His first was Angela Truman." I swallowed hard as I said her name. The image of her face masked over Lathan's rose from the underbelly of my memory. "She was a mother of three." Nothing else really stuck out—other than the fact that Lathan was wearing her face when he died. It was possible he wore the faces of his other victims, but there was no way to know. Aside from Angela Truman's, the face of each victim was still missing.

"Carmine Jenkins was his third," I continued. "Her roommate reported her missing. She was the only victim found in the lake. She was weighed down," I added.

"Is it possible Kristen Valeri is Angela Truman? Since Kristen was the first girl taken, as was Angela Truman?" Cait asked.

If my hypothesis was correct, it would make sense. "It's possible," I agreed. "But Sophia Good was Lathan's fourth victim, and Fionna Michaels was our third. So that doesn't add up."

"Maybe we aren't finished receiving the videos," Cait said, her voice full of dread. "And we haven't received them in order of disappearance, so maybe Fionna Michaels is actually the fourth person to go missing, not the third."

As disheartening at it was, Cait could be on to something. "If that's true," I said, "then our actual third victim would have been reported missing sometime in July," I said with a heavy heart. "I guess we'll find out next Thursday."

Thursday was becoming a day I rather feared. Just thinking of more videos summoned an unrelenting nausea from deep within my stomach.

"I think we should look more into this Alfa Mike," Cait said as she slid the flash drive across the table. I picked it up and twirled it in my fingers. Did I really want to know what the Deep Web thought of me? The person who took away their hero? "Do you still have the files on Lathan Collins' victims?" Cait asked.

I more than *had* the files—they were a part of me. They had become imprisoned in my mind. The information had somehow cocooned itself inside my brain. Anytime a victim's name was mentioned, the crack of the casing echoed within my eardrums. It sounded like dry spaghetti snapped in half. As if the victims were trying to break free from my thoughts. As if they wanted to be more than morbid memories trapped inside my head. They wanted their lives back.

"All up here." I tapped my temple with my left index finger.

"I was hoping for something more tangible," Cait laughed.

"Yeah," I laughed with her. "Down in evidence. I can sign them out for you. You won't be able to with a temporary badge."

I excused myself from the room and thought about the parallels of each victim as I walked toward the elevator. I pressed the "down" arrow multiple times, as if my impatience would somehow motivate the elevator to come to the fourth floor more quickly. Was all of this really happening? Lathan Collins was dead and gone, but he was still alive and thriving within my life. Would I ever truly escape him?

The elevator doors separated like a sideways mouth ready to bite into its next victim. I stepped inside and pressed the button for "B2."

The doors slid shut and the floor gave way as the elevator started its descent. A high-pitched beep that sounded like a heart monitor echoed inside the elevator as it passed each floor. I swallowed hard as I tried to block the feeling that the walls were closing in on me.

I was never one for claustrophobia, but for some reason, being in this elevator felt as if a metal vice had clutched onto me. It was tighter than a boa constrictor and narrower than an MRI machine. This feeling clung to me like a wet shirt after being thrown into a pool, and it wasn't going to pass any time soon.

The elevator slowed before it came to a stop on the lower-basement level. The upper-basement level was where the station kept its public records. The lower level was for evidence. The Lathan Collins' case was so high-profile that in order to respect the victims and their families, the unabridged versions of the case files were stored with evidence. The public was able to read abridged versions, but black lines had been placed over the personal information of each victim.

My reflection in the chrome-plated elevator doors stared back at me until the doors slowly separated. The illuminated button for "B2" quickly went out and returned to a pale gray shade. Just one more foot, and I would have freedom from this jail cell.

The poorly lit hallway stretched the length of a basketball court before it reached a door that looked more like a dead end than a passage. The door stared me down, like a bully who waited at the back of the school bus, and I cautiously took a step forward. Then another.

As my courage increased, so did my pace. The hallway grew brighter, as if I was walking toward my own light at the end of the tunnel. The strong chemical scent began to waiver as specs of dust danced under the pulsing light bulb above the door that led to the evidence room.

I opened the thick metal door and stepped inside. Even for being in the lower basement, this room was sad and lonely, like the visitors' center in an abandoned amusement park. Behind a tall wooden counter, which separated the clerk from the officer, were nine rows of metal shelving units. Each unit had three shelves packed with evidence boxes and manila folders. The folders unevenly protruded out, like weeds in a small garden.

I hadn't been down to evidence since I'd returned to work. The one time I would've needed to come down here, Abram had the item I needed. I envisioned an elderly woman in her nineties would come out from behind the counter. Her gray hair would be tussled back into a loose bun as she sluggishly walked from the counter to the shelves in order to retrieve the requested files. It would be faster if I just jumped over the counter and looked for the files myself, but I would try my best to be patient with her. I would be polite and let the woman do her job.

Resting on the counter was a logbook and a chrome bell. Next to the bell was a hand-written sign that read "Ring for Service." Although meant to be inviting, the bell sat on the counter like a four-year-old boy pouting on the steps during a timeout.

Before I could ring the bell, a faint voice called from behind the shelves.

"How can I help you?" A thin figure emerged from the shadows.

She wasn't as elderly as I thought she would be. In fact, she was quite young—almost too young to be working in such an isolated department. Her brunette hair was pulled back into a high ponytail, with loose strands that fell around her long face. She wore thick-rimmed glasses, the kind that kids used to get made of fun of for wearing.

"I need some case files, please," I said as I unclipped my badge from my belt loop. The young woman cocked her head to the side as she looked me up and down. A knowing smile inched across her face.

"Sure!" Her grin grew as I gave her my badge. It was protocol to have an ID badge scanned when taking out evidence. In the event that a file went missing, administration would have a detailed log of where it was. She looked at the photo on my ID and then back at me, her smile stretching so far across her face that all I could see was her teeth.

As she swiped my badge through the scanner, I noticed Rachel Sanzone's novel on top of her desk. The cover photo of the faceless man stood out like feces in a bag of diamonds. I no longer needed to guess why she was so elated to see me.

"Which case are you looking for?" she asked.

"C-R-fifteen-C-zero-ten," I rattled off Lathan's file number. It was standard to use numbers instead of names to prevent any files having the same name—although I knew there was only one Lathan Collins in the database.

"Okay, just a second…," she said as she wrote down the case number on a piece of scratch paper. She set the pen down and looked at me with intrigue. She lowered her voice. "Can I ask you something?" We were the only two people here, so I was uncertain why whispering was necessary.

"Sure," I said as I braced myself for a Q&A about my time with Lathan.

"I'm reading Rachel's book," she said. "It's really good. There's so much I didn't know about the case and all she went through." She spoke at the speed a teenage girl does when talking about her crush. "If you hadn't been there, who knows what would have happened to her. She thinks of you as her personal hero. We all do."

"What's your question?" I dismissed her statements. Although it was flattering, I didn't see myself as Rachel's hero—or anyone else's. A hero doesn't have nightmares after the epic battle. A hero rides off to slay the next dragon, trauma-free.

"Will you…," she paused and looked toward the ground, "…sign my book?" She looked up and locked eyes with me. Her gaze was layered with hope, as if she had just asked the most popular boy to prom.

I was absolutely speechless. Out of all the questions I had been asked in the past year, a request for my autograph was new to me. I didn't want to sign her book. Those weren't my words; I wasn't the star of the novel. As far as I knew, the Lena Evans in that story was a fictional character who just happened to have my name.

"Rachel signed it," the young woman quickly added. She turned and took the two steps needed to retrieve the book from her desk. "See?" She held open the front cover. There, written in dark permanent marker, was Rachel Sanzone's autograph, complete with a hand-drawn heart under her name. "You could sign right here, next to her name." She pointed to a blank space on the page.

"I don't know…." I slowly began to let her down. "I'm not sure if I'm even allowed to sign it, especially at work." I tried to make up a reasonable excuse. "It's not a good use of city time."

"Oh." The young woman's smile drooped into a frown. "I understand." She closed the book and set it on the counter. "Have you read it?" Her tone was dry.

"No," I said. "I was there. I know what happened." My answer may have come off snider than I'd intended.

"Right," the woman said as she picked up the piece of paper with the case number on it. "I'll get this for you." And she sulked away before I could thank her.

Although I felt terrible that I had denied her request, I knew it was for the best. If I signed one book, I would have to sign them all—if I was asked. It was better that I got myself into the habit of saying "no" before it got out of hand. If it traveled down the rumor mill that I wouldn't sign her book, then maybe no one else would ask.

From back in the corner, I heard boxes and files being moved from the shelf, and I assumed it was the young woman retrieving the file I needed. Would she think it was odd that I had requested Lathan Collins' case? Had she gone through the file herself, being a huge fan and all? It must get pretty boring down here.

After a minute or two, the young woman came out from the shadows. She was still holding the piece of paper but nothing else. She had a puzzled look on her face, as if she was trying to solve a riddle. She barely made eye contact with me when she walked up to the computer and clicked a series of keys on the keyboard. "Hm," she said to herself as she scrolled through the database. "The boxes aren't back there," she said.

"What do you mean?" I asked. How could they not be back there? All case evidence from the past five years was supposed to be stored here. After that, it went to another facility where it would remain there forever.

"They were signed out," she said as she scrolled through the screen. "In April of this year. They haven't been returned yet." She shrugged.

"Who signed them out?" The case had been closed. No one should have taken the files out. Unless an officer was bribed by the media, but even that didn't make sense. Any news story on Lathan since his death didn't contain any information that was considered privileged knowledge.

Rachel's book. Maybe an officer had been bribed for information for her book.

"Detective Ryan Novak," the young woman said. "He signed the files out on April seventh at one thirteen in the afternoon."

"Detective Novak?" I repeated. Detective Novak had retired a few days before I'd returned to work. They had used my empty office to hold his retirement party. When I came back, streamers and party favors were still taped to the walls. "Are you sure?"

"His badge was swiped. It couldn't be anyone else." She shrugged again.

"Okay, thank you." My mind raced as to why Novak would want the Lathan Collins' files. There were more than just notes and reports in those boxes; everything would have been there—including any evidence obtained at the crime scene. The only item that wouldn't have been in there was Angela Truman's face. That had been given back to the family. And the city had paid for her body to be exhumed so that she could be buried intact.

I left the evidence room and briskly walked back to the elevator. I was going to have to wait to bring this to Flu's attention. He wouldn't be back until Sunday afternoon, and I didn't want to bring this to admin's attention in case my paranoia had caused me to overreact. If Detective

Novak still had the evidence, Flu would know why. And it was best to wait and talk to him about it first.

CHAPTER | THIRTEEN

AFTER A VERY LONG day at the station, I arrived home to find Abi's side of the closet empty. Movies from our DVD collection were missing from the shelves. But all of the bowls and glasses, pots and pans, and pieces of furniture were still at the house. Either she didn't care to play "this is mine" with insignificant items, or she would save the notion of co-ownership as an opportunity to argue over the washer and dryer at a later date.

Seeing the half-empty closet—and knowing that Abi wouldn't be coming home—I was forced to face a reality of my own making. I sat alone in the living room, my heavy feelings blanketing themselves around me, and I stared into the air. There was no noise to keep me company. The only friend I found solace in was my gun, perched on the arm of the couch.

As I sat in silence, the sun slowly fell past the horizon. Tones of dark orange and deep purple cast through the living room window and danced across the floor. I stared at the colors all evening until they faded into a rich black.

I turned on the lamp beside the couch and noticed my cell phone on the end table. I needed to call Abi. I needed to talk to her and see how she was doing. I wasn't going to beg for her to come back, though part of me wanted to. I didn't want to be alone on a Friday night—or any other night— but I couldn't manipulate Abi's feelings just for my benefit. That part of our relationship was over.

With a deep sigh, I picked up my phone and called her. Little to my surprise, it went straight to voicemail. It was probably for the best; texting seemed cowardly, but I wasn't emotionally strong enough to brave a full conversation.

"It's me," I said into her voicemail and paused. I should have thought this through before I dialed her number. I didn't know what to say, only that I needed to say something. "I see you got your stuff." Another pause. "I called because…." I paused again and sighed. A million reasons raced through my head, and all I had to do was grab one.

But I couldn't do it. I couldn't swallow back the tears to tell her I was sorry. "…I wanted to see how you're doing. Things kind of got out of hand last night," I rambled. "I think we should talk—clear the air between us." I paused again. "I'll be at Bento's on Sunday if you want to meet me. Around noon?" Bento's was a casual restaurant that didn't get a lot of business, even on a Sunday. It would be a quiet place for us to talk on neutral territory. "I'm sorry, Abi," I finally said through a thick coat of tears. "I really am."

With nothing left to say, I ended the call.

Fast forward to Sunday, and here we were—two strangers who knew everything about each other, blankly staring at each other.

"Thanks for coming." I said. "I wasn't sure if you'd show up."

"I wasn't sure if I was going to either," Abi replied as she slid the chair out from under the table. Her eyes were red and puffy underneath, as if she had spent the entire morning crying. She sat on the edge of the restaurant chair, ready to bolt at any time.

A light breeze flew through the loose strands of her hair, which was pulled back into a braid. She kept a tight grip around her car keys as she crossed her arms and rested her elbows on the table. The way she looked at me intensified my already anxious demeanor. It was as if she was here against better judgment, but curiosity had gotten the best of her.

"Are you hungry?" I stalled. "We can order something."

"I'm not staying long," Abi quickly answered.

"Oh." I forced a smile. "I won't keep you then."

"You aren't," she replied. "You said you wanted to clear the air, so let's clear it." Her tone was sharp, and I could no longer hear the eggshells she walked on in her voice. She stood on firm ground, no longer afraid to put her foot down. It was enticing in a way, to see that she no longer saw me as a fragile child. Or maybe she no longer cared if I was. She was putting herself first, and I was happy for her. This backbone of hers was long overdue.

"When you came home the other night, it wasn't what you thought," I began. I needed her to know there was nothing going on between Cait and me, at least not physically. Anything emotional I felt for Cait came after things between Abi and I had fallen apart, so I didn't feel the need to apologize for cheating—because I hadn't.

"I know." Abi glared at me, and I got the sense that I was losing her attention. She wanted answers from me. But unless she started asking questions, I didn't know what to say.

For the past year, I had taken the coward's way out. I had hidden my deteriorating feelings because I didn't want to hurt her. Leading her on, however, did more damage than the truth ever could have. I had turned her into a fool. I had made her waste her time and love on someone who couldn't use it. It's not that I didn't appreciate her; I did—I still do. But what good is a bottle of wine without a corkscrew?

"It was never my intention to hurt you," I said, trying a different approach. Judging by the look on Abi's face, that was also the wrong thing to say.

"You didn't *intend* to hurt me?" Her eyebrows rose almost as high as her voice. "What *did* you 'intend' to do, Lena? Keep me around to sweep up the pieces of your broken life?" It was a rhetorical question—but one I felt compelled to deny. Had I been given the chance, I would have, but she kept talking. "It's like I woke up one morning and found this shell of a human next to me. She looked like you, and she talked like you, but she wasn't *you*." Abi took a breath and continued. "What was I supposed to do? I couldn't leave. Believe me, I wanted to. Plenty of times. But I didn't." She paused again. "I stayed because I thought maybe you would turn into *you* again." Tears lined her eyes. "I stayed because you were the life I wanted." She looked away, her jaw clenched as she shook her head. I got the impression she had more to say but was physically incapable of saying it, at least for now.

She wanted me to be *me* again. As much as I wanted to give that to her, I couldn't. She wanted me to be someone I could no longer be. The old me was gone, buried next to Lathan and his victims. I didn't know how to give her what she wanted. And that's why my heart had left this relationship long before my mind had. But I didn't say any of that to her.

In a sense, Abi and I were working toward the same goal. We both wanted me to be me again. That was our common denominator—it was the biggest thing we had in common. Now that we both knew that goal was impossible, all we had left of our relationship was a cold bed and a house full of resentment.

"All I can say is that I'm sorry, Abi." I tried to look her in the eyes, but her head was still down.

"You and me both," she said as she sniffed back tears. She gained her composure and lifted her head. "I should get going," she said softly.

"Please don't," I urged. "Don't go. I didn't want you to move out. You can come back to the house—we'll stay in separate rooms until we can figure something out." The house was in my name, but it belonged to both of us. She had spent the last eighteen months turning it into our home. It didn't feel right without her there.

"Because that always works out so well?" Abi quietly laughed. "We need our space, Lena. I'll be fine."

"At least let me pay for your hotel," I offered. Getting back together wasn't an option, but uprooting her entire life shouldn't be either.

"I'm not staying at a hotel." Abi wiped her eyes and stared at me. She began to pick at her nails, a nervous habit when she was on the verge of dropping a bomb she didn't want to. Her brother lived too far away for her to commute. If she wasn't staying at a hotel or with her brother, then she would have to be staying with someone else.

"Who are you staying with?" My mind went through her friends. She was pretty close with the couple who lived a few houses over, but I didn't notice her car parked on our street.

"I've been talking to someone for a while now," Abi slowly confessed. Whether she wanted that bomb to explode or not, it did— and all the toxic debris landed right in the pit of my stomach.

"Oh," I mustered. My face went numb as my lips inevitably formed into a frown. I tried to maintain a steady breath, but my heart sank so low into my chest that my lungs collapsed under the pressure. "Do I… do I know her?"

Did I really want to know? Confirmation either way would just be another detonation.

"No, she and I work together." Abi sighed. "This was never my intent," she added.

And there was that word again: intent. Now I understood why Abi had reacted so harshly when I'd said it. She may not have intended to meet someone, but did she do anything to stop it? Did I do anything to stop us from falling apart?

"How long have you been 'talking'?" The toxins in the pit of my stomach rose up my esophagus and scorched the back of my throat. It was a burn so hot that I was sure I exhaled fire.

"Four months," Abi answered. "It was never romantic, at least not on my end," she quickly added.

"Is it now?" my new friend, masochism, asked.

Abi hesitated to answer. "It will be. But she knows I need time."

Is that what she gave Abi these past four months? Time? How long was this "she" willing to wait? Did she know about us? About me? Every bit of my life had been thrust into the public eye, so I clung to any pieces of privacy I could. Did she, whoever *she* was, know that I wasn't the champion I so desperately tried to portray to the public?

"What does she know about us?" I didn't want to ask, but I had to know.

"Everything," Abi confirmed. "I've basically spent the last two days crying on her shoulder. So she knows everything about us," Abi said, stomping on the eggshells. "But my relationship with her isn't about you," she added.

Before I could reply, an impatient server came up to the table. "Hi, I'm Steven," a young man barely in his twenties introduced himself. He wore a black apron tied around his waist and a white button-up shirt. "Can I interest you in something to drink?"

"I should get going," Abi said, keeping her attention to me.

"And for you?" Steven asked me.

"I need a few more minutes, please."

"Certainly," he said and walked away.

"I really should get going," Abi repeated.

"Where does this leave us?" I asked, sullen-faced.

"I don't want us to be strangers." She paused. "But I need time to let us go."

I nodded and took that as a request to let her be. I wouldn't call her, I wouldn't text her. I wouldn't use her as a rock to hide under. I had to let her go, just as she had to let me go.

"What about your things at the house?" I managed to ask between tears caught in my throat. Certainly, she still had a few things at the house that she wanted back.

"I have everything I need at her house," Abi replied. Although she may not have intended for it to come out that way, I knew what she meant. Everything she needed—the things I couldn't give—waited for her at another's woman's house. Abi looked down at the table and then locked eyes with me. "I came here today because you need to know something. I was going to tell you last weekend at my brother's." She paused. I braced myself for the atomic bomb she was about to launch. "The house, the one you were in with Lathan? It sold." Abi paused again, as if trying to gauge my reaction.

"It sold?" I repeated. "Who bought it?"

"The bank has owned it for a few years," she said. "They were pretty quick to get rid of it, given the history…."

"Who bought it?" I asked more firmly. The thought of someone wanting to turn my vault of terror into a family home was so infuriating that I had become nauseous.

"I don't remember the name offhand. Michael or Mickey, I think? It was a private sale—maybe someone from the tour group? I really don't know," she said. It was oddly comforting that the house had been purchased by the West Joseph Tour company instead of by someone who wanted to raise a family there. "I just thought you should know," Abi said as she sank back in her chair, as if she regretted her decision to tell me. "I need to get going." She stood from her chair. "Take care, Lena."

I wanted to stand with her. I wanted to touch her, and hug her, and apologize for everything. I wanted to do whatever it took to keep her here—because although I wasn't in love with her, it still felt good to look at her and know she was next to me. But I remained seated. This wasn't about what I wanted. It was time I gave her what she wanted. What she needed. My cowardice had cost her happiness for too long.

"You too." I forced a smile through the tears sliding down my face. "I'm happy for you," I said. And, to my surprise, that wasn't a lie. "I hope…." I paused as I thought of what I really wanted for her. "I just want you to be happy."

"I will be," Abi said. Her stare lingered on me for just a second too long, and then with eyes full of tears, she turned around and walked out of the restaurant.

She was actually gone.

I braced myself for the impact of my life crumbling around me, but nothing happened. There was no rubble at my feet. There were no clouds of smoke. The ground remained intact. I had remained unharmed. I was going to be okay.

"Have you had a chance to look at the menu?" Steven interrupted my silent celebration.

"Yes," I lied, although I didn't need to look at the menu. I ordered the same thing every time I came here. I wiped the tears from my face and pretended to read the menu. "I'll have the 'B-L-T-&-A' with curly fries, please." I passed him the two menus that were on the table.

"And to drink?" Steven asked as he collected the menus.

"Water's fine."

"It'll be just a few minutes." Steven scribbled down the order and walked away.

I wasn't hungry. All that had just happened with Abi made sure of it. But I felt compelled to order something. And Bento's BLT with avocado was delicious. Plus, this would give me an excuse to stay here and recover from my exchange with Abi. It had been more than just a conversation—it was our final conversation, at least for the foreseeable future.

As much as I wanted to sit here and analyze every detail about Abi, my mind started to drift to another matter I had to deal with today.

Flu would be home later this afternoon, and I needed to discuss Detective Novak with him in private. I didn't understand why Novak would sign out the case file for Lathan Collins, especially on his last week at the office. Whatever the reason, I needed to discuss all possibilities with Flu before I brought it to Cait's attention.

Cait didn't know Novak the way I did—or the way I thought I did. Novak was a good detective. I trusted him. And I was sad to learn of his retirement. He was a great guy to work with. Every Monday morning, he would ask, "Is it Friday yet?" with a goofy grin. It just didn't make sense for him to have Lathan's case files.

As I waited for my food, I noticed a flat-screen television in my peripheral. It was on Channel Ten, on mute, but lines of closed captioning scrolled across the bottom of the screen. The anchor's mouth moved as I read the captions beneath her during the thirty-second promo advertising tonight's lead story.

AT SIX O'CLOCK, MORE VIDEOS OF THE CASTING CALL KILLER SURFACE.

The beginning of Kristen Valeri's video began to play. She sat in the chair as she memorized the script on her lap. Before the video could get to her horrific death, it cut to the anchor giving a sorrowful frown.

POLICE URGE ANYONE WITH INFORMATION TO PLEASE CALL.

The Casting Call Killer was becoming impatient with getting the attention he wanted. All three videos were now in the hands of the media. Being able to separate the actual killer's confession from anyone who had simply watched the evening news would be impossible now that the videos had become mainstream entertainment.

What little appetite I had was gone. I dug into my front pocket and pulled out a twenty- dollar bill. I laid it on the table to cover the cost of my food, plus a decent tip for Steven.

It was close to one o'clock, and I hoped Flu was home by now. It was at least a twenty-minute drive from Bento's to his house, so that would kill a little time in case he wasn't home yet.

As I turned onto Flu's street, I went over how I would approach him about Novak. Flu and Novak were good friends, and it would be difficult enough to point the finger at another detective, let alone Flu's friend.

I pulled into his driveway, revving my engine as I traveled up the slight incline, and put my car in park before I shut it off. Flu's truck was parked in the garage, and the garage door was up. A sigh of relief emitted from my mouth, and I stepped out of the car.

Small red berries poked through the bushes that sat neatly trimmed between Flu's two-story house and walkway. I walked up the three cement steps that led to the front door. His porch stretched as long as the width of his house, and I knocked on the red door. A minute had gone by before anyone answered. Flu stood behind the screen door, and his round belly peeked slightly over the frame of the half window. He scratched his head.

"Evans?" He opened the screen door. "Come in." He furrowed his brow and looked down his porch, as if he was expecting to see Cait with me. I stepped inside his living room. Brown carpet travelled all the way into the dining room. A deep, musky scent of bachelorism filled my lungs as I stood in his living room.

A laundry basket full of folded towels sat on the loveseat. The full-size couch sat at a ninety-degree angle to the loveseat, and the couch was aimed directly at the big-screen television anchored to the wall. Aside from the TV, his walls were bare—no pictures of family members, no knick-knacks along the windowsill. Had I not known he'd lived here for the past twenty years, I would have assumed he'd just moved in.

"Sorry for dropping by unexpectedly," I said. "How's your daughter?"

"She's good," he replied as the screen door closed behind me. "So, to what do I owe this pleasure?" he asked. I had never just stopped by his house unannounced before, so it was within reason that he questioned my motives.

"I needed to talk to you in private—outside the office."

"This sounds serious. Is everything okay?" Flu picked up the laundry basket from the loveseat and gestured for me to sit down. He sat on the couch.

"It might not be." I didn't want to taint his perspective of the situation by coming across as melodramatic. I sat on the loveseat and cupped my hands over my knees as I put my thoughts in order. "Do you remember Detective Novak?"

"Ryan?" His eyebrows raised. "Of course."

"What would you say about him?" It was in my nature to turn any conversation into an interview.

"I would say he's a great guy... one hell of a detective," Flu emphatically said. I nodded. That's what I would've said about Novak too. So having to tell Flu about my discovery was proving to be more difficult than I thought it would be. "What's this about?" Flu asked.

"I found something... and I don't know what it means exactly," I quickly added. "But I need for this to stay between us, at least for the time being."

"Sure," Flu said—although I was certain he would have agreed to just about anything in order to end his curiosity.

"Before Novak retired, did he act… strange to you?" I chose my words carefully.

Flu took a moment to think. "No," he said. "He was his normal self. I don't think he wanted to retire yet, but he knew it was time."

"Had he taken a sudden interest in any particular cases before he left?"

"Not that I'm aware of."

"Did he have money problems?" I was desperate for anything that would indicate he took the files to sell to the media. If he didn't sell them to the media, then that meant he wanted Lathan's files for personal reasons.

"Not with his pension." Flu laughed. "Seriously, what's this all about?" Flu's tone shifted, and I knew he was tired of being interviewed.

"Lathan Collins." I paused. "His case files are missing." I paused again to give Flu a chance to put the pieces together.

"Where are they?"

"I don't know. That's why they're missing," I repeated. "The last person who signed them out was Novak. In April."

"April?" Flu scoffed. "That's impossible. He retired in April."

"I know." I paused. "They were signed out on his last day."

"Novak?" Flu looked toward the ground, and disbelief decorated his face. "Have you talked to him? Called him to see what's going on?" Flu looked at me with both confusion and optimism mixed in his voice.

"Not yet. I wanted to talk to you first." I was slightly relieved that Flu also found it hard to believe that Novak could be capable of something like this. It was comforting to know I wasn't the only one.

"I have his number here somewhere." Flu looked around the living room as if his rolodex was suddenly going to come running into the room. "Geez, I haven't talked to him since he retired. Last I knew, he was moving to Florida. All he talked about was how much he wanted to buy a boat and live in the Keys. I figured that's what he did." Melancholy swept through Flu's voice. "I'll find his number, give him a call. I'm sure he just forgot to return the file and was too embarrassed to bring it back."

"Maybe," I said, although I wasn't exactly eager to believe the reason was that innocent. "We'll have to be prepared for worst-case scenario here," I gently added.

"What do you mean?" Flu asked.

Was he trying to play dumb?

"I mean, Agent Porter and I think there may be a connection between Lathan Collins and the Casting Call Killer," I answered. "The script that each victim read from…." I wasn't ready to present my theory to Flu just yet, but he needed to know the type of person we could be dealing with before he gave Novak a friendly call. "It all matches up with Lathan Collins' victims," I said. "Pamela Westlake played a grad student, and Lisa Johnson was a grad student. Fionna Michaels played a woman on the verge of divorce, and Sophia Good was divorcing her husband. Kristen Valeri played a woman going to see a mechanic, and Angela Truman went to a mechanic." I swallowed the hot saliva building in the back of my throat before I said the next sentence. "Lathan Collins was that mechanic."

Flu sat still in his seat, a slight waiver in his stature as my words sank in. Did he know the two cases as well as I did that he would be able to make the correlations? Realistically, I didn't think anyone knew the Lathan Collins case as well as I did.

"What's the worst-case scenario?" Flu asked. Although it seemed obvious to me where I was going with this, maybe Flu needed to hear the actual words. Accusing a detective, especially one as likeable as Novak, was something we couldn't come back from—especially if we were wrong.

"Worst-case scenario is that Novak took the files so that he could recreate the murders." I paused. "Worst-case scenario? Novak is the voice behind the camera."

"You don't really believe that, do you?" Flu sat back in the couch, astonished.

"I don't know what I believe. It's why I came to you first. In private." Silence rose within the room. Flu just sat there, the weight of my accusation pinning him to the back of the couch.

"I'm glad you did," he finally said. "Is there anything else?"

"No," I lied. I could've told him about the Deep Web and Alfa Mike, but I had nothing to support Novak's involvement yet. If Novak turned out to be the person we were looking for, Alfa Mike would surface soon enough.

"Okay." Flu nodded. He licked his lips, and a dry smack carried across the room. He stood from the couch. "I'll give him a call," he said. "I won't mention anything. It'll be a friendly chat just to see how he's doing. Who knows, maybe he's been in Florida this whole time." Flu forced his optimism into the situation, but it didn't bring much comfort. If Novak was in Florida this whole time, then we were back to zero suspects. "Let's sit on this until tomorrow," Flu advised. "If I can't get ahold of him by tomorrow morning, we'll look deeper into your theory."

I knew Flu wanted me to be wrong as much as *I* wanted me to be wrong. But we had to acknowledge the possibility that one of our own could be involved with the Casting Call Killer. I would've rather had no suspects than have to investigate someone I once trusted with my life.

"You and I are the only two who know about this," I informed him. "Cait doesn't know either."

Flu nodded. "Thank you, Evans." He sighed. "I'm glad you stopped by." I stood from the loveseat as he walked me to the front door. "If you don't hear from me before nine, come straight to my office. We'll inform Agent Porter and then follow up with standard procedure."

What was "standard procedure" when investigating a fellow officer? Retired or not, Novak was still family—in the proverbial sense, anyway. Flu would go to Novak's last known address to see if he was home. If he wasn't, a patrol car would be stationed outside Novak's house until he came home. Out of respect for the badge, Flu or I would conduct the interview. Based on the information we gathered, he would either be released, or formal charges would be brought against him. That thought sat like an anchor in the bottom of my stomach.

I left Flu's house with a quick goodbye and drove in silence. By three o'clock in the afternoon, I was sitting in my home office, staring at the laptop on my desk. Masking tape was still over the webcam along the top of the screen. I had promised Cait that I wouldn't go into the Deep Web without her, and I intended to keep that promise. Traipsing through a world I knew nothing about wasn't on my to-do list.

I wanted to work on the case a bit more, but I didn't need the Deep Web to do it. Regardless of whether it was Novak behind the camera, I wanted to find the next victim before we were presented with her video. If these three victims were replications of Lathan Collins' victims, then number four was still out there. Whoever was in the fourth video would be playing Lathan's third victim—Carmine Jenkins.

Carmine Jenkins was twenty-eight. She lived with her roommate in one of the nicer parts of West Joseph. She worked as a paralegal, often staying at the office late. She was the only victim to be weighed down before she was dumped in Mirror Woods Lake.

I logged into the laptop and signed into West JPD's database for Missing Persons. It was a long shot but still worth the effort to search for Ohio women reported missing in July. I typed in the pertinent details and forcefully struck the "enter" key. A low chuckle escaped my lips when the results appeared a few seconds later: only two hundred and nineteen women had been reported missing in Ohio that month.

How many of these two hundred and nineteen women had been found? Fortunately, not all missing persons ended up dead. The vast majority usually returned home within a few days.

I knew it would be a long list, but I had made the conscious decision to go through as many of these reports as I could. The women from the Casting Call Killer's videos were beautiful. Not just attractive, but drop-dead gorgeous. That's the type of woman I would search for within these reports. I needed a woman who was "movie-star beautiful," under thirty, possibly local to West Joseph.

This wasn't going to be a speedy project. I needed to review each report carefully. It was only a hypothesis that the victim would be gorgeous. And my idea of gorgeous could vary from the next person's idea. It was also just a guess that she would have been reported missing at all. Maybe her body was found the next day—maybe the family didn't even know she was missing. It's also possible she didn't have a family. Prostitutes and people who were homeless would be perfect prey for a serial killer.

By six o'clock, I had a handful of potential names—but I was only up to July 9. Independence Day was a busy holiday for Missing Persons. Drugs and alcohol played a huge part in why someone disappeared. Usually, the person wondered off in a drunken stupor, only to wake up in an unfamiliar city the next day. With no phone and no money, they would have to rely on the kindness of strangers to contact home.

I rubbed my eyes and rolled my neck as I took a break from searching through the files. This would go a lot faster if I had Cait with me. What was she doing right now? Maybe she went back to Lyons for the weekend to see her nieces. Or she could be sitting in her hotel, watching free HBO, eating take-out. She made no mention of wanting to spend time together this weekend. Even if it would be case-related, I didn't get the impression there was an open invite to be social with one another when not at work.

With a sigh, I brought my attention back to the laptop. The screen glitched and a few wavy lines swept down as the Missing Persons Reports on the screen disappeared. The cursor began to move across the screen, but I wasn't controlling the mouse. I tapped a series of keys on the keyboard. Nothing. It was as if this keyboard wasn't even connected to the laptop. No matter which key I punched, the screen ignored my commands.

Just as I was about to press the "power" button, a square window popped onto the screen. It divided into two segments, and it looked like a forum for a webcam chat. The left side of the window was completely black. On the right side was a silhouette of slender man wearing all black. His face was covered by a black mask. The background of the room was grotesquely familiar. The soot-covered walls and enclosed archways—he was in the warehouse.

I froze as I stared at the man on the screen. He sat so incredibly poised, as if he was waiting for a business meeting to begin. "Uncover your camera," the distorted voice from the videos said from behind his mask. I looked at the laptop and saw the masking tape. "Uncover your camera," he ordered again.

I broke from my trance and peeled the masking tape off the camera. Slowly, the left side of the screen filled with the contents of my office, and then I saw myself on the screen. The man in the mask leaned forward in his seat. I couldn't see the color of his eyes. The mask was tight around his face, like he was dressed as a ninja for Halloween. Over his eyes was a dark shadow, and he looked more like an apparition than a human.

"Who are you?" I asked as I stared at his image on the screen.

He laughed a demonic distortion of triumph over me. "I believe this is who you're looking for?" Multiple news articles filled my screen.

One by one, digital articles about the accidental drowning in Mirror Woods Lake coated my screen. It looked the way bacterium multiplies in a petri dish. As each article popped up, I read the content. "Wilma Reynolds," I read aloud, "accidentally drowned in Mirror Woods Lake. Reported missing on July eleventh…." I paused as more articles about her drowning appeared on my screen. After the twelfth article, the barrage stopped. I dragged my fingers over the mouse pad, and the white cursor moved across the screen, giving me a glimmer of hope that I had control of my laptop again.

I moved each article off to the side as I cleared the screen. It was like clearing the rubble after an explosion. With all of the articles moved to one side of the screen, I was able to see him again. He sat there, calm as ever, and I glared at him. I wasn't frightened to look at him. Although he was right in front of me, he was miles away. He couldn't jump through the computer and attack me. I was safe— at least physically.

"Who are you?" I repeated.

A smirk surfaced through his tight mask, and I was reminded of the way Angela Truman's skin lifted from Lathan's face when he smiled at me. The man took a deep breath and let it out. "You have five days to find out," he said. Then the video cut out. Aside from the articles on the screen, there was no trace of him.

One by one, each article on the screen started to disappear before the screen went completely black. A series of letters appeared on the screen. It was complete jargon to me, but I had a feeling those letters represented something dangerous in the tech world.

I slid my fingers across the mouse pad. Nothing. I punched several keys on the keyboard. Nothing. As I tried to gain control of the laptop, files began to delete from the hard drive. Folders that held pertinent files to this case—and every case I had ever worked on—were vanishing within seconds. My entire computer was being erased, and I couldn't do a damn thing about it.

I reached under the laptop, and the cooling vents emitted enough heat to bake a cake. I unplugged the battery cord. The laptop died in my hands as I set it back on the desk.

I had to call Cait. She needed to be here. She could fix this. I looked down at my phone, and a jolt of worry shot through my body. Had my phone been hacked too? If I called Cait, would he know? I didn't want to take the chance, but I had to call her.

"Can you come over? I need you," I breathed into the phone after she answered.

"Sure," she calmly said. "Are you okay?"

"I can't say on the phone. Just get here soon, okay?"

"Yeah, sure," Cait said. "Tell me you're okay first."

"I am," I said as I tried to calm myself. My flair for dramatics may have caused unnecessary alarm. "I just need you here," I urged.

"I'll be there in ten minutes," she said. I heard what sounded like blankets ruffling underneath her. She had to be at the hotel if she was only ten minutes away.

"I can't stay on the phone," I told her. "The door's unlocked. Just come in." And before she could reply, I ended the call.

She was at my house in seven minutes. How fast did she drive to get here? She came through the front door like a superhero running into a burning building. She was dressed in jeans and an old T-shirt, perfect for sleeping in. Her hair was pulled back in a messy ponytail, and her eyes that were usually lined in black were free of makeup. It was obvious she was in for a quiet Sunday evening.

"What's going on?" she asked when she saw me standing in the living room.

"He was here... in my laptop."

"Who was here?" She closed the front door and locked it behind her.

"*Him*," I stressed. "The Casting Call Killer. He hacked my laptop."

"How?"

"I don't know." I sighed. "The laptop is in my office—but everything is gone."

"Gone?"

"He deleted the hard drive. I tried to stop him, but I don't know if it worked." I could feel myself getting worked up again. The more I thought about his intrusion, the more I realized that I wasn't safe here. I was no longer safe in my own home.

"Okay...." Cait paused. "Tell me exactly what happened." I led her into the office and showed her the laptop.

"I was looking through Missing Persons Reports, and then I lost control of the laptop. He came on the screen, and he told me to uncover the webcam."

"But how? I tested your firewall. There's no way anyone could have hacked in," Cait said as she stared at the laptop. Her brows gathered together as her jaw clenched. "Why would he want you to take the tape off?" She looked my way, a baffled tone tinged in her voice.

"I don't know," I snapped. "He wanted to see me, I guess."

"Okay." Cait put out her hand—a calming tactic we often used toward agitated victims. "Then what happened?"

"I asked him who he was. And he just smirked at me, like I'd told a bad joke. He said I had five days to found out."

"Anything else?"

"Yeah...." I hesitated. "He showed me his third victim."

"The third victim?" Cait paused. "Who is it?"

"Her name's Wilma Reynolds. She was found in Mirror Woods Lake a few days before you got here. We thought it was an accidental drowning." Tears formed along my bottom lashes.

"It still could be," Cait said in an effort to comfort me. "He may be taking credit for a drowning to throw you off his scent."

"Maybe...." I slowly nodded. If I was getting close to finding the actual third victim, then he may have thrown out a random body just to steer me in the wrong direction. "But why? He gave us three of his victims already—why would he take credit for a fourth if it wasn't true?"

Cait just shook her head. "I don't know," she said. "But you can't stay here tonight."

"I know." For all I knew, the Casting Call Killer had snuck into my basement and was waiting to strike as soon as Cait left.

"Grab some clothes and whatever else you need. You're staying with me tonight." It wasn't a suggestion or a request. It was an actual command.

"Cait…," I protested. I couldn't stay with her. Where would I sleep? She had a full-size bed and a chair. Who was going to sleep where? It wasn't just the inclination of sex that caused my hesitation. Cait and I really weren't on the best of terms, and what would the other detectives say if they found out I had stayed with her? It would look rather unprofessional, regardless of whether they knew our history.

"Either with me or Fluellen," she said sternly. "You're not rooming alone."

"Okay," I surrendered. The only thing worse than the other detectives assuming I was sleeping with Cait is if they thought I was sleeping with Flu. And if the situation was reverse, I would want her to stay with me. Not because I would see it as an opportunity to get close to her, but because I would want to watch over her. I could protect her. "I'll get my things." I left the office and walked into the bedroom.

"I'm bringing your laptop. I might be able to see the damage that was done," Cait said as I left the room.

I grabbed a few shirts and pants from the closet, along with socks, underwear, and pajamas, and threw them into a duffle bag. As I made a mental checklist of everything I would need for a sleepover, thoughts of the masked man filled my mind.

Why would he distort his voice? Covering his face was obvious, but why his voice? Was it because I would recognize it? From what I remembered, Novak was as slender as the man in the video. If that was Novak, I would have recognized his voice. Is that why he disguised it?

I needed to wait to tell Flu about this until tomorrow morning. If Novak was in Florida and truly innocent of my accusation, then there was no reason to worry Fluellen with this. Besides, telling Flu about my video chat would also open the door to telling him about Alfa Mike, and I had a pretty good feeling Cait would make that a top priority during the meeting tomorrow anyway.

In twelve hours, everything I had worked for on this case would be taken away from me. Flu would put me in some sort of police protection, and Cait would return to Lyons. My entire life was going to shatter into pieces. I needed tonight to remain intact. Just for a few more hours, I needed to hold on to this illusion of normal.

CHAPTER | FOURTEEN

WHEN WE GOT TO her hotel, Cait began to dissect my laptop, and I went straight into the bathroom. All I wanted was to take a long, hot shower and let the stress of the day wash off me. I should have known better than to think the water would be hot or that the pressure would be soothing. What I'd intended to be an hour-long therapy session with just me and a few gallons of hot water turned into a five-minute lukewarm rinse.

I turned off the water, grabbed a towel off the rack, and stepped into the frigid air. I swiped my hand over the foggy mirror and stared at myself for a moment, then buried my face in the stiff towel. It absorbed the water that dripped from my scalp.

After I combed my hair, I put on my pajamas and walked out of the bathroom. Cait sat at the desk, her focus solely on my laptop. She had managed to open a few programs—none that I recognized, but she seemed to know what she was doing. Every few minutes, she would type a series of keystrokes, and the laptop would grind and groan in protest as another program slowly opened.

"Well?" I said as I pulled back the comforter on the bed. We hadn't discussed the sleeping arrangements, but I certainly wasn't going to sleep on the floor. And she was in the only chair in the room.

"Well," she repeated with a sigh. "Somehow he got past the firewall. I don't know how." She shrugged and turned to me. "Whoever he is, this guy is good. He definitely knows his stuff."

"More than you do?" I smirked as I sat on the bed and draped the covers over my lap.

"No." Cait laughed and turned her attention back to the laptop.

"Will the TV bother you?" I asked as I reached for the remote control on the nightstand.

Cait paused, as if my question needed time to register. "No," she said, her eyes on the laptop. "Are you hungry? We can get room service again." She picked up the menu from the desk and tossed it onto the bed. It was the same menu as the last time I was here.

175

"I'm not all that hungry," I said. "But if you are, order without me." I sank deeper under the covers and propped the pillows against the headboard.

"I'm not," she said.

And that was the rest of our evening. She, with her nose buried in my laptop, and me with my eyes glued to the television. As much as I wanted to lie in bed and watch a few hours of mindless television, I couldn't. My thoughts drowned out every show—regardless of how high I raised the volume.

My mind wandered to each victim before it got to Wilma Reynolds. I needed to read her case file before I could accurately compare her death to the other victims. Even comparing her death to Lathan Collins' victims was useless for now. I decided to use this downtime to think about the two people I did know: Lathan Collins and Ryan Novak.

How did they fit together? Why would Novak want those case files? Each thought led to a dead end. Unless Novak had been coerced into taking those files, I knew deep in my gut there was no way he could be involved.

By midnight, Cait turned off the desk lamp and turned down the comforter on the opposite side of the bed. The springs popped as she lowered herself onto the mattress and pulled the covers over her head. There had to be at least two feet between us, but I could still feel the warmth of her body. As soon as she lay down, my eyes began to close. And for the first time that night, I felt safe enough to fall asleep.

We both slept in the bed like well-behaved adults. Neither of us crossed the invisible line down the middle. My mind wasn't on sex, and I doubted hers was either.

We didn't talk much in the morning. We both showered—separately—and aside from the occasional side step as we got dressed, it was like the other wasn't there. I assumed she was lost in her own mind, trying to make sense of my laptop. I was busy rehearsing the speech I was about to deliver.

When we got to work, Cait and I sat in Flu's office—her, calm as usual, and me looking like a high school student about to be suspended. I silently repeated the plea I had rehearsed all morning. I was prepared to beg Fluellen not to take me off the case. I would bargain that another detective could take lead and that we wouldn't need Cait. The other detective and I would be just fine. We could solve the case and move on to the next homicide.

But I knew it wouldn't slide. Cait was better suited for this case

176

than I was. If anyone was going to be traded in for another detective, it was going to be me. Cait had the know-how and cyber expertise needed to keep this little engine of ours running. I was the sidekick—and easily replaceable. The only thing I had in my favor was the admiration of my colleagues. And if I didn't solve this case soon, I would lose that too.

I stared at Flu's empty chair. He was close to thirty minutes late. Maybe he was talking to Novak on the phone. Or maybe he had stopped by the bakery to bring in pastries for everyone. I hadn't eaten since yesterday, and had I known Flu was going to be late, I would have gone to the cafeteria this morning. But here Cait and I sat, in total silence and starvation.

Flu walked into his office and closed the door. Our meeting was supposed to start at nine. Here it was, nine thirty, and he didn't even have a box of doughnuts to offer as an apology.

"Thanks for waiting," he said as he sat in his chair and loosened his tie. "Agent Porter, Evans here stopped by my house yesterday. Did she fill you in on what we talked about?"

"No." Cait shook her head and looked at me. It was a sore subject between us—the fact that I had purposely kept information from her that she had a right to know about. First with Abi, now with Novak. "I was unaware she saw you yesterday," Cait added.

"Oh." Surprise caught in Fluellen's throat. "She came by to discuss the findings from your research," he said. "It seems that one of our detectives, who retired in April, was the last person to sign out evidence for a closed case," Flu said. "The evidence was never returned, which has brought some cause for concern."

"What evidence?" Cait looked at me and then back to Flu.

"Lathan's," I said as I kept my eyes on Flu.

"As you're aware, the Lathan Collins case is very sensitive, especially within our department," Flu added.

"I'm aware," Cait confirmed. "Who signed it out?"

"Detective Ryan Novak," Flu answered. "He was with West JPD for over twenty years. Heck of a guy. Someone I could really count on. All of us—we all liked him."

"Okay…." Cait shrugged.

"I asked Evans to hold off on pursuing an investigation into Novak until I'd spoken to him. Last I knew, he was in Florida enjoying his retirement." Flu said.

"Did you talk to him?" I interrupted. As much as Cait needed the backstory, I also needed to know the conclusion of this saga. We had yet to disclose my web chat with the Casting Call Killer, and my stomach was being rather vocal about my accidental hunger strike.

"No," Flu answered. "I called his number, but it went straight to voicemail. I'll call again after lunch, but if I don't hear back from him by tonight, then we can consider him a person of interest—*not* a suspect," Flu stressed.

"You have your first solid lead, and you're going to wait until tonight to pursue it?" Cait asked. "I realize this detective may have been your friend, but there are corrupt cops everywhere—we've all had the wool pulled over our eyes at one time or another."

"I understand your apprehension, Agent Porter, but you don't know him like we do," Flu said.

"That may be so, but I know what he's capable of," Cait snapped, polishing the bomb before she dropped it.

"Cait...," I said, a plea so deep in my eyes that it landed in the back of my skull.

"What are you talking about?" Flu directed his question to Cait, but she ignored him. "Evans, what's going on?"

Here it was. The last few seconds of my career—regarding this case anyway. After this, I would be placed with some rookie detective in order to show him how to properly bag evidence and the importance of proofreading case reports. Cait and the newly assigned detective would remain on the case. Maybe it would get solved; maybe it wouldn't. All I knew is that without me on the case, the victims would be forgotten. The case wouldn't be solved for them. It would be solved for recognition and a pay increase.

My heart pounded in my chest as I watched Cait answer Fluellen's question. All of her movements were in slow motion. Her lips parted to speak, and I braced myself for the impact of the explosion. "Someone hacked into Lena's laptop yesterday," she finally said. "We aren't certain who it was, but if Detective Novak is your only person of interest, we have to assume it was him."

"Hacked? When?" Flu asked me, a layer of disbelief coating his face.

"Yesterday evening... after I saw you." Maybe if he knew it happened *after* I saw him, he wouldn't be so quick to react. He wouldn't think I was keeping part of the story from him.

"Are you all right?" Flu jumped into protective mode.

"I'm fine. I stayed with Agent Porter last night. I'm fine," I assured him.

"Well... what happened?" Suspense and frustration held Flu on the edge of his seat. Did he mean what happened with my laptop? Or what happened between Cait and me? Because not a damn thing happened between us last night—and I was pretty sure nothing ever would.

"With my laptop?" I asked and Flu nodded. "I was at home going through Missing Persons Reports. I wanted to search through the women who had been reported missing during July. I came across a dozen or so that matched our other victims. After a few hours of reading reports, my screen went black. I thought the battery died or something, so I shook the mouse... and then he appeared on the screen."

"He?" Flu paused. "'He, who?'"

"The Casting Call Killer—at least, I assume it was him."

"The one from the videos?"

"Yeah." I nodded.

"What did he want?" Flu asked.

"I was looking for the third victim. Cait—Agent Porter and I think there's a fourth victim out there, someone we haven't seen a video of yet."

"But you just said 'third,' not 'fourth.' Which is it?" Flu asked.

"Both," Cait interjected. "We think the fourth victim was actually the third murder... if the Casting Call Killer is mirroring Lathan Collins."

"So you searched Missing Persons Reports to see who else was abducted in July?" Flu asked. "Smart. Go on."

"As I was looking for potential victims, the Casting Call Killer took control of my laptop, and a series of news articles filled the screen," I said.

"On what?"

"Wilma Reynolds." I paused to see if Flu would remember the name. "The woman who drowned in Mirror Lake. The one who wasn't bagged properly by the dive team?"

"Oh...." Flu hung his head in shame. "Yes. She drowned, though, didn't she?"

"Maybe she didn't?" I shrugged.

"We'll reopen her file," Flu said, "and talk to her family too. Have Abram run a scan for police calls from her address since May. Look for anything—prank calls, reports of suspicious activity in the neighborhood. Anything that seems like a coincidence to the family may be a lead to us," Flu ordered. "Where's your laptop now? Have I.T. run a scan on it."

"It's here," Cait said. "I looked it over last night, but I couldn't find much. I gave it to I.T. already. Abram's out sick, so Kevin has it,"

Cait said and I smiled.

"Yeah, sure, that's fine," Flu said as if his mind was cluttered with more important matters. "Given that information, Agent Porter, you're right—I'll go to admin right now." Flu pushed his chair away from his desk as he leaned back. "Is there anything else I need to know?"

He left a window slightly ajar for us to tell him about Alfa Mike, but all I could do was hope that Cait would let me slam it shut. Flu kept his calm over the laptop hacking, but there was no way he was going to overlook an unidentified user threatening vengeance via the Deep Web.

"There's one more thing," Cait said, her words breaking that window wide open.

"The Casting Call Killer said I had five days to figure out who is," I spoke over Cait. Maybe that piece of information would keep Flu from replacing me.

"Five days?" Flu raised his eyebrows. "Why five days?"

"We think that's when we'll receive another video," I said. "Five days from yesterday is Thursday."

"You're probably right." Flu nodded.

"Along with the 'five days' clue," Cait said, glaring at me, then turned her head to Flu, "it should also be mentioned that I found something when I searched the Deep Web forums."

"What's that?" Flu asked.

"A user, known only as 'Alfa Mike,' made a post that should be considered a threat," she said. "He wrote, 'In honor of Lathan's anniversary, a big surprise is coming.' I don't know what the surprise is," she continued, "but I find it hard to believe that it's a mere coincidence that these new murders are happening around the exact same time as the anniversary of Lathan's death."

"I find that hard to believe too," Flu agreed. "Do we have any information on this 'Alfa Mike'?"

"None whatsoever," Cait said. "As far as we know, Alfa Mike and the Casting Call Killer are the same person. And if Novak is the Casting Call Killer, and if the Casting Call Killer is Alfa Mike...."

"Yes. A equals B equals C. I get it." Flu wiped his hand over his mouth as he looked past us, his thoughts seemingly drifting into space. "That's certainly more than I was expecting to hear," he said, his eyes looking toward the ceiling. Was he thinking about my replacement? "Evans, I don't like that you've become the mouse being played with," Flu finally said.

"I'm not," I argued. "Besides, if you take me off the case, he wins...," I said, starting my rehearsed plea.

"Take you off the case?" Flu cut me off. "I'm not taking you off the case." He leaned forward in his chair. "What I was going to say is that I don't like that you're being toyed with, but maybe that works in our favor. For some reason 'Alfa Mike,' the Casting Call Killer, Novak—whoever he is—is interested in you. You're his motivation for contacting our department. It's only a matter of time before we outsmart him. The more information he gives you, the more information he gives us. And the more information we have to stop him. So I'm not taking you off the case. I probably should, but I'm not going to."

"Really?" My voice rose with gratitude.

"Really," Flu confirmed. "Instead, I'm going to get a profile on this guy. Porter, I'll need everything you have on this 'Alfa Mike' so that I can pass it along to the profiler."

"Sure thing," Cait said.

"Okay…." Flu scribbled down a few notes on his desk calendar then looked at us. "Evans, look into Novak. Everything about him—his last known address, bank accounts, cell phone. See who he's called and who's called him. I'll head up to admin and look into his personnel file. See if he has a history of mental-health issues, or if he was ever suspended. I don't think he was, but who knows?" Flu scratched his chin. "Agent Porter, work with I.T. on the laptop. We have to be quiet about this. I'm not going to ruin a man's good name because we're desperate for a lead. If either of you find anything remotely suspicious, bring it to my attention. I don't care when it is or where I am. This is top priority."

Was he serious? He was going to let me stay on the case? Before he could change his mind, I rose from the chair and opened the door. "Absolutely," I said. "I'll start now." Cait didn't stand from her chair until I'd already had one foot out the door. I wasn't going to stick around long enough for Fluellen to doubt his decision. Cait knew where I.T. was, so she didn't need me to show her the way. I was free to sit at my desk and carry on as lead detective. And that was exactly what I was going to do. First, I needed to stop by the cafeteria for breakfast.

"Lena," Cait called after me once we were both in the hallway. She was a few steps behind me, but I didn't slow my pace. Cait doubled her stride and met me at the elevator as I pressed the "down" arrow. "You left in a hurry," she said, stating the obvious.

Whether she knew it or not, I wasn't exactly happy with her. She didn't have to tell Flu about my laptop or Alfa Mike yet, but she did anyway. She might have thought she was acting in my best interests, but that was a matter of opinion.

"I just want to get to the cafeteria before they shut down for lunch prep."

"Oh...." She nodded and a silence fell between us. "I knew you didn't want me to mention anything to Fluellen about yesterday or Alfa Mike," Cait said.

"But you did anyway," I coldly stated.

"But I did anyway," she confirmed. "I get why you're mad, but you have to see it from my side. If something happened to you because Flu didn't know everything, I would only have myself to blame."

"'Flu'?" I repeated. "You're beginning to sound like one of us." I chuckled.

"Sometimes I feel like one of you."

Maybe a part of her felt like one of us because she technically was one of us. She trained here. She grew up here. Just because she'd spent the last twenty years somewhere else didn't mean West Joseph was no longer her home.

"I'm not mad," I said, waving the white flag. I was hurt. But the wound wasn't deep enough to hold a grudge. Besides, I was still on the case, so technically there was no harm done. "I understand your reasoning," I said, "I really do. But next time, let *me* handle things with *my* boss," I stressed. She was still a visitor here.

"Sure thing, Sergeant." Cait stepped back from the elevator when it opened. "Enjoy your breakfast," she said as she walked down the hallway toward I.T.

I sighed as I stepped into the elevator. Landing a low blow wasn't my intent. Neither was causing more tension between us. I had purposely kept Cait in the dark on two matters: one personal, the other professional. I didn't mean to flaunt my position in her face on top of it all. She did technically outrank me in the field, but inside these walls, I was in charge of everyone—with the exception of Flu, of course. But that didn't give me the right to squash her concerns.

Once I returned to my desk, breakfast in hand, I vowed to make things right with Cait. I would give it a few hours, enough time for both of us to finish our assignments and perhaps distance ourselves from the events that took place over the past few days. I didn't want there to be any resentment between us.

We were on our way to solving this case—and, once it was, Cait would go back to Lyons. I wanted there to be a possibility for us to continue seeing each other. After this, it would probably be just as friends. Even so, I was beginning to think that Cait was meant to be a permanent fixture in my life.

The late morning slowly crept into early afternoon as I unearthed every possible aspect of Novak's life. Ryan Michael Novak—at least we knew where the 'Mike' in 'Alfa Mike' came from—owned real estate in Naples, Florida, along with two properties in West Joseph. The first local property was the house he'd lived in while working for West JPD. The second local space was a commercial building close to downtown with multiple offices for lease.

I couldn't locate any cellular companies who had any record of a Ryan Michael Novak in West Joseph. He must've been using a burner phone. I didn't have any luck with Novak's bank records either. I needed a subpoena for his account information, and that could take up to a week. For now, I would have to scrutinize the information I had.

The addresses in West Joseph were the most probable leads, and I wanted to check out both locations. I still had six hours or so before sunset. Although that seemed like a lot of time, there was no telling what I would encounter once I got to the properties. Afterward, I wanted to come back to the station to read the file on Wilma Reynolds. Something seemed off about her being the missing victim—mostly because we didn't have a video of her murder.

As if Cait had been reading my mind, she popped her head into my office just as I was about to call I.T. to ask for her. I motioned for her to come in, and she sat in the chair across from my desk. Over the past week, it felt as if my office had become her office too. It was like sharing a dorm room where all we did was study.

I wondered if Cait would consider transferring here permanently. She had commented that she felt like she was part of West JPD. What was stopping her from making it official? I didn't know the size of her department at BCI. Maybe there were too many employees to give it the familial feeling of West JPD? We had ten detectives, Flu and I included. If Cait wanted to transfer here, I'm sure Flu would do everything he could to make it happen. She would be out of an office though. Only Flu and I had that luxury.

"I finished up with I.T.," Cait said when she sat down. "You'll want to buy a new laptop." she laughed.

"That bad, huh?" There was still awkwardness between us, but I hoped these few hours apart had helped smooth things over.

"I also looked through Fionna Michaels' laptop," Cait said. "She had responded to a few ads looking for an actress."

"Flu told me Abram was going to follow up on that," I said.

"When was that? The laptop hasn't been touched since Thursday."

"Friday," I answered. "He might've been behind, though, and was planning to do it today." I shrugged. Abram was pretty good about completing assignments. He had called off today, but I was sure he would get to it tomorrow. We were past the point in the investigation of dissecting laptops, though. We had a person of interest now. "I have two addresses I'd like to check out," I added. "One residential, one commercial."

"Whose?"

"Novak's," I answered. As much as I wanted us to be on the right trail, I didn't want this road to lead to Novak. "Are you coming with me?"

"Of course," Cait said as she stood up. "That's why I'm here, boss."

"C'mon, I didn't mean that." I understood why she was offended. I had dismissed her concern for my well-being *and* reminded her that she was merely a tourist here. "I was just worried Flu was going to pull me off the case."

"I know," Cait said. "I'll get over it." She smiled.

I grabbed a set of car keys from my top desk drawer and led the way to the garage. Our first stop would be Novak's residence. Even if he wasn't living there, the house was still in his name. If he was renting it out, maybe the tenant would have information on his whereabouts. My fear was that the house would be abandoned. If that was the case, it would be cause for suspicion that Novak was hiding out in Florida.

Large oak trees lined Novak's street as we drove toward the first address. It was a rather quiet neighborhood. Sidewalks allowed for families to walk their dogs and for children to ride their bikes safely. It was the type of neighborhood perfect for kids to grow up in or for grandparents to spend their retirement. Some homes had fenced-in yards, while others showed off their meticulous landscaping

Novak's house was toward the end of the cul-de-sac. The yard had been freshly mowed, which was a good sign. It meant someone had been here recently. The cement walkway that led from the driveway to his two-story colonial was clear of any weeds or overgrown grass. Whoever was living here took care of the outside, much like the other well-kept homes in the neighborhood. There was no cause for alarm when approaching the house. The windows were spotless, and the wicker patio chairs made the porch seem very welcoming.

I parked the car on the street and stared at the house before getting out of the car. Just because it appeared clean and inviting didn't mean we were in friendly waters. I looked for any sudden movements inside the residence. Then I looked in the driveway to see if any cars were parked there. There were none, but the garage door was closed. It was possible someone was home, but there was only one way to be certain.

Cait and I stepped out of the car and walked onto the front porch, my hand on my gun as we approached the front door. We stood on the hinged side, and I knocked five times. The screen door slapped against the frame with each knock. I listened for any noises inside, but all was quiet. After a few moments, I knocked again, this time identifying myself.

"Ryan Novak? Sergeant Evans with West JPD. Open the door," I ordered. When I knocked again, Cait walked toward the edge of the porch and looked into the front windows. She turned to me and shook her head. "West Joseph Police," I yelled into the door.

"He's not home." An elderly voice broke through the wind. I turned to the left and saw a woman standing on her porch next door to Novak's. "He isn't home during the day," she added.

"Do you know who lives here?" I stepped toward her. But there was still at least thirty feet between us, so shouting was a must.

The woman nodded. Her short, gray hair was tightly curled. "I don't know his name, but he's a young fella." I wanted her to clarify exactly what "young" meant. Given the woman's approximate age, "young" to her could have meant anyone under sixty-five.

"Can you tell me anything about him?" I asked.

"I only know that he comes home very late at night and leaves very early in the morning."

"How long has he lived here?" I asked.

"Don't know. I just moved in a few months ago."

"Does anyone else ever come by?" Cait asked.

"Someone does come over from time to time. I don't know if it's his brother, or maybe it's a *friend*. Who can tell anymore?" The woman scoffed. "He's a big guy. And they have no manners. When I was his age, if someone new had moved in next door, I would at least say hello. I've tried to go over there to introduce myself, but no one's ever home. We live among strangers. Imagine not knowing who your neighbors are. That's just how it is now, I guess." She sighed.

"Yes, ma'am," I agreed, although I didn't know the majority of my neighbors either. "Thank you for your time." I turned to Cait and motioned for her to walk toward the car.

Once inside, I picked up the radio and called into dispatch. "This is Sergeant Evans requesting surveillance at three-fourteen Dyson

Avenue. Residence seems vacant. Have patrol stay until occupant returns. Over."

White noise loomed over the radio. "Copy, Sergeant. Patrol seven is in route. Over."

"I'll wait for patrol just in case whoever lives here comes back between now and then," I said to Cait.

I kept my eye on the woman standing on her porch. She didn't seem interested as to why two detectives were looking for her neighbor. She sat on her porch as she looked over the neighborhood.

As soon as patrol number seven pulled up behind us, I turned on the ignition and drove toward downtown. Novak's commercial space was next on our list. I was a little disappointed we didn't learn more at Novak's residence. But the elderly woman had given us a little more information than we would have gained had she not been home, so that was sort of a win. At least the drive out there wasn't completely pointless.

It was close to four o'clock, and the downtown bustle was still well intact. If it wasn't for the commercial building having a designated parking lot in the back, we would have had to rely on a meter—and all of those were full. The office building was three stories high with what appeared to be two offices on each floor. Bushes lined the brick building, and a cement staircase led to a single glass door.

On the outside, mounted next to the front door, was a sign with a list of the businesses' names. Four of the six offices were occupied, leaving two blank spots on the panel. According to the sign, the building was open Monday through Friday from 7:00 a.m. until 5:00 p.m., but there didn't seem to be a doorman in the lobby to enforce the hours of operation.

I opened the glass door. Cream-colored marble floors reflected the bulbs in the chandelier that lit the room. Steel elevator doors filled the wall farthest from the door. Two hunter green sofas sat opposite of each other in the center of the lobby. Overall, the space afforded a welcoming atmosphere. Secluded but clean, with a fresh potpourri scent. Cait and I walked toward the elevators, and I pressed the only button available. The "up" arrow illuminated as the elevator lowered itself down the shaft.

The steel doors opened, and Cait and I stepped inside. The wood-paneled walls stretched from top to bottom, with a brass handrail affixed at waist-height along the three walls. We reached the second floor within seconds. The elevator doors opened, and Cait and I stepped into a small hallway with two glass office doors, one on either side of us.

On our left, at Gilman and Sons Law Firm, all the lights were turned off. The hours of operation on the door indicated they were open from 8:00 a.m. to 3:00 p.m. The office on our right belonged to a psychologist named Dr. Andrew Redman.

I led the way toward his office and opened the door. The receptionist behind the desk politely greeted us when we stepped inside.

"Hello, do you have an appointment?" she asked with confusion on her face.

"No," I said and showed her my badge. "I'm with West Joseph Police. Is Dr. Redman around? We just need to ask him a few questions."

"He's with a patient. Is there something I can help you with?" We had no right to interrupt his appointment just to ask basic questions. If he was a suspect, that would be a different story.

"Do you know the owner of the building?" I asked as I put my badge back into my pocket.

"Mr. Novak?" the receptionist replied. "I've never met him."

"Do you know if Dr. Redman has?" Cait jumped in.

"I'm not sure. I've only been here for about a year. Dr. Redman has been in this office for three years. But the only time I see Mr. Novak's name is when Dr. Redman asks me to fill out a maintenance request."

"How do you submit the requests?" Cait asked. "Does someone pick them up?"

"No. There's a mailbox in the lobby. I put the maintenance requests in there."

"What about the rent?" I asked. "Doesn't Mr. Novak come by to collect it?"

"No. It's all done by direct deposit."

Cait nodded and then looked my way as if to signal that she had no further questions. I couldn't think of any either. "Thank you for your time," I said before I turned toward the glass door.

We had a few other businesses we could question, but I had a feeling they wouldn't be much help either. If Novak had the tenants paying rent via online banking—and if he had a maintenance man to respond to any requests in mailbox in the lobby—then he really wouldn't need to be here. He could easily manage the property from Florida.

The only way we could know for sure if he was ever actually in the building was if he had security cameras in the lobby. But I couldn't recall seeing any. Besides, to gain access to any footage, we would need his permission—or a warrant.

Cait and I walked into the hallway and toward the stairwell. We took the fifteen steps up to the third floor, where we found an empty office and Shulman's Architects.

We opened the architects' door, and a plump woman, well over the age of fifty, stood in front of the receptionist's desk. She was too focused on the paperwork on the desk to notice us walk in.

"Hello, I'm Sergeant Evans." The woman's jaw clenched and her body instinctually drew back. "We didn't mean to startle you. This is my partner, Special Agent Porter. Do you work here?"

"Yes," she said. "I'm the owner. Marie Shulman."

"It's nice to meet you," I replied. "We have a few questions about the owner of the building. We won't take much of your time."

"I don't have much time to give." She went back to sorting through the paperwork. "My receptionist is on maternity leave, and I need to find a new payroll manager. But what can I help you with?"

"How long have you been here?" Cait stepped in.

"Well, I've owned the company for thirty years. But I moved into this building…," she trailed off, looking as if she might be doing the math in her head, "…seven or eight years ago."

"Do you know Ryan Novak?" I asked.

"Not really," she said without looking up from the stack of papers. "He used to come around a lot the first five years. He was very friendly, social. If we needed anything fixed, like a clogged toilet or a broken lock, he got to it by the next day."

"How often have you seen him in the last two or three years?" I leaned on the desk in order to get her attention. She looked up and let the papers fall from her hands.

"The last time I saw him was in March. It was to pick up the rent check. He was pretty good about making his rounds through the building every month. He would ask me how business was, if I had any maintenance issues, and then he would collect the check."

"Can you think of any reason why you haven't seen him since March?" Cait asked.

"No." Marie shook her head. "He sent everyone in the building an email in April, telling us rent needed to be paid by direct deposit. He gave us his routing number and account number, and that was the last I've heard of him."

"He doesn't ask about maintenance issues anymore?" I asked.

"No. We just fill out a form now. That's why the tenants across the hall moved out. There used to be a photography studio across from me. But the roof started to leak on that side, and it took almost a month for Ryan to even come out and look at it. At least I assume he looked at it. I didn't actually see him. He sent the tenants an email saying it would be repaired as soon as possible, but they were pissed. Some of their cameras and all of their backdrops were destroyed. And Ryan offered them zero compensation, so the photographers terminated their lease."

"Do you still have the email he sent you?" Cait asked.

"Yeah," Marie huffed and walked to the computer at the receptionist's desk. "You'll have to excuse the mess. Like I said, my receptionist is out, and I'm looking for a new payroll person."

"What happened to your old one?" I asked. Employees usually give two weeks' notice, which should have given Marie enough time to find a new payroll manager.

"She drowned," Marie said coldly before she looked up from the computer screen. "I found that email if you want me to forward it to you?"

"Yes, please," Cait said and fished a business card out of her pocket. "To that address." She passed the card to Marie.

"Is there anything else you need? I really need to get back to work." Marie forcefully struck the keys on the keyboard as she typed in Cait's email address.

"No," I said and then looked at Cait to see if she had anything else to ask.

"You've been a big help, thanks," Cait said as she stepped away from the desk.

We walked to the elevator in silence, and I pressed the "down" arrow. I'd hoped to get more information from the tenants than what we had, but today's trip wasn't a complete waste.

"When we get to the lobby, I want to look for that maintenance-request mailbox," I told Cait when we stepped onto the elevator.

She nodded. "I'll need some time when we get back to the station to look into the email Novak sent the architect. Check out the date and time, IP address. That'll help us locate where he sent them from. If they're from West Joseph instead of Florida, then we'll know what part of the country he's hiding in, at least."

"You can work on that while I read through Wilma Reynold's case file," I said as the elevator doors separated. Cait followed me as I walked into the lobby. The late afternoon sun sprawled across the floor, highlighting the marble.

"There," Cait said and nodded toward the opposite side of the room. To the left of the elevators, adjacent to the stairwell, was a steel mailbox with a small lock over the lid. Next to the mailbox was a metal door that read "AUTHORIZED PERSONNEL ONLY."

"Do you think Novak's office is down there?" Cait asked.

"I don't know." My shoes clicked against the marble as we walked toward the door. There was a metal latch on the outside, with a large padlock, but it wasn't fastened. I pushed down on the door's slender handle, and the cold steel absorbed into my skin as the handle turned. With little effort, I pulled the door open, and a low squeak emitted from the hinges. I peered inside. Bare white walls lined a set of concrete stairs that went down one floor.

I took a step through the doorway and held the door open for Cait to follow. The stairs zigzagged down to what appeared to be a basement. With my hand on my gun, I took the first step. It was colder here than in the lobby, and the musty scent reminded me of a boiler room, complete with sounds of leaky pipes. The echoes of dripping water bounced around the space every three to four seconds.

I walked down the cement stairs with Cait close behind me. With any luck, we would find a maintenance worker who could give us more information on Novak. But the farther down the stairs we got, the less likely that seemed possible.

As we reached the bottom step, my eyes widened and a chill raced up my spine. My voice caught in my throat, and I pulled my gun from its holster as I walked into the basement. Along the back wall were two sealed archways. Above those were glass-block windows that let the evening sunlight in.

In the center of the room, audacious and barefaced, was a dark red stain—almost the color of wine. It was at least two feet wide and slightly discolored, likely from chemicals used in an attempt to clean it up. The stain settled there, saturating the cement floor beneath it, as I stared at the ground. The longer my eyes lingered on the scarlet gore, the more my peripheral recognized the room.

This wasn't just a basement, and that wasn't wine soaked into the ground.

"Cait…." a shaken whisper escaped my lips. I walked to the stain in the center of the room and squatted next to it. A faint smell of car oil and mint filled my nose as I breathed in. The smell was light enough to stay confined within this room. Even if it wasn't, this room was completely separate. It didn't have a single vent along the ceiling. There was no way for smells or sounds to carry through the rest of the building.

Cait's shadow cast over the stain as she stood next to me. "Is that…?"

"Kristen Valeri," I answered. I knew without a doubt, this room—this tomb—was where Kristen Valeri, Pamela Westlake, and Fionna Michaels had been murdered. Cait and I were standing in the very same spot where their deaths had been filmed.

As the images of the victims flooded my mind, I understood how they could have been fooled into letting down their guard. The lobby was a perfect front for someone to manipulate their trust. It was absolutely beautiful. Nothing about the lobby or the building gave off any warning signs that danger could be lurking within.

If I had been one of the victims, I would have fallen for this scam. Aside from not having any aspirations of becoming a big-time movie star getting in the way of my better judgment, I wouldn't have thought twice about the director's intentions when I walked into the lobby. Even if I'd been asked to come into the basement, I wouldn't have hesitated. This building was full of false trust. I couldn't blame the victims for their naivety—anymore that I could judge myself for feeling as secure as they had probably felt when Cait and I got here.

We had accidentally stumbled upon the biggest break in the case. This building was all we needed to point the finger at Novak. All we had to do was find him.

I looked to the right and envisioned where the camera had been set up. There was about ten feet of space between the edge of the stain and the wall, enough room for a camera and Director Novak to audition his victims. A chunk of bile burned in the pit of my stomach.

It had been Novak this entire time. Someone I'd trusted—someone Flu had treated like family—was actually capable of this.

I took in a deep breath, something I soon regretted, and stood up. A tingling rush took over my head, and the room started to darken. Cait's hand cupped my left bicep, and she held me steady. "Careful," she said. "Are you all right?"

"Yeah." My vision slowly returned to normal. "I just stood up too fast," I added. "I have to call this in." I walked to the back of the room. The entire basement was empty, at least to the naked eye. But I knew the bodies of Pamela Westlake and Fionna Michaels were buried within the walls. That just left the question of where Kristen Valeri was buried.

I lightly traced my fingertips over the bricks that entombed the victims. How could someone do this to innocent people? How could someone do this to anyone? I've hated people in my life—truly hated them—but I could never do this. I couldn't even do this to Lathan Collins.

If their bodies were still here, it was possible their vehicles were too. The building had its own parking lot. Once we taped off the entire area as a crime scene, Cait and I could check for the victims' cars. I wouldn't be surprised if their cars were still here—out back, hidden in plain sight. Every time Novak or his accomplices came here, they would see the vehicles. They didn't need to keep a lock of hair to relive the rush of the murders. The cars were their trophies.

I dug into my pocket and pulled out my cell phone. "No signal," I told Cait. "I need to go upstair—"

I heard the door at the top of the stairs squeak open.

Cait and I quickly looked at the bottom of the staircase. A soundless stare between us was our only communication. With my gun still in hand, I silently undid the safety. I pointed it toward the staircase as echoed footsteps made their way down.

One stomp at a time, the thuds grew louder. From the corner of my eye, I saw Cait draw her gun and point it at the staircase too. The footsteps boomed louder still, and then I saw two legs dressed in brown work boots and a navy blue custodian's jumper.

I tightened my grip around the handle of my gun. Slowly, the pair of legs grew a waist, and then a torso, and finally a neck and head.

"Sergeant Evans with West JPD, put your hands up," I commanded. I had enough probable cause to make an arrest. The fact that this man confidently walked into a room where multiple murders had happened was enough to convince me that he was one of the guilty parties.

The man looked at me and then to Cait, a wide-eyed stare across his face. He looked confused, as if he didn't understand how or why we were down here. He froze mid-step as both our weapons pointed at him. He slowly put his hands up, keeping his arms bent at the elbows, and a maniacal smirk twisted from his lips.

He looked vaguely familiar, like maybe he bagged groceries at the store where I normally shopped? Except I knew he wasn't. At some point, though, I had interacted with him. His rotund belly looked most familiar. It was similar to the masked man's from the videos. That could have been how I recognized him? But his face looked familiar too.

The masked man had done the actual killing. Visions of those gruesome slaughters swarmed my mind. Kristen Valeri, strangled with wire. Fionna Michaels, gutted like a fish. Pamela Westlake, practically decapitated with the swipe of a blade.

"Don't move," I said. "Keep your hands where I can see them." I locked eyes with him and aligned my gun with the center of his skull in case he moved. I took a few steps forward.

The man looked no more than twenty-five. There was an impressionable look about him, like he could be easily manipulated into doing things he wouldn't otherwise do. He also had a guilty look about him. Sweat immediately formed along his hairline as he watched me put my gun in its holster and reach for my cuffs. He eyed Cait as she kept her firearm pointed at him.

I slapped a cuff around his left wrist and twisted his arm behind his back as I cuffed his right wrist. He was a big guy, but I had enough adrenaline to take down someone three times his size. I walked him the rest of the way into the basement with little effort. He fully complied with every move. "On the ground," I said.

The man knelt on one knee and then the other before sitting on the ground. His light brown hair was drenched in perspiration, and he obediently sat between where Cait and I stood. "What's your name?" I asked.

Nothing. He just stared at the concrete floor, tears building with each heavy breath he took.

"What's your name?" I repeated. But he didn't respond. "Can you watch him?" I asked Cait.

"Yeah," she quickly replied as she kept her gun on him.

I ran up the stairs. By the time I reached the doorway, I had two bars—enough of a signal to make the call and still be close enough to Cait in case the man tried anything.

"This is Evans," I breathed into the phone when Dispatch answered. Between the adrenaline and the unexpected cardio, I was a little out of breath. "Send over every available unit to eleven sixty-seven Staleman Street, basement level, for a ten-five."

"Copy," she responded and then repeated the address. "Available units are in route. Over."

I hung up and jogged down the stairs. Faint sirens rose from the distance. I looked at Cait as she kept her gun on the man, and I nodded. Now that we had Novak's wingman, it was only a matter of time before Novak surfaced. *We actually caught the son of a bitch*, I thought to myself. I held back a sneer as a sudden spark of triumph shot through me.

Once we got his confession—and there was no doubt in my mind we would—this would all be over. The victims' families would have closure. The citizens of West Joseph would feel safe. And I would finally be able to say I did my job.

The victims would have their day in court. The people who were responsible for the deaths of Kristen Valeri, Pamela Westlake, Fionna Michaels, and possibly Wilma Reynolds would have to suffer the consequences of their actions. This wasn't like Lathan Collins. He got the easy way out. He didn't have to be held accountable.

Within minutes, a stampede of officers raced down the stairs. As I watched four armed officers surround the man on the ground, I knew justice had won. All the work I had put into solving this case had paid off. I also had Cait to thank. If it weren't for her, who knows where I'd be? It was more than just her intuition and her Internet expertise that had led us to this moment. If it wasn't for her encouragement and support this past week, I wouldn't have made it.

This victory was as much hers as it was mine. And as much as I wanted to go out and celebrate, we had a long evening ahead of us. We had to exhume the bodies from behind the brick walls; we had to check the parking lot for the victims' cars; and we still had to interview the suspect.

After the suspect had been taken upstairs to be placed in the back of a cruiser, Flu arrived. He, Cait, and I stood back as three officers took turns swinging sledgehammers at the bricks. Pieces flew away as dust filled the room. The putrid odor of decayed flesh mixed with rotten apples seeped from the open holes in the walls. The smell was so thick that it clogged my sinuses, and my stomach churned as I held my breath until my lungs ached for oxygen. Cait and Flu had the same foul looks on their faces as they tried to breathe through the stench.

"We have a body," an officer called when the debris settled and we could see into the hole. "Female," he added as he coughed between breaths.

"We got a body here too," another officer shouted. He stood in front of the second archway with his bicep under his nose to shield his nostrils from the smell of rotted flesh. "Another female."

Flu walked to the first officer, and Cait and I walked to the second officer. I peered inside and clenched my stomach to keep the bile from erupting. There, on the cold cement floor, was presumably Pamela Westlake. The clothes I recognized from her video were saturated with blood. Although she laid face-up, I couldn't recognize her face—because she didn't have one.

Just like Sophia Good, Lisa Johnson, Carmine Jenkins, and Angela Truman, Pamela Westlake was missing her face. Her skin had been completely removed from her head. Laceration marks were carved along the edges of her face. Exposed muscle tissue and chunks of cartilage clung to her skull. Her eyelids were intact, although her eyes were still open. She stared at us. Her blue eyes looked like marbles stuffed into pockets of raw meat.

"Jesus," Flu muttered as he stepped back from his victim. I didn't have to guess as to the condition of the other body. I looked at Cait as an avocado hue washed over her face.

"Are you okay?" I asked.

She stood frozen with her eyes closed as her breath came to a steady pace. She shook her head and opened her eyes before she looked at me. "I wasn't prepared for that," she confided.

"No one's ever prepared for that." I gave her a sympathetic smile. "Was this your first?"

She slowly nodded.

"If you need to leave," I said, "it's okay. No one will fault you."

"No." She paused and swallowed hard. "I'm okay." She walked the two steps past me and joined Flu with the other victim.

"We won't be able to positively identify the bodies until we run the dental records," Flu said in a low voice. He walked toward me, and I got the impression he was blocking me from seeing his victim. "Is yours…." He didn't finish the sentence, but I knew what he was asking.

"The same as Lathan Collins?" I locked eyes with him. Why would he keep me from seeing the body? After everything I had seen and witnessed, what could possibly throw me over the edge that hadn't by now?

"Lena," Cait called, and I broke my stare down with Fluellen.

I stepped past Flu and stood next to Cait as I looked inside the tomb. Another body lay on the cold cement floor, clothes saturated in blood, skin completely removed from the head.

"Fionna Michaels," I said. I could identify her body based on the clothes from her video. I turned to face Flu. "We'll stay with them until Crime Scene and the Coroner get here," I told him.

I wasn't going to leave them alone. They had died alone, and they had been buried alone. It was time they were surrounded by someone who cared for them. I wasn't going to allow Novak and his protégé to make them suffer anymore.

"Okay," Flu agreed. "They should be here soon."

The three of us stood guard in front of the graves of Pamela Westlake and Fionna Michaels as the responding officers headed upstairs. And as much as I wanted to join them outside—and I knew Cait and Flu did too—we stayed. We stayed for the victims, for their families, and to prove that, even in all this horror, there was still kindness in the world.

MICHELLE HANSON

CHAPTER | FIFTEEN

"HE ISN'T TALKING." FLU flopped himself into the chair across from my desk. He held a manila file and looked at me. "We've switched out officers, played 'good cop, bad cop.' Hell, I even gave him moral justification for the murders. Still—nothing." Flu sighed. "Novak has a tight lid on this kid, that's for sure."

"Did you get a name out of him yet?" I looked up from Wilma Reynolds' case file. I had been staring at her file for more than thirty minutes, but I had yet to actually read a single word of her report.

After we had returned to the station, Cait and I had brought the suspect into the interview room. She and I had taken turns asking questions, but all he did was stare at us. Even when we'd asked his name, his only response was the same blank, maniacal look he'd given us when we'd found him in the basement. It was like looking at a doll: a motionless face with lifeless eyes.

Flu thought the suspect's presumed obsession with me and Lathan Collins was the reason for his silence. So he pulled me and Cait out of the room—and replaced us with himself and another detective.

It did bring a little satisfaction to know the other officers were having just as hard a time getting him to talk as Cait and I'd had, but it would've been nice to get him to at least say his name, even if we weren't the ones who'd gotten it out of him.

"James Coffer." Flu sighed as he tossed the manila file onto my desk. I made no attempt to look at it. "We ran his prints to find his name," he added.

"Any priors?" I asked.

"It's all there." Flu gestured toward the file he'd chucked onto my desk. "One theft charge from three years ago. He stole a jacket from the mall. No jail time. Just ten hours of community service." Flu shrugged. "He's compliant for the most part. He just refuses to talk." Flu sat deflated in the chair. "Where's Agent Porter?" He looked at the empty chair next to him.

"I.T."

Cait had gone to I.T. to research Novak's emails and to run another scan on my laptop. She said was determined to find out how Novak was able to hack past my firewall, but I had a feeling she was simply trying to keep her mind occupied. The shock of seeing her first dead body—especially in the condition Fionna and Pamela were in—would stay with her for the rest of her life. It was one thing to see a photograph or even a video of a murder. It was on a completely different scale to see the result in person.

Crime Scene had taped off Staleman Street and had canvassed the property for evidence. I was right about the parking lot: Three of the seven cars belonged to victims. The vehicles had been tagged and towed to impound, and they would be kept there for an indefinite period of time. Once the cars were no longer needed for the trial, the families could have them back.

"Well," Flu said, "we have enough to hold him for seventy-two hours before we have to charge him or let him go." He shook his head, worry and grief weighing down his face. "We got a search warrant for Novak's residence in West Joseph. The team's there now. And admin contacted Naples PD. If—," Flu corrected himself, "when they catch him, they'll contact us." He paused. "They'll hold him for questioning. And, if need be, we'll make arrangements to have him brought back to West Joseph for formal charges."

I understood the worry and the grief that haunted his face. The worry stemmed from not having a murderous mastermind in custody yet, but the grief—Flu, and this entire department, was about to lose a trusted friend. All the fond memories we had of him were now tainted. Flu had twenty years of memories with Novak. Within a single second, they had been ripped away.

"I'll let you know if this kid starts talking or if we hear from Naples." Flu stood from the chair and lingered. I got the impression he was looking for any excuse not to be alone but that he'd run out of reasons to stay.

"Are you doing okay?" I asked. I had never seen him this affected by a case before.

"Yeah." He stiffly nodded—and then his hardened exterior broke. "It's just… you think you know somebody, and then they do something like this." He sighed and shook his head. "Maybe I should have known. He doesn't have a wife. No kids. Nothing to keep him *good*." He paused. "Maybe if I was a better friend. Talked to him more often…."

"You saw those women," I reminded him. "You saw what he did to them. Nothing you could have said or done would have cured *that* kind of monster inside him."

"Maybe." Flu sighed and left my office without another word. I didn't know if he was going to cry or punch something—or both—but I was certain he needed time alone. Flu was a caring person, but he didn't let people see his vulnerable side.

I brought my attention back to Wilma Reynolds' file and flipped through the pages of the report. The coroner had ruled it an accidental drowning and noted there was slight discoloration on her left bicep, possibly from a bruise. It was large enough to be a handprint but too faint to be sure. Her body had suffered a lot of damage from being submerged for almost two months—not just from waterlogged skin but from fish and insects nipping at her flesh.

Wilma Reynolds had been reported missing on July 11. According to her husband's statement, she hadn't come home from work that Saturday. So he'd stopped by her office, but her car wasn't in the parking lot; he figured she'd gone to the grocery store and forgotten her phone at work. He told the police that he'd called her cell every fifteen minutes until two in the morning. But when she still hadn't come home the following day, he filed the Missing Persons Report first thing Monday morning. He'd also stated that it was rare for her to go into work on a Saturday.

July 11 was a popular date to go missing. That was the same date Kristen Valeri had been reported missing. Assuming Wilma's husband and Kristen's boyfriend both had to wait the mandatory forty-eight hours to make their reports, then Kristen and Wilma went missing on the same date. It was highly probable that Kristen had filmed her audition on a Saturday, but how would Novak have time to orchestrate two very different murders in the same day?

I leafed through the individual pages of Wilma's report until I came across her employment history. There, at the very top, was her most recent employer: Shulman's Architects at 1167 Staleman Street.

Wilma worked in Novak's building.

Had Wilma Reynolds walked in on Kristen Valeri's murder? The building was normally closed on weekends, so Novak would have been very surprised to see a tenant stop by. Did she hear Kristen in the basement? Is that why there were those jumps in Kristen's video? Regardless of how she found out about Kristen, the connection was clear: Wilma Reynolds' place of employment was also Kristen Valeri's crime scene.

But if Wilma was supposed to represent Lathan Collins' third victim, Carmine Jenkins, how did her murder fit in? Wilma probably hadn't responded to any ads looking for actors, so Novak would've had to change his MO. And Wilma wouldn't have sat in front of a camera as she read from a script. Her murder was more spontaneous. Novak saw an opportunity to kill two birds in one day, and he took it.

Carmine Jenkins had been the oldest of Lathan's victims. Wilma was thirty-one. Pamela Westlake was the oldest victim so far, so that wasn't the connection. Carmine had been reported missing by her roommate, and Wilma had been reported missing by her husband. But that didn't matter either; if this was an opportunistic kill, Novak wouldn't have known who would've report Wilma missing. Wilma worked as a payroll manager, and Carmine was a server. Nothing there. Wilma's body had been found underwater… and Carmine Jenkins had also been found underwater. She was the only victim of Lathan's who had been weighed down.

The coroner's report noted that Wilma's ankle had been wrapped in algae. And it would've been possible for Novak to wrap the algae around her ankle, assuming she'd been unconscious when they got to Mirror Lake. But why go through the trouble?

Signature killers work from a script. They become obsessed with the process. Novak worked from an actual script—he went so far as to write the words he wanted his victims to say before their demise. Why would he abandon his audition for "Carmine" and replace her with an opportunistic kill? Had he not yet found an actress to play Carmine?

I massaged my temples with my fingertips and took a deep breath. The strain of dealing with today's discoveries—and having to figure out Novak's twisted mind—was taking its toll. As exhausted as I was, every part of my body craved alcohol. And lots of it.

I needed to embrace the part of my brain reserved for fun.

"Hey. You got a minute," Cait said as she walked in and sat in the chair across from my desk.

"Sure." I leaned into my chair. I needed to tell her about the connection between Carmine Jenkins and Wilma Reynolds, but it seemed like whatever Cait had on her mind was more urgent.

"I found something on your hard drive," she said. "A tracking program. I don't know how long it's been on there, but it's a newer program. Less than a year old."

"How did it get there?" I assumed Novak was behind the tracking device. He was able to hack into the laptop's camera after all.

"I'm not sure. It's third-party software, usually installed in-person. But maybe you could have clicked on a link and accidentally downloaded it."

It was possible but not likely. I rarely clicked on links if I didn't know who it was from. "Who would have sent it?" I asked.

"It could have been from your bank? Or an email that looked like it was from your bank? Something like that," she said. "Typical phishing scam, easy to fall for."

That was more probable. I requested account information from banks all the time, and usually they responded via email, with a link or an attachment to download. "Why didn't I see the software?"

"You're not supposed to." Cait smirked. "It lies dormant until certain programs are opened." Cait paused and worry filled her eyes. "There's something else," she said with caution coating her voice, and I got the impression that this "something else" was more perilous than the tracking program. "I was able to recover some of the data and programs from your laptop, and I went onto the Deep Web again. I thought if Alfa Mike was the one who'd hacked you, then maybe he would brag about it in the forums."

"Did he?" My curiosity piqued.

"No. No one's taking credit for the hack." She paused. "If Alfa Mike was making noise, I wouldn't be as alarmed."

I understood what she met. If Alfa Mike had taken credit for the hack, then we would know who to keep a watchful eye on, so to speak. But the fact that the hack has remained anonymous meant that it could have been anyone. It's a lot easier to watch one person than it is to watch one thousand.

Cait continued, "It makes me worry there's something else planned—something he doesn't want us to know about just yet," she added.

Our suspect had three names: the Casting Call Killer, Alfa Mike, and Ryan Novak. According to one of them, I had five days left to find out who he truly was. I wasn't exactly sure what would happen on the fifth day, but I knew it would be big. Another video, maybe? More gruesome than all the others?

"I discovered something too," I said, hoping that focusing on our progress would overshadow the unanswered questions. "Wilma Reynolds, the woman who drowned at Mirror Lake?"

"The one the Casting Call Killer claimed?" Cait asked.

"Yeah. I found a connection to Lathan Collins' third victim, Carmine Jenkins. Wilma Reynolds worked at the building on Staleman Street. She and Kristen Valeri were reported missing on the same day. And Wilma told her husband she was going into work that day. What if she walked in on Kristen Valeri's murder?"

"It's probable," Cait said, "but how does she match Lathan's the third victim?"

"She wasn't intended to *be* the third victim. I think the Casting Call Killer just saw an opportunity and took it. But Carmine Jenkins *was* the only one weighed down—and Wilma Reynolds was submerged underwater. It could be circumstantial, but I don't think it is."

Cait slowly nodded. "Has he talked yet?" She gestured toward the interview room.

"Not yet." I shook my head. "They're holding him for the full seventy-two hours. Hopefully someone can get him to talk."

As I watched Cait, her face still awash in worry, I realized that her concern for this case stemmed from more than just human decency. A euphoric sense of trust came over me. I knew she genuinely cared about my safety. I could trust her with my life. If it really came down to it, I knew she would put her life before mine. That's what made her a great a partner—and someone worth loving.

I looked at the clock above her head. It was almost 7:45, and neither of us had eaten since this morning. "Are you hungry?" I asked, although food wasn't my only interest. I felt the need to celebrate the break in the case, and Cait deserved to be a part of that celebration.

"I don't think I'll ever be able to eat again," Cait said. "Not after seeing those women today." She had a sullen look on her face. "But I could use a drink?" Her face quickly beamed at the thought.

Anything I needed to work on could wait until tomorrow. My brain was too fried to actually comprehend words anyway, so staying would be a waste of time. Dinner and a few drinks would help clear my head.

"I'm ready when you are." I stood from the desk. Cait rose from the chair and waited for me to walk into the hallway before she followed. As I closed my office door, Flu came walking toward us.

"Are you heading out?" he asked.

"Yes," I replied. "I have my phone if you need me."

"That shouldn't be necessary," he said. "The search team just called—Novak's West Joseph house is clean. No sign of him. It's immaculate too. No prints... not even on the remote control."

That didn't make sense. The old woman next door said someone was definitely staying there. "What about Naples?" I asked.

"He doesn't live there. At least not in the residence that's in his name. That place is rented to a family of four. They were questioned about Novak's whereabouts, but they said they've never met him. They just transfer rent money into his bank account each month."

Flu was just as perplexed about Novak's vanishing act as I was. How could Novak be everywhere and nowhere at the same time?

"You two worked a long day—I don't mean to keep you," he said before heading back to his office.

It seemed that no matter how many clues we uncovered, it was never going to be enough to find him. Our biggest chance was James Coffer, and he wasn't talking. At least for now he wasn't. Spending the night in a cold, cement jail cell usually worked in our favor when we needed a suspect to talk. It was a ghoulish glimpse into the suspect's potential life if he or she didn't cooperate. If James was involved with the murders, he would spend the rest of his life in prison, no matter how much he cooperated. But parole was still a possibility—at least, we'd let him *think* parole was a possibility. I would do everything I could to make sure the Casting Call Killer and his partner would never see the outside world again.

"Still want that drink?" I joked as Cait and I walked toward the elevator.

"More than anything," she said with a smile and pressed the "down" arrow.

The elevator reached us within a matter of seconds—the only perk to working late. As we stepped inside and the doors closed, I felt my guard go down. I was no longer in work mode. Details of the case still lingered in my mind, but I was technically off the clock and able to unwind.

When we stepped off the elevator and into the parking garage, I noticed three news crews parked in front of the station. I didn't have to guess why they were there. Reports had leaked that West JPD had discovered two bodies, and each broadcasting station was determined to be the first to find out the names of the victims. But that information wasn't going to be released until Flu had spoken to their families. That could be why Flu was still there.

I kept my focus on the news vans as we walked through the parking garage toward our cars. I bumped into Cait every few steps. "We'll take my car," she said. She must have noticed where my attention was. The reporters knew my car, and they would follow me. If I left with Cait, hopefully they would see my car in the garage and think I was still at work.

The taillights to Cait's silver Lexus blinked as she clicked the "unlock" button on the remote control. I opened the passenger's side door and sat in the seat, greeted by stale air that felt surprisingly good. It was mid-September, and evenings had become chilly. It was too hot during the day to wear a jacket, but by evening, I usually regretted not wearing one. I preferred warm nights to cold ones, and I wasn't looking forward to winter.

Cait started the car and backed out of the parking spot. The section of the garage where she'd parked was completely vacant. She followed the signs that led to the exit and rolled down her window to swipe her temporary parking pass at the gate. The sun had just begun to set, and the purple clouds swept across the horizon. Images like this made me appreciate the beauty in the world—even when the people in it only showed ugliness.

"I only know of two restaurants," Cait said when we turned onto the main street. She drove right past the news vans, and the crews were completely oblivious that I was in her car. "They're both across the street from my hotel," she added.

"That's fine," I said. "Your choice." It was best that we stayed close to her hotel anyway. It wasn't my plan to get drunk, but I wasn't exactly opposed to the idea. Knowing there was a bed within walking distance made the idea more appealing.

I hesitated to start a conversation with Cait. The last thing I wanted to talk about was the Casting Call Killer, but what else could we talk about? The case consumed our lives—it was the reason we were always together. And aside from the case, the only other thing going on in my life was my break-up with Abi—and I doubted Cait wanted to know that I had met with Abi only yesterday.

Cait could talk about her personal life. She said she wasn't dating anyone, so there was no fear of hearing about another woman. A dull ache that felt a lot like jealousy crept through my veins as the thought of Cait with someone else entered my mind. It had been a long time since I had actually felt jealousy. How foolish of me to feel envious of a fictional woman. Cait was single. I was single. There was absolutely no reason for envy.

Now that the case was on its way to being solved, I could actually feel. I could grieve over Abi—or, if I wanted to, I could pursue something with Cait. But why go down that road?

"Do you mind if we don't talk about the case?" I asked when Cait parked the car in the lot at her hotel, which was within walking distance of DiCello's, an Italian restaurant with an impressive wine list.

"Sure," Cait said as she turned off the ignition.

We both stepped out of her car and walked the three blocks to the front entrance of DiCello's. A blanket of stars covered the sky as night set in. Soft candle light shone from the two picture windows on the front of the building, and the thick wooden door to the restaurant was propped open.

The hostess, who was undoubtedly still in high school, greeted us with a warm smile.

"How many?" she asked.

"Two," Cait said.

"Right this way, please." The teenager picked up two menus from behind the hostess stand and led us through a maze of tables. We followed her toward the back of the restaurant, where she placed the menus atop a small table set for two.

We hadn't requested a secluded area, but I'm glad we were here. It was next to the restroom but quiet enough that we could have a decent conversation. The glowing votive candle, the bud vase with a single pink rose, and the white linen tablecloth cast a romantic mood.

"Your server will be right with you," the hostess said before she walked away.

Cait took a seat first. I scooted the wooden chair away from the table and sat down. I opened the menu and held it at chest level, as if I was using it as some sort of shield against Cait. It was ridiculous, really. I was treating Cait as if she was some type of perpetrator that I needed protection from. As if her stare could penetrate through my chest and capture my heart.

I lowered my menu, chest and heart fully exposed to the woman across from me, and I perused the dinner options. The more I read, the more hungry I became. I looked at Cait, who had her eyes locked on the wine list. If I knew Cait as well as I knew wines, she would choose a bold Chianti. And after the day we'd had, she deserved it—regardless of the cost.

"Anything look good?" Cait asked as she set the wine list down.

"Either the chicken marsala or the chicken parm," I replied. "You?"

"The Antinori Chianti," Cait answered.

A sly smirk crept from the side of my face. Maybe it was just because I knew my wine, or maybe it was because I was really getting to know Cait again. The way she moved and the way she thought—it had become second nature to me. I was beginning to know her as well as I knew myself, and a huge part of me really liked it.

"Are you ordering food?" I asked, my eyes landing on hers. They sparkled the same way crystal accents do from a chandelier.

"Probably the eggplant parmesan," she answered, and flirtation rose within her smile as our eyes remained locked on one another.

Before the feeling could grow, we were interrupted by our server.

"Good evening, I'm Brian," he said as he arrived at our table. "I'll be your server tonight. May I start you off with a glass of our house wine?"

"I'll have the Antinori Chianti please," Cait said.

"Excellent. Glass or bottle?" Brian asked.

Cait paused as she seriously thought about her answer. I could see her mind trying to calculate how much she actually wanted to drink tonight.

"Will you have some too?" she asked me.

"Sure," I replied. I was more in the mood for cabernet, but chianti would do just fine.

"Bottle," she finally answered.

"Perfect. And are you ready to order, or would you like more time with the menu?" Brian asked.

"I'm ready," I said, more toward Cait than our server. "I'll have the chicken marsala please."

"And I'll have the eggplant parmesan," Cait said when Brian turned to her.

"Excellent," he said as he collected our menus. "I'll be right back with the Antinori."

I looked at Cait, disappointed that the moment between us had vanished. It was probably for the best. What could really become of us?

As I sat there, fully open for the flirtation to return, I realized that what I'd felt only a few minutes ago was something I was used to feeling in this type of setting with Cait. The last time she and I were in a nice restaurant together, we were madly in love and in our twenties. What I felt was nostalgia for her—for us, all those years ago—and for that peaceful time in my life.

I also felt relief.

We had a suspect in custody, and most of the stress of the investigation had been lifted. The void that stress had left behind was ready to be filled with other emotions—such as gratitude. And I was well aware that gratitude could often be mistaken for love.

As much as I wanted to spend this evening with someone I was in love with, I couldn't force these emotions onto Cait. Nor could I lead her on. She had tried to create a personal relationship with me when she first arrived, and I had sternly reminded her that part of us was dead. Somehow, though, it felt resurrected.

"If we can't talk about the case, what would you like to talk about?" Cait asked. I hadn't noticed that while I was compartmentalizing my feelings for Cait, an awkward silence had lingered above the table.

"I don't know." I blushed. And that was the truth. I was perfectly content just being around Cait, even if we were silent. I didn't necessarily have to fill our time with polite chatter. But Cait was a conversationalist—she needed to be actively engaged with someone. "Why don't you tell me how you got the assignment?" I asked, putting the burden of speaking onto her. If she wanted to talk, then she could do all the work.

"I thought we weren't supposed to talk about the case?" she teased, a glimpse of flirtation lifting her voice.

"We aren't." I coyly smiled.

Before Cait could come back with a quip, Brian appeared from the shadows with the chianti. He showed us the bottle then twirled the corkscrew in his hands as if he was a contestant on a talent show. The candlelight bounced off the chrome mechanism as he twisted it into the top of the bottle. The cork rose with an almost imperceptible pop. He tilted the bottle against Cait's wine glass, and the crimson color reminded me of the tarnished blood that stained the basement floor. I closed my eyes.

I had to keep the gory details of the case at bay. I couldn't let them consume the night or me. I deserved to have one evening to myself. I needed a clear head if I was going to take on interrogating James Coffer tomorrow.

"Thank you," Cait said after she sampled the wine. Brian poured my glass and then moved back to fill hers. I opened my eyes and watched the liquid flow from the bottle. I no longer saw the blood from earlier today. It was just wine pouring from a bottle. The evening belonged to me again.

"Your entrées should be ready soon," Brian said as he set the bottle on the table and walked away.

Cait picked up her glass and smelled the contents inside before taking another sip. She seemed rather pleased with her choice as she set the glass down. She looked across the table at me and smiled. I could tell the silence between us was screaming in her head.

"Have you been here before?" Cait asked, dodging my question once again.

"I have."

"I don't remember this being here when I lived here. Is it new?"

"New to you," I answered. "It's been here for about ten years."

Cait nodded before she took another sip. "It used to be an arcade?"

"Yeah, that's right," I remembered. It had been a long time since I thought about the arcade that used to be here.

"We went there a few times, didn't we? To the arcade," Cait clarified.

"We did." I paused, remembering the past. "You were really good at the shooting games." I laughed. Cait could balance the plastic pistol in one hand and a drink in the other—and still hit the target with perfect precision every time.

Cait laughed to herself. "I remember you being pretty good too."

The trip down memory lane was unexpected but actually enjoyable. I had forgotten what it was like to be on the receiving end of Cait's attention. I had her undivided attention on the case, but this was different. This was *us*, stripped of our badges and sense of duty. There was nothing keeping us here except the fact that we both wanted to be. That's the feeling I had forgotten during all these years—what it felt like to be wanted by Caitlyn Porter.

"We had a lot of fun together," I said with a soft smile. I picked up my wine glass and brought the rim to my lips. My breath echoed inside the glass.

"We did," Cait agreed as she and I both took a drink. "I wish we had longer together," she added.

"We could have," I challenged and set the glass down.

"At that age, it would have been too hard." She shook her head. "I had my sights set on Lyons, and you had West Joseph."

Was she serious? *She* broke up with me. *She* couldn't commit to me. And now, twenty years later, she's going to act like our careers were the reason we grew apart? I would have followed her anywhere in the world just to be near her.

"For what it's worth," she said, "I'm sorry for the way things ended."

And there it was. Her usual vague apology for being an ass. Maybe it was better not to point the finger of blame. I had zero regrets with my decision to stay in West Joseph. I was needed here; I belonged here. She had her path, and I had mine.

It was best not to play the what-if game.

As I looked at Cait, I kept my focus on the fact that we were here now, enjoying one another in a way that I didn't think would ever be possible. I just didn't know why she was here—or, better yet, why she *chose* to be here.

"You didn't answer my question," I reminded her. "How'd you get this assignment?"

208

"How did I get the assignment?" she repeated, a stalling tactic guilty people often used during an interrogation. But what was she guilty of?

"Yes," I confirmed and took a sip of wine. I looked into the glass. It was good wine. So good that a second bottle was tempting.

"It was presented to my section," she said. "And it sounded interesting, so I volunteered to take it," she added defensively. Cait's armor weighed down her shrug. Her story was an abridged version of Flu's, who had used the phrase "pulled rank" to describe her decision.

As I watched her fiddle with the stem of her wine glass, I debated whether to pry for more information. I had a feeling she was hiding something, and I wanted to know what it was.

"No one else wanted the assignment?" I asked, knowing all too well what the answer was.

"I'm sure others did." She squirmed. "We don't get too many murder investigations across our desk—at least not one this complex."

It seemed like a logical answer. She took the case because it was filled with thrills and excitement. I doubt she fully knew what she was getting herself into though. Death isn't as horrific when the details are merely written in ink.

"Knowing what you know now… knowing that you would see what you saw today… would you still have taken the case?" I asked.

"Honestly?"

"Yes." Of course I wanted honesty.

"Yes and no." She sank into her chair. "'No' because seeing those women… in person… who would volunteer to see that?" Cait paused. "And 'yes' because…" Cait looked up from the table.

"The eggplant parmesan," Brian said as he set her plate down, "and the chicken marsala." He placed the plate of mushroom-covered chicken and a side of fettuccini in front of me.

"Thank you," Cait quickly said, almost as if she was thanking him for interrupting us. Did she not want to tell me the reason why she still would have said "yes" to the case?

"Can I get you anything else?" Brian asked.

"No, thank you," I said.

"Enjoy," he said then walked away.

As much as I wanted to find out Cait's answer to my question, I was just as consumed by the aromas of our meals. That first glass of chianti had found a home in the bottom of my stomach, but that didn't satisfy my appetite for actual food. And if I was going to keep my wits about me after a second glass—let alone a second bottle—I needed the noodles to soak up as much of the alcohol as possible.

Cait alternated between small bites of eggplant and large gulps of wine as we ate in silence. The food was too good to pause for conversation. Brian came back to check on us and asked if we wanted another bottle. After some hesitancy, I shook my head, and he walked away. Two glasses each was more than enough to polish off the night.

After dinner, Brian cleared our plates and seemed rather happy that we declined dessert. I assumed we were his last table and that staying an extra twenty minutes wasn't something he was interested in, even if it meant a larger tip.

He placed the check in the middle of the table. Just as I reached for the black leather booklet, Cait swooped in and picked up the check.

She opened the booklet and read over the receipt before digging into her back pocket and pulling out her credit card. She set the card inside the booklet and placed it on the table.

"What do I owe you?" I asked as she took her last sip of wine.

"Nothing," she said and set down her glass. A tiny drop of red wine slid down the inside of the glass and landed at the bottom.

"Cait, I can pay for myself."

"I know," she said, "but I got it. You can get it next time."

I knew better than to argue with her. Once Cait made up her mind, that was that.

"Thank you," I said, admitting defeat—though there was something victorious in the thought of "next time." Did she want there to be a next time? And in what setting? Our one rule was not to talk about the case, and we could barely oblige. What would there be for us to talk about after we solved the case and Novak was locked away forever?

"I'm glad we parked at the hotel," Cait said.

"Same here," I added. We may not have been drunk, but neither of us would have passed a sobriety test.

Brian picked up and returned Cait's credit card within a matter of minutes. She signed the receipt, and we were quickly on our way back to the hotel.

I was still a bit too wired to call it a night, but I wanted to be at my best tomorrow, and I needed as much sleep as I could get. I assumed she was too inebriated to drive me back to my car at the station. I could take a cab, but there really wasn't a point to it. I already had fresh work clothes in her hotel room. I had slept there last night, and nothing had happened. Why would tonight be any different?

Cait and I walked side by side through the restaurant's parking lot.

My body was at the perfect temperature to shield the chilly air that followed us across the busy street and through the hotel's parking lot. It was a little after nine o'clock, and the lobby had quieted down for the day. We walked past the front desk clerk toward the elevator, and the abrupt odor of chlorinated pool water startled my senses.

As we waited for the elevator, I studied Cait from the corner of my eye. Maybe the wine convinced me that I was more stealth than I actually was, but Cait didn't seem to notice my stare. She stood patiently in front of the elevator doors, and a sophisticated demeanor fell upon her. She had been so confident when we first met—but who wasn't at twenty-three? The world had yet to show us how cruel it could be. But now, as a veteran to the world's viciousness, she still stood poised and dignified. She possessed the type of attitude I was wildly attracted to.

The elevator doors slid open, and Cait and I stepped inside. Here we were, alone in an elevator, full of wine and lust. At least I was. But I knew once the wine wore off, so would this thirst to be with her. And one night wasn't worth the chaos it would bring in the morning.

"You never told me why you still would've taken this case knowing what you know now," I said once we reached the door to her room. She slid the plastic card into the slot, and a mechanic melody echoed in the hallway before the door unlocked.

"I didn't?" She looked over her shoulder at me and smirked as she walked into the room.

"No, you didn't," I confirmed.

The lamp on the nightstand was on when we walked into the room. The curtains were open to have let sunlight in during the day, but now, only the glare from the lampposts outside came through. Her window overlooked the shopping plaza that the Casting Call Killer had used to send those first two videos. The third video had come from another plaza, and I made a mental note to visit that location tomorrow if we had time.

Cait walked to the window and closed the curtains. The room darkened slightly as I walked to the side of the bed I had slept on last night. My pajamas were still folded on the nightstand. I gathered them in my hands and walked into the bathroom. I wanted nothing more than to get out of my work clothes and slip into Cait's warm bed.

As I shut the door, I picked up my toothbrush and coated it with a glob of toothpaste before turning on the sink water. I scraped the brush over my teeth and tongue, scrubbing the fuzzy film out of my mouth. After I brushed my teeth, I looked at myself in the mirror and took a deep breath. For a few seconds, I felt completely at ease. There was no need to have my guard up. I took my gun out of its holster and set it on the counter before I undressed.

I put on my navy blue sweatpants and an old white T-shirt. Not even two *bottles* of wine could make someone feel sexy in this outfit. But that was what I appreciated about Cait. I didn't have to be sexy around her. I could be myself.

This wasn't our first date; it wasn't a date at all. But, even if it had been a date, we knew and respected each other enough that we didn't need lingerie to enhance the mood.

I ran my fingers through my hair before I opened the door and walked out of the bathroom. Cait stood in the middle of the room and held her pajamas in her hand. I was sure she was just as ready for bed as I was.

"If you really want to know, I'll tell you," she said as I walked past her. We both stood in the center of the room.

"Really?" I asked skeptically. The way she'd avoided the subject earlier, I got the impression that the answer would either embarrass her or incriminate her.

"Really," she said. "When I heard that you'd been abducted by that madman, by Lathan Collins, every gruesome thought of what he could have done to you raced through my mind. You and I hadn't spoken in years, and probably never would, but to know the possibility of never being able to see you—or even just being able to talk to you again—was gut wrenching. You may not have been my first, but you were certainly the first woman I loved." Cait stifled back a tearful chuckle. "A part of me has always held on to you. And it wasn't until I thought I had to permanently let you go that I realized how much you still have a hold on me." She paused and walked toward the bathroom. "So, to answer your question," she said when she got to the bathroom door, "I still would've said 'yes' to the case... because, even after seeing all the blood and guts and gore, I would be with you." She leaned against the doorway, and her confidence hooked its claws into me. "I would give up the comfort of my entire life just to spend one day in the chaos of yours," she added.

Her admission paralyzed my entire body. As I stood there, absolutely speechless, she bowed her head and retreated into the bathroom. The door closed and the faint sound of water flowing from the sink filled the room.

A burst of euphoria rolled through my body and engulfed my heart. Cait wanted to be with me. The *real* me. She had witnessed the madness and disarray of my life—and, instead of wanting to run from it, she wanted to embrace it. She didn't want to fix me, and she didn't want to stay out of pity.

Her words were exactly what I needed to hear. Maybe I wasn't as damaged as I thought. I had convinced myself that I was repulsive to be around and to look at. I was damaged goods. No one would put in the time to get past my bullshit and embrace the real me.

But I was wrong. Someone was willing to do all that and more. Cait's words were a testament that I was someone worth wanting and someone worth loving. In a single sentence, she had stripped the armor from my skin and left my heart completely exposed. In that moment, I didn't mind being naked and vulnerable in front of her—because I needed her. I trusted her. I loved her.

But more than all that, I wanted her. I wanted her the way she wanted me the other night. I wanted all of her pressed against me. I wanted to feel her lips against mine, her hands on my skin, her breath upon my neck. I wanted to make her feel as good as she had just made me feel. But I didn't want to do it with words. I wanted to do it with my lips, my hands, and my tongue. I wanted to be the person who controlled her body tonight.

Although my entire being ached for her, I knew that's all it could amount to. This want couldn't grow to fruition. I couldn't act on these feelings. Above everything else, we were partners—platonic, working partners. But weren't we both mature enough to separate our personal lives from our professional ones?

The creak of the door handle broke my trance, and I looked in her direction. I would thank her for her words, hug her goodnight, and leave it at that.

As I took the first step toward the bathroom, Cait stepped into hallway, and I felt my platonic intentions disintegrate at my feet. Her hair was pulled back into a low ponytail, with loose strands around her face in disheveled layers. Her black pajama pants fit perfectly around her waist, backside, and legs. Her white tank top clung to her breasts and stomach. I had never noticed how tone her body was, especially in her arms. The feminine bulge in her biceps accentuated the curves in her body. As I took in her beauty, my heart slowed, as if it forgot how to beat. That's how strikingly spectacular she looked.

I stepped over the ashes of my virtuous plan, and I confidently strode toward Cait. The controllable ache I felt for her moments ago had transformed into an insatiable desire. It ignited a fire so deep inside me that the addiction I felt for her burned my skin. Every step toward her had purpose—and that purpose was to kiss her for as long as she would let me.

She had her back to me as I approached her, and she didn't feel my presence until I was only inches away. She turned around, surprised to see how close I was, but she didn't step back. Instead, her bewildered stare invited my lips on hers.

I leaned in to kiss her. With a mere millimeter between our lips, she brought herself closer to me. Her lips landed hard on mine, and she opened her mouth as wide as mine was. She wanted this kiss to happen just as much as I did. She wanted me just as much as I wanted her.

Cait controlled the kiss for only a second. I cupped my hands around her jaw and held her in place, and my tongue entered her mouth. Her breath escaped through her nose, and she took a deep breath. Then she wrapped her hands around the back of my neck and brought my body closer to her. We danced in a circle down the hallway toward the bed as we fumbled for control of the kiss and of ourselves.

She somehow managed to press my back against the wall, and she held me in place. We stood there, kissing and breathing into one another. She grabbed at the ends of my shirt and lifted it to my neck before she paused. In order for my shirt to come off, we had to stop kissing—if only for a fraction of a second, to let the fabric pass over my head—but she didn't want to break from the kiss. And I didn't want her to.

It was as if the force of her mouth against mine was the greatest pleasure I had ever known. If I wanted to feel more of this ultimate pleasure from her, I had to lose the shirt. I let my fingers slip from the sides of her face and took hold of my shirt in her hands. I didn't pull back from her lips. Instead, I lifted the shirt between us—a temporary barrier between our mouths, and I pulled it over my head. It fell to the floor as Cait pressed her warm chest against my naked flesh.

The curve of my lips struggled to keep from smiling. My hands reclaimed the sides of her face. I paused briefly to catch my breath. She took the opportunity to hitch my leg around her waist and twirled us back onto the bed. I grabbed the waistline of her pants as she hoisted my head to the pillows.

As I anticipated our reckless and passionate kisses to resume, she smoothed my hair away from my face and looked at me. Her eyes fixed on mine, and a warm smile travelled over her mouth. She leaned her head down with grace and timely precision and softly kissed me. The animalistic desire between us had settled, and I was left with a slow romantic burn that cooled my senses. She kissed me as if she intended for this night to never end. She caressed my face in a way that's reserved only for the enamored. She kissed me in a way that persuaded my heart to love again.

I brought my hands to the back of her head and rolled her onto her back. As our momentum grew, so did our kiss. The unrestricted kissing commenced. Although I enjoyed the tenderness, my body ached too much to take my time with her. I needed to taste more of her. I nipped and kissed her neck as I breathed my way down her chest, kissing and caressing her breasts with eager affection. Cait separated her legs, and my lower half gently landed against her. I had an open invitation for my hands and tongue to travel inside her.

I bowed my head before I placed my lips on top of hers. The way she tasted, and the way she moved, was exactly the way I wanted her. I pushed back the strands of hair from her face and smiled at how eager she was for me to be inside her. Regardless of what the morning brought, right here—right now—I knew I was able to feel love. Cait was the cure I had been looking for. And I was going to spend all night making sure she felt as good as I did.

CHAPTER | SIXTEEN

I RUBBED SLEEP FROM my eyes and took a deep breath. My head sank further into the pillow, and the crinkle of down feathers echoed in my ear. Heartening warmth wrapped itself around me. It felt as if a dozen towels fresh out of the dryer had been tossed on top of me.

I watched the clock rotate to 7:58 a.m. In two minutes, the alarm would go off, and I would have to leave the sanctuary of Cait's embrace. She lay behind me with her arm draped over my side. Her hand was tucked between the bed and my breast, and her left leg was sandwiched between mine. Her face was against the back of my neck, her breath warming my skin as she breathed in and out.

We fit perfectly together.

The ache I had for Cait last night was very much still alive. Every time I moved, a satisfying soreness pulsated through me. It was a pleasant reminder of where she had touched me last night. She had kissed, licked and bit every inch of my body, but I still craved her. I still wanted more.

The clock clicked to 7:59 a.m. I had one more minute to be with her. One more minute to feel safe.

I didn't want to move. I wanted to stay confined in her arms for the rest of the day. The thoughts of her hands on my body, her lips on my skin, and her breath in my ear were tempting enough to unplug the alarm clock and forget about the real reason we were together. But she wasn't here to caress my back, kiss my lips, or lick my skin. She was here to help me catch a serial killer.

As that thought pierced its way into my heart, the alarm clock emitted a series of high-pitched beeps. It was 8:00 a.m. Time to pull myself away from Cait's splendor in order to fight the cruelty in the world. By the fifth beep, Cait tightened her hold on me and stretched her legs down the length of the bed. She rolled onto her back, her naked body covered by the comforter, and she sat upright.

I felt her look at me before she traced her fingertips down my neck, along my exposed arm, and stopped when she reached my waist.

"Did you want to shower first?" she asked.

"No, you go ahead," I said as I pressed the "off" button on the alarm clock.

"Any word from Fluellen about James Coffer?" Cait asked as she stood from the bed.

I turned to look at her. The pale sunlight illuminated her body as she waited for my answer. It was next to impossible to formulate a response. I was absolutely fascinated by her beauty—and knowing that only a few hours ago I had touched her and tasted her clouded my mind with thoughts of doing just that. I was more than tempted by her subtle seduction; I was completely captivated by it.

"No," I answered, although I wasn't certain that was the truth. I hadn't checked my phone yet. But if Flu had called, I would have heard the phone ring. "We'll find out for sure once we get to the station."

"Are we headed there first? I thought you wanted to check out Mirror Woods Plaza," Cait reminded me.

I instinctually braced myself for the cannonball that would inevitably explode inside me at the mere mention of Mirror Woods. Whenever it went off, the agony from the memories would shoot into my stomach, and the blast would rise to the back of my throat, burning my esophagus as if I had taken a shot of battery acid.

But this time, when my body tensed in preparation for the explosion, there was nothing. Hearing Cait say the words "Mirror Woods" had the same effect on me as if she had asked me about adopting a kitten. There was no burning. No anger. No bomb in the pit of my stomach.

"I do," I said as an unfamiliar feeling of calm nestled inside me. "We can head there first," I added.

Cait nodded before retreating to the bathroom. The door closed behind her, and the strident echo of water beating against porcelain roared from the bathroom. I rolled onto my side, the cold air hitting my back where Cait was only a few moments ago, and I looked out the window.

The tall buildings along the horizon blurred through the sheer curtain as my eyes fixated on the bleach-colored sunlight. I thought about my lack of reaction to Mirror Woods. Even now, just thinking about that baleful place brought no painful reminders. I wasn't angry, and I wasn't scared. My breathing remained normal. Had this been last month—or even a week ago—I would've been running to the bathroom to splash water on my face in an attempt to keep myself from falling into a full-blown panic attack.

As I contemplated the difference between now and then, thoughts of Cait swarmed my mind. She was the difference. In the past two weeks, Cait had built a fortress around me so tough I was ready for battle. I knew I could trust her, and that trust led to the overwhelming desire I now had for her.

Just one night with Cait did more for me than six months of therapy. Cait should be charging me a co-pay and billing my insurance company. My weekly session with Dr. Rosenthal was scheduled for tomorrow morning. But as I laid there, the sound of Cait showering behind me, I couldn't shake the feeling that I no longer needed Dr. Rosenthal. I dreaded going to her sessions—not because she didn't help me, but because she made me relive a night I would much rather forget. With Cait, I didn't have to relive the night. All I had to do was face it. And I could do that, now that I had her by my side.

If I made it through the entire day feeling this confident about Mirror Woods, then I would cancel my appointment with Dr. Rosenthal. I didn't want to give Cait all the credit for my progress—the majority of it was my doing, but something new was growing inside me. It was strong, ready to heal the wounds that had weakened my mind.

The abrupt turn of the shower handle halted my thoughts. I sat up. The comforter rustled as I stood from the bed and walked toward the bathroom door. I knocked twice. The door quickly opened. Cait stood in front of the fogged mirror, a towel wrapped around her otherwise naked frame as she brushed her teeth. We made eye contact through the mirror, and I smiled at her before stepping into the shower.

Beads of water trickled down the walls and glass door as I turned the shower on. Hot water rained down from the spout, and I ran my fingers through my hair. Cait watched my reflection in the mirror, a seductive smirk spread from the corner of her mouth as her eyes traveled down my body. It was as if she knew she had an unspoken invitation to join me. But she chose not to. The case took precedence over our mutual thirst for each other. She tapped her toothbrush along the edge of the sink before she tightened the towel around her and walked out of the bathroom.

Until this point, I had forgotten how nice romance felt. I didn't want flowers or jewelry. What Cait gave me was much more tangible than the traditional romantic gestures. She gave me attention and compassion. She gave me patience and kindness. She gave me back my confidence.

She didn't look at me as if I was an injured puppy. She knew I had some issues to work through, but that didn't influence the way she treated me. She trusted that I could do my job—and, more importantly, that I could do it well. She saw the cracks along my surface, but she knew I was stable enough for her to put weight on.

By the time I had gotten out of the shower, Cait had already dried her hair and gotten dressed. The bathroom was too small for both of us to get ready in at the same time. Cait stayed in the bedroom while I brushed my teeth and got dressed in the bathroom.

I pushed the thoughts of what it would be like to get ready with Cait every morning from my mind. It wasn't fair to put such expectations on her. We had spent one night together. I couldn't sentence her to a lifelong love affair with me. That's where I went wrong with her twenty years ago. I wasn't the same naïve twenty-year-old. This Lena knew Cait needed her space and independence. This Lena knew not to expect more than just one night.

"What's the game plan?" Cait asked once we were both ready to go.

"Interview employees at the plaza," I said. "Maybe they'll remember James Coffer being there Wednesday night. If we get a hit, we'll ask the employee to ID James at the station. If not, then we'll head back to the station to interrogate James some more," I added.

We left the hotel and walked back to Cait's car, which was still parked in front of DiCello's. It took us about twenty minutes to drive to Mirror Woods Plaza. We spent most of the journey going over the types of questions we would ask the employees.

When we reached the plaza, I noticed it was much smaller than the West Joseph shopping plaza we had staked out. Mirror Woods Plaza had only five shops, each no bigger than the size of a small carryout restaurant. If we had continued down the road the plaza was on, we would have ended up at Mirror Woods Lake—the dumping site for Lathan's victims.

The last time I was here, Flu and I had been investigating the cause of Wilma Baker's death. And as soon as Flu and I had reached the entrance of Mirror Woods, my body had immediately tensed. My palms had become saturated in clammy sweat, and it had been almost impossible to breathe. Had it not been for Dr. Rosenthal's breathing exercises, I might not have survived that panic attack.

But here I was: one hundred feet from Mirror Woods, and I was fine. My breathing was normal. My hands were dry. My body was at ease. I didn't need to breathe in and out, in and out. I knew exactly where I was, and it had zero effect on me. If Cait wasn't here with me, it might be a different story, but she was the shield I needed to maneuver through these haunted woods.

It was easy to deduce which shops had Wi-Fi. The Tackle and Bait Shop was quickly crossed off the list, as was Moore's Lake House, which sold beach towels, bathing suits, and sand pails. They had no need to offer free Wi-Fi to entice consumers' interest. A deli was sandwiched between a coffeehouse and an electronics store. Both the deli and coffeehouse offered free Wi-Fi. It was possible the electronics shop did too, but I had strong doubts.

Nine of the two dozen or so parking spaces in the plaza's lot were full. I assumed three of the cars belonged to the employees of the stores that were already open at this hour. It was half past ten; the bait shop and Moore's Lake House didn't open until noon during the week.

The plaza didn't give an overly inviting feel to customers who were eagerly awaiting a day at the lake. Above the doors of the shops was a warped and weathered awning made of wooden planks. It stretched across the length of the plaza, giving the shops a cabin-like feel. It was an attempt to stick to the theme of Mirror Woods and the cabin rentals deep within.

We got out of the car and headed toward the plaza. The cedar scent of cabin walls filled my lungs, and I was reminded of a hamster cage. A faint fragrance of mildew loitered the walkway of the plaza. It guarded the door of each shop like a silent soldier protecting its kingdom.

We walked into the coffeehouse, and the bright aroma of coffee beans masked the hamster-cage scent. My eyes scanned the patrons. A man and woman, each in their late twenties, sat at a tiny table for two in the back. They were just as immersed in their cappuccinos as they were in their conversation. They drowned out the boisterous espresso machine, as only true regulars knew how to do.

The barista behind the counter smiled as Cait and I approached. His apron, tied loosely around his bulging waistline, had a series of coffee stains embedded in the fabric, as if those stains served as a badge of honor—a tribute to the excellent service he had provided over the years.

"I'm Sergeant Evans," I greeted him, and his smile quickly faded when I flashed him my badge. "This is Special Agent Porter." I gestured to Cait and ignored his abrupt retraction of customer service. "Can we ask you a few questions?"

"Certainly," he said. He composed himself by wiping a clean coffee mug with the dishtowel that had been draped over his shoulder.

"What's your name?" I asked.

"Dan Gresko." Specs of white splashed throughout his full head of charcoal-colored hair.

"Were you working here Wednesday night?" I asked.

Dan cocked his head to the side and looked upward. "Yes, I was here Wednesday night. I worked four to close."

"What time is close?" I asked.

"For the customers, eleven o'clock. But for me, midnight."

"Were you busy that evening?" I reached into my back pocket for my phone.

"Not that I remember." He paused. "We usually get a wave of customers between six and eight. But by nine, everyone has gone home or takes their order to-go."

"Would you recognize someone from that night?" I used my phone to sign into West JPD's employee portal, where I could pull up mugshots.

"Depends. If it's a regular, sure." Dan set the coffee mug down and flipped the towel back over his shoulder.

"What about him? Is he a regular?" I showed the barista James Coffer's mugshot.

Dan leaned over the counter and squinted at the photo. "I've never seen him," he quickly replied.

"Are you sure?" I kept the photo in front of him.

"Yeah, I'm sure," he said and backed away from the counter. "There's something about his eyes—I would have remembered that face," Dan added. "What did he do?"

"We're not at liberty to discuss that," I informed him.

"He must have done something big if you're going through all this trouble looking for him."

"Do you remember anyone who was here Wednesday night? Especially around the ten o'clock hour? He or she would have been using a laptop."

"Around ten?" He scratched his chin. "Not that I recall. It's pretty empty in here after nine. By ten, I'm usually wiping down the tables and getting ready to lock up."

"Are you the owner?" Cait stepped in.

"No," Dan said. "I'm the manager—been here more than seven years."

"Do you have any cameras on-site?" Cait continued.

"Yes, but the tapes are only good for forty-eight hours. If we don't save what's on them, they're recorded over."

This was quickly becoming a dead end. Dan didn't remember seeing James Coffer, and we were three days past the expiration date on the surveillance cameras. If Coffer *was* here, without Dan being able to give a positive ID, there was no way for us to know.

Unless James bought something while he was here.

"Are you able to access sales receipts?" I asked. "If a customer used a credit card, would you be able to look it up by name?" I asked.

"Sure. But technically you would need a warrant—or the owner's permission." Dan crossed his arms over his chest. "But you two seem desperate. And I think being the manager for seven years give me the authority to give permission," he added. "What name are you looking for?"

"James Coffer," I answered.

"I'll see if it comes up," Dan said. "Do you want anything in the meantime?"

"No, thank you." I smiled but soon regretted the decision. A caffeine headache was starting to form just above my temple. It would have been a conflict of interest to purchase coffee here, but as soon as Cait and I finished interviewing the plaza employees, we would stop at another coffeehouse.

The floorboards squeaked as Dan stepped away from the counter and walked toward the small wooden door adjacent to the cash register at the end of the counter. It led to a small office that could barely fit a desk and a computer, let alone a human. He shuffled through loose receipts on top of the keyboard. He sighed as he sat in the chair and typed in whatever he needed to in order to log into the system.

As Dan searched for Coffer's name, I scanned the coffeehouse. Movie posters from Hollywood blockbusters were framed and evenly hung on the walls. In the back corner, by the couple sipping their drinks, was a large bookcase stuffed with books in an organized mess.

Cait had lost herself in the bulletin board near the front door. It was filled with miscellaneous advertisements for boat rentals, psychic readers, and an array of other services like dog-walkers and lawn-mowers. I walked toward her but didn't need to be as close to the board as Cait was to recognize one particular service. The pamphlet for West Joseph Tours hung prominently in the center of the board. It made sense for the company to advertise here. This was the last retail plaza before entering Mirror Woods.

"They can help you next door," Dan said to Cait. He had returned sooner than expected. I turned and saw him standing behind the counter holding a single receipt. "The deli next door runs the tours," he added.

"No." I forced a smiled. "That won't be necessary." I walked back to the counter as my heart tried to find its natural rhythm. I was more startled by Dan's return than I was to see the tour pamphlet, but the reminder that people actually celebrated Lathan's brutality was also disconcerting. "Did you find something?" I gestured to the receipt in Dan's hand.

"Not under James Coffer," he said as he peered at the receipt. "The only sale we had after nine o'clock that night was from a Ryan Novak for seven dollars."

"Ryan Novak?" I repeated. The surprise in my voice must have summoned Cait to join the conversation.

"How long was he here?" Cait asked.

"He left before close," Dan said while looking at the receipt. "Maybe around a quarter after ten?" he surmised.

"Are you able to email us a copy of the receipt?" Cait continued.

"Sure. But wouldn't you rather have a hard copy?" Dan held out the receipt.

"Email would be better," Cait insisted and then handed him her business card. "To this address, please," she added.

Dan took Cait's card with mild hesitation and then walked back to the office with a submissive stride. With each step, I could feel his regret for helping us intensify. What he thought was going to be a simple task, a favor to law enforcement, had turned into extra work for him.

"We could have taken the hard copy," I quietly said to Cait.

"I know, but this way we'll have the shop's IP address. We can match it to the one that's on the video," Cait said.

"So not only do we have a receipt placing Novak at the IP address, but we also have proof of who owns the IP address." I nodded. It was smart—and something I hadn't considered.

"I sent it to your address," Dan said as he came out of the office. "Is there anything else I can help you ladies with?" The annoyance in his voice was a clear indication he wanted us to leave.

"No," Cait said. "You've been very helpful. Thank you."

Cait led the way out of the shop, holding the door open as I walked out behind her. She had managed to get exactly what we needed. Although, without Dan's cooperation, it wouldn't have been as easy. That didn't change how impressed I was by her investigative skills. She was cunning. One step ahead of the witness. Something I'm sure she learned at BCI.

My curiosity for the West Joseph Tours was grander than my admiration for Cait though. As we walked past the deli, a train-wreck reaction turned my head to look at a different bulletin board. This one was affixed to the outside wall between the coffee shop and the deli.

Pamphlets ruggedly stuck out from the plastic holder below the bulletin board. Pictures of previous trips were encased behind the glass covering the outdoor board. Guests of the tours posed in front of the bus as if they were about to enter an amusement park. And maybe, in a way, at least to them, they were. The tour treated Mirror Woods as if it was some sort of adventure. Each dumpsite was a new thrill. The guests may not have physically gone on a roller coaster at each stop, but the excitement and scare of one was certainly there.

I knew better than to look inside the pamphlet. It would only drudge up memories I was trying to get past. But I was able to keep my cool when I saw the entrance to Mirror Woods, so maybe I was strong enough to face other reminders as well.

Inside the pamphlet was the price breakdown and map for the tour. For $39.99 per person—only $12.99 for those twelve and under—the bus would drive to all four dumpsites, Lathan's garage, and each victim's residence at the time of their disappearance. It was such a repulsive and hideous display of human greed. To not only capitalize on someone's death, but to flaunt their voracity in front of the victim's families—in front of their homes—was enough to make me nauseous.

Just as I was about to put the pamphlet away, I noticed a new addition. The "Grand Tour," at $59.99 per person, went to the abandoned home and showed tour-goers "how it all ended that night," according to the pamphlet. A photo of the building was next to the price, along with testimony from past guests.

"West Joseph is my Graceland," one guest was quoted as saying.

"Fun for the whole family," another quote advertised.

The "Grand Tour" allowed guests to get out of the bus and walk the property. And, for an extra ten bucks, an actor dressed as Lathan Collins would take a photo with you.

I suddenly remembered that Abi had told me the house had been recently purchased. She couldn't remember the name of the buyer, but she had assumed it was someone with the tour group. This proved it.

I was curious, however, to know how *they* knew "how it all ended that night." The thought of some actor dressed as Lathan coming down the steps—as tourists voluntarily shackled their ankles to the basement wall—brought a fury so wild that I could feel my skin rip apart.

They must have gotten their information from Rachel's book. Other than me, she's only person alive who knew exactly what had happened that night. Was she so desperate for money—or healing—that she needed to include those details?

A sudden and sharp tingling sensation stabbed at my hands and forearms. It felt as if a million pins were being pricked into my skin. The pamphlet fell from my hands as I walked away from the shop. Cait was only a few feet in front of me. A dark haze cast over my eyes as she continued to walk toward the car, and my throat tensed when I tried to call her name.

Now that I was no longer under the awning, I felt the sun's volcanic rays. It felt like a fire was trapped inside the clouds, and the flames hovered above me. No matter which way I tottered through the parking lot, the heat continued to attack me. It had latched onto my skin—and if I didn't get to the car soon, my blistered skin was going to burst.

Beads of sweat formed along my scalp as I took larger steps toward the car. I looked at Cait, to see if she was also on the verge of melting, but she didn't seem bothered by the sun or the intrusive way it tried to liquefy us.

I felt crushed beneath a hundred burning logs. The fumes from the fire filled my nose and poisoned the air. I gasped—but there was nothing to breathe. No oxygen to fill my throbbing lungs. My heartbeat accelerated. One beat too fast, then two beats too fast. It didn't cease until my pulse felt like one horrendous pound. The thump echoed in my ears and shattered my vision like a hammer against glass.

The car. Where was the car? Everything that was once in front of me was now gone. Nothing but pure blackness consumed my eyes. I tried to blink away the blinding darkness, but it remained. I was cocooned in a blanket of peril, and there was no escape. I couldn't find Cait. I couldn't find the car. I was trapped here.

Thoughts of the actor dressed as Lathan pelted my mind. Then I heard his voice. The taste of metallic tar saturated my saliva. "Sergeant Lena Evans," he hissed.

His snarled breath was hot on my ear and burned my neck to a degree that, had I not known better, I would have sworn he was here with me—right on top of me—holding my vision hostage as he shoved me to the ground.

A surge of adrenaline coursed through my veins. It felt as if a million spiders were crawling under my skin. I tried to slap them away. I wanted to claw at my skin and crush them with my hands, but my limbs were too paralyzed to move. I was utterly frozen.

"Lena…," he repeated in the same grotesque growl. "Lena…"

A force grabbed at my arms, and I bowed my head to keep my

face from aligning with his. I couldn't look into those arctic eyes again. I couldn't see his face—or Angela Truman's face—in front of mine. I squeezed my eyes so tight that tears streamed down my cheeks.

"Lena?"

I heard my name again. But this time it didn't sound like him. It was rough and dominant, but with a hint of kindness that coated the tone.

"Lena." The coarseness had faded. "Breathe."

I felt pressure against my chest, just above my heart. Then the light touch of two fingertips slid down my neck and stopped at my jugular, as if he or she was checking my pulse.

"You're having a panic attack," the gentle voice said. "Just breathe."

As if the cocoon around me had broken open, I felt my chest rise as I took a deep breath. The oxygen in the air had been restored. I could breathe again. With each breath, portions of my vision returned. The ground slowly rebuilt beneath my feet. The iron clasp around my heart opened. The fire in my veins subsided.

"Cait?" I asked as the shadowy figure came into focus. Her hands, cupped around my biceps, held me in place. I looked at my surroundings. I was no longer inside a black hole.

"Yes," she confirmed.

I took another deep breath and exhaled. The gentle mid-September breeze was back. It blew through my hair and cooled the sweat along my face. I looked at Cait as I breathed in and out, in and out.

"What happened?" she asked.

"I don't know." I shook my head. "I'm okay," I added. I placed my hands over hers and slid my arms out of her grasp.

"Are you sure?" she asked as she steadied my backside along the car.

"Yeah…." I nodded. "I could use some water." The fire had scorched my throat, and each word I said scraped over my raw skin.

"Are you okay to wait here? I'll go get you some," Cait said as she continued to hold me in place.

"Yeah." I nodded again.

She let go of my arms and headed to the coffeehouse. I felt completely drained. If I wasn't leaning against the car, I would have collapsed to the ground.

I may be able to be *near* Mirror Woods, but being in it was a different story. Each blade of grass was a trigger. The house where it happened, the tour groups, the dumpsites—all of it. How foolish was I to think I already had overcome that night.

It didn't matter if I was happy and on the brink of falling in love. It didn't matter how many lives I saved. I was going to hear that ugly, vile voice every day for the rest of my life. I couldn't cancel my appointment with Dr. Rosenthal. If I was going to beat this—if I was going to beat *him*—I still needed her too.

MICHELLE HANSON

CHAPTER | SEVENTEEN

ONCE THE PANIC ATTACK dissolved, Cait offered to drive us back to her hotel. She knew I was in no shape to work, and I agreed with her. However, I didn't want to spend the rest of the day in her hotel room. I wanted to be in my own house, in my own bed. The familiarity of the four walls I called home was the serenity I needed.

So Cait drove us to the station. And after I convinced her I was okay to drive myself home, she pushed my hair behind my ear and kissed my forehead. The quick tenderness of her kiss was exactly the reassurance I needed that she wasn't going to leave.

Walking into my house felt like sitting in my car after it had been broken into. I hadn't been in my house since Sunday—when the Casting Call Killer had hacked into my laptop—and the spoiled stench of violation still stained the walls and muddied the floors.

But this was my home. I wasn't going to allow the Casting Call Killer, Novak, Alfa Mike, or any other player in this twisted game take away the one place where I could feel safe. My life and my sanity had already been compromised. But my home was mine.

I spent the reminder of the evening in a light sleep, and I forced myself awake in the middle of the night when I felt a dream form. I didn't have the strength to conquer whatever was hiding within my psyche. Whatever that thing was, it wanted to come out. Its sharp claws were ready to slash into my chest and rip my soul to shreds. A nauseating beast that reminded me once again I needed to keep my appointment with Dr. Rosenthal.

So here I was.

"How are things?" Dr. Rosenthal innocuously asked from behind her notepad.

I traced a rhythmic "8" pattern with my index finger into the arm of the chair's micro-suede fabric. Dr. Rosenthal sat idle as she reviewed the notes from our last session. I toyed with the notion of telling her that I'd wanted to cancel my appointment. That I had thought I didn't need

228

it. That I had thought one kiss from Cait had cured the disease inside me.

What I'd thought was stupid.

My mind was just as heavy and clouded as it was the night I'd escaped Lathan's lair. No blast-from-the-past love affair could shield me from that kind of storm. If I was going to get beyond this—if I was going to truly survive what had happened—the antidote had to come from within.

I blinked away my thoughts as I formed a response. What *things* was she referring to? So many *things* had happened since the last time we'd spoken—and that was just a week ago. She knew nothing of Cait, and she barely knew the truth about Abi. If I told her about my episode yesterday at Mirror Woods Plaza, she would want to try exposure therapy again. And, if I had anything to say about it, that was no longer an option.

"Things are things." I hesitated to commit to an adjective.

"Are you able to elaborate?" Dr. Rosenthal set the notepad down on her lap.

"No," I said brazenly.

"Lena." It was clear that Dr. Rosenthal was in no mood to coddle my romance with ambiguity.

"I thought things were getting better, but yesterday…."

"What happened yesterday?" she asked.

"I…." The room fell silent as I thought about what had happened. The burning under my skin. The black hole that consumed me. "I had another panic attack."

"You can always call me if you need to," Dr. Rosenthal offered. "I'm not just here for you during our sessions. I'm here anytime."

"I know." I nodded. Her offer, though part of her job, stirred a resounding sensation of sincerity. If yesterday's panic attack had taught me anything, it was that I wasn't ready to go without these sessions. "I would have," I added, "but I was close to cancelling my appointment."

"Why?"

"I've felt a lot better this past week."

"Could it be because our sessions are working?" Dr. Rosenthal asked with a smile.

"Maybe…." I played along. Deep down, I knew I was feeling better because therapy was the best medicine, not my adoration for Cait.

"Do you know what brought on your panic attack?" Dr. Rosenthal readied her pen.

I nodded. "Cait and I were at Mirror Woods Plaza—" I cut myself off. I had accidentally said Cait's name. She had become such a constant figure in my life that including her in the facts of the story came naturally.

"Cait?" Dr. Rosenthal scanned her notes.

"Cait's my partner on this new case," I volunteered. "She's a Special Agent in the Cybercrimes Unit with the Bureau of Criminal Investigations," I added.

Dr. Rosenthal nodded and jotted down a few notes. "What were you doing at Mirror Woods Plaza?" she asked.

"Following up on a lead." I had to be vague because it pertained to the case. The fact that the emails had been sent from an anonymous server hadn't been made public yet, and it was still considered privileged information.

"Just being at Mirror Woods Plaza brought on a panic attack?"

I got the impression Dr. Rosenthal knew I was holding a vital piece of information hostage.

"No, not just *being* there." I paused, debating how much to divulge. "I saw something. Something that reminded me of that night."

Dr. Rosenthal remained silent, which told me everything I needed to know. I had progressed too far to resort to a tight-lipped session. My relationship with Dr. Rosenthal had been built on trust and accountability. We were long past the days of her pandering to my being immature and obstinate.

"I saw a pamphlet for West Joseph Tours," I finally admitted.

"You've seen those before," Dr. Rosenthal replied. "What was it about this one?"

"The tour now stops at the house where Rachel was."

"And where you were," Dr. Rosenthal reminded me.

"Yeah. Where I was."

"How did that make you feel?"

"That part didn't bother me," I said. "I expected it in a way. If the owner of the tour is cold-hearted enough to take tourists to the victims' dump sites, what would stop him from profiting off the house as well?" A thin wall of tears formed behind my eyes.

"Then what was it?" Dr. Rosenthal pressed.

"Once they're at the house, the tourists can get off the bus and take pictures of the property, and..." I cleared my throat, "and pose with an actor dressed as Lathan Collins. Like it's fucking Disney World, and Lathan is Mickey Mouse."

"How did you handle seeing that information?"

"Not well," I retorted. I took a deep breath and let the growing hostility dissolve under my skin. "The panic attack came on so fast. I didn't even know it was happening until I was in it. I didn't have time to count or breathe," I added.

"How did you feel?"

"Like I was on fire. Like my lungs had shrunk to the size of peas. And then everything went black."

"Yes, but *how* did you feel?" Dr. Rosenthal emphasized.

"How did I feel?" I paused. "I felt angry. More than angry—I was livid. I wanted to strangle the people involved. I wanted to watch all signs of life leave their bodies. And I wanted to be the one who did it."

"Could that anger have been a reaction to another emotion?" Dr. Rosenthal asked.

"Maybe?" I paused as I thought about what I had felt during the attack. "Fear?" I guessed.

"What brought on that fear?"

"Seeing him," I replied. "I knew it wasn't *him* in the pamphlet, but it was the thought of him. The presence of him." I swallowed back the memory. "I know the fear Lathan instilled in his victims because I *was* one of his victims. And these people—the organizers of the tour, and even the guests of the tour, they treat what happened to me and the other victims as if it's there for their entertainment. Like it's a goddamn haunted attraction." I paused and took a deep breath. "Maybe it is. It's scary and it's frightening, and the real danger stops inches from their faces. They get to go home when it's over," I continued. "But it wasn't a haunted attraction for me. It was reality."

"This is the first time you've verbally acknowledged that you, too, were one of Lathan's victims," Dr. Rosenthal pointed out. "Why do you think that is?"

"I don't know." I shook my head. "Because I'm not ashamed of it anymore." I shrugged.

"What made you ashamed of it before?" Dr. Rosenthal brought the pen in her hand down to the notepad.

"Because I'm not supposed to be the victim. I'm supposed to be the hero."

"Do you still want to be the hero?"

"No," I confessed. "At the time I did, but not now. Not anymore."

"Why? What's changed?"

"Everything." I dismissed all specifics. But everything *had* changed. I didn't feel the need to be the hero anymore because West Joseph now had someone who was better at it than I was. Even if Cait was only here temporarily, she was well suited for the role.

"During our last session, you stated that you blamed Abi for what happened with Lathan Collins. Do you still feel that way?"

"A part of me does, yes," I answered honestly. Now that Abi had made her way into the conversation, it was only a matter of time before Dr. Rosenthal would ask about our relationship. I would have to tell her about everything—including Cait.

"You also stated that you wanted to make her proud to be with you," she continued. "Is that still the case?"

"No," I replied.

"Why not?"

I took a deep breath and exhaled loudly. The subject that I had wanted to avoid was now sitting on my lap. "Abi and I are no longer together," I said matter-of-factly. "She moved out. She's with someone else," I added, spraying the blame all over Abi.

"How does that make you feel?" Dr. Rosenthal began to write again.

"Relieved in a way."

"How so?"

"Because I no longer have to see the pity in her eyes when she looks at me. I no longer have to force a feeling that wasn't there." The more freely I spoke about Abi, the better I felt. It was as if the tight pressure between my brain and skull shrank with each word I said.

I no longer had a best friend or anyone I could confide in. There was Cait, but given the circumstances and the dual role she played in my life, I couldn't talk to her about Abi. For the past week, I had kept my thoughts and feelings about Abi to myself. And it was too complicated to sort through alone. But with Dr. Rosenthal, I could lay it all out.

"What feeling did you force with Abi?" Dr. Rosenthal probed.

"Being in love with her," I replied. "When Abi and I first met, it was so easy to love her. She's beautiful and kind, smart and generous. She was everything I could have asked for. And then Lathan Collins happened." I paused as I thought about how that night truly affected me. "After that, it just felt like our relationship was made strong because I was weak."

"What made it strong?"

"Abi, and her determination to make it work."

"What changed?" Dr. Rosenthal shifted in her chair.

"I was finally too much for her?" I shrugged. "I could only bend her back so far before she snapped," I added. "Every time she reached for me, I slapped her hand away."

"What was it that made her leave?"

"She thought I was having an affair." I laughed through the tears. I could barely handle one relationship, let alone two.

"Were you?"

"No," I quickly said.

"Why did she think you were?"

"My partner, Cait…," I began. "She was over late one night. We were working on the case. A few glasses of wine happened, and it was decided that it would be better if she stayed the night. Abi came home to find Cait in my pajamas and me standing next to her with two glasses of wine. I can understand why Abi thought what she did, but it was nothing. Abi stormed out. And when I chased after her, she ended things."

"It feels like there's more to this story," Dr. Rosenthal pushed.

It was a mystery even to me as to why I wanted to keep Cait a secret from Dr. Rosenthal. And not only from Dr. Rosenthal, but from the world too. I had matured into the skin that kept my private life a secret. I didn't keep it hidden from just the media that lurked outside my front door, but also from anyone who could use it against me.

But I truly believed I could confide in Dr. Rosenthal. And I hoped I wasn't wrong.

"Cait and I have a history…." I started to tread down a rocky path of trust. "She was my first girlfriend—my first love—my first everything," I said. "Before she and I could really become something, she moved to Lyons, and I stayed in West Joseph. And up until last week, we hadn't seen or spoken to one another in twenty years."

"What was that like—seeing her again?"

"Surreal," I said the first word that came to mind. "Staring at someone I thought I'd never see again. Past emotions mixed with present ones," I added as I thought more about the answer. "When she left for Lyons, she just left. No real goodbye or an offer to go with her. I don't know if I would have gone with her, but I wasn't even given a chance to consider it. For the first few years, I thought about what I would say to her if I ever saw her again. I'd tell her how much I hated her for making me love her, and how much I resented her for leaving. But when I saw her, none of that mattered."

"Why?"

"Because we're different people now."

"What's your relationship with Cait now?" Dr. Rosenthal nudged.

"Professional…." I paused. "And… romantic." I hesitated to reveal my true feelings, but this was something Dr. Rosenthal needed to know.

"Is it wise to mix both worlds?" she asked. I could sense a hint of concern in her voice.

"No, it's not," I answered truthfully, "but it's different with us." And that was also true. "Cait will always put the case before herself, and so will I," I defended. "Neither of us is going to let one night get in the way of our entire lives."

"One night," Dr. Rosenthal repeated. "So, this is new?"

"Yes," I confirmed. "Very new and *very* unplanned."

"How long have you two been working together?" Dr. Rosenthal asked.

"This is our second week."

"In less than two weeks, you went from partners to lovers." Dr. Rosenthal glanced at her notes. "And in these two weeks, you wanted to cancel your appointment. Are the two related?"

"Yes…." I avoided eye contact to shield myself from her clear connection.

"I'm glad you didn't cancel," Dr. Rosenthal added in her usual supportive demeanor. "The high of a new relationship can make us feel on top of the world." She smiled at the thought. "Can I ask: How does Abi fit into this?"

"She doesn't," I quickly replied. "Abi and I knew we were over before Cait was even assigned to the case," I added.

"How do your feelings for Cait differ from your feelings for Abi?"

I shook my head. "I'm not ready to admit my feelings for Cait."

"Why not?"

"Guilt, I guess?" Maybe that's why I wanted to keep Cait a secret. I wanted to hide the guilt I felt for loving her. I tried so desperately to feel love again for Abi because I felt as if I owed it to her. It was a debt I knew I could never fully repay. I was so laden with guilt that I had shut the idea of happiness from my mind. I was convinced that Abi was my last chance at love. And I stayed because I thought it was be with her, or be with no one.

And then Cait happened.

I was too scorched to ignite a new love—but, with Cait, she was the spark I needed to rekindle a love that had burnt out.

"I'm concerned about your relationship with Cait," Dr. Rosenthal said bluntly.

I just stared back at her. I was caught off-guard by her severe tone. I was so used to Dr. Rosenthal's supportive approach to everything I said. But not this time. What did Dr. Rosenthal think would happen?

That I was swimming in a bottomless lake—and that it was only a matter of time before I tired and drowned?

"The timing is alarming," she continued. "Starting a new relationship this soon after a trauma raises some trepidation. But it's also the intensity of the feelings," she added. "I understand you two have a complicated history, and I'm concerned there may be some confusion."

"How so?" I challenged.

"Cait makes you feel good, and that's something you haven't felt in a long time. So I understand the desire to want to be with her." Dr. Rosenthal paused. "Usually, those who suffer from PTSD purposely take risks and put themselves in dangerous situations, most commonly with drug and alcohol abuse. But I feel your relationship with Cait is risky in and of itself. It's risking your case and your career, it's risking your progress, and it's risking your heart."

Part of me could understand why Dr. Rosenthal would warn against getting involved with Cait. It was unethical to be in a romantic relationship with a partner, but it was something that happened so often that my career wasn't in true jeopardy. And my feelings for Cait did initially cloud my commitment to therapy, but I had found out the hard way that I still needed my weekly sessions with Dr. Rosenthal. Risking my heart, however, wasn't something I agreed with.

Dr. Rosenthal knew nothing of Cait. All she knew was what I told her. Granted, my quick recap of our history didn't make Cait seem like the greatest of people. But I knew Cait for who she truly was. She was kind, trustworthy, courageous, and smart. Dr. Rosenthal had no right to criticize this relationship because she didn't know Cait the way I did.

"I know what I'm doing," I defiantly replied.

"I truly believe that you believe that." Dr. Rosenthal paused. "I'm no expert in love, and we have no control over when it happens. I just want you to be careful, Lena. Right now, you're on the road to rediscovering yourself, and that's a positive. I'm not discouraging you from walking that road. And I'm not surprised that you and Cait have fallen into a relationship, especially given your history together." She paused again and a closed her notepad. "There are things from your past that you want to move on from, Lathan being the most pertinent. But there are other areas in your life you may be seeking closure for. You have an opportunity for a new beginning—to emerge as a healthier self. You've made a lot of progress, and I don't want to see you throw that away."

The cause for Dr. Rosenthal's concern finally revealed itself. She was worried Cait would distract me from the gains I had made in my therapy.

"I won't," I assured her. It was encouraging that she was rooting for me, but she had to know that I wanted to get past this more than anyone did.

"How are you sleeping?" she asked, changing the subject. "During our last session, you mentioned nightmares."

"I have good nights and bad nights," I said. "More bad than good."

"Do you remember your dreams?"

"Just one." The memory clogged my mind. "I was trapped the backseat of my car with Lathan," I said. "The doors wouldn't open, and the car was surrounded by fire."

"Fire has come up several times in your dreams," Dr. Rosenthal recalled. "What do you think it means?"

I shook my head and shrugged. "Fire means destruction, passion, and anger," I repeated from my last session. I purposely left out that Cait was in the dream too. If fire really did represent passion and destruction, then it could have easily served a dual purpose: passion for Cait, destruction for Lathan.

"We're just about out of time," Dr. Rosenthal said as she glanced at the clock on the wall. "I want to thank you for being so honest with me today, especially about your feelings for Cait and admitting that you had considered cancelling your appointment," she added. "Will I see you next week?"

"You will," I confirmed.

"Good." She smiled as I stood from the chair.

I reached into my front pocket and pulled out my phone. I had silenced the ringer throughout the session, but now it was time to return to the real world—even if that world was filled with murder and madness. I peered at the screen and saw three missed calls from Cait within the last five minutes. It was unlike her to call with such urgency and not leave a message. Before I could call her back, Cait's name came across the screen again.

"Evans," I answered. It was difficult to determine the appropriate answer. This was my work phone, so professionalism was a must. But it was Cait on the other end—she could be calling for personal reasons.

Every part of me wanted her to be calling for personal reasons. Maybe she just wanted to hear my voice—or she was curious as to when I was coming in. I was desperate for an indication that she could be as much into this blossoming relationship as I was. But judging by the amount of times she had called, I knew this wasn't going to lead to anything good.

"Lena," Cait said, her tone despondent. "We got a notice of a new Missing Persons Report." The caution in her voice left me frozen as I stood in the empty lobby of Dr. Rosenthal's office.

"Who is it?" I asked. If Cait was calling about a Missing Person, then it had to pertain to our case—or, worse, someone I knew. Thoughts of those closest to me ran through my mind as my heart teetered between panic and fright. If the Casting Call Killer was still in game mode, he would use my weakness against me. And my weakness was to go after those I loved. "Cait, who is it?" I demanded after her pause lapsed into stalling. I clenched my jaw as I prepared myself to hear the name.

"Rachel Sanzone," she answered. A rush of rage and defeat infected my vision. My hands trembled as I held the phone against my ear. "Fluellen and I are headed to her apartment now," Cait added. Her voice pounded against my eardrum as I took in her words. "I'm sorry, Lena."

"What's the address?" I managed to muster as the shock slowly wore off.

My blood boiled to the point that it felt like razorblades flowed through my veins. Novak was determined to make sure I played this game whether I wanted to or not. He took the one piece that was sure to lure me into his trap. Rachel wasn't just a pawn—she was the queen. She was the prize I had taken from Lathan, and she was the prize I was going to take from Novak too.

"I'll text it to you," Cait said. "Come as soon as you can."

CHAPTER | EIGHTEEN

I PULLED INTO RACHEL'S apartment complex, and several police officers greeted me as they scanned the property. One officer in particular was in charge of sectioning off the scene with caution ribbon. The yellow tape swayed in the wind as he tied the loose end around a neighboring tree. I assumed the area he sectioned off belonged to Rachel: a first-floor apartment with a small patio overlooking the parking lot. The bright sun reflected off the beige siding, making sunglasses a requirement instead of an accessory. I parked in a vacant spot a few feet from where the caution tape ended and got out of the car.

Next to the three patrol cars was Fluellen's vehicle. I didn't see him combing the grass for clues with the other officers, so I assumed he and Cait were inside waiting for me. It was odd to see such care for a Missing Persons Report. Usually this type of operative was reserved for an actual crime scene. As far as I knew, Rachel was only considered missing—not abducted.

The officers patrolled the property with the same grace as ballerinas do, meticulously watching their every step as they scoured the area for clues. With their latex-gloved hands, they looked behind bushes and small pine trees that decorated the outside of the complex. The scent of fresh mulch lingered in the air. I was hopeful that if someone did abduct Rachel, then that someone was clumsy enough to leave behind a footprint.

But the better part of me knew that was unlikely—because the likelihood was that Ryan Novak was Rachel's abductor. As a police officer, Novak had hundreds of break-ins under his belt. He was an expert when it came to detecting clues, which meant he would be an expert in hiding them too. His precision was a skill I had truly admired… until now.

I ducked under the caution tape as I stepped onto the cement walkway that led to Rachel's door. Her apartment was the first in a row of three. Each apartment was shaded by a large awning. The letter "A" was prominently displayed on Rachel's green door, which was wide open. Three deadbolt locks had been installed over the chrome door handle. The frame was still intact and showed no signs of forced entry. If someone had kicked in the door, the wood frame would be splintered. The door was also missing any signs of damage; there wasn't even a shoe print.

I stared at the three locks on Rachel's door. One lock was standard for an apartment complex, but the other two—those were Rachel's doing. And I understood why. I had suffered only a few hours of Lathan's torment. Rachel, however, endured five days of it. To this day, she probably saw him every time she closed her eyes. Those three deadbolts were here for extra security and for peace of mind, and it would take more than a few kicks to break through this door.

As I lingered under the awning, Flu's voice echoed through the small foyer. Inside, to the left, was a navy blue couch with bright floral accent pillows. Next to the couch was a matching recliner that had a crocheted afghan draped over the back. A few dirty dishes had collected on the coffee table in front of the couch. The walls were decorated with mass-produced paintings. It livened the place up, but the apartment was void of anything personal. No pictures of family or friends. To the right, I saw a galley kitchen and an adjoining dining room. Junk mail and local ads were mixed in with dozens of unopened letters that sat atop the dining room table.

In front of the doorway was a hallway that I assumed led to a bedroom and bathroom. Before I could make my way to the back of the apartment, Cait and Flu walked out of a room and down the hallway toward me. Their faces were both wounded with worry. Behind Flu and Cait was a man wearing a dark brown suit. His salt-and-pepper hair was slicked back, and genuine concern weighed down his frown as he walked behind Fluellen.

"You say you haven't spoken to her in a few days?" Flu asked the man as the three of them walked toward the front door. Cait and I briefly made eye contact, and I had to hold back the instant smile that seeped from my lips whenever I saw her.

"No, not since Sunday," he answered.

Flu nodded. "Kelly, this is Sergeant Evans. Evans, this is Kelly Stewart, Rachel's publicist."

"It's nice to meet you," I said.

"Sergeant Evans," Kelly said and extended his hand for a shake. "Rachel speaks very highly of you."

I half-smiled as I shook his hand. "Thank you," I responded.

"What time on Sunday did you speak to her?"

"Oh, early," he said. "Maybe ten—ten thirty?"

"How did she seem?" I asked.

"Fine." Kelly shrugged. "She can be quiet at times. She has good days and bad days," he added.

"Good days and bad days?" I repeated.

"She has PTSD... from what she went through," he added as if it should be common knowledge.

He didn't have to explain further. I knew what those good days and bad days felt like. I also knew there was no way to tell if a day was going to be a good one or a bad one. What started as a good day could quickly turn into a tsunami of terror and distress.

"You said she was 'fine' when you last spoke to her," I said. "What does 'fine' mean?"

"She was happy. She was in good spirits," Kelly answered. "She was looking forward to having a few days off from the book tour." Kelly turned to Fluellen. "We've been to signings at almost every bookstore in the state during the past two weeks."

"That has to be exhausting," I said.

"She was starting to feel it." Kelly chuckled to himself. "I came by last night—she hadn't been answering my calls since Sunday evening. But I'm used to it. It's not unusual for her to shut her phone off for a few days, especially when she has a bad panic attack."

"Was she here last night?" I asked.

"Not that I know of. I knocked a few times and called her cell phone, but no answer. I thought she was at her boyfriend's house." Kelly shrugged. "We had to leave for Cincinnati this morning for another book signing, so when she didn't answer this morning, I called you guys."

"Did you try her boyfriend's house?" Cait asked.

"I don't know where he lives," Kelly answered.

"Do you have a key to her apartment?" I gestured to the door.

"No," Kelly said.

"Maintenance let us in," Flu said. "They have keys to the extra deadbolts."

"It's part of the lease agreement," Kelly added. "My apologies for bringing this to your attention, especially if it turns out to be nothing. But this isn't like Rachel."

"No, we appreciate your concern," Flu said. "We'll call you if we have any more questions. You're free to go," Flu added.

"Thank you," Kelly said and looked at both Cait and I before leaving Rachel's apartment.

"I didn't want to say anything about the Casting Call Killer in front of him," Flu said, lowering his voice to almost a whisper. "But with the recent murders, and your belief that the killer is replicating Lathan Collins, I'm treating this as an abduction. Better to be safe than sorry."

"I agree," I said. "Are there signs of a break-in?"

"No," Cait replied. "*If* she was abducted, she had to let the person in."

"Captain?" An officer interrupted from the doorway and motioned for Fluellen to walk outside with him.

"Just a second," he said to the officer. He lowered his voice again. "Let's find Rachel's boyfriend," Flu said to Cait and me. "And I don't want anyone talking to James Coffer without me," he added. He turned to walk away with the officer.

"*If?*" I turned to Cait. "You sound like you don't believe she was abducted."

"I don't know. I'm just not convinced."

"Why not?"

"It just doesn't seem right. Someone like Rachel, who obviously has trust issues," Cait said and motioned toward at the three deadbolts, "wouldn't just open her door to anyone."

"Yeah," I agreed, "she had to know the person."

"But even that doesn't fit." Cait sighed. "She has trust issues, so she isn't going to open herself up to new people. Whoever she opened the door for, she must have known for a long time—probably since before she was taken by Lathan Collins."

"Okay…"

"And it's unlikely that someone she's known since before Lathan Collins would abduct her." Cait scanned Rachel's apartment, a perplexed look on her face. "There's no sign of forced entry, no sign of a struggle anywhere in the apartment. If she left, I think she left willingly."

"But why?"

"Maybe her boyfriend surprised her with a weekend getaway?" Cait suggested.

"But her boyfriend would've known she had a book signing to go to this weekend," I argued.

"Maybe she was tired of being this town's entertainment." Cait shot me a look. She knew that's how I felt, but the difference between Rachel and I was, Rachel wanted the attention—she wrote a whole damn book about it. She wasn't trying to forget what she went through. "A romantic weekend getaway with no phones, no adoring fans…" Cait trailed off, and I started to get the notion that she was hinting as to what we could do this weekend. But, again, Rachel and I were different.

"No." I shook my head. "Rachel wouldn't leave without telling someone," I said. "Her family went through the anguish of her disappearance once already. She wouldn't do that to them again. Not on purpose."

"Maybe you're right," Cait said, but her tone didn't match her words. It was possible Cait was on to something. I haven't allowed myself to trust anyone new since I was taken by Lathan. Aside from Dr. Rosenthal, everyone in my life I had met pre-Lathan. Even Cait. I was so untrustworthy of new people that my heart had to rummage through the rubble of a past relationship in order to feel again. If I hadn't already known Cait, I never would have allowed myself to trust her enough to fall in love.

Cait let out a shallow breath as she looked around the empty room and pushed my hair behind my ear. For just a moment, she was no longer Special Agent Porter, and I was no longer Sergeant Evans. We were Cait and Lena—two women enjoying the excitement of a new relationship. "How are you feeling?" she asked.

"I'm good." I tilted my head so it could land in the palm of her hand. She caressed her fingers against my scalp, and I was completely helpless to her touch. I always felt my best just after a session with Dr. Rosenthal, but with the added bonus of being with Cait, my distress level was at a twenty out of one hundred—the lowest it's ever been since that night with Lathan. "Are we done here?" I asked when Cait let her hand fall from my head.

"Yeah. We searched every room before you arrived. There's nothing here," she added. "Flu's going to keep an officer stationed outside the door as a precaution."

"I'll drive us to the station," I said. "If Rachel was abducted, it's probable that James Coffer knows by whom."

With a trusted nod, Cait followed behind me as I walked out of Rachel's apartment. I noticed Flu speaking to Rachel's mother. I had met Mrs. Sanzone the night of Lathan's death. She had introduced herself in the hospital hallway and thanked me for saving her daughter. Dark circles had made a permanent residence under her eyes, and although she had been emotionally exhausted, she was also ecstatic that her daughter was alive.

Mrs. Sanzone appeared to be rather upset with Fluellen. Her white hair was pulled back into a messy bun, and bug-eyed sunglasses hid her eyes. She was a petite woman with a frail frame, and I was sure that her already-bruised heart couldn't handle another disappearance. As she spoke to Flu, she wiped away tears that slid under her sunglasses. She dabbed a crumpled tissue at her reddened cheeks as Flu spoke.

Given the current circumstances, I decided to avoid Mrs. Sanzone. I didn't want her to see me, in case I would only remind her of Rachel's first disappearance. Seeing me might make her regret thanking me for saving her daughter—because maybe I really hadn't saved her. Maybe I had only postponed the inevitable. If Rachel was abducted a second time, there was only one reason for it: someone wanted to finish what Lathan Collins had started.

As soon as Cait and I returned to the station, she went to I.T. to review Rachel's phone records. I stayed in my office to read the log notes that detailed James Coffer's behavior while in custody.

He still wasn't talking to officers, but that didn't matter. His actions said almost as much as a confession would have; he had been calling the same phone number that Pamela Westlake had called before she was reported missing. Presumably, it was the burner phone that belonged to the man in the videos with the distorted voice. West JPD had also called the number several times early in the investigation but received the same outcome James received now: disconnected.

I had been sitting at my desk for almost ninety minutes waiting for Flu to get back from Rachel's apartment. The anticipation ate away at my skin. We were wasting valuable time. If James Coffer knew something about Rachel's disappearance, we needed to act fast.

"Evans," Flu said when he finally tapped on my office door. "I see you got a copy too." He motioned toward log notes I had been reviewing. "What do you make of it?"

"It isn't enough to charge him," I said. Any decent public defender would argue that the phone number was circumstantial at best, and the case would be dismissed. We needed something more than a smoking phone number to pin four murders on James Coffer. "Have you spoken to him?" I asked Flu.

"Not since yesterday when I showed him a picture of Novak to gauge his reaction, to see if Novak looked familiar to him…."

"And?"

"He acted as if he'd never seen him before." Flu shook his head and stepped inside my office. He sat in the vacant seat across from my desk and draped a few sheets of paper across his lap. "We got the profile from the Feds," he said. "The one I requested on the Casting Call Killer."

"Is that why you wanted us to wait to talk to James?"

"Yes," Flu said, "but I also wanted to talk to someone close to him before we made another attempt at an interview," he added. "I've been on the phone with James' mother for the past half an hour."

"Any luck?"

"She was informative." Flu nodded. "She said he's been rather aggressive and that the behavior started about a year ago. She said it's manageable for the most part, but he's easily irritated—punches walls or kicks furniture when he gets upset."

"Has he displayed that behavior here?" I scanned the log notes.

"No," Flu said. "His mom's concerned, but she didn't seem surprised that we were holding him. Most moms say, 'It can't possibly be my son, he's such a good boy,' but not her." Flu paused as he gathered his thoughts. "She also said everyone calls him Jimmy."

"Is that all you got out of her?" Skepticism scorched my tone. Flu didn't come in here just to tell me his nickname.

"No." Flu paused. "When I asked her about his interests, she said that Jimmy talked about Lathan Collins a lot. He printed off articles about the murders, went on the site tours almost every weekend and...." Flu sighed as he took another pause.

"And...?"

"And Jimmy talks a lot about you too," Flu finally said. "His mom also added that his most prized possession is Rachel's book. He was so excited to have her sign it."

"Jimmy Coffer," I repeated to myself. That name sounded more familiar than James Coffer did. His face seemed vaguely familiar to me, but it wasn't until Fluellen mentioned Rachel's book signing that I remembered exactly why I recognized him.

Jimmy Coffer had approached Cait and me outside the Bistro on Labor Day. It was the same day that Rachel was having her book signing at Volume One Bookstore.

Anger growled through my body. Not just at Jimmy Coffer, but at myself too. Approaching me was just a game to him. He had stared me in the eye, a fake smile slapped on his face as he caressed my ego with false intentions. He had acted star struck as he saturated our short conversation with adoration. He had even gone as far as to ask about the Casting Call Killer. Little did I know he was actually asking about himself—or at least someone he was working with.

"Anything else?" My jaw clenched.

"He doesn't have a lot of friends," Flu continued, "except that he hangs out with a guy named Michael."

"We should question Michael."

"We should. But Jimmy's mom didn't know Michael's last name," Flu said. "She said they've known each other for about a year. She said Michael's a nice kid, in his late twenties, and is also obsessed with Lathan Collins." Flu crinkled his forehead and exhaled quickly as if he had just made a sudden connection.

"What?"

"Something Mrs. Sanzone said this afternoon," Flu answered. "Rachel's boyfriend. His name is Michael." Flu paused. "Could be something—could be nothing," he added. "Anyway, I've read over the profile." Flu held up the stack of papers on his lap. "Something just doesn't sit right with me. All the physical evidence points to Novak, and I've come to terms with that. But the profile doesn't fit."

"Profilers have been wrong before," I said. "The profile for the D.C. Shooter was way off."

"I know." Flu nodded as his shoulders fell into an unsettled demeanor. "The profile has the unknown subject listed as a white male, early twenties to late thirties, outgoing but doesn't have a large social circle." Flu paused. "Novak is in his sixties and had more friends than he knew what to do with."

The part about the unknown subject's age bothered me too. It would take a physically fit person to be able to move a dead body from one crime scene to another. Even if the perpetrator had help—from someone like Jimmy Coffer, for instance—it would still require a great deal of agility and stamina to move a body. Novak wasn't in the best physical shape. Thirty years as a detective can take its toll.

"What else does the profile say?" I asked.

"He is, or once was, a local resident of West Joseph," Flu muttered.

"That fits Novak," I chimed in, followed by a dirty look from Fluellen.

"Higher education, probably in electronics." Flu looked up from the profile. "Novak could barely turn on a computer, let alone hack into somebody's web cam," he defended.

"Could Jimmy Coffer be the one in charge of the electronics?" I asked. "We're not just dealing with one killer—we have two," I reminded him.

"The profile was very clear that the offender is organized. Has a stable work history, likely to have served in the military. Jimmy Coffer's work history is scattered at best. He works at a menial job—"

"At a building *owned* by Novak," I interrupted.

"Jimmy lives with his mom, lacks social skills, and has below-average intelligence. The profile doesn't match either one of them—at least not enough to convince me we have all the players involved," Flu said.

"So we're looking for a third person?" I asked incredulously.

"I don't know." Flu shrugged, and fatigue clouded his eyes. "Read over the profile and meet me in the interview room in twenty minutes." Flu stood from the chair and walked out of my office.

The profile was exactly ten pages long. Each page explored a different part of the unknown subject's psyche. As I read over what Flu had already summarized, parts of our conversation whispered in the back of my mind.

Both Rachel and Jimmy were associated with a man named Michael—last name unknown. The name Michael was also associated with the case. "Alfa Mike" was a possible alias for Novak. But Jimmy's mom said Michael was in his late twenties, and I doubted that Rachel would date a man Novak's age.

Fluellen also stated that Jimmy's aggression started a little over a year ago—the same time he started his friendship with Michael. Something else about "a year ago" stuck with me. That's when Lathan Collins was killed. If Jimmy were as big of a fan as he seemed to be, it would make sense that that could be the cause of his aggression. Losing a role model, even one as disgusting as Lathan Collins, was a lot for someone to deal with.

Bile brewed in my stomach as that thought festered. If Jimmy was demented enough to consider Lathan Collins a mentor, then West JPD had to proceed with extreme caution. He may not have displayed any violent tendencies while being detained, but that didn't mean he wouldn't in the near future. It would just take one trigger for the real Jimmy Coffer to surface.

Rachel's boyfriend, Michael, also lurked in the back of my mind. It wasn't exactly unheard of for a young woman to date a much older man. Novak was very charming and friendly. I wouldn't be completely surprised if he caught the attention of a beautiful young woman like Rachel.

If Rachel was dating Novak, it was possible she had called the same number that Jimmy had been calling—the same number that belonged to the Casting Call Killer. I slid my chair back as I stood from the desk. Cait was in I.T. going over Rachel's phone records. If Rachel did call that burner phone, there would be record of it.

As I walked out of my office and toward I.T., I thought about the traits listed in the unknown subject's profile.

It was likely he had a military background. But neither Ryan Novak nor James Coffer had been in the armed forces.

The suspect was believed to be outgoing yet without a large circle of friends. Novak was very outgoing but had a very large circle of friends—at least he did while he was with the department, and I found it hard to believe he was friendless in Florida. Jimmy Coffer only had one friend, according to his mother, but he wasn't outgoing at all.

The profile also mentioned that the subject would have a post-secondary degree, most likely in electronics. As far as I knew, Novak's one and only degree was in criminal justice. It's possible he could have studied electrical engineering in his free time, but I wasn't convinced. And the brief interactions I'd had with Jimmy didn't exactly give the impression that he could build a computer.

I walked into I.T. and saw Kevin on the left sitting at his desk and Cait on the right sitting at Abram's desk. The I.T. department looked more like a dorm room than an office. Kevin and Abram had their separate sides of the office, with their desks facing opposite directions so that their backs were to one another. Posters filled with computer humor were affixed to the cinder-block walls.

Kevin had his dark brown hair pulled back into a low ponytail. A half-eaten sandwich sat inside a plastic container on his desk. I lightly knocked on the door as not to startle either of them. Both Cait and Kevin were in their own worlds as they worked independently.

"Cait," I said as I approached Abram's desk, which was less cluttered than Kevin's desk but which may have been due to the fact that Abram hadn't been here all week.

"Yeah," Cait said as she peeled her eyes from Rachel's phone log.

Before I could ask her about the burner phone, I saw something next to Abram's desk that I had never noticed before. It could have been pinned to the wall for months; I hadn't visited the I.T. office since I came back to work.

Tacked to the wall behind his monitor was a poster of a military soldier's silhouette. The soldier was facing an amber sunset as he held his rifle high in the air in a victorious pose. To the left of the soldier, just beneath the glowing sun, was the military phonetic alphabet.

"He's ex-military," Kevin said as he wiped the crumbs from his mouth.

"Oh." I nodded. A fact about Abram I didn't know.

"You okay?" Cait asked as I continued to stare at the wall behind Abram's monitor.

"Yeah…," I said slowly, my eyes glued on the poster.

A for "Alpha," B for "Beta," C for "Charlie." It wasn't until I reached the letter M that my heart sank. M for "Mike."

I glanced back at the letter A, just to verify what I already knew. A for "Alpha."

Alpha. Mike.

Alfa Mike.

I closed my eyes as the fear of what was becoming so blatantly obvious rose inside me. I *knew* the phonetic alphabet. We had learned it at the academy and used it in dispatch. How could I have missed this? How could I have let a careless mistake counter twenty years of hands-on experience?

"Sergeant?" Kevin turned and stood from his chair.

"Lena, are you okay?" Cait repeated.

"Yes." I opened my eyes. "Where's—" My voice went hoarse. "Where's Abram now?"

"He took the week off," Kevin said. "He called on Monday to say he was using a few vacation days. I don't blame him. That guy works his ass off."

Abram Myers had taken a sudden vacation the same week that Rachel had gone missing. It could be a coincidence, but the coincidences were piling up against him. Aside from his initials being A.M., the profile fit. Military background, organized offender, outgoing personality, late twenties, higher education in electronics.

As clear as my suspicion felt, I couldn't just blurt it out like I was playing a game of Clue. I had to be certain. I had already accused Novak of the murders; adding Abram would only make me look like a mad woman desperate for a lead.

"Are you close with Abram?" I asked Kevin.

"For forty hours a week, I guess we are." Kevin shrugged. "We don't do anything together on the weekends."

"What does he do on the weekends?" I followed up.

"He goes bowling, spends time with his girlfriend," Kevin answered.

"What's his girlfriend's name?" I was more afraid to hear the answer than I was shocked to learn that he actually had a girlfriend.

"He doesn't talk about her much. It starts with a P, I think. Maybe an R? I don't really know. Paula, Ruth, Rose…." He rambled off random names. "Rachel…."

"Does he hang out with anyone else?" I interrupted.

"Not since Novak moved to Florida."

My already sunken heart collapsed further into my chest. "He's friends with Novak?" My voice shook.

"Kind of." Kevin shrugged again. He was clearly oblivious to the vital information he was privy too. "He and Novak didn't really start hanging out until Novak's retirement party." Kevin chuckled to himself. "Novak came in to turn in his badge, and the two started talking about Novak's boat and all the fishing he was going to do. I think they went out for drinks afterward," Kevin said. "It's too bad Novak moved—they really got along. Abram kinda looked up to him, ya know?"

A symphony of static noise filled my head. It sounded as if a radio was trying to tune into a station. Slowly, the static subsided as my thoughts arranged in my head. Flu had mentioned there was a possible third suspect. Someone who was the brains of the operation. Someone who fit the parts of the profile that Novak and Jimmy didn't.

That someone was Abram.

"Thank you," I said to Kevin as I stepped out of the office. Cait remained seated at Abram's desk, a confused look on her face, as I turned to walk to the interview room.

With each step, my pace increased until I was jogging. Supporting evidence swarmed my mind as I put the pieces of the puzzle together. All the times the Casting Call Killer was one or two steps ahead of West JPD were because of Abram. Abram supplied Cait and I with the list of abandoned warehouses. He could have already been at the warehouse; he placed the shovel under the door and smashed the car window with a brick.

He also knew when Cait and I would be at the plaza to try to catch the person sending the videos. He knew to go to a different plaza that night in order to keep his MO the same. It was part of his signature to send the videos on the exact same night, but he wouldn't be able to with Cait and me on surveillance duty.

Abram could have easily hacked into my laptop. He was the one who had given me the laptop in the first place. He could have installed a program to watch my every move, and I would have been none the wiser.

And then the most damning evidence came to mind: Abram was technically the last person to have Novak's badge. Kevin had witnessed Novak turning it in to Abram. It was protocol for I.T. to collect and deactivate all badges from former employees. Abram could have waited a few days before deactivating Novak's badge so that he could use it to sign out Lathan Collins' case files.

As certain as I was that Abram was our third suspect, I knew Fluellen wouldn't be as easily convinced. As I practically sprinted down the hallway toward the interview room, I passed the bulletin board with department information, including new hires from the past year. Abram's photo was still on it.

I reached for his cocky-grinned picture and tore it from the board. It ripped at the corners where it had been stapled, and the paper wrinkled at the side as I tightly held it in my grasp. The only way I was going to convince Flu that Abram was a part of this was to show Jimmy Coffer Abram's photo. His reaction alone would tip the scales.

I bulldozed my way through the first door that led into the interview room. A detective watched from behind the one-way mirror as Flu asked Jimmy questions. Jimmy sat in a metal chair bolted to the ground, his hands cuffed to a table also bolted to the ground. His lips were pressed so tightly together that not even tissue paper could be worked between them.

Flu stayed hovered over Jimmy as I barreled through the second door like an invincible warrior. Jimmy's eyes widened as he stared at me, complete shock soiled his face. Flu also had a similar expression as I made my grand entrance. I walked up to the table, my breath heavy, and I slammed Abram's photo onto the table in front of Jimmy.

"What's his name?" I shouted.

Jimmy looked at me, then the photo, then back to me. Panic paralyzed his body as his eyes darted back and forth—to me, to the photo, back to me. He squirmed in his chair as he tried to free his cuffed hands.

"What's his name?" I yelled again, moving further into Jimmy's personal space. It was a fearless but stupid move. Even with cuffed hands, Jimmy could still attack.

"Evans," Flu stood tall as he scolded my behavior.

"We have him. In the next room." I ignored Flu as I filled Jimmy's head with lies. "He's talking. He told us everything," I continued.

Jimmy's face contorted into a mask of anger. His eyes burned black as he scooped the photo in his hands and crumpled it in his fists.

"Fuck you!" Jimmy screamed in my face as he stood from the chair. He kicked outward, but the bolted chair stayed in place. He pulled and yanked at the cuffs that bound his hands. The table moaned at his attempts to pry himself from the shackles. "Fuck you!" Jimmy shrieked again. Spittle flew from his lips as deep red marks formed along his wrists from the cuffs. "He wouldn't. He wouldn't talk!" Jimmy's breathing rapidly grew as he gasped for air. "Fuck you," he sobbed. A lost and confused cry escaped his lips. "You stupid, bitch!" Jimmy screamed. "You took Lathan from us. You took him from us!" he cried. "I hate you. I hate you, you stupid bitch," Jimmy repeated as his scowl seared into me. He was a rabid dog trying to break free from his chains. "Mike would never turn on me." His sobbing continued. "He never would," he repeated, almost as if he was trying to convince himself rather than us.

Jimmy sat down in the chair and buried his tear-stained face in his hands as he sobbed into himself. Flu stepped to the side so that he could see what had invoked such a reaction.

The way Flu lost his balance when he saw Abram's photo, I thought I was going to have to call for medical. Flu took a deep breath and let his head fall forward. It hung there for a few seconds as he stared at Abram's photo, disappointment and discontent embedded in his skin.

"I hate you," Jimmy repeated in a whispered snivel. His outburst had physically exhausted him—and the harsh, but false, realization that Abram had turned on him was more weight that his fragile state could handle.

Flu turned his gaze to me, his eyes thinly outlined with tears. "A word?" he said as he walked toward the door I had barged through only moments ago.

I glanced at Jimmy as he kept his face buried in his arms. He had calmed slightly, but the stream of tears remained. I followed Fluellen into the hallway, perplexed as to what he needed to say to me in private.

"What the hell was that?" Flu shouted, and all the detectives within hearing distance looked at us. I glanced behind Flu's shoulder and saw Cait standing in the hallway.

"Flu, I—"

"No," he cut me off. "You are pointing the finger at an officer. Another one!" Flu continued to shout. "First, it's Novak. Now, it's Abram?" he said as if he didn't believe my allegation.

"Flu, you *saw* Jimmy in there." I searched his eyes for the captain I knew and admired. He had to be in there somewhere. "Jimmy's behaving as if I just shot his father in cold blood."

"That stunt you pulled is unacceptable." Flu lowered his voice once he realized we had an audience. He took two steps away from me and breathed deeply a few times before returning. "I'm willing to go along with this, but when are you going to stop pointing the finger at your own people?" he barked.

Flu walked to a vacant chair in front of his office and flopped down. "Damn it," he groaned. "We can't even trust our own people." He sighed, and I understood his explosion, as unwarranted as it was.

He'd trusted Novak. He'd trusted Abram. He'd trusted two people who were likely responsible for at least four murders. What did that say about Flu as a captain? As a human? "I'll get a warrant for Abram's place," Flu said, his voice calmer. "Have Agent Porter scan his computer."

"Can you get a warrant based off a photo?" I asked.

"I'll get the warrant," Flu snapped. "Charge that piece of shit in there with all four murders." He stood from the chair and went into his office, slamming the door behind him.

CHAPTER | NINETEEN

I STOOD IN ABRAM'S front yard alongside Flu and Cait. The morning dew had yet to evaporate, and it clung to the tops of my shoes. It was roughly eight in the morning—two hours after Flu had received approval for the warrant.

As we stood in the front yard, I scanned the exterior of Abram's burgundy ranch-style home. It was pristine and polished, much like I had imagined it would be. The landscaping was flawless. Not a single blade was higher than the rest. Had I not felt the grass firsthand, I would have thought it was Astroturf.

The walkway to Abram's front door curved to the right and led straight to a weathered welcome mat that sat upon his small porch. The front windows were spotless, though the curtains were drawn, so no one could look inside.

Cait, Fluellen, and I stood in the front yard as one of the three uniformed officers knocked on the front door. The other two positioned themselves on either side of the door with their guns drawn. The officer knocked five times, a steady slap that pounded on the wood frame of the screen door as he announced his presence.

"Abram Myers," the officer said. "West Joseph Police Department. We have a warrant."

No response.

The officer knocked again. "West Joseph PD," he repeated. "We're entering the home." The officer pulled his gun from the holster and steadied it at his side as he opened the screen door. He jiggled the handle to the front door; to our surprise, the door opened when the officer turned the knob. It wasn't even locked.

Either Abram had left in a hurry and didn't have time to lock the front door, or we had an open invitation to come inside. Whatever the reason, I knew I wasn't going to like what we would eventually find.

The officer turned and looked at Flu before he stepped inside. Flu nodded, and the three officers walked inside the home with their guns aimed and ready to fire. Within several minutes, an officer stepped back outside. "It's clear, Captain," he said.

Flu stiffened his posture and walked up the three steps that led to the front porch. Cait and I followed behind as if we were his trusty sidekicks. When we reached the front door, I looked at Cait. She had probably been on searches before with BCI, but nothing to this caliber. I worried that she wouldn't be mentally prepared for whatever we'd find.

I worried that I wouldn't be prepared for what we'd find.

The front door led straight into his living room. It was a typical bachelor-pad set-up. A sixty-inch flat screen television served the as focal point of his living room. Game consoles and multiple media devices were neatly aligned in the large entertainment center that enveloped the television. Two recliners faced the entertainment center, and I had visions of Abram and Jimmy sitting there late at night as they played various video games filled with violence and murder.

Toward the back of the living room, there was a large couch and an end table. The black leather couch looked unused, like it was only there for show. The table was tucked between the couch and wall. On top of the table was a picture frame that showed Abram and presumably his girlfriend spending a day at the beach together. The closest beach to West Joseph was nine hours east. Abram had on a red windbreaker and gave a wide grin as he loosely held his arm around her shoulder. Upon a closer look, I noticed that his girlfriend was, indeed, Rachel Sanzone.

She looked happy in the photograph. She was naturally photogenic, but there was a genuine joy in her smile. It was full of radiance, and she appeared to be truly in love with Abram. She was nuzzled up close to him, either in an effort to keep warm on what seemed like a windy day, or just to be nearer to the one person she trusted most. She looked much younger than she did now—though a year's worth of PTSD can really age a person. But still. There was innocence to her smile. She had yet to learn what true fear was. She had yet to meet Lathan Collins.

I remembered Cait had stated that Rachel's abduction might not have been an abduction at all—at least it didn't start out that way. If Rachel had left voluntarily, it would have been because she had known her alleged abductor for a long time and trusted that person completely. And that trust would have deep roots.

If Abram had started dating Rachel before her five-day stay with Lathan, his obsession with Lathan may have stemmed from trying to protect his girlfriend. Perhaps I had pegged Abram all wrong. Maybe he took the investigation into his own hands after Lathan was killed. He had access to the case files, and he's computer savvy—maybe all of this was to protect the person he loved.

I had been thinking of Abram as the enemy, but perhaps he was actually on our side, helping us from the shadows. He could have been the person who'd anonymously sent us the videos, hoping we would catch the killer. He knew that if he addressed the videos to my attention, I would make certain the killer was caught. He could have created the Alfa Mike persona in order to gain Novak's trust. But why wouldn't he just come to me or Flu with his findings? Why did he choose to leave breadcrumbs instead?

"Lena," Cait said from behind me, then paused as if something else had caught her attention. She picked up the picture frame and stared at it. "Is this Rachel?"

"Yes."

"Did you know they were dating?" she asked as she set down the picture frame.

"No." I shook my head and turned to her. "Do you think Abram's the one who sent us the videos?"

"It's possible. But why?"

"To protect Rachel." I gestured to the photograph.

Cait gave an uneasy smile. "Flu wants us to head through the kitchen. The officers said that's where Abram's home office is."

I glanced over Cait's shoulders and saw the officers leading Fluellen through the dining room and then into the kitchen. I looked at Cait and nodded before joining Flu on his quest toward the office.

Both the dining room and kitchen were spotless, much like the rest of the house. I thought about the profile of the Casting Call Killer, especially the part about him being well organized. Everything about Abram supported the fact that he could be the Casting Call Killer, but it was my hope that he loved his girlfriend so much that he was willing to do anything for her—and that hope kept me from wanting to believe he was the real culprit.

"In here, Captain," the lead officer said as he opened a door just off the kitchen.

The room felt like an afterthought—an extension built onto the house after Abram had moved in. The wood-paneled walls made the windowless room feel even darker. The only light was a tall lamp in the corner of the room. A large bookcase rested against the wall next to the desk where the computer sat. The desk was free of clutter; the entire house looked like it was staged for an open house.

Although motionless, Abram's computer was somehow eerily full of life, and chills ran through my body. It was as if its sole purpose was to breathe evil into this world—all it needed was someone to do the heavy lifting. The chrome-colored dual monitors sat on top of the desk and matched the keyboard and mouse. The screens just sat there quietly, as if patiently waiting for one of us to approach.

Cait pulled back the office chair after she stretched latex gloves over her hands and fingers. The gloves snapped around her wrists as she took a seat in front of the computer. The three officers had stationed themselves throughout the house, in case Abram or someone else decided to stop by. Flu stood next to Cait as she began her investigation into Abram's hard drive.

Cait turned on the monitors, and I glanced around the room for any signs of Abram's psyche. If Cait was going to be able to figure out Abram's password, it would take several tries and a lot of time. Maybe there would be something in the room that would help us decipher the password.

Next to the desk was a large bookshelf the same height as the door. Every shelf was full of books. A drafting table was against the adjacent wall. A few writing utensils stuck out of the pencil holder. I didn't think of Abram as an architect, but I was finding out a lot about Abram I hadn't known before today.

"There's no password," Cait announced with surprise, and my attention was brought back to the computer.

Flu and I took a step closer and peered at the monitors. She was right. Abram's computer wasn't password protected. It was utterly defenseless to any spying eyes. Someone like Abram, an expert in computers and cyber security, would know the importance of having a password. Instead, he left this piece of machinery completely vulnerable.

Cait looked at Fluellen, and he nodded for her to continue. Icons for basic programs, like email and word processing, neatly aligned on the left screen. On the right screen was a program that was very familiar—though it didn't come standard with the computer. It was the same program Cait had installed on my laptop so that we could access the Deep Web.

The background of Abram's screens was a photograph of the abandoned home where Lathan had housed his victims. It was the same house where Rachel and I had been held captive. I stared at the photo, completely dumbfounded as to why Abram would have chosen that particular picture as his wallpaper. It could have been his motivation to help catch Novak, but that didn't quite fit. Rachel probably would have seen this computer, and I doubted she would've appreciated seeing that house again. My jaw instantly clenched when I saw it, and I was sure that

Rachel would've had a similar reaction.

"It shouldn't be this easy," Cait mumbled to herself. "He would have a password. Everyone has a password," she continued to mutter.

It was the equivalent of leaving his doors unlocked—which was something he had also done. Abram had made it too easy for us to gain access to his home and computer.

He must've known the only way we would've entered his home was with a search warrant. So it was possible he didn't see the need to keep us locked out. That only would have slowed down the process; Abram must've known that if we were already here, we would get in eventually. Maybe unlocking his door and removing his passwords were his way of further assisting the investigation—or raising the white flag? But if that were the case, then where was he? He should've been at the station giving a statement if he truly wanted to help.

I watched Cait click on the Deep Web program. "If he's involved in the Deep Web," Cait said, "he'll have a hidden webmail account."

"Hidden webmail?" I repeated.

"It's just like email but hidden in the Deep Web. It doesn't leave a trace," she added. One by one, emails loaded onto the screen. She scrolled down a long list of emails, and I glanced at how far back they dated.

The message started two weeks after Lathan Collins' murder spree began and ended the day before his death. But that wasn't the only odd part of the emails. Every incoming message was from the same person. I leaned in further so I could see the screen more clearly, to ensure my eyes weren't playing tricks on me.

Every single email was correspondence with Lathan Collins.

I took a deep breath and held it as my heart pounded in my chest. The beat intensified as disquiet grew in my stomach. I could feel my throat spasm as it gave in to the nausea rising in the back of my throat.

Cait placed the mouse over the first email and let it hover, as if she wasn't quite sure whether she wanted to open it. I wasn't sure if I wanted her to either. Doing so would only confirm any involvement between Abram and Lathan. I still wanted to believe that Abram was on our side. I wanted to believe that one of our own wasn't capable of this.

I wanted to believe the impossible.

"Open it," I urged. As much as I wanted to live in blissful ignorance, we had to know the truth. Maybe somewhere in those emails would be a clue as to where Rachel was. The Casting Call Killer—either Novak, or possibly Abram—stated we had five days to figure out who he was. Today was the fifth day. It was also the fifth day that Rachel had been missing. And if the Casting Call Killer was following Lathan's MO, then Rachel's fifth day would be her last.

Cait opened the email and read it to herself.

"Abram's introducing himself to Lathan Collins," she said aloud. *"'I watched your video. Good stuff, man. The way that bitch screamed.'"* Cait continued to read in a low monotone.

"Video?" Flu interrupted. "What video?"

I didn't see a video attached to the email, but I did remember Cait's assertion that the murders were somehow related to Deep Web entertainment.

"Cait theorized that Lathan recorded his victims' deaths," I spoke up, "and then uploaded them to the Deep Web for either payment or entertainment. Maybe both."

"Why would anyone do that?" Flu asked. "Why would anyone watch?" He paused. "Read the rest." He gestured to the screen in front of Cait.

She clicked through multiple emails and scanned the body of each message for highlights of the conversations between Lathan and Abram. "It's mostly Abram praising Lathan for his 'work.' He refers to him as 'an artist with impeccable taste for his craft,'" Cait said as she continued to scan. "This one, here." She opened another message. "This one goes into great detail of one of the murders."

I looked at the date on the message. "That was sent a week after Sophia Good was reported missing," I recalled.

"Lathan skinned his victims, correct?" Cait asked.

"Correct." I nodded. "Except Sophia wasn't skinned. She was fully decapitated."

"I know," Cait said with anguish. "Abram offered Lathan six thousand dollars for her head."

"Jesus Christ," Flu muttered as he took a step back. He ran his hands over his head and gripped what little hair he had as he tried to compose himself. "Agent Porter, stay here and go through the emails— make a copy of each message before we leave. If Abram slipped through our background checks, we have to assume others have too. We can't trust his computer won't be tampered with while it's sitting in evidence," Flu commanded.

As Cait downloaded the emails onto her flash drive, I looked around the room again. Now that I had been standing here for quite some time, it felt strikingly small. It could have been the fact that there were three of us in the space, but there was something else about it.

"Evans, search this room for anything that could possibly link

Abram to the murders or to Lathan Collins," Flu continued. "And I'll let the officers know we'll be conducting a full search of the rest of the house." With that, Flu left.

I stared at the bookcase to the right of the computer and eyed it from top to bottom. Nothing seemed unusual. Books of different sizes and colors were neatly placed on each shelf. I walked toward the bookcase and scanned the titles. Almost every book was about a specific serial killer. Those that weren't about murderers were medical books about human anatomy and body decomposition.

I knelt down to examine the bottom shelf. Only one book resided there. I reached into my pocket and pulled out two latex gloves. I slipped them over my hands before I picked up the beat-up, leather-bound book. The cover was blank as well as the majority of the pages. This was a journal—most likely Abram's personal journal. I flipped through the pages that had writing on them.

Rambled thoughts had been scribbled onto the first one hundred or so pages in thick black ink. There was no organization to the journal. Some pages had sketches of Mirror Woods Lake, other pages told a story of just how troubled Abram's mind was. As I started to read his thoughts, my eyes and my heart stopped when I saw a familiar name: Pamela Westlake.

Then another: Fionna Michaels.

Wilma Reynolds.

Kristin Valeri.

Next to each name was an explanation of how Abram had lured the woman to meet him for an audition. It was exactly as Cait and I had surmised: He'd posted an ad for female actors to audition for lead roles. The auditions had been held at Novak's property downtown, and that was where the murders had taken place.

What I couldn't find in his journal was an explanation of how Novak was involved, or why he specifically sought out actors. I flipped to the beginning of the journal and read each page more carefully.

Musings on 'Lathan's craft,' as Abram referred to it, had been neatly penned, as if his admiration for Lathan was so great that sloppy handwriting would have been an insult to Lathan's memory.

Past the pages with the drawings of Mirror Woods Lake was a detailed plan to commemorate Lathan's legacy. It was Abram's intent to bring Lathan Collins to celebrity status—and to use that newfound fame to secure a movie deal to further preserve Lathan's memory. It was an absurd plan. Then again, given the general population's intrigue and interest with serial killers, maybe it wasn't as ridiculous as it had initially come across.

Abram's plan mainly consisted of recreating the murders in hopes of gaining national attention. That's why he purposely sent the videos to the news stations, and that's why he sent them to West JPD, addressed to me. I was also part of Abram's plan.

According to his diary, he wanted to use my small-town fame as a way to secure a place in the spotlight. I was an obvious choice in his strategy because I was known for one thing in this world: beating Lathan Collins. And there was no better way to ensure nationwide recognition than to make me the focal point of a copycat murder spree.

As I perused the journal, something on the floor caught my attention. Multiple scratch marks were etched in the wood along the edge of the bookcase, as if the bookcase had been moved back and forth dozens of times. The scratches created a quarter-circle pattern.

I placed the journal back on the bottom shelf and stood up as I slid my hands along the frame of the bookcase. My fingertips skimmed the edge of the wall as I felt around for a lever or a switch that would release the bookcase from the wall. I pushed my fingers between the wall and bookcase, nudging it forward slightly in order to peek behind it.

"Did you find something?" Cait asked as she turned away from the computer.

"Yeah," I answered as I pulled the bookcase further from the wall. "Tell Flu to come in here?"

Cait nodded and left the room. The bookcase made new scratch marks as I dragged it across the wood floor. A burst of cool air seeped from behind the bookcase as the back wall was fully exposed—except there wasn't a back wall. The office felt so small because half the room had been concealed behind a dummy wall; the bookcase served as a secret doorway.

The dichotomy of Abram's house was just as demented as he was. The exterior resembled a home that was warm and inviting, much like Abram's exterior. It was bright, with flowers and landscaping, and great care had been taken to preserve the purity of the home.

Inside, however, this hidden room revealed exactly who Abram was. Although it was just as immaculate as the other rooms in the house, the décor, for lack of a better word, was unsettling.

A stale scent filled the dusty room, which was lit only by a sliver of sunlight cutting through a gap in the drapes. A navy blue armchair and matching couch were pushed against the far wall. Between them was an end table covered with tousled newspapers and magazines.

The off-white walls housed several floating shelves of different lengths and heights. They were evenly leveled and free of unwanted clutter. What was on the shelves sent chunks of rancid disgust racing to the back of my throat. I covered my mouth with my hands as I stared at the horrific sight.

"Jesus H...," Flu said as he entered the room. Cait followed closely behind him. We all stared at the same shelving unit. Flu's mouth hung open as he stared wide-eyed at the gruesome presentation ceremoniously displayed before us.

Three clear shadowboxes, like the kinds used to display autographed sports memorabilia, sat on the top shelf. Four more shadowboxes were on the shelf just below it.

Inside each shadowbox was a tattered and decayed face. We were staring at the combined seven victims of Lathan Collins and the Casting Call Killer.

Each victim's skin and hair had been fitted over a Styrofoam head. Pupils and lashes had been delicately painted onto the mannequins' faces to make them appear more lifelike. The flesh resembled the waxy brown texture of a mummified corpse. Wrinkles created dark grooves in their skin as their painted eyes stared into emptiness.

Lisa Johnson, Carmine Jenkins, and Sophia Good resided on the top shelf. Until now, it had been a mystery as to where Lathan Collins stored his trophies. There should have been a fourth shadowbox on that shelf—one that held Angela Truman—but her face had been returned to her body so that she could rest in peace.

The bottom shelf held the faces of the Casting Call Killer's victims. Their faces were less damaged and decayed than the flesh of Lathan's victims.

Pamela Westlake, Fionna Michaels, Kristen Valeri, and Wilma Reynolds neighbored one another as their painted eyes, too, stared into the blank abyss before them.

As grotesque as it all was, there was clearly a certain care that had been taken with each face. Abram undoubtedly cherished these trophies. He had spent a lot of time and tenderness in creating this tomb for his treasures. Each victim's hair had been brushed and held in place with barrettes. Not a single strand was out of place. He was methodical in the handling of his prized possessions. The display resembled a ritualistic adoration—as if he believed these women had died for the greatest reason on earth: to serve as "a testament to Lathan Collins' talent" as Abram had described it in his journal.

"Flu...," I breathed out as I looked toward the corner of the room; another shadowbox sat solo on top of a plant stand. "Novak isn't the Casting Call Killer." My adrenaline kicked in and sent my chest rising.

"How do you know?" Flu followed my stare.

Inside the shadowbox was Novak's decapitated head. His eyes were shut, and his bottom lip drooped into a frown. His gray hair was severely disheveled—the exact opposite of how the female victims were presented. There was no attention paid to Novak's remains. He was cast to the side, not even worthy of being on the shelf.

Flu slumped back as the blow of looking at his friend knocked the wind out of him. A heavy silence fell upon the room as we looked at the demonic display of death before us. Anger and sadness simultaneously rose within my body. I wanted to cry and punch and kick and wail at the person responsible for this. I wanted to do the same to Abram that he had done to Novak and these women, so that he would know what it felt like. But death was too humane for him. Abram deserved to suffer. He deserved to endure the cruelest torture possible, but I wasn't convinced anything I came up with would fit the type of brutality he was capable of.

"Don't touch anything," Flu mustered as he broke the sickening silence in the room. "We'll get Crime Scene here for photos and bagging." He scanned the tomb one last time with an agonizing look on his face, and then he left the room.

A low chirp hummed from behind me, and I reached into my back pocket to pull out my cell phone. "UNKNOWN" loomed across the top of the screen as I stared at my screen.

"Hello?" I answered the call and raised the phone to my ear.

"I see you found who you were looking for," Abram breathed into the phone. I looked around the room for any sign as to how he could've known the exact moment we stumbled upon his sadistic crypt. "Behind you," he said. "Top corner."

I turned around and looked up. There, in the corner of the room, was a small camera overlooking his shrine of faces, like a security guard keeping a watchful eye over Abram's most cherished belongings.

"This spoils my plan. You weren't supposed to find me until tomorrow," Abram playfully said.

Everything I had wanted to say to Abram, to the Casting Call Killer, or to Lathan Collins, escaped my mind. Just seconds ago, I had wanted to rip into him, to claw my hands deep into his chest just to see if he actually had a heart. Now, I was frozen. Not with fear, but with such disbelief that Abram actually found it humorous to call me. He taunted me with me such euphoric arrogance, the kind reserved only for a malicious monster—which he truly was.

As threatening words of hostility filled my head, I brought the receiver closer to my mouth. "Why?" I asked. Sorrow and frustration tangoed in my heart. As good as it would have felt to spit insults at Abram, I needed to know his reasons. I needed to know what could possess another person to do something like this. "Why? Why would you do this to these poor women? To these *innocent* women?"

"Poor women?" Abram repeated. "They served the greatest purpose imaginable," he said. "They had meaningless lives, and I gave them purpose." Pride rose within his voice.

"You can't honestly believe that," I countered. "Lathan is not someone to idolize. He took your girlfriend for Christ's sake."

"Took her?" Abram's voice rose with laughter. "I *gave* her to him." I bowed my head in defeat. There was no use in reasoning with him. Tears welled behind my eyes as the madman on the other end of the line spoke. "You just *had* to be the hero?" he continued. "You couldn't have just left it alone." He paused, and then there was a sudden shift in his tone. "She was meant for him," he growled. "Rachel belonged to him, and you took them *both*." The hatred in his voice swelled, as if I had robbed him of the only thing he ever loved. Maybe I had. By killing Lathan, I had deprived him of ever knowing happiness again.

"Where is she?" The words shook as my body trembled with fury.

"Where she's always been," Abram retorted.

He was toying with me again, throwing out breadcrumbs in the form of riddles. Where has Rachel always been? She's been home—she's been safe. At least physically, she has been. Mentally safe was a different story. If she and I had anything in common, it's that we were still trapped in that basement, figuratively speaking. We were still being held against our will by Lathan.

"The house," I answered. I remembered Abi telling me that someone had recently purchased the home. She couldn't remember the name, but that didn't really matter. Abram was full of aliases.

"Come alone," he hissed into the phone before a brief pause. "No...." His voice shifted. "Bring Agent Porter with you," Abram ordered. "Someone needs to audition for Rachel."

Before I could counter his demand, the line went dead. The abrupt silence left a deafening pierce in my ear. I slipped my phone back into my pocket and looked at Cait. Her face was consumed by curiosity. My mind spun as I tried to pinpoint the words to explain the conversation. Abram's voice echoed in my head as I thought about Rachel and the peril she was in.

If Abram was recreating the murders, then he needed to recreate that night. And there was no one better to play the victims than the original characters themselves. But if Abram needed Cait to audition for Rachel, that meant Rachel was no longer alive. A burst of anger and despair shot from my body, and I cupped my hands over my mouth to hold it in.

"Lena?" Cait took a step closer to me.

"No." I shook my head. "We have to go," I said in a low voice. If Flu, or anyone else, was within earshot, I didn't want to be overheard. This was something I needed to do alone. Not because I wanted to, but because I had to.

If Rachel was alive, showing up to the house with the entire police department would be a guaranteed death sentence for her. If Abram saw Flu and a pack of police officers behind Cait and me, I would be responsible for Rachel's execution. Abram wanted this battle to stay behind closed doors. And if I wanted to give Rachel a chance at survival, I had to play by Abram's rules.

"Okay…." Cait nodded. "Should we tell Flu—"

"No!" I quickly cut her off, my voice still in a whisper. "You have to trust me on this. We just need to leave. Now."

"Lena, what's going?" Cait sternly asked. Her feet firmly planted on the ground as she matched my whispered tone.

"I'll explain in the car," I said as I walked out of Abram's lair. I could feel the painted eyes of each victim staring at me, as if they second-guessed my decision to not tell Flu.

Why didn't any of them understand why I had to do this alone? Rachel was my responsibility. She trusted me to keep her safe. She believed in me one year ago, and I had a feeling she believed in me now. I wasn't going to do anything to jeopardize her life. I wasn't going to do anything to fail as her hero.

The weight of the victims' judgment eased as Cait walked behind me. She had become a shield from their stares. Crime Scene would be here soon, and the remains of each victim would be taken away from here. They would be stored in an isolated section of the evidence room until after the trial, but at least they would no longer be here—in this room, in this hell.

My heart pounded as I walked lightly through Abram's house. I felt like a teenager sneaking out past curfew. Each step was carefully calculated so as to not land on a creaky board. Walking into my dad—or Flu, in this scenario—was the last thing I wanted to do, although it was highly inevitable.

Cait and I had made it back through Abram's kitchen and dining room without running into anyone. All we had to do was make it past the living room and to my car, and I would be able to explain everything. My hope was that Cait understood enough to not talk me out of this. Because there was no talking me out of this. If Cait didn't want to help me, then I would drop her off on the side of the road and fight this war alone.

As we turned into the living room, I saw Flu standing in the middle of the room talking to the two officers. Crime Scene must not have arrived yet, which was a bonus on my end. Crime Scene would want my account of what we'd found, and that would only delay my rescue mission. And that's exactly what this was. I was going to rescue Rachel; I was not going to recover her.

"Did you get everything downloaded?" Flu asked when he saw Cait and me in the living room.

I turned to look at Cait, another silent plea darted from my eyes to hers. Please… just go along with the plan. "I did, yes," Cait answered after giving me a dubious look.

"We're headed to the station," I cut in with a lie. "There's something in a case file I want to reread now that we're certain Abram is behind this."

"Message me the second you find what you're looking for," Flu said. "Crime Scene should be here in less than ten minutes."

A surprise breath of relief escaped my lips, and I quickly smiled to cover any trace of my deceit. This was easier than a kid sneaking out of her house. This was sneaking out of the house when her parents were out of town—and left the car keys by the front door.

We still had to make it to the car before we were in the clear. The euphoric sensation that I got past Flu without having to further explain myself only made my heart pound faster. He didn't even watch us leave. Once I had given Flu my answer, he just nodded and continued his conversation with the officers. It was as if he knew there was no reason not to believe me—not to trust me.

That was why this was so easy: Flu did trust me. He believed I would do what was best for the department, for myself, and for the victims. And that's why I had to lie to him. I had to do what was best for the victims, even if that meant doing the worst for myself.

Before Cait could extend the conversation, I bolted out the front door with the hope that she would follow. My car was parked directly across the street. Thirty feet stood between saving Rachel or Abram finishing what Lathan had started. Cait's footsteps down the short set of stairs fell in unison with the pounding of my heart. She was still behind me. She was going to come with me, and with no questions asked—so far.

I shoved my hand into my coat pocket and grabbed my car keys. I clicked the sensor to unlock the doors and opened the driver's side door once I saw Cait walk around to the passenger's side. She seemed as worried and concerned as I was. She knew it was her duty to protect those who needed it, but she didn't have to go into that duty blindly. I needed to tell her the truth, but doing so could gravely affect Rachel.

Once inside the car, I turned the ignition before Cait put her seatbelt on. Without even checking the side mirrors to see if there were any cars behind me, I pulled away from the curb and drove down Abram's street. I kept my eyes on the road in front of us. I didn't want to see Flu in the rearview mirror in case he'd decided to come outside for a few more questions.

The farther I drove, the more I pushed on the gas pedal. It was a quiet residential area that wouldn't take too kindly to someone speeding down the road, even if that someone was a detective on the verge of catching a monster. But I didn't care. I had somewhere to be.

"Lena, slow down," Cait insisted. The click of her seatbelt echoed in the car. I eased my foot off the accelerator, and the car slowed to a slightly less offensive speed. "Who was on the phone?" She turned her body toward me as she sat in the passenger seat. She was not letting herself settle in for a nice joyride. She knew I was headed somewhere with purpose and that this journey would certainly lead us to a destination filled with danger.

"Abram." I avoided her stare.

"Why didn't you tell Flu?" Cait looked out the rear window, as if she thought Flu would still be within eyeshot. "He needs to know," she added.

"I know." I nodded.

"Turn around… or call him…"

"I can't."

"Why not?" I could feel Cait's eyes searching me for a logical explanation. "What did Abram say?" Cait's plea turned to concern.

"He has Rachel." I finally took my eyes off the road and looked at Cait. Her stiff posture deflated into a stewed slump. "The Casting Call Killer told me we had five days to figure out who he is. Today is the fifth day." I brought my eyes back to the road, then to Cait again. She didn't seem to understand the correlation with the fifth day. "Lathan Collins kept his victims alive for five days," I reminded her. "Rachel has been missing for five days."

I weaved in and out of traffic as I continued driving toward Mirror Woods. Cait wasn't familiar with the area. So if she believed we were headed to the station, she wouldn't know I was going the opposite way.

"Why would Abram do that to his girlfriend?" she asked.

"I found Abram's journal in his office," I confessed. "It explains everything. He wants to carry on Lathan's legacy... his plan... so Lathan can become a pop-culture icon. He wants Lathan to have the same level of fame as Manson or Dahmer. And he thinks the only way to do that is to tell Lathan's stories through a series of copycat murders."

"That's why he has Rachel." Cait answered her own question. "That's why he wants you...." Her thoughts trailed off as she took in our surroundings. "Where are we going, Lena?"

"Mirror Woods."

"Mirror Woods?" Cait's words were laden with confusion. "Why? You told Flu we were going to the station."

I sped through the entrance of Mirror Woods, and the first of the fallen autumn leaves blew around the car's tires. For the most part, Mirror Woods was one long road that led to a dead end. But along that mile-long road were obscure service roads that led to boating docks and hiking trails.

"I know." I kept my eyes on the road. "Abram has Rachel. She's at *the* house in Mirror Woods. I can't leave her there."

"You aren't. We can call for backup," Cait bargained.

"You just have to trust me."

"Call for backup." Her demand was grim. As much as I wanted to argue with her, I knew she was right. I needed to turn the car around—or at least pull over and call for backup. I eased my foot off the gas and prepared to turn down the next service road. "I don't know what crusade you're on to get yourself killed," Cait continued, "but I'm not going to—"

Before she could finish her sentence, a speeding force, like a meteoroid travelling at the speed of light, rammed into the passenger side of the car. Glass from the window shattered around Cait. It created an aura of shimmering crystals around her frame. Her hair blew forward as the force of the speeding object pushed her closer toward me. Then the dashboard snapped from the front of the car. It crushed together like an accordion. I gripped the steering wheel as the entire car was pushed off the road by the massive force that seemingly came from nowhere.

Cait's body was locked in place by her seatbelt, but her arms and head flailed forward. I kept my focus on her face as the world outside started to spin. Loud clashes of metal hitting pavement echoed through the car as it tumbled onto its side, as if we were a pair of shoes cycling through the dryer.

The driver's side airbag exploded from the steering wheel and ricocheted off my face. It pummeled me harder than a punch in the nose. My skull shot back into the headrest as the car slid onto its side. Sparks of metal danced in the street as the car skidded into the trees. The roof dented inward, pinning Cait's head between it and the seat.

My vision faded in and out, and the throbbing in my head was so severe I was sure that something foreign had been imbedded under my scalp. I fought to keep my eyes open. I had to help Cait. I had to get us out of there.

As I looked in her direction, all I could see was a blurred abstract of her frame. Cuts on her face from the shattered windows slowly dribbled blood down her cheeks. It was hard to tell if she was breathing. Her eyes were closed, and I couldn't hear her breath. All I could hear was a high-pitched ringing throughout my head.

She hung in her seat like an unconscious soldier dangling from a tree in his parachute. She was completely unaware and unresponsive to the dire state we were in. I could see the tips of the trees from outside her window, and a few puffy white clouds that slowly blew by. The bright morning was becoming dull and dark, as if black paint was being brushed over my eyes.

I mustered all the strength I had in my body to try to free Cait, but my limbs felt encased in cement. I was trapped in this car. *We* were trapped in this car. My arms and legs were completely useless. A wave of nausea coursed through my stomach as my head tipped to the side. Just before my vision went pitch black, I saw a pair of legs covered in navy blue overalls walking toward the car. I let out a low breath as my lungs and heart went still, and the darkness consumed my eyes.

CHAPTER | TWENTY

A JARRING CHILL IN the air crept up my spine as my eyes slowly opened. I winced at the constant throbbing in the back of my head, and I blinked my vision into focus. Slowly, the cold, damp room came into view. A single light bulb hung perfectly still. It wasn't bright enough to reach all four corners of the room, but I didn't need light to know where I was. The putrid mildew smell, the chillingly cold air, and the familiar cement walls told me everything I needed to know.

I reached down and felt my ankle. It was the confirmation I needed for this palpable situation. Wrapped around my ankle, binding me to this basement, was a steel cuff—much like the one around my ankle one year ago. I rested my head against the cement wall as I came to terms with the realization.

My chest ached as my lungs expanded, and I opened my mouth to breathe more air. The bridge of my nose pulsed in unison with the throbbing in my head. I brushed my fingertips under my nostrils. Hardened and congealed blood had set into my upper lip. I was able to breathe from only one nostril, a clear indication of a broken septum. No doubt a casualty from the airbag.

As I looked around the room, I noticed the wall across from me. The same articles about the Faceless Killer that resided there a year ago were still on display. As improbable as it was for those articles to be there, I knew why they were there. Crime Scene had taken everything in this room when they collected evidence last year, but if Abram had Lathan's case files, he could have easily put the articles back on the wall.

The mementos in the room were here on purpose. Abram wanted to recreate that night. And he needed me in order to do it.

I had fallen directly into his trap.

This was exactly where he wanted me to be: shackled to the same wall that Lathan had cuffed me to. The easy access into his house, the lack of a password on his computer... all part of his plan to get me here. His manifesto on the bookcase, the phone call demanding I come here... all so that I would willingly drive to Mirror Woods—where he could run us off the road.

Us.

Cait and me.

A burst of adrenaline shot through my veins as I frantically scanned the room for any sign of Cait. The edges of the space were too dark to see if she was here, but I knew better than to think she'd be propped in a corner. I knew why Abram wanted Cait with me: so that she could play the part of Rachel.

Lathan had shackled Rachel by the staircase, and I knew that's where Abram would have Cait. I stared in the direction of the stairs and sat very still as hope filled my heart. I begged to hear any sound that Cait may be down here with me—and, even more, that she was still alive.

The single bulb's light spread to the staircase, but the stillness of the air offered no resolve regarding Cait's whereabouts. If she was alive, her breath was too shallow to hear.

"Cait," I whispered, but I was greeted by silence. "Cait," I called again as I crawled closer to the staircase. My journey was quickly cut short when the cuff around my ankle tightened. I looked back at the shimmering metal vice as it mocked my attempt to break free.

A flash of the car crash invaded my vision, and I remembered the look on Cait's face as we were struck. There was no doubt that Abram was the cause of that crash. It was his way of rendering us helpless in order to bring us to this goddamn house. I couldn't tell if Cait was breathing when Abram hit us from the side. If she was, Abram would have brought her here too. I just had to find her.

And I clung to that belief like a magnet to metal. I needed to believe Cait was alive. If she wasn't, her death was on my hands. I was the one who fooled her into coming here. I had blindly taken her to Mirror Woods. And if this was where she met her end, then I was the one who drove her to it. Whatever happened to Cait was my fault.

I sank back as I looked up the staircase. If Abram was here, I didn't want him to know I was awake. He had me in this basement for a reason. If he really wanted me dead, he would have killed me already. I knew he had different plans for me, and those plans required my being alive.

I reached back to pry the cuff open, but it was like trying to snap a tree trunk in half. The cold metal embedded itself into my skin as I tried to break it open. If I was going to get out of this cuff, I was going to need a key. Or something flat enough to pry the lock open.

The underwire in my bra. That worked the last time. I felt under my breast, but my bra was gone. There was nothing between my shirt and skin. Abram must have taken it. I swallowed back the sickening thought of Abram reaching under my shirt, touching my bare skin. Lathan hadn't sexually assaulted his victims, and there was no evidence to prove the Casting Call Killer had either, but the thought of Abram working his fingers against the metal clasp felt just as violating. And, what's worse, I wasn't going to be able to make a DIY key out of underwire this time.

There were so many ways Abram could have known how I'd gotten myself out of the cuffs last year: Rachel's book, the reports in Lathan's files, the records kept on the department's server. It was also possible that Rachel had told Abram herself. I could only imagine how many times Rachel had told Abram the story of her captivity—under the impression her boyfriend was lending a sympathetic ear, but really for his own debauched amusement.

Lathan had thought to check my pockets for anything I could use to break the chains open, but that didn't mean Abram did. I dragged my hands over my pants pockets. They were completely smooth to the touch. The pockets inside my blazer were also empty. My gun, cell phone, and badge were missing too.

I sat back against the cement wall and took a deep breath through my mouth. I had to remain calm. Controlling the situation was the only weapon I had at this point.

Abram may have been able to move me—and hopefully Cait—to this house without being detected, but there was no way he would have been able to clean up the mess from the accident, or to move the car without someone seeing him. Mirror Woods was deserted in the early to late morning, but by mid-afternoon, it was a hotspot for hikers and nature enthusiasts.

Someone would see the wrecked vehicle and report it to the police. Once the officer ran the plates, it would come up that the car was registered to our department. Flu would remember that was the car I had driven to Abram's this morning. He would think it was rather suspicious that the car I was driving was found in Mirror Woods but I was nowhere in sight. He knew the Casting Call Killer was a copycat of the Faceless Killer. It was only a matter of time before Flu figured it out and checked this house. I just had to wait.

But there was the subject of Cait. If she was here—and alive— every second I wasted put her further in jeopardy. If she needed medical attention, she couldn't wait for a Good Samaritan to call in the crash. She couldn't wait for Flu to connect the dots. Her rescue had to happen now.

I reached down and felt the cuff again. Even if I had to break my ankle, I was going to get out of this restraint. I pushed the cuff down my ankle, and the cold metal dug into my skin. I clenched my jaw as a surge of pain attacked every part of my body. I took another deep breath and forced the cuff down further. The skin around my ankle broke. A cry escaped my lips as I let my breath out. I paused as the pain settled.

I had moved the cuff less than a millimeter, and it was the worst pain I had ever felt, like razor blades had been shoved into my skin, digging deeper into the muscle with each push. I cupped my hands around my ankle and squeezed. I hoped the pressure would alleviate some of the pain. My fingers rested along my boot and landed against the zipper. My pinky finger lightly skimmed the thin, flat pull tab of the zipper.

The thin, flat pull tab. The thin *and* flat pull tab. If I could break the pull tab off the slider, that might be exactly what I needed to pick the cuff's lock.

I gripped the tab between my thumb and index finger and twisted it to the side. I felt the slider bend as I twisted harder. The tab imbedded itself into my skin as I applied more pressure. It felt as if the pull tab had sunk so deep into my skin that it rested against bone—but it hurt less than sliding the cuff down my ankle.

I rocked the pull tab back and forth, twisting it with all my might. I took another deep breath and held it as forced the pull tab to break through the slider. A low snap echoed in the otherwise quiet room as the tab broke from the slider. There, between my index finger and thumb, was a possible key to my escape.

I lowered it to the cuff and pushed it into the keyhole. I pried it back and forth until I felt the lock give way. The cuff loosened as the release opened. I gripped the cuff in both hands and pulled it open. The shackle fell to the cement floor with a low rattle, and I stared at the restraint with euphoria.

I was free.

Excitement rose through my body, but before I could stand, a slow clap sounded from the darkest edge of the basement. I turned my head to the corner opposite the staircase and peered into the darkness. The clap picked up speed until it sounded like one-man applause. As my eyes adjusted, I saw a shadowed silhouette against the wall. The clap continued.

The shadow took a step toward the light. All I could see were tan work boots and the bottoms of blue coveralls. The same pants I saw walking toward the car after the accident. The man clasped his hands together as he took another step forward. I could only see his torso.

"I'm impressed."

"Abram," I muttered. But before I could come back with any type of retort, he bolted from the shadows like a dragster and screeched to a halt as he knelt in front of me.

My mouth fell open as my eyes swelled with tears at the horrific sight in front of me. I immediately recognized the person in front of me—the face that covered Abram's.

Rachel Sanzone's pared skin had been stretched over Abram's head, masking his face with hers. His hazel eyes peeked from the open sockets where Rachel's eyes should have been. I stared into his pupils, and a kaleidoscope of terror stared back at me. I shook as anger and grief grew inside me.

Everything I feared was right before my eyes. I failed the one person who needed me the most. I didn't rescue Rachel from Lathan; I only prolonged her torture. A year's worth of PTSD and sleepless nights as she relived that nightmare every day—all because of me. Everything Rachel did to survive her time with Lathan was for nothing.

Abram paused in front of me, as if he wanted me to marvel at what he had done. He looked proud of his achievement, and his smile beneath Rachel's cheeks proved it. He sucked in a deep breath as his sinister smile widened.

Bile rose from deep within my stomach and scorched the back of my throat. Tears welled over my eyes and poured down my cheeks. "No...." I quietly sobbed. As I locked eyes with the monster before me, all I could see was Rachel. Her once beautiful face stretched into a massacre of carnage over his. What this sick beast did to her was more grotesque than anything Lathan had done. Abram took his girlfriend's trust and used it against her. He manipulated and tortured her. He made her suffer through excruciating betrayal because he had a grander plan in mind.

And she went through all of it because of me.

I was supposed to protect her. I was supposed to save her. If I had figured out who the Casting Call Killer was just a few days sooner, Rachel would still be alive. She would still have her face.

Anger jump-started my heart into a blind fury, and I lunged at Abram. Tears streamed down my face as hatred coursed through my veins. He was nothing more than a predator attacking a child—a coward feasting off the weak. Disgust raged through my body as I fixated on ending him. I visualized pulling his limbs from his body, hearing the hollow rip of skin tearing from skin.

He sneered as I clasped my hands around his throat and squeezed. I squeezed so hard I could have crumbled a brick into dust, but Abram just continued to laugh. My arms shook as all my strength went into the grip I had on him. I wasn't doing this for me. I was doing this for Rachel, and for the four other women he'd murdered. They were the strength I needed to end him.

My hands were still around his throat when he brought his fist back and fired it like a cannonball against my already broken nose. A gruesome cracking rang through the room as I shot back against the cement. My head hit the wall, and I slumped to the ground. As I gasped for air, the taste of mildew filled my mouth, and I lay in the fetal position as I succumbed to the womb of his madness.

Abram stood above me, his fists clenched and his breath heavy. I tried to stand. My numb limbs caved under my weight, and I collapsed to the ground again. "Get up," Abram growled. "Get. Up." His voice rose with distinct loathing.

As I steadied myself, he grabbed my hair. His fist pressed against my neck as he yanked me back. It felt as if my scalp was going to rip from my skull as he pulled me up. I stumbled as he dragged me up the stairs. My knees banged against each step as I was forcibly taken hostage.

I knew where he was leading me, but I didn't know why. Up the stairs, past the door, was where I had fought Lathan and barely won. As Abram led me upward, I grabbed at his firm grasp on my hair and tried to pry his fingers loose. He was too strong. When he reached the top of the stairs, he pushed the door open and shoved me through it. I fell to the floor and slid along the linoleum.

I crashed into the dilapidated kitchen cabinets, and Abram immediately brought me to my feet again. He dragged me alongside him then shoved me onto a wooden chair in the center of the kitchen, which led straight into the wood-paneled living room. That's where I saw Abram's horrifying artistry displayed.

Taped to the living room walls were newspaper clippings, much like the ones downstairs. These articles, however, were editorials about the Casting Call Killer. My eyes drifted from the articles down to what was in front of the wall—a casket surrounded by dozens of thick, white candles. Each candle sat upon individual iron candleholders, ranging in height from two to four feet tall. The flames flickered in the drafty space, creating a dramatic glow around his altar.

Interspersed within the candles were three white plaster podiums, each three feet tall. On top of each podium was a single Styrofoam head. They were the same as the ones in Abram's secret lair, minus the painted eyes.

I followed the candlelight until I reached the main focal piece: the casket. The lid was propped open, revealing an off-white silk sheet and matching pillow. The mahogany wood reflected the candles' glow, and my lungs stopped mid-breath as my eyes widened. Resting inside the coffin was what was left of Rachel Sanzone.

Her body was intact, except for her face. She wore a light purple dress, and her arms and hands were neatly folded over her chest. Her eyelids were the only skin remaining on her head. Stubborn chunks of muscle and tendons decorated her skull as she lay motionless, like a plastic doll tossed aside.

My heart sank to the pit of my stomach as I stared, horrified, at the grotesque display. Nausea rendered my limbs lifeless. Abram appeared in front of me and plopped a stack of papers on my lap.

I looked down. There, upon my lap, was the script to Lathan's story. I brought my eyes up to Abram as I glared at his audacious attempt to turn me into his pawn.

"Page seventy-three," Abram directed from behind Rachel's face. I defied his command as he walked toward the kitchen counter, which served as a divider to the living room. With his back to me, he pulled out a camcorder attached to a tripod. In a rhythmic stride, almost as if it was part of a dance, Abram placed the tripod ten feet in front of me. He pointed the camcorder in my direction. "Page seventy-three," he repeated with a stricter tone. He turned on the camcorder.

I looked at him the same way a rebellious student looks at a mandatory homework assignment. I was not going to be a part of his game. I was not going to be the final brush stroke he needed to complete this sadistic painting. If he wanted me to read this script, he was going to have to move my cold, dead jaw and read it for me.

Abram believed he was in control of the situation. He was in control with Pamela Westlake and Fionna Michaels. He was in control with Wilma Reynolds and Kristen Valeri. He even had control with Rachel.

But not with me.

He was able to overpower his victims because he had their trust. He falsely dangled their dreams in front of them. He also had an assistant. He had neither in this scenario. I took his sidekick from him. And he did not have my trust. I was already aware of the evil inside him.

He did not have control.

As my defiance filled the room, so did Abram's obvious frustration. He walked toward me with heavy feet and grabbed the script from my lap. He fumbled through the pages until he landed on the correct page. He scooped my hand in his and slapped the script inside it. We stared at each other as the battle for control continued.

"Read it," he snarled.

I peered down at the pages in my hand, and I silently read the words that described Abram's admiration for Lathan. Lathan was more than Abram's mentor; he was his heart and soul. Lathan was the reason Abram lived.

"How could you love a monster?" I cried. "What he did to those women—what you've done to those women. Carmine Jenkins, Angela Truman, Lisa Johnson—"

"Those women?" Abram shouted. "*Those* women humiliated him. They laughed at him, so *he* laughed at them. He took their skin and wore it, laughing the entire time."

"They laughed at him?" I repeated. It had been difficult for us to piece together Lathan's motives. Murders that heinous were usually lust-fueled. But with Lathan's victims, there were no indications of sexual assault.

"Lathan was a brilliant man, and they treated him like an imbecile," Abram replied. "They're not laughing now, are they?" He smirked from under the mask.

During the course of the initial investigation, we'd discovered that Lathan had a history of being bullied. He'd been tormented in middle school and high school. He'd even been expelled for bringing a knife to school—in an admitted attempt to physically hurt the kids who'd taunted him. If he did feel belittled by these women, it could have sent him into heightened sense of rage.

"Read!" Abram's demand impaled my thoughts. Then he paused, as if he'd just reached a malicious epiphany. "You need a scene reader." He grinned. He took a few steps away from me and disappeared behind the wall that separated the kitchen and living room. My heart froze as scraping sounds soured the silent air.

A high-pitched squeal belched from behind the wall as Abram reappeared. He was dragging a chair behind him as he re-entered the kitchen. With a loud plop, Abram placed the chair adjacent to the camcorder.

Tied to the chair, with her mouth taped shut, was Cait. Her face was bruised and cut from the accident, but she was alive. At least, she appeared to be. She sat bound to the chair in a lifeless slump. If she was dead, though, Abram wouldn't have gone to the trouble of incapacitating her.

The hope that Cait was alive was exactly the fuel I needed to rise from this weakened state and overpower Abram. The last bit of strength inside me amplified. With the script still in my hand, I tackled Abram like a linebacker on steroids. He fell to the ground as I landed on top of him, and pages of the script scattered around us as our crashing bodies knocked the camcorder and tripod to the ground.

We rolled on the floor, our limbs intertwined, as we wrestled for control. We both threw frantic punches in an attempt for domination. I braced my body for impact as one of Abram's lucky blows collided with the side of my rib cage.

I choked on my own breath as it launched from my lungs, and Abram stood up. He stretched his long arms in front of him and curled his fingers around my neck. With the strength of what felt like a dozen men, he picked me off the ground and shot me against the kitchen wall.

I clamped my hands around his as he held me high above the ground. My legs kicked out as I tried to break free, but each strike to his shins and legs was like a toddler kicking a steel pipe. I couldn't break free.

Abram tightened his grip around my neck as I wrapped my fingers around his. I gasped for air as he continued to hold me in place. His eyes were full of rage, and I prepared for his vengeance. It was only a matter of seconds before he inevitably crushed my throat.

I was sparring with a demon. And I was losing.

I looked past Abram, past Rachel's blood-soaked hair matted against his head. I focused on the newspaper articles on the wall behind him. Every name on that wall was because of me. Had I done my job correctly, all of those women would be alive right now. Abram's victims were a casualty of my careless detective work. And if Lathan was still alive—if I hadn't gone into the house alone last year—Abram might not have sought revenge for his hero's death.

Maybe I deserved to be here, captive in Abram's clutch. This was my doing. And I should know what it's like to be the one to suffer at Abram's hands.

As the room grew dark, I made peace with my demise. I would no longer be responsible for this murder investigation. I would no longer disappoint the victims or their families. Even if I could catch the bad guy, I wouldn't be able to beat him.

A black haze coated my vision as my focus returned to Abram. He tilted his head as he stared at me. He looked at me with such wonderment, as if he couldn't believe he'd actually won. I squeezed my eyes closed as I prepared to hear the crunch of my crushed esophagus.

Abram took a deep breath, and I pictured his sinister smile as it crinkled the corners of Rachel's lips. It was the last surge of energy he needed to destroy me.

I instinctually gasped for one last breath as the force of Abram's grip lightly loosened. I opened my eyes. Why won't he just kill me? It's what he's wanted since the beginning.

Abram's arms shook as he held back the might within his hands. He wasn't allowing himself to kill me. Maybe this was all part of his game, to torture me into briefly believing I was going to live.

But that didn't match the look in his eyes.

It was as if I was his favorite toy—and killing me would kill the only thrill he had to live for. Tormenting me and stalking me had become his obsession. I had become his obsession. And if he killed me, he would no longer have a purpose.

Why did he care, though? He would soon find a new obsession. Once he'd completed his mission of solidifying Lathan's legacy, he would continue his mayhem. He had more than a taste for it. It was more than an addiction. It was a part of him now.

My eyes drifted from Abram, past Rachel's ceremoniously displayed body, and over to Cait. Once he was finished with me, he would move on to her. Even if she was already dead, that didn't mean he didn't have plans for her. Those three Styrofoam heads on those three podiums had a purpose. They were there to display Abram's handy work. It didn't take a police sergeant to figure out one was for Rachel, one was for me, and one was reserved for Cait.

She didn't deserve to be part of Abram's perversions. She deserved to be laid to rest in peace and intact. Her family didn't deserve the burden of knowing she had been part of some psychopath's cruel sport. I was the one who brought her here, and I had to be the one to get her out.

The image of Cait's raw flesh drooping over a Styrofoam head as chunks of blood clung to her sliced skin drove a rush of adrenaline directly to my core. The will I needed to live awoke with a ferocious desire to obliterate Abram for good.

As that spark ignited, Abram's grip tightened around my throat. My hands fell away from his, and I placed my hands on top of his mask. I peeled Rachel's raw skin from Abram's face; pieces of her fell to the ground like strips of frayed fabric. There, beneath her torn skin, was Abram's true self: still a monster, but no longer hiding behind a mask.

If he was going to commit these acts, it wasn't going to be under a guise. The hellacious beast inside him was going to be on display, just as he displayed his victims. He was going to have to face his true self.

Streaks of dried blood stained the exposed parts of Abram's face, and he emitted a low growl as I slammed my foot against the wall and pushed myself toward him. He staggered as my full weight of my body shoved him back, and he tripped over the fallen tripod, sending both of us to the ground.

We landed against the casket, knocking candles off their holders and onto the floor. The candles continued to burn as they lay on their side. Pages of the script caught fire. One candle had fallen into the casket. Flames rose as the silk sheet caught fire.

Disoriented from the fall, Abram looked around the room. His face contorted with confusion, as if he didn't understand how he'd lost control. I brought my knee back and struck the side of his face with my foot. The rubber sole of my boot collided against his cheek. His body shot six feet back as he flew across the floor.

Before I could stand up, Abram scrambled to his feet. The wood-paneled walls were alive in a blaze of golden fury as flames engulfed the living room. Abram, now standing, choked on the thick smoke that blackened the room. His chest rose and fell as he took a few deep breaths, inhaling more smoke than air.

His eyes finally found me, and he hurled himself toward me. As his body soared into the air, I grabbed the tallest iron candleholder and raised it between us. The iron spear pierced Abram's chest, cracking his rib cage as the spike of the candleholder tore through him.

I held the iron steady as Abram's slumped body inched down the spear. Blood gurgled in his throat as he reached his arms forward and wrapped his hands around my neck again. He squeezed as he continued his slide down the iron spike, but his limbs were rapidly losing strength. Blood gushed from his fatal wound, and I fought to keep the candleholder upright as Abram's lifeless body lowered onto mine.

I took a deep breath as I heaved the candleholder, along with his body, toward the floor. His hands were still clasped around my neck, and I turned to my side and faced him as I pried his fingers from my throat.

Abram was dead.

As I stared at this vile creature, my skin began to burn. I looked around the living room. It was completely in flames. The newspaper articles on the walls had burned into the wood paneling. Rachel's corpse blazed a fiery glow as it, too, burned.

The room cracked and hissed as the fire took over. I sat up to get away from the flames. And I saw Cait. She was still unconscious, tied to the chair. With my last ounce of energy, I hobbled toward her and grabbed the back of the chair. I dragged her through the kitchen and toward the backdoor. It felt like I was pulling a cruise ship across desert sand, but I wasn't going to give up. She wasn't going to be Abram's last victim.

Each step sent an excruciating stab through my ankle. Inch by inch, I slid the chair through the kitchen until I reached the backdoor and pulled it open. Fresh air blew into the house and ignited the flames even higher. The fire had traveled into the kitchen, scorching the decrepit cabinets. I pulled Cait outside and dragged her fifty feet through muddy grass and collapsed to the ground.

With my face pressed to the dirt, I sucked in clean air until my lungs felt like they were going to burst. If I could sleep for a millennia, it wouldn't be long enough. The slight chill in the air succumbed to the heat that escaped the burning house, and I closed my eyes. Someone would see the fire and call for help. All I had to do was wait.

I was safe. Cait was safe.

And the Casting Call Killer was finally burning in hell.

EPILOGUE

A STEADY STREAM OF mourners trailed through the cemetery and made their way toward Novak's closed casket. His portrait, was displayed on top of the casket, was surrounded by dozens of single red roses that his friends and coworkers placed around the picture frame. Flu and I were in the front row, and I could see the sorrow on Flu's face as it reflected off the black coffin that was barely five feet in front of us.

It had been three weeks since we'd discovered Novak's body, but that didn't make laying him to rest any easier. To avoid a trial that surely would've ended in the death penalty, James Coffer had made a plea deal with the prosecuting attorney. In exchange for telling West JPD where Novak and Kristen Valeri were buried, he would be sentenced to life in prison without the possibility of parole. I wasn't happy with the plea, but for the sake of Kristen Valeri's family, I agreed to the sentencing.

Kristen Valeri and Ryan Novak had both been buried deep within Mirror Woods. If James Coffer hadn't escorted West JPD to the exact location, their graves never would have been found. Even the cadaver dogs had a hard time picking up a scent. After both bodies had been discovered, James Coffer was put in the back of the cruiser and driven to the station—where he was promptly transferred to a maximum-security prison.

I stared at the coffin, and the sound of weeping officers echoed through the crowd as we listened to stories about Novak. It was hard not to laugh through the tears, as every story was filled with love and humor. Novak had been a great detective, and an even better man. The circumstances of his death could never take away how cherished he was within our department. Knowing that brought some comfort to this day—though not a lot.

The remaining leaves on the trees were boldly colored in orange, red, and yellow hues. The dry leaves on the ground scattered about the cemetery. They collected around our feet and fell into the six-foot-deep hole that would soon be Novak's final resting place.

I slipped my hand between Flu's arm and waist and leaned against him. He provided great shade from the afternoon sun, but he was also a shield from my own emotions. There was no doubt that some people here thought I should be the one in that coffin. I could feel the other officers' glares pierce into my back. They would have easily traded my life for Novak's. He had become collateral damage in a war that had nothing to do with him. He shouldn't have paid the price for my life, but he did. And that was something I was going to live with for the rest of my life.

"Captain?" An officer gestured to Flu.

Flu took a deep breath, and I let my hand slip from his elbow. He cleared his throat and adjusted his tie, then stood up and took two steps forward. He turned to face the crowd. His eyes were red and filled with tears, and his sorrow-stricken face looked as if it weighed two hundred pounds. He glanced down at the ground, kicked at a loose pebble by his shoe, and shoved his hands into his pockets. For once, he wasn't a captain about to deliver a speech to his unit; he was a man grieving for his best friend.

"Ryan Novak was...." Flu paused as he looked at the crowd with a blank gaze. He took a deep breath and let it out as he turned his head toward Novak's picture. "Ryan Novak was the kind of man who would have given his life for any one of us," Flu said as he turned back to face the crowd. "In all my years as an officer, I have yet to meet someone who has a purer heart than Novak. Not a day goes by that I don't think, 'How could I have prevented this?' I was his captain, and I let him down. But the truth is that there's only one person who could have prevented this, and he chose not to. Novak spent the majority of his life doing what he loved. He helped people. He saved people. No one can take his good name away from him, and no one can destroy how he will be remembered." Flu bowed his head as if he was saying a silent prayer, and then walked back to his spot next to me without saying another word.

Flu's brief but powerful eulogy lingered over the crowd as we all sat in silence. The weight of Flu's words sank deep into my heart. It seemed Flu also felt responsible for Novak's death. But he was right—the only person responsible for Novak's death was Abram. It was going to take some time before my guilt came to terms with that fact, but hearing Fluellen acknowledge who was truly to blame provided a jumpstart on letting that guilt go.

As the funeral ended, I caught a glimpse of Cait in my peripheral. She was in the far corner of the back row of attendees. She was dressed in a black pantsuit, and she smiled at the few detectives from West JPD that she had met while investigating the Casting Call Killer.

This was the first time I'd seen her in three weeks, and that was mostly due to my own actions. Cait had called and texted me several times, and I ignored every single one. The remorse of putting her life in jeopardy made it impossible to speak to her. I wanted to hear her voice, and I wanted to see her face, but I didn't want to deal with the shame I felt for risking her life.

It was fortunate for me that she had gone back to Lyons shortly after her quick stint in the hospital. From what Flu had told me about that night, the park ranger saw the smoke and drove toward the flames to investigate. He then called the fire department as soon as he saw the house engulfed in flames. During a quick perimeter check, the ranger found Cait and me unconscious in the backyard.

My stay at the hospital had been longer than Cait's. Doctors had released her after only two nights of observation, but I had been there for almost a week. Due to the sensitivity of the case, two security officers had been stationed outside my door to ward off any nosey reporters. The only person authorized to visit, aside from the nurses and doctors, was Flu. Even if Cait had wanted to see me—and I'm not sure whether she even tried—she wouldn't have gotten past security.

Upon my release from the hospital, I had been granted twelve weeks of medical leave. During that time, I was expected to heal—not just physically, but also mentally—from what had happened with Abram. I could have been given an eternity, and that still wouldn't have been enough time.

I was consumed not only with the guilt from practically driving Cait to her death sentence but also with complete uncertainty. I had fought two beasts, and I had barely won both times. But I was no more of a hero than I was before. I wasn't a detective because I enjoyed the glamour of a job well done; I was a detective because I wanted to make West Joseph a safer place to live.

But I didn't see myself staying in West Joseph much longer. I couldn't. It had become a swamp filled with toxic memories. The more I trudged through the murky waters, the more I realized I was never going to be happy here. I would never be free of Lathan or Abram's torment. I had become a prisoner of West Joseph. And although I was the warden of my own jail cell, I couldn't find the strength to turn the key and let myself out.

Without West Joseph, though, I had nothing. I was no one. My entire identity was dependent on the success of my career and the notoriety that came with it. If I wasn't Detective Sergeant Lena Evans, who was I?

I wasn't ready to retire, but it felt like West JPD was ready to retire from me. I brought too much peril to the department and to the officers within it. Novak was a testament to that statement. And so was Cait.

I stood up and moved off to the side when the memorial service ended. I watched Cait maneuver through a herd of mourners as they made their way to their cars. If Cait had seen me standing here, then she would have come over—unless she took my obvious hints that I didn't want to speak to her. I knew she had something she wanted to say to me, probably something along the lines of how could I have been so careless with her life? But whatever she wanted to say, maybe she knew Novak's funeral wasn't the place to say it.

I turned my back to Cait and the rest of the officers and walked further into the cemetery. Off in the distance, less than fifty yards away, was a frail woman in front of a tombstone. Fresh dirt was beneath her feet. She hugged herself in a loose embrace as she stared at the marble stone, as if hypnotized by its presence. As I studied the woman, I realized I didn't need to read the name on the tombstone to know who she was.

"Rachel's funeral was yesterday," Flu said from behind me, and I could feel him gesture toward Mrs. Sanzone as she stood in front of her daughter's grave.

"Did you go?" I kept my back to him.

"I did." He paused. "I'm a little disappointed I didn't see you there."

"Flu." I turned to face him. "What would I say to her?" I asked, referring to Mrs. Sanzone. Although somewhat rhetorical, I was interested to hear his thoughts. I had gone back and forth on the notion of attending Rachel's funeral. But knowing I would have to see Mrs. Sanzone—her exhausted and permanently tear-stained face—was what ultimately confirmed I wouldn't attend. There was nothing on earth I could say to her that would have brought any comfort. There was nothing that I could do that would bring her daughter back. I knew I was the last person Mrs. Sanzone wanted to see. I may not have been able to save her daughter, but I was able to keep my distance, to spare her the agony of seeing me.

"Sometimes just showing up is all you need to do," Flu replied. "Why do people go to funerals? To show they care about that person. That's what she needs right now," he added, "to know that people loved her daughter, and not just because of what Rachel went through, but because Rachel was someone worth loving." Flu paused, and a peaceful calm wrapped itself around us. "I'm glad you came today," he said after a few moments of silence.

"I think you're the only one."

"Why's that?" Flu kept his gaze across the cemetery.

"I know the other officers blame me for Novak's death."

"Why would they blame you?"

"It was Abram's obsession with Lathan, and eventually with me, that brought him to West Joseph."

"Abram made his choice," Flu said. "You didn't make it for him." Flu looked at me. "No one blames you, Evans."

"It doesn't feel that way."

"When you come back from leave, you'll see nothing has changed. No one feels differently about you."

As much as I wanted to confirm that I was coming back, I couldn't bring myself to say it. Deep down, I already knew I wasn't coming back. My time there was over, and Flu needed to know it.

"I'm not coming back," I looked at Flu.

Flu studied my face and searched my eyes with his. "You still have time to think about it," he said in a dismissal of my verbal resignation.

"No, Flu... I'm not coming back," I repeated with more assertion.

He nodded and sulked into a silence quieter than the cemetery. He stared at me as his eyes began to water. He took a deep breath and let it out as he blinked back the tears. "Where will you go?" he asked.

"I don't know." I couldn't look at him.

"You're a good detective, Evans... too good for West Joseph. I'm actually surprised you stayed as long as you did." He paused as he stared at the horizon. "I'll let admin know, but you'll have to put in a formal resignation."

"I know," I said. "Thank you." I looked up at him. I wanted to thank him for more than just his kind words. I wanted to thank him for accepting my resignation with encouragement, and for not pressuring me to stay to fulfill his own selfish reasons. Flu and I had a great working relationship. We respected each other, and we valued each other's opinions. Whatever my next career move was going to be, I knew it was unlikely that I would find a superior who was also a mentor and friend. "Are you headed home?" I asked.

"Not yet." Flu shook his head. "I'm going to stay here for a bit longer. It's nice here. Quiet," he added. He took a moment to collect himself, then turned to face me "Take care of yourself, Evans." He reached out his hand.

"I will." I placed my hand in his. "You too."

He squeezed my hand before he let it slip from his. In that simple gesture, I knew that if I ever wanted my job back, it would be waiting for me.

As I made my way toward my car, I noticed the cemetery was mostly empty. My car was the only one within view. But leaning against my driver's side door was Cait. She had her arms crossed over her chest as she kept her focus in my direction. When I reached the curb, I looked down the street for her car. She was parked several car lengths ahead of mine.

Her demeanor read as non-confrontational, though I found that hard to believe. She wanted to confront me about something, and I knew it wasn't going to be a friendly chat. My palms began to sweat as my heartbeat increased, and I started to take smaller steps toward my car in order to delay the inevitable. In the near future, I was going to have to face Cait, and it was very apparent that the near future was now.

"You heal nicely," Cait said, referring to my broken nose. It had only taken a few days for the swelling to go down, but the bruising had lasted a few weeks. Novak's funeral was the first time I was able to be in public without the physical signs of my battle with Abram displayed across my face.

"It still hurts like hell when I sneeze," I replied, and a smile instantly formed. It was impossible not to smile when I saw Cait. She could burn holes into my eyes with her stare, and I would still grin like a schoolgirl in love. But as much as I wanted to believe that she was here for a pleasant conversation, I knew better. "Let's hear it," I said, slicing through any niceties she had prepared.

"Hear what?" She stiffened her posture. "That it's nice to see you? That it's nice to know you're doing okay?" she snidely offered. "I'm fine, in case you wondered."

Her tone told me she was angry enough to re-break my nose in one punch if she wanted to, but she didn't need to resort to physical violence; her words could hurt more than any blow she could have thrown.

As she stared me down, I studied her face. She still had tiny scrapes from the car accident along her cheekbones. It made me wonder if that was the only part of her that had yet to heal.

I knew her well enough to know that she was a forgiving person, if only because she didn't want to seem weak by hanging on to past emotions. But I had a feeling she wasn't worried about appearing vulnerable right now. Her resentment was all the force she needed to confront me. Emotional weakness didn't exist in this moment.

"Cait...." I paused as I tried to come up with an apology sincere enough to warrant her forgiveness.

"I won't keep you," she said, interrupting my thoughts. "I just wanted to see if you were okay. And to give you this." She uncrossed her arms and gave me a small business card hidden in her hand.

It was a card I was already familiar with.

Along with news stations and reporters who had called my phone incessantly, I had also received a plethora of calls during the past three weeks from publishing companies who were interested in my story. The same company that had published Rachel's book had been the most persistent—and it seemed they had also gotten to Cait.

"Are you writing a book?" I asked as I looked at the business card. Thoughts of Rachel flashed through mind. As much as I hated the idea of Rachel's book, it wasn't until now that I was actually glad she wrote it. Not because I wanted the public to know what those moments with Lathan were like, but because I wanted the public to know Rachel. I wanted her to be remembered for something. Even if that something was tainted with Lathan's stench, at least the public got to know how brave she was for telling her story.

"No," Cait assured me. "This isn't my story to tell." She smiled at me. "You need to get this demon out of you, Lena. Maybe sharing it with the world will help you do that."

I met her advice with silence.

"Well, it was good to see you," she said before she turned to walk away.

I didn't know where Cait was going. I knew she was going back to Lyons, but I didn't know what that meant for us. A meteor of regret collided against my chest and filled my heart as I watched her walk away.

If I didn't stop her from leaving, I knew I would never see her again.

And I knew my time with her wasn't over.

We had been through too much together to let it end this way. She had become a permanent fixture in my life, and I didn't want her to fall through the cracks of my stupidity.

"Cait?" I called after her. She stopped and turned to face me. I took that as my cue to walk the ten feet between us to try to repair what I had so selfishly broken. "I'm so sorry," I said. "I'm sorry for not telling you where we were going. I'm sorry for not calling you back. I'm sorry for almost getting you killed—"

"Almost getting me killed?" she repeated. "Lena, you didn't almost get me killed. I almost got myself killed."

I searched her eyes to see if that's how she truly felt. Nothing in her stare convinced me she was lying. But how could she believe *she* was the one responsible for putting herself in danger? I was the one who withheld where we were going until it was too late.

"Before we were hit by the car, you said I was on a crusade to get myself killed," I reminded her.

"I did." She nodded. "And if that car hadn't hit us, I would have added that I wasn't going to let you do it alone." Cait locked eyes with me. "Is that why you thought I was calling you? To yell at you for taking me to Lathan's house?" She cocked a smile. "Nothing would have stopped me from going into that house with you."

"You really don't blame me?" I asked as a wave of insecurity receded.

"No," she confirmed with a light laugh. "I understand why you went to that house alone the first time."

She had asked me that question over lunch our first day on the case. She had been so enthralled by the way West Joseph residents treated me. She asked me why I had gone to the abandoned house without calling for backup, and I dismissed her question without giving her an answer. I was embarrassed to reveal the reason why I had gone alone. It was something I knew she wouldn't understand.

"It was more than just the adrenaline rush of wanting to catch the fucker," Cait continued. "It was wanting to *be* the one who actually caught him. I get it. This case became personal—more personal than it should have. I wasn't just fighting for the victims… or for you… I was fighting for my reputation. Abram had one-upped us so many times, I wanted to prove to everyone that I could beat him—that I could own him—and that I could do it by myself."

I looked at Cait as she confirmed all of my motives for going into that house alone the first time. She also confirmed why I was stupid enough to do it again with Abram. This case *had* become personal—just like Lathan's case was. It criticized my investigative skills, it insulted my credibility, and it attacked my self-image. Detective Sergeant Lena Evans had become synonymous with the word "hero." And as much as I tried to humbly brush that title off, I actually enjoyed having it.

Over the course of the investigation, Cait and I had endured the same experiences. We were better detectives—and better people—because of it. She was the only person in the world who understood what I went through, and she was the only person who knew what it felt like. Having that bond made me fall in love with her even more.

But the difference between Cait and I was that she wasn't going to live the rest of her life as Abram's victim. She was going to live it as his survivor. And that was something I needed to do too. I had spent so long living as Lathan's victim I didn't realize I had the option to live as his survivor.

"Thank you," I said. She gave me more than the forgiveness I was seeking. She gave me permission to forgive myself. "All things considered, I really enjoyed working with you."

"Is that all it was to you?" Cait smiled. "Work?" Her tone shifted to a flirtatious pitch.

"No…." I grinned and shook my head. My gaze caught hers, and we stared at each other in silence. Our smiles translated what our words couldn't.

"I'm sure we'll work together again," Cait said with optimism.

"Maybe not." I hesitated to end the romanticism in our conversation, but I wanted her to know. "I just resigned from West JPD. I'm not staying here."

"Where will you go?" she asked with a sudden look of shock on her face.

"I don't know." I nervously smiled. Leaving West Joseph had never crossed my mind before. It was the only place I'd ever known.

"If you don't know, then maybe you'll consider BCI. We have an opening for a Special Agent," Cait offered. A sudden surge of elation filled my heart. Here I was, talking to someone who had made it out of West Joseph. She was the example I needed to convince myself it was possible. What's more, she had invited me to join her at the Bureau of Criminal Investigation. That invite meant I wasn't just a temporary fling to her. Even if our relationship was over, our partnership wouldn't be.

"What would that mean for us?" I boldly asked.

If I had the entire world in front of me, I wasn't going to settle for somewhere and someone who didn't want me. I didn't want to leave West Joseph because I was running away from something. I wanted to leave because I was running toward something. My career choice pretty much guaranteed a job wherever I moved to, but it didn't guarantee I would find someone to love. These past few weeks proved I was ready to be in love—and I was only ready because of Cait. She showed me a world I had long forgotten and reminded me of the grace I need in my life.

"It would mean a lot for us, Lena. Whether you move to Lyons or to London, I'm not going anywhere. Not this time." Cait walked the few steps between us and took my hands in hers. "I'll see you Friday night," she added as she took my hands in hers.

"What's Friday?" I searched my mental calendar but came up with nothing.

A coy smile rolled across Cait's lips. "You owe me dinner, remember?"

I mimicked her infectious smile as she confidently walked toward her car before I had an opportunity to decline.

The remnants of Lathan Collins and Abram Myers would travel with me, but they would no longer be the anchor that held me back. There was life worth living outside of this town, waiting for me to find it.

OTHER PROJECTS BY MICHELLE HANSON

Red Rue

Rue died more than 100 years ago, on the night of a rare Red Moon, and generations of evil Hunters have been chasing her ghost ever since. The Hunters need her spirit in order to unlock the gates of hell. So it's up to her human friends Katie, Hardy, Justine and Stella to find a way to save Rue, before all hell breaks loose. Literally. But the farther Rue's friends go to try to save her, the more Katie realizes she has feelings for Rue.

Red Rue is written and directed by Michelle Hanson, and is produced by Albertane Elm.
Season 1 is available for free on on Youtube at youtube.com/redrueseries
Season 2 will be available for free October 22, 2018

Final Girls

What happens when a lesbian couple are the two remaining survivors, but there can only be one final girl?

Final Girls is a short parody film on the final girl trope. It is inspired by the *Friday the 13th* films/game.

Final Girls is written and directed by Michelle Hanson, and is produced by Fearopoly Films.
It is available for free on Youtube at youtube.com/fearopolyfilms

Gül Girl

In the 1950s, the unmarried daughter of the town's wealthiest man gave birth in the barn behind her house. Unbeknownst to her, her father had promised the baby to the church in exchange for the doctor's silence. When the baby was born, the young woman was too weak to fight the men who stole her baby, and she died within a few hours. Legend has it that her spirit still searches the property for her missing baby.

Today, four road-tripping twenty-somethings find out why some ghost stories are nothing to joke about.

Gül Girl is written and directed by Michelle Hanson, and is produced by Fearopoly Films.
It will be available on Youtube at youtube.com/fearopolyfilms October 31

Veho
His Destination Is the End of Her Journey.

A driver for Veho, a ride-sharing company, unwittingly picks up an unknown serial killer. What begins as idle chitchat on an ordinary drive turns into a full-on psychological thrill ride with torturous twists and turns.

Veho is written and directed by Michelle Hanson and produced by Fearopoly Films. *Veho* will be released late Fall 2018 and will be available for free on youtube.com/fearopolyfilms

ABOUT THE AUTHOR

MICHELLE HANSON is a writer, director, producer, and photographer. She writes detective novels so her degree in Criminology can be put to good use. Michelle is an avid fan of the horror genre, and spends most of her free time volunteering at a local theatre. Her photography has been published in newspapers and online magazines/blogs.

Michelle is the creator, director and writer of the supernatural lesbian web series, *Red Rue*. She also wrote and directed *Gül Girl*, and the upcoming psychological thriller, *Veho* (**Fearopoly Films**).

Michelle is married, and has two dogs and three cats. She hopes to see her novels turn into a movie or television show one day (Netflix, are you listening?).

Follow Michelle on:
Instagram: MLRED219

Follow her projects on:
Twitter: Fearopoly
Instagram: Fearopoly

38357476R00172

Printed in Great Britain
by Amazon